I0680185

An Open Enemy

*Book Three
of the Souls of
the Saintlands*

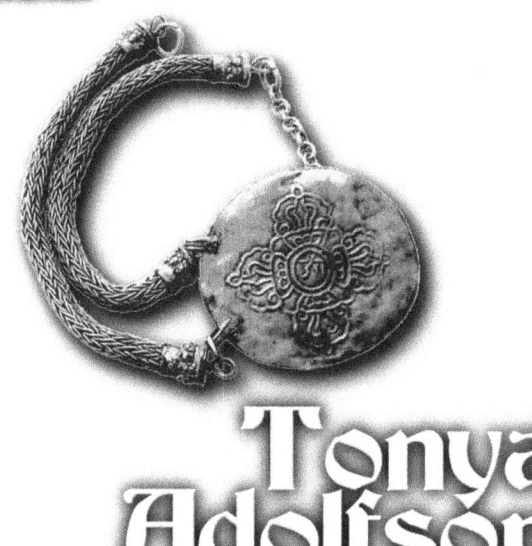

Tonya Adolfson

Published by Fantastic Journeys Publishing,
Boise, Idaho
PUBLISHING HISTORY
E-Book released through Kindle
Soft Cover trial edition March 2013
Mass market edition/ XXXXXX

Cover art: Photo of fabric by William Sparks
Created in Gimp 2.6 by John Farmer
Cover Art copyright by Fantastic Journeys Publishing
Interior Art by Suzette Snyder
Edited by Brady Sparks and Julia Stidolph
Content copyright ©Nov 2012 Tonya Adolfson.

All rights reserved. No part of this book may be used or reproduced in any form or by any means, electronic or mechanical, including photocopying, recording, or by any information storage and retrieval system, without prior written permission from the publisher, except in case of brief quotations embodied in critical articles or review.

Published in the United States of America.

ISBN: 978-0-9855766-3-9

The sale of this book without its cover is unauthorized. If you purchased this book without a cover, you should be aware that it was reported to the publisher as "unsold or destroyed." Neither the author nor the publisher has received payment for the sale of this "stripped book."

The characters and events portrayed in this book are fictitious. Any similarity to real persons, living or dead, common or deific, is coincidental and not intended by the author, unless, of course, I know them.
No Augustinians were harmed in the making of this book, though a few folks were roughed up a bit.

Reviews for the Souls of the Saintlands Series

Thine Enemy's Eyes

"I loved it I stayed up late several nights 'cause I had to know what happened! Its a great read with excellent pacing and such entertaining and rich characters. I loved the rich world she created and the details used to make it stand out. I cannot wait to read the second book to learn more about the characters and places mentioned! I highly suggest this book."
Maryanne Durant, Amazon Review

"I cannot wait for the next book, and hopefully, subsequent books to follow."
Steve Nunez, Dragonfleet Studios

"Tonya Adolfson's debut novel is incredible! Full of intrigue, wildly imaginative characters and set in a medieval fantasy world of such authenticity it blew me away. I would heartily recommend this to anyone, and can't wait until the second novel comes out!"
I. J. Smethurst, author of the *E.D.F Chronicles*

"The plot has interesting twists and turns to keep you going straight through the book. When it ends, it leaves you wanting more."
Shelley Wolf, Amazon Review

"...good political intrigue... good action scenes... Not to mention one of the heaviest cliff hangers I've seen in a while."
The William Jones Review

An Unpolished Gem

"In a perfect follow through to Thine Enemy's Eyes, Ms. Adolfson continues to illustrate just how sticky the politics and personalities of her world really can be. She never lets go of you, even after the book is done. Just when I think I have a character figured out, they surprise me; I can't even tell how many sides to this story there are. I can't wait for book three!"

Julien McBain, author *Ghosts of the Past*

"It is difficult for second books in a series to have the same weight as the first. This is the rarer case of the second book surpassing the first."

Christopher Garcia, editor of *the Drink Tank*

"This book is just as captivating as the first book in the series. Again I was so enthralled with the characters, plot twists, and story line that I litterally couldn't put it down and finished reading it in one day..."

Chalyse Padigimus, Amazon Review

"I love her writing style. She creates this world that becomes real to its readers. Oh and then there are these great characters with such richness and depth you cannot help but to love and in some cases hate them! She has written it in such a way you have no idea where or who, if anyone, the main character will end up with. There is such a depth in the story you just cannot put it down. I read it in a matter of hours. I know these are books I am going to read again and again throughout the years. It has to be a great book for it to have that kind of status on my bookshelf."

Maryanne Durant, Amazon Review

"Love the way the characters grow and mature. Can't wait for the next book!"

Shelley Wolf, Amazon Review

Also by Tonya Adolfson

The Souls of the Saintlands Series
Thine Enemy's Eyes
An Unpolished Gem
An Open Enemy
To Thine Own Self*

*Coming Soon

For Todd, one of the two
finest men I've ever met.

And for my Daddy, who is
the other one. He helped the
first American walk in
space, saved the world
through revamping the U.S.
decryption center during the
Cuban Missile Crisis, and he
really did the yard arm thing.

Acknowledgments:

First and foremost, I'd like to thank all the people who were inspirations for this book:

Gwen for Gwen, John for Raven, Dartanian for Alexander, Jeff for James, Misha for Emmy, Morgan for Alan and Johannes, Rod for Xeno, Shanna for Fierah, Stephanie for Belladonna, Erik for Dom, Jared for Draethen, Dave for Octavius, Morgan Wolf for Morgan Wolf, Aaron for Duncan, Adam P for Ambroise, John for Myrgen, David for Henri, Jennifer for Ce'Nedra, Daddy for Thessius, Kim for Ysabel, Joe for Nicaise, Jenn for Flora, Aggie for Aggie, and all the hundreds of friends and family that have been contributors to this book. Your work has been amazing and your lives inspiring.

A big shout out to the most amazing editors a gal could have: Brady and Julia. Brady does the technical editing but you, Dear Reader, have Julia to thank for the Skyrim-level books, religions, calendar, and appendices. Without her input, this world was far less rich.

I'd also like to thank Gwen J. and John F. for endless hours of inspiration and consultation. Thank you guys!

Thanks to Shannon Galarneau for being my agent and helping me fulfill the dream of Fantastic Journeys Publishing. I'd also like to thank Steve "Warky" Nunez for all his enthusiastic support.

And finally, to my wonderful family: Morgan and Misha, for being so tolerant of Mommy's work; to my Daddy, Ray Lamar Manley, for inspiring me to tell stories for the sheer pleasure of my audience; to my Mom, Rosemary Virginia Manley, for reading historical romances; and to the Great and Powerful Todd, for being everything a Prince needs to be.

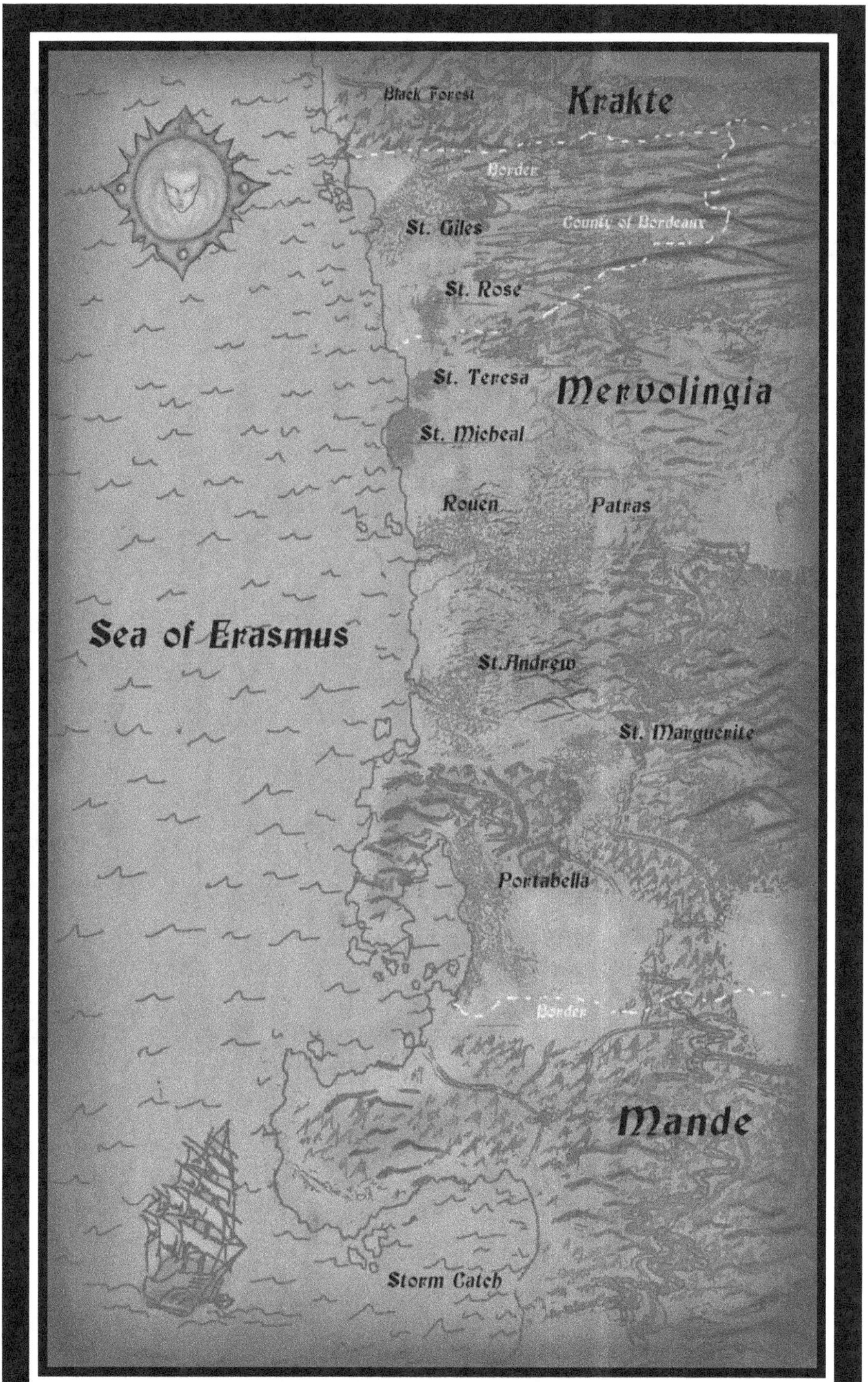
Black Forest
Krakte
Border
St. Giles
County of Bordeaux
St. Rose
St. Teresa
Mervolingia
St. Micheal
Rouen
Patras
Sea of Erasmus
St.Andrew
St. Marguerite
Portabella
Border
Mande
Storm Catch

The Siren's Song is a book of sayings and prayers offered to Calista, the goddess of the Sea. Many sailors know these because they have been put into chanties used to keep timing on the pulling of ropes and working of sails.

Book One

"An open enemy is better than a false friend."
The Siren's Song of Callista

I warn you, if you bore me, I shall take my
revenge.
J.R.R. Tolkien

One

"Death is never at a loss for occasions."
The Siren's Song of Callista

"Wait! You can't behead me! Traitors must be hung!"

Spencer smirked. "Trust me. For you, I think His Majesty will make an exception."

The cell door was closed and Myrgen de Sablonierres heard the scrape of iron tumblers sealing his fate. His clothes still showed evidence from the fall he had taken in the street while trying to escape. He looked down, brushing the small pebbles from the heels of his hands. The back of his left knee hurt where the hilt of the guard's dagger had dropped him and he had a slight limp that he was only barely aware of at that moment. He wiped the dirt off his thighs and looked around at the condition of the cells here in St. Marguerite. It held a place to sleep and a place to pee but the only light in the room came through the barred window in the iron-strapped wooden door. The scent of old urine and old straw dominated the room, and the air tasted of iron and wood. He stepped to the back and sat on the bunk built into the wall. He leaned his scuffed elbows on his scuffed knees and shoved his hands into his long dark hair which was punctuated by a pale brown shock from a recent experience. He had no idea how he was going to get out of this one.

A knock on the door woke Nicaise le Saviage and drew him from his bed. His thick, dark head of hair coupled with the inability to grow any on his face revealed his foreign heritage but the fact that he had no religious qualms to killing made him the one and only choice for local executioner. He pulled on an exotic long coat of black and maroon brocade against the chill of the midnight air and stepped over to the door. A guardsman stood in the hallway. Nicaise squinted at the man and rubbed the back of his neck. "Yes?"

"An execution is scheduled for dawn."

"I figured. I don't get midnight visits from men otherwise. What manner?"

"Beheading, sir."

"Beheading? I don't recall any trials."

"A traitor was caught in town. The Vicar has ordered his death personally."

"Hunh. Odd request. Usually traitors are hung. However, an enemy of the State does get special treatment. Okay. I'm on it..." Nicaise started to close his door and his curiosity got the better of him. "Hey Aaron, who is this fool who has incurred the Vicar's personal wrath?"

"Myrgen the Grey."

"The former Kingdom Chancellor? Where did they find him?"

"He was on a ship bound for Caratia. Some woman captain was giving him sanctuary."

Nicaise blinked. "The *Enigma?*"

"Yes, I think so. You know her?"

"I've run across her once or twice. All right then, I'll see you in the morning."

Nicaise closed his door and glanced around the room a moment, then grabbed his socks and boots and pulled on some breeches, fastening them with skill bred from haste. Socks and boots were restored to his feet and he buttoned the Caratian long coat over his bare chest. A simple black hat hid his features in the night and he stepped out to the street.

Nicaise slipped easily into the late night movements of the bustling port city. He glanced at the road to his right, which led to the local tavern, then to the left where the docks creaked in the night air. He decided to assess the situation first, maybe see if he could talk to Octavius, the *Enigma's* First Mate. If anyone would know what was going on, it would be him. This ship and her Captain had saved his life and the lives of sixty men a few years back. His Captain, Ramirez de Santiago, in a suicidal depression, had gone insane and tried to blow up both ships with all hands. Nicaise wasn't going to sit by while anyone in her care was in danger.

He turned left and strode to where the black ship was moored. Three guards stood at the end of the dock and two more flanked the gangplank leading to the ship.

"Rhys! How are you?"

"Nicaise?" The guardsman waved to the executioner, Rhys's bald head fitting neatly inside the regulation helm. Nicaise remembered the challenges for fitting Rhys' sizable skull. The man was tall and broad with a proportionate head and shaving it was the only way to fit the helm. "Good to see you!"

"What are you doing wearing the Guard Captain tabard? I thought you left the guard and became a herald?"

Rhys glanced down, tugging the bottom of the baldric across his chest, denoting his rank in the Baron's guard. "Sir Conrad von Zuberbueler was recalled to Krakte with the death of our Queen. Baron Robert had the Vicar give me this position to keep an eye on things. We're looking around for a Mervol knight to take over here. However, with this duty right now, I might fetch on with the King himself. He's here in town."

"He is? Why?"

Rhys shrugged. "I dunno, but he's up at the Vicar's manor right now with the Captain of this vessel. Why are you up at this hour?"

"Spencer knocked me awake. I guess I have work to do tomorrow."

"That would be the traitor, Myrgen the Grey. He is responsible for the death of King Charles."

Nicaise cocked his head, nodding to the *Enigma*. "A traitor to Mervolingia was on this vessel? Did the Captain know who he was?"

Rhys glanced over his shoulder and nodded. "Yes. Apparently, he was there under diplomatic sanctuary but the Vicar got him to step off the ship. Once he was back on Mervol soil, he was arrested."

Rhys's features showed little interest, but Nicaise caught a slight disapproval. Rhys wasn't one to let people know his real feelings so for distaste to leak out, the action must really sit wrong with the man.

"It seems rather surprising though. I was told it was to be a beheading. Traitors are hung."

"I guess he wants to impress the King with being efficient. He's up at the Vicar's spa with the Captain right now."

Nicaise glanced up to the ship and saw Octavius stroll over to the railing to see who was talking to the guards. A flicker of recognition crossed his face and Nicaise inclined his head barely enough to show Octavius he had his support. "So, the King is in St. Marguerite. This should cause a stir. "

Rhys shrugged. "I imagine Their Excellencies will be here by morning, outrunning their retinue. This is one of the reasons why they wanted me to serve on the guard for a while after Sir Conrad left. They received word that His Majesty was out scouring the kingdom for a wife. If he showed up here, they wanted someone on hand to take care of things and get word to them."

"This isn't the sort of thing Robert would normally support. And Ariel's never attended an execution. Are they in accordance to what Morgan is doing? I realize he's their Vicar, but this is a bit unprecedented. Doesn't he worry he'll anger the Baron and Baroness?"

"I think maybe the King ordered it. They wouldn't go against the will of the King. He holds their fealty, after all."

Nicaise nodded. "Yes, of course." He gestured to the ship. "So, why the guards here then?"

Rhys nodded towards the manor house on the other side of town. "Vicar Morgan told us not to let anyone on or off the boat. I guess he doesn't want them leaving before the execution."

Nicaise looked at Octavius. He knew the man's predicament. The *Enigma* never sailed without all hands. She didn't leave her people behind. If Myrgen the Grey had been accepted as part of her crew, then the Captain would not allow his execution, King or no King. "Then all hands are on board?"

"No idea. We're just here to keep everyone in place until dawn."

Octavius shook his head and Nicaise nodded, understanding the meaning. The First Mate made a gesture like drinking and Nicaise understood. The rest of the crew was at the taverns. He clapped his hands together. "Well, I'd better get back to bed. I just wanted to see what the story was."

Rhys nodded. "I promise I'll tell you the details over an ale when I find out the rest."

"Thanks Rhys." He nodded to the guardsman and went back down the road to the tavern.

Ysabel opened the door to the manor house of the Vicar of St. Marguerite where she lived and served His Honor Lord Morgan Wolf. She had just seen him in town, arresting a man. She knew this was her only chance to tell the captain of the *Enigma* that the man given sanctuary there was being jailed. The Stâpâna Catriona Moriarity had already earned her respect when she had told everyone at dinner she believed Myrgen was innocent. Myrgen was accused of murdering the brother of the very monarch who was honoring her. To still hold strong her beliefs impressed Ysabel. It was this king's brother Myrgen was accused of murdering, and the reason he was king now. To risk war with Mervolingia over an accused killer meant she was either very foolish or very informed. Ysabel didn't believe Catriona was foolish at all.

Ysabel knew Morgan Wolf. He was a good, kind man, a good administrator and a very honorable person. If he was arresting his own brother for treason, he must have no choice.

She hoped the Stâpâna could help. His Majesty had seemed very smitten with the lady but Ysabel now doubted his attention. She feared it was a distraction so Morgan would have time to betray his family.

She crept up to the Stâpâna's bedroom and knocked carefully. Her previous attempt to return a necklace that had fallen from the dignitary's things had proven unsuccessful and Ysabel feared the King may have the good lady in his room to make certain he kept track of her. She didn't want to risk her life interrupting the king needlessly but if he was defiling this woman, she had to stop it. She stood at his door, trying to build up the courage to knock. Instead, she listened at the door, trying to make out noises. Unfortunately for her, the rooms here were practically soundproof. She couldn't even see flickering light beneath the door.

Maybe she is somewhere else in the manor. She could have gotten hungry or be in the privy. I should check first.

She went downstairs and checked the kitchen, the bathing area and the downstairs privy before looking at the stairs again. She glanced at the parlor, just to make sure it was empty. She noticed an open document on the Vicar's desk in the dancing light cast by a small lamp. She stepped into the room. She had cleaned this room while the King had been bathing. There had been no decree on the desk.

She picked up the official looking document, glancing around because a woman reading was unholy, and recognized most of the words:

Be it known by these… that Alexander…, King of Mervolingia, does at this time make this decree:
That the former Kingdom…, Myrgen de Sablon…, is hereby… a traitor to the Crown. If he is…, then at dawn the day following his…, he is to be… with extreme …for high crimes against the State. Anyone giving him rest or …will be …an accom… to …and will bring the… of this Crown upon their household.
Done this third day of Elmos, …1574.

Alexander Angloume, Rex

She turned the decree over and saw it had not been delivered to the Vicar through the Royal Messenger. It had apparently been hand delivered, and judging from the date, written that day. *No wonder the Vicar arrested him with such animosity. He was protecting the rest of us.* Still, she wasn't certain she was right. The larger words might have a different meaning than she thought. She needed to get this to the Stâpâna. She would know what to do. Ysabel folded up the decree and put it in her pocket. She doubted the Stâpâna had known this. Judging from her well made, but well-used, regular clothing, she didn't spend her time in court or sitting a throne of any kind. And she took good care of her things. She had been very specific that her things be returned to her ship. She doubted, with taking such care of clothes that were common, that Catriona would discard a human life she fought to protect.

What if the Stâpâna is actually in love with Myrgen? That must be it! Otherwise, why would she have given the man sanctuary on her ship? The King was merely getting rid of the competition for her heart. Ysabel now felt the nerve to pound the King awake. She would not stand for this, not in her good Vicar's home.

"Ysabel, what are you doing?"

She turned, the panic not hidden in her face, as she looked the Vicar in the eye.

Two

"Your shipmates are your brothers, regardless of the Captain."
The Siren's Song of Callista

Nicaise stepped into the Fair Winds tavern and scanned the room. He spotted several sailors from the *Enigma*, a couple of whom were former crewmates from Ramirez' ship, the *Crimson Veil*. He recognized Thessius, the First Mate on the *Veil* and sat down at the bar next to him. The barkeep came over and nodded greeting. "Nicaise, what brings you out this late?"

"Hey Martin. Eh, one of the town guards came by my place tonight. Told me about some fella being dragged off that black ship in the docks. I'm supposed to execute him tomorrow at dawn." Out of the corner of his eye, he saw Thessius stop swallowing on his beer a moment, then begin again.

"Yeah? What'd he do?"

"Treason. Apparently, he escaped from somewhere up north and the Vicar found him and coaxed him off the ship."

"He's a smart one, that Morgan Wolf. That's a good way to give himself a good name with the King. He was in here today, you know?"

"Who? The King?"

The barkeep nodded, gesturing with pride. "Yep, some fella dragged him in off the street and said he was the King of Mervolingia. At first I didn't believe him but Owen pulled out a silver piece and sure enough, it was him! Couldn't believe my eyes. Luckily, the Vicar came by a few minutes later and took him in. I was frightful scared our accommodations weren't up to royal inspection."

"I heard he was in town. This is a very auspicious day for St. Marguerite. The Vicar has the black ship under guard. I wonder if he suspects other criminals on her?"

The barkeep shook his head. "I've never had any trouble with those men. In all my years of keeping this tavern, that's one ship I like to see pull into port."

Nicaise finished the ale he ordered and put a silver on the bar. "Thanks Martin. That should help me sleep now." He stood, with a very quick look over at Thessius. Thessius nodded to his former crewmate and Nicaise left the tavern.

"Your Honor!"

Morgan looked her over. "Going somewhere, Ysabel? At this hour?"

"No. Not really… I…"

The girl was nervous, like she had just been caught in the act. *Exactly what had she been doing?* Morgan could see she was dressed to be out in town instead of in night clothes or the clothes she had worn when she attended the Stâpâna at dinner or in the spa.

Also, Ysabel rarely left the manor after dark. Too many ruffians and she had been attacked by bandits a few years back. Her husband, Spencer, was a guard at the jail, and that security was one of the reasons why she had been attracted to him. Morgan's eyes marked the room, looking for anything missing.

"I was thinking of going to see Spencer. He's on duty tonight and I thought I would bring him something." She turned to gesture towards the fire in the fireplace. "I was just checking on the fire to make sure the coals were properly banked for the night."

Morgan looked at her shoes and knew immediately she was lying. There was dirt and mud on the sides, not soot, as would be present if she had fiddled with the hearth. The fireplace looked undisturbed. The inside hem of her cloak had smudges of mud upon them as well. Her dark brown hair had a bit of dirt on it and her hands had a smudge of mud as well, like she had crouched or touched something on the streets.

She gestured with her left hand while her right one stayed clenched around something, which he noted because she was right handed. He stepped over to her and grabbed her wrist.

She struggled to get away but Morgan kept a tight hold on her. He twisted her wrist and she cried out, opening her hand a little. Morgan caught a glimpse of what she held and pried her hand open. The necklace with the key lay discovered in her palm. Morgan picked it up and looked at her, holding up the necklace, then turned an accusing gaze upon his servant.

"This belongs to the Stâpâna. I saw it on her neck when she entered my home. What are you now, Ysabel? A thief? Within my own walls?"

"No, Your Honor." Her eyes were wide and tearing up a little from his grip. "I found that in the salon. I didn't want it to be missed so I was taking it back to her ship where her other things were taken earlier this evening."

He reached down and grabbed her cloak, exposing the wet, muddy edge that he could now smell reeked of alley mud and garbage. "You've already been *out*. And in an alley, from the smell of you. *What were you in here looking for?"*

"Nothing, I swear it! Let me go!"

He twisted her arm behind her and stayed to the side, out of kidney punch or kicking range. He moved over to the desk to grab some twine to tie her hands and realized the decree from the King was gone. He looked at her, then finished his task of binding her hands behind her. The twine, though thinner than rope, was easier to catch under the bones of the wrist, digging into a pain point and bringing the prisoner to a more reasonable point of view. He then reached into the belt pouch on her waist, looking for the decree. He found a secret pocket sewn into her skirt seam which crinkled and pulled out the stray decree.

"Not a thief, eh? Then what were you doing with this?"

Ysabel stopped struggling against the bonds as each movement caused her more pain. "That… That decree… it is against your brother…"

"Yes. I'm very aware of that."

"Is that why you went to see him, to trick him off the ship so you could arrest him?"

"What is going on with that traitor is not your concern. He put all our lives in danger when he decided to betray the King."

Ysabel turned pleading eyes upon him. "Please, you have to let me tell her. I… I think the King may be only doing it to get rid of him. I think, maybe, she's in love with him."

"With whom? My *brother?* Please. Don't make me laugh. If she is, then I'm sparing her getting stabbed in the back by that fiend. Myrgen is a manipulating scoundrel, who lies or tells the truth interchangeably, whichever will get him what he wants. He's a selfish criminal who has managed to get away with smearing my family's good name for years. This end was inevitable, Ysabel. He just took a bigger bite than I expected."

"But she gave him sanctuary. The King is just using her to get to him."

"What the King is doing is his own business! It's none of ours."

She looked into her employer's eyes. "Please, sir, you're a good man. Don't let this happen."

Morgan hesitated, his blood ties fighting against his fealty oath. It was possible the King was indeed using that ship Captain to get to Myrgen. He didn't like that thought because he truly felt the King cared for her and that she returned the emotion. If that was the case, well, Morgan couldn't interfere.

"I am the King's man, first and foremost, as per the oath of office I took. I *must* uphold his law and he did not tell me to stay my hand. Brother or not, it is the King's Will that he be executed at dawn of the day after he is caught. He handed me this decree when you were bathing the Stâpâna. It's in his own hand. He wrote it here and handed it to me, in this very room. I can't ignore it and I can't deny it or my entire household is forfeit. That's you, Spencer, your children, Lysette, even the Duke and Duchess. I'm sorry, Ysabel, but when faced with the safety of my brother or the people in this house, I'll choose this family over him."

He maneuvered her before him, and escorted her to the door.

"Wait, where are you taking me?"

"To the prison. That way, you'll be with Spencer and he'll keep you safe. I need to make sure you aren't around His Majesty when he wakes. He's clearly in a killing mood."

Alexander lay back on his pillow. "I'm sorry, Catriona. I don't know what's wrong with me." He put his soft healer's hands across his royal blue eyes and shook his head. His barely blonde hair, rather like his bed partner's long wavy locks, had given up the pretense of fashionable behavior. He rather liked having her hair cascading loose. So often, it was bound in a braid to keep it out of her way.

His body was that of a young king, still trim from training and exercise, before the rich diet and hours of forced inactivity on the throne had the chance to steal the muscle. Despite his years of traveling the ports searching out the woman beside him, the recent winter had taken the calluses and suntan from his flesh. He had always traveled incognito so as not to become a target for kidnappers, but, as Prince, it was easier to get away with it. As King, he would not be so lucky, as today's activities had shown.

Catriona raised up on her arms and hovered over his chest, smiling. "Guilty conscience?"

He loved her voice, which could vary between liquid velvet and silken poison, depending on the subject matter. The Caratian accent was always there, even though she came from the isles of Latia, near the Mandian coast. He liked it because it sounded exotic while still being understandable. He felt certain she would sound exquisite by his side in the halls of Mervol court.

Her dark hair fell over her shoulders and onto his chest, accentuating the soft brown of her skin. Despite her beauty, he could see the weather in her features from being at sea. If she kept

14

on with this life, she would be ancient in appearance before she was forty. She took care of her skin as best she could, but being soft in the hard environs of wood and hemp ropes was detrimental. Her hands were always protected when she was dressed in order to be pleasurable when she was not, and Alexander appreciated that especially now.

"Please. This is embarrassing enough." He touched the face of the woman he loved and shook his head. *How could this happen? How could I not be able to perform when I'm finally, at last, with the one woman I would stop the world to be with?*

Catriona looked at his bare chest with shimmering emerald eyes, and ran a finger along his sternum. "I don't know for certain, but maybe it has something to do with your trip through the shadows." She shrugged, looking into his eyes again. "Who knows what that does to people?"

He took her hand and kissed the finger she had been using on his chest. Although she was hiding it from him, he could tell she was actually unsettled by this as well. He took her into his arms and lay her down beside him. As a matter of fact, he knew exactly what that place did to people. His Power of Sovereignty, granted him when Charles released it, had several properties, one being a shield which held dark things at bay. As a regular Shadowalker, Duncan McVryce had brought the King to St. Marguerite in an instant, but Duncan's body showed the effects: Swirling blackness within his eyes, like ink in water. Allowing the shadow to take him, it seemed the shadow gave something as well. Alexander wasn't certain what that might be and he didn't want Catriona to find that out.

He needed sleep, and that would fix everything.

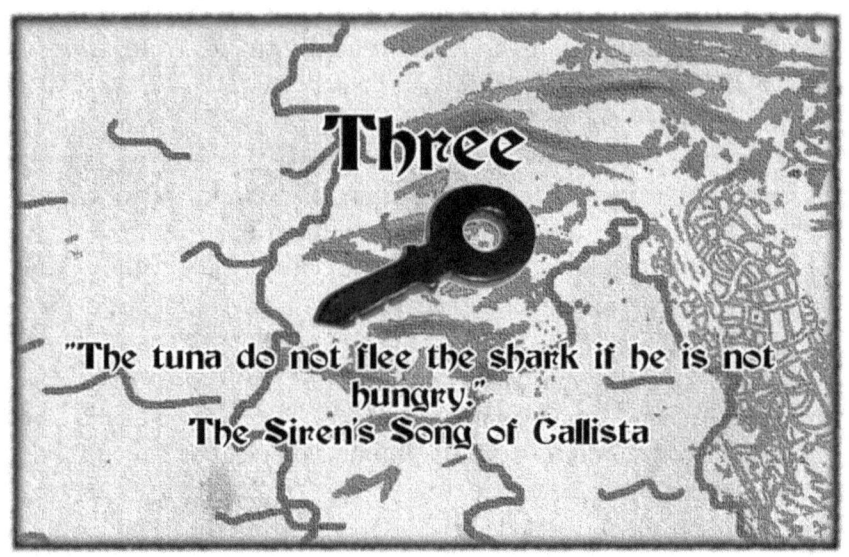

Three

"The tuna do not flee the shark if he is not
hungry."
The Siren's Song of Callista

Alistair Hapsburg MacGlarren, former Crown Prince of York, closed his eyes and rubbed them. *This is not how I planned this part if the day.*

He opened them again and looked at the image on the curtains of sheer silk draped around his circular bed. Alexander was finally falling asleep, Catriona by his side. Alistair was not pleased with this outcome. The earlier part pleased him quite a bit though, so it balanced out. As an agent of Karma, that was appropriate.

"Was that really necessary?"

The scent of cedar and sandalwood caught his senses. He looked at the image of the Woman beyond the silk. Her voice was elegant which made him want very much to touch her, yet he had not even gotten close. However, the weight of the responsibility that had come from meeting her here had completely ruined his death. "Which part?"

"His ill performance with her?"

Alistair held up his hands, showing his palms. "Hey, that was just the stress of the situation, I'm sure. Besides, that's the purpose of Karma, isn't it? I can't tell the number of times I was repaid for a good or bad deed through the timing of an outcome. That's all that I messed with, the timing of his actions, and frankly, just the first one. The rest was his own inadequacy."

The Woman cocked her head and put a hand on her hip. "Did you think the same when it happened to you?"

He returned his attention to the figures *on* the curtains rather than the one behind them. "I have no idea what you're talking about."

"That union could have settled the whole problem. United the forces of Heaven and Earth, preventing a war. The child that would have come from that coupling…"

"*Would have destroyed her.*" Alistair frowned at the image of Catriona on the silk. "Besides, she's the Stâpâna, not the Dûcesa."

"But she could be. Drake won't live forever and if she takes the throne of Caratia, then it could unite the two largest faiths in the world."

Alistair snorted. "The Augustinian Church won't tolerate a faction that believes a person can pray directly to Heaven and *not* go through the Saints. It will hardly be inclined to live in peace with a Dirt Worshiper."

"Fair enough." The Woman disappeared from the silk, leaving Alistair alone again.

He remembered his conversation with Raven Grasshair the day Alistair was killed and came to this place between life and death. Alistair believed that the First Dûcesa, a great servant of the Land, had been reincarnated. Raven had been her Stapan once, her protector. Upon looking at Catriona, Alistair was certain Raven would be able to tell if the First Ducesa was back amongst the living.

If the Dûcesa has returned, he thought, *I owe it to her to let her have her own mind in this.*

Myrgen heard a pounding on the door to the Magister's Office. "Open the door! I have another prisoner!"

The squeaking hinges spoke of entry and he heard his brother's voice more clearly. Myrgen got to his feet and looked out the small window, straining to see who he had chosen to arrest now. *Please be Catriona.*

Morgan spoke to the guard. "This woman was found with a necklace that didn't belong to her. Please lock her up until we can sort this out."

Myrgen's heart leapt, then dropped as he heard the woman speak. "Vicar, please. Don't do this."

"I must. I'm sorry, Ysabel."

The guard seemed to be a bit surprised by the person in question. "Ysabel? Vicar, there must be some mistake."

"I know she's your wife, Spencer, and I'll do all I can to get her cleared of these charges in the morning. Right now, I have other matters to spend my attention upon."

"But..."

"*Lock her up, Spencer. Please.*" A pause, then, less angry, "I'll take care of this in the morning."

Ysabel didn't seem satisfied with this option. "Spencer, this is a lie. He's going to execute someone..."

"Silence! If you don't want to end up on the chopping block next to him, you'll hold your tongue."

Myrgen had heard that tone before. Morgan was near the breaking point and Myrgen needed to do something, fast. He sneered through the small window in the door to his cell. "Give it up, Ysabel. Once he sets his mind to it, my brother is unmovable."

He saw Morgan turn and look down his direction. He shoved past the girl and the guard and came down to glare through the bars at his brother. "You want this girl to share your fate? Your familiarity with her can make her an accessory to your treason, *brother.*"

"If being related to me isn't enough to damn you, then *this* isn't enough to damn her." Myrgen glowered at his brother. "You should watch your step, Morgan. The King is very unforgiving to those who overstep their bounds."

"Come dawn, your petty little opinion will no longer be assaulting my ears. However, if you think for a second I won't make your final hours so full of pain you'll beg the Saints for a faster sunrise, think again." Morgan pointed at Myrgen, a leather thong with a small black stone key upon it dangling from his hand. "You put our entire family at risk, not to mention my office here and the Baron and Baroness I serve. This girl has a family too, but her life is forfeit if you acknowledge her. Brother or not, I will not tolerate your treasonous choices endangering everything in my world."

Myrgen's eyes grew wide at the sight of the key and his heart skipped a beat. *Catriona's necklace, the one that opened the stone wall! If I can get it, maybe I can escape.* Unfortunately, Morgan noticed the reaction and looked at the necklace in his hands. "What? You know what this is? Who it belongs to?"

Myrgen's mind tumbled and landed quickly on its feet. "Get that unholy thing away from me. I don't know how you got it, but keep it away from me. It's cursed."

"Cursed? She was wearing it."

"But she's the only one it obeys, the only one who *can* remove it. It's a sacred artifact of Caratia. Only the Stâpâna is allowed to touch it. Anyone caught with it will be put to death."

"Well then, maybe I will have her find this on you herself."

Myrgen's eyes grew wide and filled with terror. He hoped Morgan's spite would cause him to throw the thing into the cell with him.

"Or maybe I should put it on someone else instead." Morgan walked over and started to put it over the girl's head.

Myrgen cried out. "No! Morgan, don't! Put it on me. Don't do this to her."

Morgan looked at his brother and smiled, then put it on the girl, whose eyes were wide with fear. Ysabel started breathing heavily and panicking, but she didn't reach up and take the thing off, or even block the movement. It was then that Myrgen figured out her hands were tied behind her back. Myrgen slammed the door with his fist and closed his eyes.

"See, I didn't get the impression that the Stâpâna was the murdering sort. After all, she spared *your* traitorous life."

"Then clearly you don't know her."

"Maybe not, but I suspect this is probably a family heirloom or keepsake from a past, *or present*, lover."

Myrgen blinked, not certain what that jab meant. The Vicar threw the girl into the cell next to his brother's and turned to impress a vicious smile upon the former chancellor. "However, should you be telling the truth, now, you'll have the pleasure of hearing her dying screams as your Stâpâna enforces her duties, knowing it was your fault she's dead. Had you kept your mouth shut, *I* would have handed it back to her. Thanks for saving my life, Brother." Morgan walked off and with a passing comment to the guard, left the building.

Myrgen could hear the girl through the hole in her door, crying. He looked out his door to see if there was a guard within earshot, and it looked clear. "Ysabel, can you hear me?" He kept his voice low to avoid calling attention to their conversation.

The girl was breathing in ragged steps but she must have moved closer to the door because Myrgen could hear her easier now. "Yes." The girl's breathing calmed. "Yes, I can. Are you Myrgen de Sablonierres?"

"Yes. How do you know my name?"

"The Stâpâna mentioned you. You are the Vicar's brother. His Honor's surname is actually de Sablonierres, though he goes by the name the townsfolk gave him when he first arrived, Morgan Wolf."

"That actually confused me when I first saw him here. I knew the name Morgan Wolf from doing the King's correspondence but didn't realize he was my brother." He could hear her grunting in her cell. "What's wrong?"

"Nuffin'…" Her voice was muffled, like her mouth was full. A couple minutes later, she spat and put both hands on the small bars on her cell door. "By the Saints, my hands may never recover all feeling."

Ah, she freed herself. Talented girl. "Did you pick your lock?"

"Huh? Oh, no. My hands were tied, not shackled."

"Oh. Still, that's only slightly less impressive."

"Well, don't be too impressed with me, Master Myrgen. I wasn't able to alert the Stâpâna to your plight."

"You didn't find her?"

"Well," Ysabel shuffled in her cell, "she wasn't in her room. Could she be on the ship?"

Myrgen shook his head. "No. My brother staged some guards there and told them not to let anyone on or off. She wasn't on when I was taken. She might be in town though. If she finished dinner up at the manor house, she could have changed into her Captain's clothes…"

"Actually, no, she couldn't have. I was told to send those back to her ship. That was the reason I was in that alleyway, in fact. She had dropped her necklace in a potted plant in the salon when she had bathed and I wanted to make sure it wasn't missing when she returned to the ship."

Myrgen was about to ask who told her to send the clothes away when Ysabel continued.

"Speaking of which, is it true what you said about this necklace? Will she really kill me?"

"Huh? Oh, no, I don't think so."

All movement stopped in Ysabel's cell. "You don't *think* so?"

"Well, to tell you the truth, I've never seen her without it. And I can tell you it's probably an artifact of her country, or at least of her religion."

"Religion? Who's symbol is this? Dunstan? He's the Patron Saint of jewelers and locksmiths. It would explain the onyx key."

"Well, no. It's not quite like that, I guess. Caratians don't worship the Saints. They aren't Augustinian."

"You mean they're Emilianites? Those arrogant people who believe they can speak directly to Heaven and bypass the Saints?"

"No. I mean they worship the Land there."

Ysabel was silent for a moment. "The… land? You mean, like dirt? Are they farmers or something?"

"No. Well, actually, yes, like the dirt. I'm not certain about it, but Catriona worships the Land. For her, the Land is as active in her life as the Saints are in ours. More so, from what I've seen. I could pray all night to Saint Dunstan and not be magically released from this locked cell."

"Are you saying the Land would?"

"Well, that's the theory I would like to check. Here, toss me that necklace, would you?"

He heard movement in her cell, then silence. "How could he?"

Myrgen shifted against the door. "How could who what?"

"How could the Vicar put this on me, after you told him it would mean my death?"

"Clearly he spent time in the Stâpâna's presence. He said she didn't strike him as the murdering sort."

"You said she was. Are your experiences with her different than the Vicar's?"

Myrgen exhaled, trying to figure out what to say to this frightened girl. *Was Catriona dangerous? Oh yes. Did this girl need to know that? Probably not.* "Ysabel, look. I needed that necklace you're wearing around your neck. I needed it here, not back where Ca… where the Stâpâna was." He swallowed, not certain he wanted to say this next thing. It wasn't true, and might, therefore put his soul in jeopardy, but frankly, this girl had been put through enough.

"And I think he did it because he realized I wanted it here. If he did anything else, it would have meant he was committing treason as well. He is bound by a fealty oath, Ysabel, but he's always been a better man than me."

"How do you know?" He saw her hands wrap around the bars of her cell window. "How do you *really* know she won't kill me for having this? Caratia is a barbaric place! I've heard they only have one sentence for crimes and that is death. If she is an important person there, how can you know she doesn't have the same requirements placed upon her now?"

Myrgen shrugged. Truth was, he didn't know if what he said was true. Caratia *was* barbaric in their practices, according to rumor. Myrgen had never been there, but stories abounded of the Dûce, a dark, imposing man of huge stature and black features who ruled the Land-worshiping populace with an iron grip. His laws were straight-forward but his punishments were brutal. Most penalties for crimes were death, from petty theft or adultery to rape and murder. That Catriona called that place home simultaneously caused him great curiosity and trepidation.

"Because I know *her*, Ysabel. She can look into a person's soul. She'll know you didn't steal the necklace."

"What? How can she do that? See a person's sins?"

"I don't know, but she's done it to me."

Ysabel shifted again. "Does it hurt?"

"Only if you're lying."

"Does the Vicar know she can do this?"

Myrgen heard an unasked question in her voice, but he wasn't sure what it was. However, he had time to talk, at present. That wouldn't be the case if dawn actually came. And he really needed her trust if he was going to get that necklace. "What are you really asking, Ysabel?"

"There was a decree in the parlor. I tried to bring it with me but His Honor found it on me. He said it had been written by the King himself in that very parlor while the Stâpâna was being bathed and readied for dinner. It had the official seal of Mervolingia even. He told me the decree said you were to be executed at dawn of the day following your capture. Lord Morgan is trying to protect us because if anyone aids you in any way, the Crown would do something to them and their families."

Myrgen blinked, understanding joining him in the cell and settling in on the straw mattress. "That's why the rush. I thought it was a grudge that Morgan was exercising." *Apparently, my brother wasn't the one exercising the grudge.* Alexander had told him back in Rouen that he would abide by Catriona's decision to protect the fugitive as long as he was aboard the *Enigma.* Putting the decree right in front of Morgan probably required his fealty oath to be enforced. It was part of the Power of Sovereignty to have laws enforced when dealing with someone in fealty. Luckily, the fealty oath was as easy to break as deciding you don't want to follow the King's Will, and one was free.

Myrgen sighed. And that fealty was what had made Morgan enforce the King's laws. Well played, Alexander. You really are a D'Medici after all.

"I also think she might be in love with you."

Myrgen pulled out of his thought process. "Er, what?" He felt the understanding he had just been feeling flit away like a sparrow after another branch.

"The Stâpâna. I think the King wants her for himself, but she cares for you. That's why he's doing all this. To eliminate you as competition."

"What in the world would make you say something like that?"

"Can you think of a better reason for the King to be so intent on insuring your death? At dawn of the morning after your capture? So if, like tonight, you are arrested late in the night, you won't have time to warn her. He's making sure she's occu...pied..."

Myrgen caught the pause. "I thought you said you didn't find her?"

Shuffle. "I didn't, but I didn't get the chance to look everywhere."

He blinked, suddenly feeling pain and rage in his belly. He shook it off. He had told her to go and to be with Alexander. He had *told* her to go, that she truly did love the man. He shouldn't be angry to discover she did. "How can I be this stupid twice?"

"I'm sorry."

Myrgen leaned his head on the cell door. "No, Ysabel. No... It's my fault. I thought... I thought he was a good man, worthy of her. I'm just not sure if I'm right anymore."

A pause. "Can I ask you a question?"

Myrgen shrugged. "Certainly."

"What did you do?"

He sighed. "I was stupid. I fell in love with the Queen of Mervolingia, who was friends with my sister, Tanglwyst. Tangl got me a job in the palace as the Kingdom Chancellor to give me the chance to be around the Queen. Then, one night, they came to me, saying the king had hurt the queen. The prince, Alexander, had given her healing herbs to stop the bruising so no one at court would know, but I was furious that this person I thought the world of could be abused. I felt this was not a suitable ruler for the kingdom. So, I withdrew my fealty in my heart and found I could act against the king. I plotted his assassination. Unfortunately, I was deceived on several levels, and it went badly for me. I was caught and while they were waiting for the Queen Mother to return home before trying me in court, I was rescued."

Movement near the end of the hallway indicated the presence of a guard in the main foyer and Myrgen realized he had forgotten to keep his voice low. *No need to give them reason to start the execution early.*

Ysabel seemed to realize the same thing because she lowered her voice as well. "Why would they wait?"

"Do you know who the Queen Mother is? Catherine D'Medici. One of a long and prestigious line of poisoners, torturers and murderers. These people thrive on intrigue. They are experts.

24

So, I imagine they were waiting for her so she could decide my fate."

"How horrible. How did you escape?"

Myrgen thought about the night almost three ten-days ago, where, after being beaten half to death by the watch captain Nicolai Moriarity, Catriona's now late husband, he had been rescued by Catriona herself through the use of that little black key. "I'm afraid I can't disclose that information. Suffice it to say, I was given a second chance at life, and I was truly hoping to have a bit more time to atone for my sins than three short ten-days."

"You said you were deceived?"

Myrgen pursed his lips. "Yes, but honestly, it serves me right. I haven't always been the upstanding citizen with a noose around my neck you find before you." He smiled and the small joke coaxed a small snicker from his jail mate.

"Well, I think you need to get smart because I'm not certain he's a good person to be with her anymore. He seems to give the impression he's a good man, but anyone who would plot like this is a bit too evil for my comfort. And I find, despite her odd religion and country, I rather like the Stâpâna. She treated me like I mattered, even though my circumstances didn't require it."

Well put, my lady. I feel the same. "Look, don't worry. I'll figure a way out of this. I'm pretty clever, you know."

"I really don't know." He saw her hands let go of the bars in her cell window and heard her relax. "But if the Stâpâna felt inclined to trust you, I do too."

Myrgen smiled, actually reassured by her faith in him.

Start thinking, M'Lord Clever. You need to figure out a way to get both yourself and that girl out of this prison and alert Catriona and her entire crew to be on board the Enigma before dawn, all from the confines of this cell. And the night isn't getting any longer.

Four

"The sirens only claim the guilty. To the innocent man, they are sweet music."
The Siren's Song of Callista

Thessius stepped out of the tavern and pulled his collar up around his ears, then stepped over to where Nicaise was standing. He lit a pipe and took a puff. "Nee-cayse."

"Thessius."

A couple sailors left the bar quietly, nodding to the men on the way past. Nicaise recognized them as crewmen of the *Enigma*. One went left, up the street towards a different tavern.

"Soa, ye desaided ta stay ashore after we drooped ye hair, eh?"

Nicaise smiled. Thessius had a heavy Yorkish accent that seemed to have bred with a Glarren one in an attempt to create almost a different language all its own. He had sailed with the man for two years and was surprised that, after more than a year ashore, he could still understand him. Barely.

"Yes. My fellow citizens seem to prefer having a savage as their executioner. It doesn't hurt that my race counts coup in the form of souls freed to the Great Cycle in the interest of justice. I get a better life in my next incarnation because I released the souls of wrong-doers so they could be reborn, to try again. It has turned out to be equitable."

"Yeh, ay kin tell ye don' seem ta mind it." Four more sailors left the bar, followed a few moments later by two sets of two. A group of them were coming down the street from the other tavern in the company of the sailor who had gone there a few moments before.

Nicaise glanced at them and then back at Thessius. "The ship is guarded on the docks. They aren't letting anyone on or off."

Thessius puffed on his pipe. "Ayr they watchin' both sides o' th' ship?"

Nicaise furrowed an eyebrow. "Doubtful. She's docked in the far slip. Nothing but harbor on the other side of her."

"Then I ain't worried, Mate."

He took another draw on his pipe as a couple more crewmembers meandered towards the docks.

Nicaise waited until Thessius finished his pipe. As he did so, he noticed several crewmen talking down near the docks. One of them nodded in the direction of the *Enigma* and the guards posted at the end of the gangplank and dock. One of them leaned in to say something, and the others nodded. They walked down to the third dock from the ship, then walked to the end and each, one by one, slipped into the water from an open mooring area.

Nicaise did not react to the brilliance of the plan, but he was still glad they didn't decide to fight the guards. Nicaise remembered the *Enigma* had ladders on both sides, and that they were only drawn up on the side next to the dock for exactly this kind of occasion. Within a few minutes, Nicaise saw one of the sailors that had been on the dock before walk up to Octavius, the First Mate. They waited a bit longer as Thessius drew out the smoking of his pipe. Eventually, Octavius stepped over to the guard rail of the ship and nodded to the two men.

"So, do Port lawrs oan sailors who git arrest'd git enforc'd in St. Marguerite?"

Nicaise nodded, not looking at the other man. "Oh yes."

Thessius emptied his pipe on the street and tucked it into his coat. He kicked off from the wall and finally turned to face his friend. "Shell we, then?"

Nicaise nodded. "Which method?"

"Th' one from St. Giles'd work well 'ere, don't ye thank?"

Nicaise shook his head. "Somehow, I knew you were going to suggest that." He stepped over in front of the open door to the tavern and took a deep breath. "Go."

Thessius grabbed the front of Nicaise' coat and yelled, *"No one talks 'bout the Capt'n laike thet!"* Then, he punched Nicaise across the jaw, knocking him into the tavern.

Catriona awoke and listened to the sounds around her. It was different being in a real bed on the land and this bed was extravagant, to be sure. Alexander was sleeping finally and she was grateful. She kissed him and got up, her need to use the privy pressing. He stirred as she got out of bed and he reached out for her. "Where are you going?"

"The privy. I'll be back."

He nodded and closed his eyes again. Within seconds, he was back to sleep, a slight snore escaping his lips. She smiled and looked around. None of her clothes were here and she wasn't about to get back into that behemoth of a dress just to go to the privy. She saw a dark, lavish silk robe hanging on the door to the wardrobe and grabbed it. Her slippers from the gown were simple enough to slip into so she put those on. She tied the robe closed and slipped out the door.

She found the privy easily and used the facilities, which were very nice for a manor house where no royalty actually lived. It was probably a holdover from the pampering of the salon. The privy was well lit and held a novel, a mirror and some grooming tools like a brush, tongue scraper and teeth cleaner, with a sink and pitcher for face and hands. More of the soaps were here and she was very impressed that they scented the room so the privy did not stink of the middens. She made use of the facilities and all the tools, cleaning them and returning them to their proper places when she was finished. The flavors of rich food always turned foul smelling in the stomach and she was grateful for the dish of cloves left in the room. She checked the mirror to make sure she didn't have black flecks of clove in her teeth and stepped out of the privy.

She started down the hallway when she heard the sound of people talking at the front door drifting up the stairways.

"I'm looking for the Captain of the *Enigma.* I was told she was here?"

Catriona didn't recognize the voice of the man speaking but she recognized Lysette's when she answered. "Yes, I think she is but she's gone to bed by now. You can't come in here disturbing her, Owen."

Catriona walked towards the conversation as the man insisted he had official business and Lysette insisted otherwise. As she looked over the railing near the steps down, she was surprised to find the man was wearing a city guard uniform. She called attention to herself as she descended the stairs. "I'm the Captain of the *Enigma.* What can I do for you, Officer?"

The guard snapped a bow to her as Lysette curtsied. "I'm sorry, Stâpâna," Lysette tossed a glare at the guard, "Officer Owen here says he has business with you of an official nature."

"Indeed, Lady. One of your crewmen has been arrested and owes damages. It is the law in St. Marguerite that the Captain of a ship be notified immediately if crew are arrested and damages are owed."

Lysette bristled. "I highly doubt they mean disturb the Captain from bed the first night they have had to be ashore, Owen."

Catriona smiled. "Actually, it cites *especially* under circumstances like those, Lysette. It tends to save on supplies for the prisoners because the captains tend to be harsher ministers of justice than the city is allowed, once their crew are back on board." She looked back up the stairs, checking to be sure Alexander had not discovered her still missing and come looking for her. She didn't want to inconvenience him and frankly, she suspected the arrested crewman to be needing to speak with her. Her crew knew better than to break laws in a port such as this. "Well, we'd best be going then."

"My lady!" Lysette's horror at venturing out in the robe and slippers was audible as she looked the Stâpâna up and down.

Catriona shrugged. "I'm sorry, Lysette. My clothes were returned to my ship."

"I could help you get dressed in your dinner clothes, my Lady."

Catriona leaned in and drew her into her confidence. "Unfortunately, that would mean waking His Majesty. I'd rather just deal with this and return later before he misses me." She patted the servant woman's arm. "You cover for me, would you?" Catriona looked at the guard. "Shall we, Officer?"

The guardsman offered his arm to her and they stepped into the midnight air.

Myrgen raised his head as he heard the guards bringing in another prisoner. *Saint's Blood! Is it always this rough around here?* The guard opened up the cell on the other side of Ysabel's and tossed the prisoner in. "You stay put now until your Captain shows up."

"Now, ye din' go an tell me Capt'n, did ye? She'll 'ave me 'ead."

Myrgen stood up and went to the cell door. "Thessius? Is that you?"

"'Ey! Master Myrgen. Now who did ye 'ave ta beat up ta git tossed in 'ere?"

"More the other way around, Thessius. Did you say the Captain was going be showing up here?"

"Aye. T'is th' lawr 'ere."

Myrgen heard the guardsman lock the cell and then leave.

"So, the Stâpâna is coming here?" Ysabel's voice was nervous and shaky.

"'Ey, 'ey, don' wairry, m'laidy." Thessius dropped his voice to keep the guard from taking interest in the conversation. "Th' Cap'n ain' gonnae be 'urtin' me. I was jus' sayin' tha' ta let Myrgen know I were 'ere."

"And let me tell you, Thessius, I'm glad you are."

"So, d'ye 'ave a plan or am aye yer best bet?"

"Well, getting the Captain here will help. Ysabel here has the Key."

Myrgen saw Thessius' nose poke through the bars on his door window. "Wait, this gal has th' Key? Th' Onyx Key?"

Ysabel still managed to keep her voice low but her excitement from this adventure was obvious as Myrgen's fate at dawn. "Yes. It's right here."

"Ye maight wanna gait rid o' it afore she gets 'ere then."

Myrgen blinked. "What? Why?"

"'Cuz thet's a precious artefect o' 'er coontray. She's oblaishud ta take ta task any'ne who tooches th' thing."

"I'm sorry. What did he just say?"

Myrgen smiled, aware that only his gift for languages enabled him to understand half the things Thessius ever said. "I think he said you should give it to me."

"That's not what it sounded like he said."

"Trust me, Ysabel. You want that Key in my hands when she gets here."

Myrgen could practically hear the blood leave Ysabel's face.

"Er, yeh... 'At's wh't aye sed."

"You said you weren't serious, that you were just saying that to get the Vicar to give you the Key."

"Lucky guess."

"Well, ye maight wanna git on thet. When aye were arrested, th' guardsmen sen' a fella oop ta git 'er."

"I quite agree." Myrgen put his fingers through the bars on the window. "Ysabel, can you get your hands through the bars?"

She messed around a bit in the cell, then poked the necklace and much of her small hand out the bars. She tossed it and Myrgen felt it hit his fingers and then it was gone, the leather thong making a silent *thop* as it hit the ground. "Did you catch it?"

"Um, no." He got down on the floor and looked under the door. The thong was there, but the Key was gone. He was about to ask about it, to see if Ysabel had taken the Key off when he saw the top of the Key sticking out of the ground, attached to the necklace. The Key had entered the earth as if the solid ground Myrgen knelt upon was mere illusion.

By the Saints, this really is a gift of the Land. And obviously, Catriona doesn't need to be holding it for it to work. I might be able to get us out of this.

Alistair crawled back into the bed area. He didn't dare leave this situation unmonitored for long. The Woman had told him she would help him maintain balance. He didn't really know what that meant. He was in Karma's Hand, wherever that was, and had come to this place when he died in perfect balance. The Woman had told him he was here to judge the situation and when it was in balance, he was supposed to do something. It was something he wasn't sure he wanted to do.

He looked at Catriona. The Woman had mentioned something earlier, something that was now catching his mind. *The child of that union... Was Catriona ripe to get pregnant?* He looked at the curtains on the other side, calling up the image of Myrgen.

I like that a lot better. He cracked his knuckles. This was going to take some work.

Five

"Fire can save or damn the whole ship."
—The Siren's Song of Callista

Myrgen got up and looked around the room for something to use to snag the necklace and found a piece of stiff straw poking out of the mattress. He pulled it and found it possibly long enough. Now it just needed to be stiff enough. He reached under the door and caught the loop of the thong but the straw bent when he tried to move the necklace.

"What's happening?" Ysabel's fear had left her voice, to be replaced by nervous curiosity, but she was remembering to keep her voice low.

"I'm trying to snag the necklace, but the straw isn't strong enough."

"Use more than one piece. Tie them together, like a faggot of sticks."

Myrgen looked up and then back at the necklace. "Smart girl."

He went back to his mattress and pulled several more straws from it. Some of them were too short to use but a few had promise.

Now to tie them with something. He glanced around, running his hand through his hair. A hair caught on a snag in a fingernail and he pulled, freeing it. Then he glanced at the stray and ran his fingers through his hair several times, pulling out those which were destined to abandon him anyway. With about a dozen strands with which to work, he wrapped the straws into a sturdy bundle.

He went back over to the door and resumed his position. The girl was right and the added strength of the extra straws brought the thong to within reach. He pulled it into the cell with him and picked it up. There, like he remembered, was the small onyx key Catriona had worn on her neck the night she rescued him from the cell in Patras. The night he had openly declared his defiance to the will of the Crown of Mervolingia. The night he had kissed her for the first time.

The night his life had changed forever.

He swallowed, and clutched the key, then went to the back of the cell. He put the key against the stone wall, where it soaked into the rock like a drop of water into a sponge. He pushed against the stone, but it did not move. He pushed harder, then kicked it. Nothing. He put his head against the stone. *I can't open it. By the bleeding Saints and Martyrs, I can't open it.* He slammed his fist against the wall, but it responded to him like he was hammering his fist against a stone wall, and he realized in that moment, he was probably going to die.

He took the key from the wall and held it in his hand, his heart heavy. The stone key winked at him in the dim light and he pressed it to his lips, trying, for just a moment, to connect with her, to feel her presence, or smell her perfume. Then the door to the Magister's Office opened and his wish was granted. He heard her voice.

"Captain Rhys, you didn't need to escort me personally."

"I couldn't have a visiting ambassador wandering unescorted in such attire without proper guard. The Baroness would kill me."

"I was hardly unescorted, Captain."

"Ah, but you don't know Owen like I do. Allow me to say your attire was commanding far too much of his attention."

Footsteps down the hall, one set soft, one set hard.

"Had you allowed me upon my ship to change clothes, I wouldn't have been wandering about in such attire." They stopped in front of a cell. "Thessius. I would have expected this from you."

"It seem'd th' proper thing ta do, Captain."

"Captain Rhys, since I do not have my belt pouch with me, I will have to pay for his release in the morning. Is it a problem for him to stay here tonight?"

"Of course not ma'am, but your word is as good as gold here, Lady. Should you wish to take him with you and administer your own justice, that is the law here in St. Marguerite."

"I beg ya, sir, please, let me 'ave one final night of peace 'ere in yer jail."

"Quiet, you." Catriona's voice was appropriately harsh but Myrgen had to smile, nonetheless. *If they only knew.* "Yes, Captain, if he could stay here, I would appreciate it. Since I'm not able to get on my ship right now, it wouldn't do to have him wandering the streets and getting into more trouble. Is that all?"

"Er no, not really. While you're here…"

More steps, closer this time.

"This young woman was found in possession of an item of yours. She said she was trying to return it to your ship but the Vicar thinks she might have been stealing it."

"What was this item?"

"Uh… A necklace, I think."

"Where is this item now?" Catriona's tone was sharp and the young Captain of the Guard seemed to believe he was walking on dangerous ground.

Myrgen decided to show his hand. He stepped over to the door to his cell. "I have it, Captain."

Catriona's face drifted into view and he had to admit that if he had to see nothing else before the axe met his neck, this was a good final vision. Her long black hair was unbound and had a sexy tousle to it. She had bathed and been pampered a bit and her features were enhanced beyond his ability to imagine. She was almost as beautiful as she had been when they were in the bath house in Rouen. Clearly an artist of the highest measure had chosen only to outline her already full lips and her deep green, exotic eyes. She scanned him and he realized when she faltered in her harsh outward show that she had just read his thoughts like he had spoken them aloud.

She looked at the necklace he was holding up and recovered her façade before turning to the guard. "It appears your evidence against this woman has changed recipients, Captain. I see nothing to impugn this good lady's name. I would recommend you release her."

"I will let the Vicar know, Ma'am. He will undoubtedly release her in the morning."

"Good." She turned back to Myrgen. "As for you, I don't know why you set foot on Mervol soil again, but you have clearly chosen your fate and in doing so, inconvenienced myself and my entire crew by banishing us from our ship until you are disposed of. Don't make it worse. Give me back my necklace."

Myrgen stepped back. "Come get it." He put it on his neck.

Catriona's eyes never left his as she spoke to the guardsman. "Captain Rhys, open the cell."

"My lady, that is incredibly ill-advised. This man is a traitor to the Crown, wanted for murder. I can't put you in danger."

"The item he has is an artifact of my country. I have to have it."

Rhys exerted his leadership qualities then and Myrgen gained a respect for the man as he stood up to Catriona. "Then I will remove it personally tomorrow, from his corpse, if I must. You will not enter. I'm sorry."

"Your interference could be seen as an act of War, Captain."

"Then the King will execute me as readily as he would if I let anything happen to you. Either way, I'm dead, but I'd rather have died protecting you than explaining to His Majesty that I let the woman he was," he paused to glance down at her scant attire, "*entertaining* tonight be attacked by a known enemy of the state."

Myrgen blinked at the veiled blackmail threat and watched the next part of the exchange carefully. *Well played, sir. Stupid, but well played. My money's on that she'll kill you for threatening her like that.*

She took a deep breath. "Then perhaps we need to have His Majesty come down now and take care of this."

Rhys frowned. "I'm sure it will keep until morning,"

Myrgen snorted. "Before or *after* my beheading at dawn?"

Rhys glanced at the cell, then back at the dignitary before him. Myrgen saw his blink stutter and wondered if Catriona used some sort of Land Worshipping magic upon him. Then he shook his head.

"I'm not the right person to make that judgment. Luckily, I have him in the next room. Please wait here while I get the Vicar."

Catriona glared into the cell and crossed her arms. "Take your time."

Six

"If the maid kisses and calls not the guard, thank
her."
The Siren's Song of Callista

Catriona stepped forward as soon as Rhys was out of sight.
Myrgen came rushing to the window on the door. She reached
through the bars, her fingers touching his.

"We've got to stop meeting like this," he smiled.

She smiled at him and nodded, matching his volume. "I agree.
This is getting to be a habit with you. Hand me the key."

He did so and she placed it in the lock, closing her eyes to
concentrate. The sound of stone scraping metal caused him to
glance down the hall for guards responding to the sound. No one
seemed to be moving their way but he heard Rhys's voice. The
tumblers fell as she turned the key.

She pushed open the door and it screeched. The sound of a
chair scraping the floor caught both their attention and she ducked
into the cell with him. She put her back to the wall beside the door
hinges as the guards in the other room discovered the door open.
She grabbed Myrgen and pulled him to the wall in front of her,

then closed her eyes. The guards entered and Myrgen stopped breathing as the guards glanced over the cell, at one point looking right at them. They searched quickly, then left, closing the cell door. "The prisoner has escaped!"

Rhys glanced in. "How? And what about the Stâpâna?"

"She's not here. He must have taken her as a hostage. Tell the King!"

They ran off and Myrgen looked down at Catriona as she held his robe in her fists, concentrating. She opened her eyes and brought her gaze to him. There was a moment, like so many these days, where his thoughts went immediately to an intimate place. Her body beneath the silk robe was far too accessible and far too appealing to keep his desires in check. Her look did not seem to imply a desire to stop him. He leaned in as she tilted her chin up to meet his lips.

"Cap'n! Ye there?" Thessius' timing could not have been more precise if he had been standing in the cell with them, and Myrgen stepped back to a more respectful distance.

Catriona glanced down at her open attire and pulled it closed as Myrgen averted his eyes. "Uh, yes, yes I'm here."

"How'd you keep them from seeing us? We were right here."

She patted the wall behind her. "Stone wall coupled with a trick of the light. They glanced behind the door but didn't move it to check."

"If they had?"

"Then you would have had to improvise."

He hazarded a look at her backside as she stepped over to the wall between the cells, entertaining the thought. She touched the stones, like she was searching for something. "What are you looking for?"

"A communion stone, one with Land in it. The farther away from Caratia, the harder it is to find, but there's almost always something of the Land in real stones."

"Can't you just unlock the door again?"

She looked at him. "You see a keyhole on this side?"

He looked at the door and saw she was right. "You didn't have a key before. Can't you just open the cell the same way?"

"I could, but then we'd be charging through a room full of guards into a street full of guards."

"Yeah, that would be stupid." His eyes were fastened on the robe and decided he quite liked her new attire. "So, you going to keep that?"

She looked back at him, then down at the robe. "Why not? It's not like I have something else to change into right now." She looked back at him. "Although I suppose I could commandeer your shirt and robe."

He stepped in closer and lowered his voice. "Wouldn't you have to take that off in order to wear my things?"

She smiled and focused on the task in front of her, finding what she needed. She placed the Key on the wall and turned it. The stones fell open like they were on an invisible hinge, much to Ysabel's surprise.

She stepped back as Catriona stepped through. "By the Saints! How did you...?"

Catriona put her finger to her lips. "I'm just passing through to my crewman. I wouldn't want you to be charged with a jail break." Catriona looked at Ysabel. "Unless you *want* to come with me. I don't know if the Vicar will be inclined to re-employ you after this. However, as of this moment, Ysabel, you've done nothing to jeopardize your standing as a Citizen of Mervolingia. If I leave you in here, you can't be implicated."

Ysabel looked at Catriona, then at Myrgen as he entered her cell. She swallowed and shook her head. "Thank you, but no, I'll stay here. You're right. But my lady, may I say you have an ally here, should you ever need one." She looked at Myrgen. "You too, sir."

Myrgen bowed. "Thank you, my lady."

Catriona put her hand on the girl's shoulder and smiled, then her visage returned to business. She stepped up to the wall on the other side and did the same opening technique on the wall.

Ysabel leaned towards Myrgen. "I see now what you meant about the Land being active in her life."

"Well, keep that to yourself. Here, she'd be tried as a witch."

The cell housing Thessius cracked open and he poked his head through.

"Ah, so tha's wha' ye look laike." He looked Ysabel over and nodded. "Not quite wha' I expect'd."

Ysabel frowned at him. "What's that supposed to mean?"

"You're pre'ier. I wasn't expecting ye ta be this pretty because they called ye a servant. Ye smell nace too."

Ysabel looked Thessius over and got a small smile on her face. "Um, so, I should just stay here?"

Thessius fetched her around the waist with a move so smooth, it pulled Myrgen up short. "I could kidnap ye, if ye like…" Then he kissed her like he had just the one kiss to show her what she was going to be missing.

Catriona closed the wall to his cell, then walked past him and Ysabel like this was simply the way things were done. "You coming, Myrgen?"

"Er, y, yes, yes." He turned from the spectacle. "Right behind you." He stepped through the opening in the wall and glanced back through the hole. "Thessius, I think we're leaving now."

He ended the kiss and released his victim. "It's been splendid, m'Lady." Thessius bowed and stepped through the wall. Catriona scanned the girl, then closed the wall. Thessius looked at Myrgen. "What? Haven't ye ev'r want'd ta do somethin' like tha'?"

Catriona cleared her throat while Myrgen decided he should pay attention to what she was doing to get them out of the cell. He turned to look at her pressing her hand against the wall. Her shapely back was to the men and Myrgen had trouble breathing for a moment. "Never crossed my mind."

"Righ'."

Catriona pulled the wall toward her this time and very carefully peeked outside, which merely enhanced the view from behind. "It's clear. Let's go, gentlemen."

The two men stepped outside and Catriona reached in and grabbed the Key from the wall before sealing it again. She nodded towards the end of the alley and the three of them moved quickly and quietly between the buildings. At the end, she looked around and waited a moment as someone shouted and entered the front of the Magister's Office. Myrgen recognized his brother's bellow and he realized they were a wrong turn away from capture. He looked at Catriona and waited for her signal.

She motioned and the three ran across the street to the next alley. They made their way near the docks. When they got within sight of the ship, he noticed that the guard had been increased since Myrgen was taken. Now there were five men guarding the docks and they looked prepared for a fight. "It looks like my brother stopped by here first."

"We can't get to the ship." Catriona looked around for an option.

Myrgen glanced up the street, then back at the ship. "Contact the spirit of the ship, like you can when you're on board."

She closed her eyes, then shook her head, opening them again. "Too far."

"There's a proximity requirement?"

"Obviously, or I would have known the instant your brother arrested you instead of Thessius having to get captured in order for your situation to be brought to my attention. I'm certain Alexander had every intention of keeping me with him until well after dawn."

"Aw, aye doot tha' Grymalkin 'ad any inklin' this were goin' on, Cap'n." Thessius looked at Myrgen. Myrgen realized the crewman didn't know about the decree. An alleyway while trying to escape probably wasn't the best setting to shatter his current illusions regarding Alexander. Thessius looked at Myrgen, then back at Catriona, a little less certainty in his voice. "Did 'e?"

She looked at her friend and swallowed before returning to her vigilance. "I don't know. I can't read him."

Myrgen had suspected Catriona might have been in intimate surroundings with Alexander due to the attire she chose for this rescue. She was too aware of people's opinions and thoughts to allow herself to be compromised like this. Alexander had made sure, if she was summoned away, she would have to either be put in a compromising position, probably so he could come to her reputation's rescue, or that she would have to rely upon his royal endowments to achieve her ends. Regardless, Myrgen no longer believed Alexander was the valiant savior he once did.

Still, Myrgen had hoped that perhaps she was sleeping in her own separate chambers. It stung to have it confirmed that she was indeed with the man. Although Myrgen had no claim on her, it didn't change the fact that he still cared for her quite a bit.

Thessius stepped over to her and surveyed the docks. "I 'ave 'n idea, but I sure wish tha' Ysabel gal were 'ere fer it."

Myrgen looked at the crewman. "Why?"

"'Cuz she's goin' ta 'ate tha' she missed this." He backed away from the pair and ducked back the way they came, turning at the street.

Myrgen looked at Catriona. "Did you see what he was going to do?"

She shook her head. "Only that it was something to tell his children and that he hopes he gets a chance to have them."

"Should we go get Ysabel?"

She looked behind them. "You think that's who he had in mind to make them with?"

"Hey, you're the soul reader. If you don't know, how should I?"

"Good point."

A voice came from nearby and Catriona and Myrgen ducked back into the alley. The voices were definitely guards because they were shouting instructions to search all the alleyways and doorways. Catriona fingered the Key on her neck and looked around. Most of the buildings around them were wooden, not something the Key would work upon and they searched for a stone wall to use. Myrgen spotted one and pointed it out, but it was across a very wide main thoroughfare from where they were currently hiding. She stopped toying with the Key and shook her head. "It wouldn't work. There's no Caratian citizen on the other side who needs my help."

"I'm not Caratian, Catriona, and you've used that Key to help me twice now."

"Remember that tirade you went on to Nicolai in the prison in Patras? When you said you'd rather spend the rest of your life on bended knee before me than pay another moment's homage to the Mervol Crown?"

"That's all it takes?"

"Caratia is not Mervolingia. We don't require the people's fealty to rule. We are there because the Land has chosen us. Without its approval, none of this works."

Myrgen was about to mention the stone-hiding trick as an interim solution when a movement caught his attention. Thessius was walking out on a yardarm that stuck out over the dock toward the *Enigma*, whose yardarm was about four feet away from the one he was on. "By the Saints and Martyrs. Can the Land help *him* fly?"

Seven

"To escape the burning ship, you must swim through the sharks."
The Siren's Song of Callista

Catriona turned and saw at what he was looking. Her eyes grew wide and she grabbed Myrgen's hand. Thessius walked casually over to the yardarm end, measured the distance, then backed up and ran. The leap was a short one for someone not forty-feet in the air, and apparently, the sailor's skill in climbing and running the rigging had stolen his fear in this situation. He landed on the *Enigma's* yardarm and rushed along its length to the mast. Within a minute, he was safe on the deck and the guards around the area were none the wiser.

Myrgen and Catriona exhaled and he looked around to make sure they hadn't been stumbled upon. "Ok, so he's safe, at least until they search the ship. That still doesn't get us on board and even if we were, it wouldn't get us out of the harbor."

"Trust me. Having him on the ship right now just enabled us to succeed. He used to be First Mate on a ship with a very clever Captain. They had more than a few ruses for situations like this.

Now we just have to avoid capture until he and Octavius figure out something."

Octavius came to the stern and looked out into the city. Thessius pointed to the alley she and Myrgen were hiding and Octavius nodded. Thessius handed him something and Octavius opened it, fussing with it a moment. He held up a ball and Catriona squeezed Myrgen's hand. "Interesting choice…"

"A ball? Is that supposed to draw the guards' attention?"

"Um, you might say that."

Octavius lobbed the ball as far as he could down the dock area and the ball hit a few feet in front of the store across from the pair. It exploded with a splash, igniting upon impact with the ground. Fire sprung up everywhere the fluid touched and Myrgen pulled back as it occurred to him that the guards were going to be running their way. He drew Catriona down to the other end of the alley, looking into the street to make sure no guards were coming their way. Shouts from the guards near the *Enigma* filtered down the alley and the two stepped out of the alley just as the guards got to the end of it to put the fire out.

When they got to the street, he realized they had a shot at getting to the ship but they had to hurry. The fire was starting to spread a bit and the light was getting brighter. Very soon, the street would be flooded with citizens, guards and light. Then the ship would be cut off. They sprinted to the dock. As they got there, Myrgen heard a shout from a guard. There was a thump behind them and Catriona stopped moving forward, almost falling. They looked back to see a dagger pinning the silk into the docks. The material was strong and the dagger had caught it between the planks on the dock.

Catriona glanced back at the guards who were taking notice of their flight attempt. One of them was a larger man with kind, but very sharp eyes. She looked at the dagger. "That guy's good."

Myrgen saw the man who had dropped him with a dagger throw to the back of his knee. "Yeah, I know."

She glanced down the street to the distraction and then kicked off the shoes toward the street. She untied the robe and dropped it to the dock, then ran up the gangplank, completely nude. It took a moment for Myrgen to recover before he followed her. On deck, she shouted to her crew. "Gentlemen! Get us ready to sail! Octavius!"

He came running over to the edge of the upper deck rail and stopped when he saw the Captain's undressed state.

"Are all hands on board?"

Silence greeted her as all conversation and activity stopped for a moment. She repeated her question. "Octavius! *Are all hands on board?"*

"Uh, yes! Yes, Captain!"

"Then get us under weigh! *Now!"*

Myrgen took his robe off and put it on her unclothed form. As soon as she was covered again, the spell was broken and her crew started moving like they had a timeline. She turned to him. "Thanks. I hadn't thought of that."

"It took me a minute as well. Go. I'll help get things going here." Myrgen ran over to the gangplank and hauled it up as the foresail was unfurled to give the ship some movement. The fire and mayhem in the streets covered their own activities as several other ships were shouting orders to their skeleton crews to get their ships away from the fire. Catriona disappeared into her cabin and the ship was away before the guards realized she was moving. Myrgen went up the aft castle next to Octavius and Thessius. "Nice move, using alchemist fire. Haven't made that for a while."

Octavius turned to him. "You know how to make that?"

"Yeah."

"Good. Then at the next opportunity, you need to replenish our stores. That was our last one."

"Done." Myrgen looked out at the fire and saw something he really didn't want to see. "By the blood of the Saints. Alexander."

He pointed at the man moving down the street from the rich end of town. He was wearing the breeches and boots from the night before. His shirt without the doublet was untucked and he walked with purpose, his sword drawn. He pointed at Myrgen with the sword and Myrgen realized at that moment that, had he still been a sworn member of the Mervol populace, he probably would have leapt off the ship with Catriona in tow. A small wind caught the smallest fore sail and moved the ship away from the dock in a quick lunge. By the time Alexander reached her side, she would be too far from the dock to leap onto.

Alexander strode onto the dock, his boots striking the boards like they were trying to call up sparks. "Myrgen! Release Catriona and bring her back!"

The King's voice was not as practiced from years of addressing the populace at court as his brother or Myrgen had been, but the intervening and increasing space did not diminish the sound of his anger and Myrgen heard that as it was intended.

Myrgen answered with actual practiced ease. "She's not my prisoner, Alexander!"

"I'll charge you with kidnapping! You won't be able to pull into port in any city in the country! The crew will *die* without supplies, and it will be *your fault!*"

"Return to your D'Medici world, Alexander. You tried to trick her, like you tricked me! You're just mad because she saw through it!"

"You're pathetic, Myrgen! She'll never love you! You're not good enough for her!"

The mainsail dropped and the breeze from the city pushed them easily. The distance was finally getting great enough that even Alexander could no longer project enough to be heard. He looked down at the dock and picked up the robe that was cast off. He pointed his sword at Myrgen again, then ran the blade through the robe, slicing it in two. He threw the shreds to the ground and turned his back on the fleeing ship.

Myrgen watched as the fire started to spread. The guards discovered the worst way to put out a fire of this nature was to throw water on it. He watched Alexander shout out to the men, who kicked dirt onto one of the places with splash over from the alchemist fire. Unfortunately, the guards didn't seem to understand and kept throwing water until the fire started getting ahead of them. A single look back at the ship indicated the King's rage was following the fire's lead. He kept glaring at the fleeing ship as Morgan Wolf came running down the street towards him. Myrgen turned to Octavius and Thessius. "The city watch is going to have their hands full tending to that fire. We should be safe. I'm going to check on the Captain."

Both men nodded and Thessius shook his head. "Ai don' know if ai've ev'r seen a man th't angry b'fore."

Myrgen glanced back at Alexander. "Look right here. You'll see another one." He turned away and went down the stairs to the main deck.

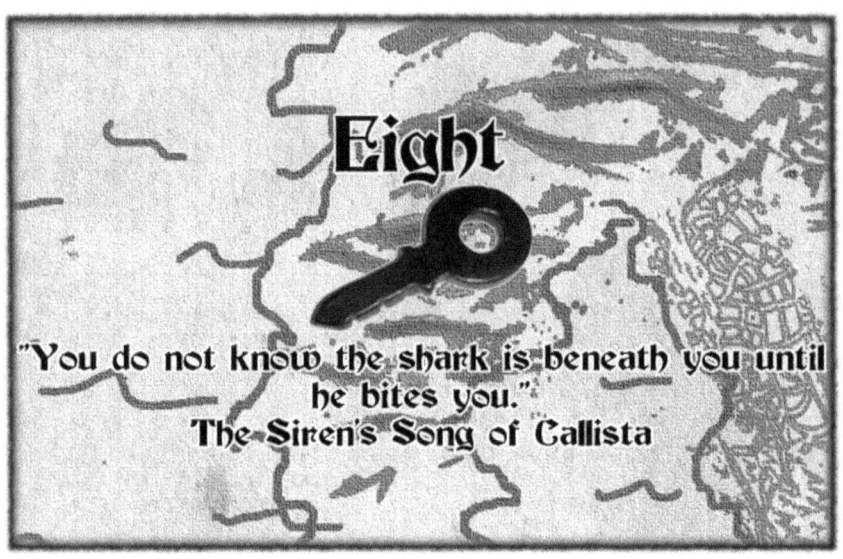

Eight

"You do not know the shark is beneath you until
he bites you."
The Siren's Song of Callista

Myrgen knocked on the door to Catriona's cabin and entered when he heard her call.

"Hey, are you all right?"

She looked up from where she was sitting, pulling on her boots. She had gotten into a black shirt and long, thick hose that didn't get in her way when she worked the rigging. She had braided her hair to get it out of her way, a hasty job which showed in several missed hairs that softened the look around her face. Her coat was draped over the back of the chair at her desk.

"So to speak. I could hear Alexander shouting at us," she shrugged, returning her attention to her boots, "well, shouting at you, but I couldn't make out what he was saying."

Myrgen folded his arms and leaned against the door. "Nothing I wouldn't expect from him at this point. He threatened to ban your ships from Mervol ports so you couldn't re-supply."

She sat up, a look of concern striking her features. "That would be a problem. A lot of my people depend upon trade with these ports."

"I don't think he'll do it. He wouldn't want to alienate you. Not after what he just tried to do."

She stood and pulled on her coat, not meeting his eyes. "I don't know what you mean. He didn't try to do anything."

Myrgen looked askance. Could she seriously be defending him? "For someone who is able to see into people's souls, how can you possibly be so naïve? He tried to keep you occupied while he had me executed, after sending my own brother to get me off the ship, in direct defiance of your pact with him."

She looked away, grabbing her sword belt and putting it on. "Maybe your brother suggested it." She buckled the sword into place.

"No, all he had was a decree that Alexander apparently wrote while you were bathing, one that declared anyone who rendered me aid forfeit to the wrath of the Crown. I'm pretty sure I could read off the exact wording, since I've seen one or two of them before regarding a certain massacre a few years back." He stepped over to her. "Don't you understand? That decree puts you and this entire crew, and their families in danger for helping me. He can hold them hostage, to make you return and he did it while you were bathing, when he knew where you were."

Catriona looked into his eyes, then returned to her task of getting dressed. "Look, you don't know him. He's not like that."

His eyes widened while his brow furrowed. "I beg to differ. My experiences with the man tell an entirely different story. That man sent my own brother to trick me off the ship so he could arrest and execute me before you even knew I was in trouble. Alexander counted on the guilt from that to drive you into his arms. And if that didn't work, he was going to destroy your ship. That kind of treachery, that kind of betrayalshouldn't be allowed to touch you, much less marry you."

Myrgen knew, in the back of his mind, that he should be intimidated by this woman, that she was no one with whom to trifle, but he found he could no longer hold his tongue.

"Frankly, with your ability to read me, I had decided long ago not to hide things from you and I'm not going to disguise my feelings on this subject, especially not after tonight. I have let Alexander have his last opportunity to deceive you, and I'm determined to make you see the side of him you keep turning away from.

"Catriona, I watched that man cut down the last woman I loved after deceiving her. I've watched that man do unspeakable horrors simply because he wanted something. He's his mother's son, and that woman is a D'Medici all the way. He was raised by her to be the best manipulator possible. Think about it! Do you really want Alexander raising your son to become like Marco Giovanni?"

Myrgen stopped, realizing he may have just gone too far, bringing up the man who had raped and almost killed her when her son was born. Her look was cold and she continued to dress herself.

He looked away a moment. "I'm sorry. That was rude, but the fact remains that he has a side he doesn't show you, but I've seen it up close." He pointed to her. "So have you, when he cut Elizabeth down. He was cold and calculating. That was Catherine's blood running through icy veins, giving him the ability to put aside his emotions to do what he felt was necessary."

"And you don't think that a good thing for a King to be able to do?"

"I don't think it a good thing for a husband to be able to do, or a father, especially not one with you."

"And you'd never do that to me? That the burden of the Crown is not yours so you would never have to choose between me and the good of thousands of lives? Is that where you're going with this, Myrgen? Are you trying to tell me my heart would be safer with you than with him?"

"Yes! Yes, I think I am!" There. I've finally said it. Myrgen's heart was pounding in his chest, the hope that she would see that he loved her so powerful, it would take a single pause, the slightest hint of that latent passion they had seen in the prison or on the deck or anywhere in the past few ten-days to catapult him to her for that third, eternal kiss.

Her eyes grew dark and cold against the passion he was feeling. Her voice became that same silken poison from their first meeting.

"Why would you think I would be safer with a man so weak willed, he fell prey to a Fae spell cast by a human girl?"

He straightened up, slapped back to reality by the validity of her comment. He blinked, running his hands through his hair as he stared at the floor. "Good shot. You got me there, Catriona. You have successfully deduced my greatest fear."

She looked away from him, and didn't comment.

Myrgen shook his head "You know, ever since Alexander told us about the spell Gwen cast, I have been afraid that it was the source of all this emotion I've been seeing and feeling. This intense attraction, the sleepless nights, even the random occasions where we've kissed. I've fought it because I figured it was the same thing every sailor on your ship went through." He looked at her. "Except that you were returning those looks, those kisses. That night in St. Andrew? How many of your crew have spent the night with you?"

"That's not fair, Myrgen. We were set up."

"You had the chance to send me away. You didn't. I think about it now and I realize that, even if Gwen cast a spell to open up our hearts to love, there's one thing that makes that unbelievable."

She looked at him, her breathing quickening. "What?"

"That it was Alexander that told us about it. A man who would destroy anyone in his way to get to you. Don't you see, Catriona? He's tried it the nice way. Now he's delving into his darker side. He'll gladly use your crew against you to get his hands on you. By the Saints, Catriona, he traveled with a shadowalker, who tried to kill us, to get to you. He could have gotten him on this ship and destroyed it."

"Ridiculous."

"How so?"

She turned an angry glare on Myrgen. "Because Alexander doesn't know anything about the special nature of this ship. That's privileged information. Frankly, only a handful know about it and four of them are on this ship right now."

"What about the decree?"

"Well, that's another matter entirely. If it exists, it could cause trouble with the crew."

"If it exists?" Myrgen was trying not to get upset over this but her defense of the man was getting the better of him.

"Did you see it?"

"No, I wasn't the one up at the manor house getting bathed for his pleasure. I was the one being threatened with beheading at dawn."

"That's not my fault, Myrgen. You knew you had sanctuary here and you knew he had it in for you. Why would you ever set foot off this ship?"

"Because I figured he would leave me out of it once he had you!"

"Apparently not, since he wrote the decree before he took me to bed!"

Myrgen blinked, the admission hanging there like the echo of a musket. He felt defeated, destroyed. Even though he had figured they were together, his heart had just kept dodging the concept, hiding behind plausible scenarios. Suddenly, he felt sick again and he wanted to leave. "I need to get out of here. I just can't bear the thought of him, and you... Good night, Catriona."

"Excuse me? You told me to go to him. You told me that I was in love with him."

He looked at her. "Then what am I doing here? Why are you putting your relationship, your life, your ship and your crew in jeopardy if you love him?"

"I don't know!" She turned from him, pacing. "I don't know. I can't seem to sort out the way I'm feeling right now."

"Well, take this as a clue to the solution: You were in his bed tonight."

"I was in bed with you in St. Andrew, Myrgen. Nothing happened there either."

Myrgen shook his head and looked at her. "What do you mean nothing happened there 'either'?"

"He didn't... He couldn't get it up... with me..." She looked crestfallen, like Alexander's inability to perform with her had damaged her.

He looked her over. She still wore the make-up and although the scent on her was not the one with which he was familiar, it was still pleasant. He envisioned her in the robe, her hair unbound and a little tousled. He had barely been able to contain himself in the cell when she pulled him to her. Every movement on the ship had stopped when she had called attention to the fact she was nude on the deck. Even now, he could feel the twitches of life in his breeches.

He shook his head. "I'm sorry. I'm not buying that. It's just not possible. I look at you, at the way you looked tonight when you came to the jail and I can barely remain a gentleman. You're the love of his life."

She stepped over to her sea chest and pulled out a pair of leather gloves. "Yes, well, I guess that wasn't enough."

"No, it just proves he has no right to be with you." It was unintentional, but the statement came out harsher than he had expected. Apparently, his vitriol over Alexander's betrayal was still too dominant in his heart to be kept from his voice.

Catriona turned to face him in a swirl of anger. "He has every right to be with me. He has been there for me when no one else was and deserves forgiveness and leniency and anything else he desires. And he doesn't need to be disparaged by a traitor to his Crown who tried to murder his brother so he could sleep with the Queen."

"Well, at least when I actually got the chance to bed the woman I loved, I was man enough to take her!"

"And you think you're man enough to succeed where he failed?"

He saw the challenge in her eyes and walked over to her. "Hell, yes."

She backed up against the chart table, dropping her gloves, her hands gripping the edge as he prepared to claim her at last. His desire for her was screaming for release and the sharp intake of breath from her caused her chest to rise in anticipation. He grabbed her around the waist and leaned down, drawing breath by her neck. Her skin still held some of her own scent and it was softer than it had been before. Her eyes closed and she let her head fall back, exposing the fact there was little between him and heaven beneath her shirt. He pulled her sword belt, undoing it in order to free her shirt for access from below. His lips followed the curve of her skin as he fought with the leather strip, finally freeing it to gravity's will as a moan from her encouraged him.

The sword belt hit the floor with a clang and was pushed aside by Myrgen's boot. He slipped his hand under the edge of her shirt and pressed it against the small of her back, his fingers spreading to keep control. His other hand went to the back of her neck, slipping easily into that pampered hair. The shudders in her muscles betrayed her desire. His was just as evident, pressing against her. He ran his lips along her neck, denying her that final kiss they both wanted, prolonging the intensity, reveling in it. He would kiss her right before he went inside her. There could be no doubt at that moment.

She looked at him, eyes intense, flashing, and her eyes narrowed, seeing his plan. "You bastard."

"Oh, you'll be calling me more than that soon." He let his lips linger just out of reach of her lips, his hand at her neck gripping lightly into her hair to keep his strategy intact.

Her voice caught in her throat as he rolled her head to the side to give him access to her neck. Her fingers gripped the table as he commanded pleasure from her flesh. He raised his eyes and saw a flash from shore, then heard a boom. A black ball in the distance became bigger. He pulled her off the table and threw her to the floor beneath him as the cannon ball shredded the stained glass and ceiling. Suddenly, there was yelling from the crew above, obvious through the new hole torn in the deck above them and the sounds of the ship creaking under fire tore through his ears.

He looked her over. "Are you all right?"

Her face had a few cuts on it but nothing serious. The chart table had shielded them from most of the blast. She looked around. "Someone shot us."

"Yes."

He lifted himself off her and looked out the window. Another shot blasted through the air from a different part of the city. They heard it hit outside in the water. He helped her to her feet and she grabbed her sword from the floor, strapping on the belt in far less time than it took him to remove it. Myrgen ran to the door, moving her in front of him. They ran out onto the deck as chaos erupted around them.

"Octavius!" Catriona ran to the helm, Myrgen quick on her heels.

"Captain! The city is firing on us!"

Myrgen looked back at the city. "It looks like Alexander's decree is carrying more weight than he expected. They mean to execute us all."

Octavius looked at Myrgen. "What decree?"

Catriona shook her head. "None of that matters right now." She turned to Myrgen and pointed. "Get that sail up and get us out of range before they start firing the chain shot!"

"Aye Captain!" He looked at a couple deckhands who were lost in the surprise and pressed them into service.

Alistair looked around, his fury flipping his hair around. "That was unfair!"

"You interrupted my plan. I get to interrupt yours."

"You planned to get her pregnant and make her have to marry Alexander?"

The Woman sat on the bed behind him and wrapped her arms around his waist, laying her head on his shoulder blades. Her scent was *so* familiar but he just couldn't place it.

"It could solve a lot of problems. A country devoted to Heaven, even with its little civil squabbles, and a country devoted to the Land. Stâpâna is a high rank in Caratia, and would go a long way in swaying the Dûcesa. If the Dûcesa chooses not to battle, and the Champion of Heaven chooses not to battle, none of your friends or family will have to suffer a war. Is that not what you said you wanted?"

Alistair frowned and turned back to the scene before him. In St. Andrew, when he was still alive, Alistair set Myrgen and Catriona up to be together, playing tricks to get the two of them in the same bed. Although it didn't end up quite as planned, they left St Andrew together. He had thought they would have at least shared that third kiss he prophesied would be the one that sealed them together. Now, the tricks seemed to be stronger magic and higher stakes. This was getting too complicated and he wasn't sure where the lines were drawn anymore.

Hang in there, Myrgen. It's not over yet.

Catriona closed her cabin door behind her, more than a little embarrassed by the display on deck. She hugged Myrgen's robe to her as she leaned against the door, letting her heart shake off the adrenaline. Her mind wasn't processing yet and she felt she needed more than anything for it to get to work on that. Her thumb rubbed the fabric and she glanced down at the covering.

It was in such bad shape. The fabric was torn and the color nothing like it used to be. It was a telling contrast to the robe Alexander had provided. Yet she had so readily cast the fine one aside for this ragged one. She wondered if it was a sign.

She pushed off the door and went to her sea chest. Her clothes which Ysabel returned were there, but Catriona shunned them for the time being. She was still unsettled by the incidents at the spa and the idea of being in the same clothes felt wrong. She slid the coat from her shoulders and pulled fresh ones from the chest.

For a moment, she imagined strong hands on her as the fabric fell to the floor. Myrgen had been so close to her in the jail cell, so warm and available. It would have taken so little to let herself go in his arms. She blinked, shaking off the inappropriate thought. This was nothing more than sexual frustration.

Her last sexual encounter before Alexander had been just as unsatisfying. When Alistair had been about to take her in St. Andrew, that ridiculous Passion Sap Gwen had allegedly put in her drink tossed all that aside. She was still embarrassed that she fell for that. The herb gave the impression of bleeding from recent wounds, or, if no wounds were present, from the eyes and ears. It was developed by Mandians to preserve the virtues of their rich daughters during kidnappings. Like nearly everything in the Saintlands, the Mandians and their deceitful ways had ruined free will and immorality.

Bastards.

She shook her head and closed her eyes. Her exposure on deck was sure to start a fresh round of the Morning Ritual. She wasn't sure if she shouldn't join in. There were worse things than dumping a bucket of sea water on your head to quell such urgings. Feeding them, for example, would be beyond detrimental. She needed to be in her right mind around here. And right now, her mind was anywhere but in the right place. She was either going to get in a fight or get in bed.

And the Land help whoever was the focus of either.

Nine

"Thank Callista after a storm, even if she spares you not."
The Siren's Song of Callista

Alexander ran up to Morgan Wolf and the cannon his guardsman was manning. A second guard was loading the next ball. *"What are you doing?"*

"I'm executing the traitor and all who give him quarter, Sire, as per your decree."

Alexander looked at the Vicar, then at the harbor as another cannon fired near the center of the dock district. "No! You have to stop! You'll kill her!"

Morgan grabbed Alexander by the collar. "I *can't!* You made a decree, Sire. You handed it to me, knowing I would have to fulfill it or renounce my fealty to this Crown. Since I can't do the latter, I'm bound by that oath to do the former." He released the King's shirt. "I did what you wanted. I arrested my brother and gave the order to have him executed at dawn. I hate to be the one to point it out, but that sky isn't getting any darker."

Alexander looked into the eyes of his subject and looked around as another boom ripped the sky. The guardsmen lined up the cannon and lit the fuse. Alexander kicked it, barely moving the muzzle. It went askew, shooting just to the right of the target. "Stop!" He turned to the other rises with cannons on them, shouting. "Stop! I command it!"

"The spoken word at a time like this won't work, Your Majesty. They, like me, are channeling your rage, your power, your will. They will destroy my brother at all costs, because they have no choice."

Alexander turned to look at Morgan and saw he was holding up a piece of paper, folded and a little rumpled from transit. It was the decree.

"If you truly want to save her life, you have to destroy this. No one else can."

Alexander looked at the ship trying to get away, a hole already in the captain's quarters, that beautiful window of stained glass ripped to shreds. *Catriona might already be dead.* He grabbed the decree and threw it to the ground, then took the torch for the cannon and set the page afire.

A wave of light went out from the decree and for a moment, all was silent, like someone had taken away his hearing. Then the sounds of life around him filtered back. He looked at Morgan. The Vicar nodded and then started giving orders for all guards to tend to the fires still burning in the street. The two guards ran off to the street where the alchemist fire had been thrown and began to fight it in earnest, but the neglect of those on duty had threatened the other parts of the city. Citizens were bringing buckets of sea water in fire lines to douse the fires. Having the twelve men manning the city's harbor defenses finally join the lines seemed to make the difference.

Alexander watched the *Enigma* get further out of reach. He had been so close, but he got greedy. He'd let lust, pride and envy take their turns at his soul, and had lost it all. He turned to look at the city in flames around him and felt the rage of his folly consume him. Morgan put a hand on his shoulder.

"Thank you, Your Majesty. You did the right thing."

"How can you say that?" He let his eyes return to the face of the man who had put his own brother in prison. "How can you possibly say that?"

"Because realizing you have done something wrong, and then setting it right is always the right thing to do."

Alexander looked after the ship as it sailed out of sight around the horn of the harbor. "I've lost her."

Morgan patted him on the shoulder. "Maybe you were never meant to have her." He looked at the fire, which the city's forces were finally getting under control. "I have to get down there. Why don't you return to the manor and get some rest?"

"What if someone's hurt down there? They'll need a healer."

Morgan smiled. "I'm sure they will. Come on. Let's get to work."

Catriona looked over the aft castle at the shoreline as the city's forces stopped firing. The fire that Thessius caused was still burning and Catriona found it odd that the guards had chosen to spend manpower on trying to sink them instead of tending to their own. She looked at Octavius. "Is she all right?"

The First Mate looked over at the helm and closed his eyes. "She's tore up, Captain. Couple of those shots got through, though nothing that would take her down. She ain't bleeding."

"Good. We're going to need to go ashore at first light, get some repairs done to her. I'm thinking we might need to focus and make all haste to Caratia."

Octavius nodded. "Yeah, I'm not thinkin' we'll be all that welcome in any more Mervol ports." He looked at her. "What in the realm of Callista would make them abandon a threat like a fire to attack a fleeing ship?"

"Myrgen mentioned a decree Alexander had written and given to the Vicar. It commanded the townsfolk to destroy Myrgen and any who give him refuge."

"So he wrote a decree that would make a city let itself burn to the ground instead of let us escape? What's that mean for the next port we pull into?"

"Nothing. We won't pull into port again until we're out of his jurisdiction. I won't risk it."

"You don't have to." Myrgen dropped from the rigging above their heads. "I saw a flash before we got out of view. I think he destroyed the decree."

"How do you know?"

Myrgen pointed to the thinning glow as the citizen's focused upon the fire in town. "They stopped firing. I saw a flash of light right before the cannons went quiet."

Catriona looked at Octavius. "Is there any way to confirm that?"

"No one on this ship has fealty to Mervolingia over you, Captain. I never knew it was in place before, or I doubt Myrgen would have been allowed off the ship." Octavius looked at Myrgen. "He has the power to make a decree that will cause citizens to forsake their own safety?"

Myrgen folded his arms and nodded his head. "That's the Power of Sovereignty that Elizabeth was after. You see why it would have been a horror if she had gotten her hands on it instead of the false one?" He turned to Octavius. "The former queen tried to steal that Power before Alexander claimed it, but the Chancellor of the kingdom is always given a false ritual that's designed to exhaust the thief and give them an artificial sense of the Power. It leaves them vulnerable for the moment when the real heir claims the Power."

Catriona shuddered and Myrgen figured she was remembering the scene in the Royal Crypt when Alexander ran Elizabeth through for her betrayal. She hadn't died there. She died hanging on the wall of the city as a reminder to traitors not to threaten the Crown. Myrgen had never really seen the harsher side of Alexander until that moment. He suspected it was more the influence of that much power than the D'Medici side of his breeding.

Octavius noted the solemn pall that settled on the two and took a deep breath. "Well, it's ended now. We're still in range of their cannons. He must have called off the attack."

"Not with a Decree in place. You saw the city forsake its own structures to attack us. Even a verbal order wouldn't outweigh that decree. He had to destroy it before they would have listened. It's a failsafe against someone incapacitating the Crown and issuing an order as the next highest authority." Myrgen looked at Catriona. "Besides, even if he did remove it, who's to say he won't write another one tomorrow, saying execute me on sight? It's bad enough I might have put this crew, their families, and everyone in your company at risk."

Octavius blinked, the surprise of such an intense hatred from Alexander etched into his features. "What the hell did you do, Myrgen?"

"The worst thing I could have, apparently." He reached into his belt and pulled out his gloves, healing his hands from the small offenses he had sustained in the attack. "I made him king." He pulled on the gloves and went to help the crew clean up the debris from the attack.

Myrgen grabbed the heavy end of a cargo crate and helped move it back in place. The deckhand, Draethen, was going for his bo'sun's rank and he used the opportunity to practice tying the cargo to the deck. Myrgen looked around and saw the rest of the deck cargo was all but returned to place. Most of it had stayed put, but some flying shards of railing had cut through the ropes of two areas. He was glad they hadn't gotten around to damaging the masts. He looked at Draethen. "What's chain shot?"

"Cannon balls with chain attached to 'em. Destroys sails and masts."

"By the Saints. I can see why she wanted us out of range for that."

"Oh yes. If they had hit us with the chain shot first, we would have been dead in the water. The next volley of round shot would have sunk us."

Myrgen blinked. That was a good point. *Why wouldn't they use that first, if they truly wanted to sink us?* It was enough to make him think that perhaps his brother had managed to shake off the decree's influence. Their parents hadn't raised weak children. "Hey, if you're good here, there's a mess in the Captain's quarters. A cannon ball took out the back wall."

"She get hurt?"

"No. I caught sight of it before it hit and managed to get her under cover of the chart table. Window's destroyed though."

"Damn. I liked that window."

"Yeah, me too." He went down into the hold and got a broom and dust pan. Several men were down there, patching a hole in the side of the ship. Half the food supplies were shattered into pieces and water was everywhere. Black gun powder, a collateral casualty from the look of it, floated on the top of the couple inches of water. One of the sailors was mentioning a missing crate of nails.

Myrgen went back up top and found Draethen. "You free now?"

"Yeah. The Bo'sun's got the other set of cargo. Whatcha need?"

"There's a pretty big mess in the hold. You wanna take these and get that glass from the floor in the Captain's room while I help out down there?"

"You sure you don't want me to help out in the hold instead?"

Myrgen looked over at the Captain, who was returning to her cabin. He had been well on his way to bedding that woman and right now, they were both needed tending to the ship. If he were to be alone with her now... "No, I think I'll be more productive down here." He pressed the broom and dustpan into Draethen's hands and turned heel to help mend the ship.

Ten

"Those that are claimed by the sea become part of the sea. But those who must repent grow fins and teeth."
The Siren's Song of Callista

Catriona stepped into her room and looked over the damage. The stained glass window was a total loss and the ceiling had a chunk bit out of it. There was a hole in the wall that she shared with Myrgen's cabin and she could see the cannon ball on the floor, having narrowly missed the bed but not the desk. She imagined, of the two, the damage was more severe to the thing he used the most. A knock at the door called her attention and she saw Draethen standing in the doorway with a broom and a dust pan. He looked around the room as well.

"Damn. Myrgen wasn't kidding."

Catriona nodded. "Where is the Chancellor?"

"He's in the hold, helping out. Said there was some damage there too. He figured he'd be more productive down there."

"He's probably right. Look, I can handle the clean up here. Why don't you see if you can do something about the deck right above me? I don't want it caving in on me in the night." Catriona took the broom and dustpan from him

Draethen nodded. "Aye, Captain," and he left.

She looked around to see where to begin and set the dustpan on the desk. She began to brush the pieces of glass off the chart table, the charts having been rolled up while they were in port and put in the case on the wall along with their tools. She paid close attention to getting the glass off the custom woven upholstery material that was a tapestry of charts and maps, realizing the glass shards had already cut some sizable holes in the window seat. The chart table had bits of glass embedded in the wood and she realized, if Myrgen hadn't pulled her to the floor, she would have been severely injured, if not dead. The path of the cannon ball may or may not have hit her, but either way, the large pieces of glass and lead were pretty lethal. *Thank the Land the argument had taken that turn.*

She shook off the desire to follow that thought. There were things to do, and she didn't need to be distracted by dwelling on Myrgen during the daylight hours. Her nights were full enough, though clearly, they were both interested in bringing those out of the ether. *The way he touched me...* A small moan slipped from her throat and she opened her eyes, blinking. They had a very serious problem on their hands right now, and she needed to focus.

She swept up the shards of glass and tossed them out the window. It took several loads. She thought briefly about saving the bigger pieces, the intact ones, but that turned out to be foolish. Even the piece with the name, "Galadorn", had a crack across the center. As strong as the reinforced pieces of glass were, they were no match for a flying ten pound ball of heated metal. She eventually got all the wood chunks, lead and glass cleaned up off the floor and she leaned back, stretching out her sore muscles. Draethen had apparently been pulled onto a different job because the damage to her ceiling was as yet unfixed. She decided to see what was commanding his attention.

She had discarded her sword belt for cleaning purposes and thought about putting on her Caratian long coat for going out on deck, but frankly, it was too impractical. The black shirt she was wearing was loose over the thick hose she preferred when she was on ship. Her hair had decided to send out scouts from the braid, so she undid it to re-secure them. She got her brush out of the drawer of her desk where she kept her toiletries and walked over to the silver mirror on the wall between her room and Myrgen's.

The hole from the cannon ball was still there and it occurred to her that, with him working in the hold to get things repaired, he would undoubtedly be far too tired to clean up the mess in his own quarters. She took the broom and the dustpan and went into his cabin. The first thing she wanted to get rid of was the cannon ball. This ill-timed thing managed to interfere with her getting a certain itch scratched, one for which she was now quite primed. She felt her nethers twitching with the thought of Myrgen thrusting between her thighs, the intensity with which he had come at her catching her fancy again. Every cell in her body screamed in desire and she fantasized briefly about coming to him in the night and straddling his hips like she did in her dreams.

The smell of him was everywhere around her and she kicked herself for being so concerned with decorum when he had lain beside her in the inn back in St. Andrew. He had been there to protect her. He had stayed battle dressed and kept his hands to himself, but nonetheless, she had woke up in his arms, resting on his chest. She should have given in to their desire at that time, but she had been too prudish to let herself go.

That part of her irritated her. The Giovanni had cursed her not to want the touch of a man, his rape of her stealing her desire for human contact. Nicolai's gropings had been disappointing because he had wanted her to be someone else, and Alistair was not the right one to lift this curse. His desire to lay with her former employer, Tanglwyst, had caused a gross error of judgment, one that had caused hundreds of men to pay the price for his lust.

Alexander was first man in years to touch her without visions of the rapes seizing her mind.

But Myrgen, ah Myrgen was different. He had been straightforward from their first meeting. He was a conspirer, someone who did bad things to people. He had killed before, as had she, and for his own reasons as well. He had done his research concerning her, had figured out, or been tipped off to, what her weaknesses were, who her associates were and what she could do. He knew how to stop her, but she could see that he had not wanted to involve her or her son at all. As soon as he had a chance to get her son out of harm's way, he had taken it, without regard to the consequences to his own life. It was for that reason that she had gone back to save him.

But she had also gone back because Anika had told her she must, that the one she was to be with was trapped back in the palace. Catriona believed then as she believed now, that the person to whom Anika was referring was Alexander. Unfortunately, he was still trapped, but this time, by his role as King, and that was entirely her fault. When Armand had given Charles the antidote to the drug that made him appear dead, she should have demanded Charles return to the throne. But she didn't. Alexander already had the Power of Sovereignty. He was King, and nothing could change that. It, apparently, was *his* destiny.

Catriona knew that feeling. The power of the Land was in her own life, her own hands, as it was in her Dûcesa and Dûce's, as it was in every Land Worshipper's. Anika had been given the Heartstone by the Land. If the Heartstone said she needed to be with Alexander, then the Land had chosen him for her. She believed the Land knew best. It was the basis for all she knew to be true.

She looked around the room, only this time with a bit more despair. Myrgen excited her in ways she never knew she could feel, but when weighed against the Will of the Land, the desires of passing mortals meant very little. She needed to get Myrgen home, where he was safe, and then return to Alexander to be his queen. She figured the marrying of the Stâpâna to the King of Mervolingia would unite the two kingdoms, coupling the greatest source of sustenance with the greatest means to defend it. There must be a war coming.

Suddenly, she realized that was what must be going on. The Land and Heaven uniting, with some dark shadow cult vying for control. Perhaps the Fae nation was going to be attacked, and only by uniting the mortals could the devastation be stopped. Octavius said the ship was especially vulnerable and Alistair had ran to check on Gwen, whom she had not realized was in town, after the attack by Duncan. Gwen was heavily invested in the Fae nation. The touch of someone shadow-tainted could destroy her, and likewise, this ship. Catriona leaned back against the wall of Myrgen's room, stunned by the insight she had just received. It would explain a lot. Perhaps the shadow cult had put Myrgen in her way to interfere with her relationship with Alexander, as a distraction. If she betrayed Alexander with Myrgen, then the shadows would score a victory, and the Fae nation would be in danger.

Catriona owed her life, her ship and her sanity to the Midsummer King, Corrigan Starshadow. He had rescued her in the Galadorn forest from evil creatures who had wanted to violate her. They had become friends and he had trusted her with his daughter's life and essence. He had given her the pitch that enchanted this ship and put her on the path to find her home in Caratia. She had built that window to remind her, every day, of the friendship she had with him. He guarded the tree that gave the *Enigma* life. She couldn't let him down.

She looked around and realized she needed to leave Myrgen's room. Being here was inappropriate. If he were to return, he might want to pick up where they had left off. She knew now she couldn't do that. He was easily everything she desired, which just made the case against him stronger. She pushed off the wall and slipped out the door. She needed to get some wood, to patch the hole in the wall between them. Such access would only tempt her from her course now that she had figured out what the cosmic forces were trying to say.

She turned from his room at the door, then closed it firmly behind her.

Eleven

"Cast your wish on a stone into the sea on your first voyage. Then hope you sail, never finding that stone."
The Siren's Song of Callista

Myrgen moved the last of the debris into the half barrel where the repair crew was storing the pieces. He knew of a couple places where there was lighter damage and some of the pieces of wood here would be useful there. At the very least, he knew there was damage in the Captain's quarters, and it would be wise to make sure she had everything she needed before tossing this stuff overboard.

The lumber patching up the hole in the ship, far too close to the waterline for everyone's comfort, was being sealed with pitch to make it waterproof. He wasn't sure if this was a temporary fix or if it would be permanent, but he imagined he would learn that when the damage reports came in. One thing was certain, this was no ordinary accounting job.

"I'm going to see if anyone needs this wood." He bent down to pick it up, surprised to discover he actually could.

"You need any help with that, Myrgen?" Ambrois, the ship's cook, dusted his hands on his pants, looking at the Chancellor.

"Well, I can get it right now, but thinking about it, I'm not sure I can get it up the stairs without a little assistance. Thank you, Ambrois."

"Hey, not a problem. The smell of pitch kinda turns my stomach, especially the temp stuff." He reached over and took one of the rope handles Draethen had tied around the half keg so it could be carried out.

"So this is just a temporary fix, then?"

"Oh yeah. If we can get her back to Caratia, they'll get her fixed right up. Then we'll use the Galadorn pitch to seal the new boards."

Myrgen walked towards the stairs. "The Galadorn pitch?"

Ambrois nodded. "Comes from a special tree in the Fae forest, I guess. Makes the ship stronger. This is the first time I've ever seen this much damage to the *Enigma.*"

"You want to go up first?"

"Sure. You certain you can handle the weight?"

"I'll put it on my shoulder. That will even the yaw so we don't lose any of the boards."

Ambrois helped him get it on his shoulder, then took the other handle and started up the stairs. He stopped at the top and lowered his grip so the keg could be slid onto the deck as Myrgen crested the stairs. A rip split the air as the bottom of the keg caught on his sleeve and tore it half off. He set the wood down and examined the tear. There was some blood rising to the surface from the edge of the keg catching on his skin as well. "Bloody hell."

"Myrgen, you need to watch your language. You're losing that cultured edge you came on board with." Ambrois smiled.

Myrgen nodded. "I'll watch that." He pulled off the shirt and looked at the scratch on his shoulder. He closed his eyes a moment and healed it away. Such a minor wound was almost dismissible, but he didn't want it to turn septic before he attended it. Better to handle it immediately.

"You got another shirt?"

Myrgen shook his head. "I'll have to repair this one tomorrow morning. I'll be right back." He walked over to his room and opened the door. He noticed the night air immediately and looked to the right at the hole through the wall. He looked to the left and saw the cannon ball near the back of the room and the path of the thing right through the desk. It was a good thing his sea chest had been on the other side, at the foot of his bed. He dropped the shirt on the back of the chair and went back to the door.

Catriona pulled up short, right outside in the hallway. She was completely dressed again, boots, coat, gloves and sword all in place. "Myrgen. I thought you were still in the hold."

"Finished." He looked back in his room. "There's a hole in my wall."

"Yes."

"There's also a cannon ball in my room."

"Well, you didn't have one of your own yet. I thought it might add to the décor."

Myrgen smiled. At least she was still willing to joke with him, despite the argument and the siege on the ship. He hadn't given the argument between them much thought until just that minute. He found he was a little unsure about how to proceed now. *Was the moment lost? Is she just going to assume that being with me is cursed?* "I'm sorry about the damage to the ship."

She blinked at him a moment, then frowned. "Yes, I suppose you really are responsible, aren't you? We probably need to get you off the ship before someone gets killed."

He smiled and nodded. "Well, I wouldn't want the crew to decide I was cursed. You have some very superstitious sailors."

"That's actually part of the definition of a sailor: swearing and superstitious. Just don't tell them why we were fired upon and I think you'll be safe." She smiled and then her eyes drifted to his lips. She blinked and instantly adopted a colder demeanor, straightening to the posture he remembered from watching her deal with merchants and strangers.

The sudden change confused him. "Are you all right?"

"No. Not really."

"You want to talk about it?"

"I'm afraid I can't. Not with you."

"Is it about me?"

Catriona blinked slowly, a tell of hers which meant she was thinking.

"And what happened right before the cannon ball?"

Again, the blink, this time with a breath.

"You're not comfortable with that, are you?"

She didn't answer. He took that to be a yes.

"I'm sorry. My aggression… It must have reminded you of Giovanni."

"No." She touched his arm, the intimacy coming back in a moment. "Of course not. That creature never crossed my mind." She looked at her hand on his arm and retrieved it as if trying to regain her distance. "It has nothing to do with you or what you did. It's…" She frowned, casting about as if trying to tell him something he wasn't going to want to hear. He could think of only one thing that she could say that would be a problem.

"It's Alexander."

She turned her gaze from him, her eyes closing against his ire in speaking the name.

He nodded. "I see." He rubbed the back of his neck and glanced out onto the deck. "After all he's…" He sighed, dropping his hand. "Never mind."

She looked at him again but he chose this time to be the one not to meet her gaze. She was probably reading his feelings but he was so tired right then, it didn't really matter. It had been a rather long night. "You off to bed, then, Captain?"

"Not with the ship in this much pain. It would be inappropriate." She walked past him to the deck and got some boards from the half-keg he left there. He looked back at the hole connecting their two rooms and exhaled. He joined her there.

"I'll tell you what. I'm not really tired, so why don't you take my room until I can get yours repaired? I plan on pulling a night shift anyway."

She looked at him a moment. "You're lying. You're actually very tired."

"I know. Just give me this one, will ya?" He looked into her eyes and she held them a moment, then nodded. He did likewise. "I'll take a few minutes and board up the hole so the breeze is gone and I'll see about getting your room repaired tomorrow."

She looked down at the boards she had grabbed and he reached out for them. Her hands held them a moment, as if she were still thinking about doing it herself. "You don't need to give me your bed, Myrgen."

"Understand, Captain, I'm not doing it for you." Her eyes returned to his and they connected again, like before the attack and his voice softened. "It's the only way I'll ever be able to wake up and smell you next to me."

Her voice dropped as well and he could hear the internal struggle she was waging. "Isn't that what you got back in St. Andrew?"

"Yes, but I don't sleep there every night. I only wish I did." He took the boards and slipped past her down the hall to her cabin. He turned the knob and stopped, feeling her behind him, still on deck. He looked at her, begging her to read him so she could keep her distance. She nodded. *Can you at least tell me why?*

She reached up and touched the stone key at her throat with one hand and the pommel of her sword with the other. He understood. The Land had told her otherwise. It only seemed logical after getting the ship fired upon and endangering the lives of every crewman's family through association. He had to trust Catriona's assessment that Alexander would not go after those still ashore.

She shook her head, then glanced around the ship before coming over to him. "It's not what you think, Myrgen. Anika told me, back in Patras, that I was supposed to be with Alexander, that it was what the Land had told her. That's why I returned to the palace after I got Alan out of there."

"Oh." Myrgen looked down at the wood in his hands. "So this isn't entirely your choice, then."

"It is not my preference, but it is my choice."

He looked at her glimmering green eyes. "And if you *had* your preference?"

She took a breath, her eyes on his lips, then closed them. "It would be inappropriate…"

"To hell with inappropriate!"

They glanced at the deck to make sure no one was listening in on this exchange, then Catriona nudged her chin in the direction of her quarters. He stepped in carrying the wood and dropped it on the floor by the hole in the wall. "I'm sorry. I just…" He turned around and Catriona pushed him up against the wall next to the hole.

She moved in close to him, the scent of her skin rippling across his senses. She had pulled the tie out of her hair when she stepped into the room and it tumbled free like the wind. Her nose skimmed the surface of his neck, her breath heating up more than his throat and her lips ran along the throbbing of his jugular. She lingered near his ear and touched her lips to his lobe, whispering. "Remember what you were planning to do to me before?"

He nodded.

She brought her lips across his cheek, threatening to brush against his lips but staying just out of contact. He wanted to kiss her, to possess her like he had before but something stayed his hand. She was going somewhere with this and he wanted to know where. She lifted her emerald gaze to his waiting eyes and closed them, the familiar look of guilt returning to her features.

No, nononono don't, don't stop!

"Consider us even." She lowered her head, pushed off of the wall and walked out the door.

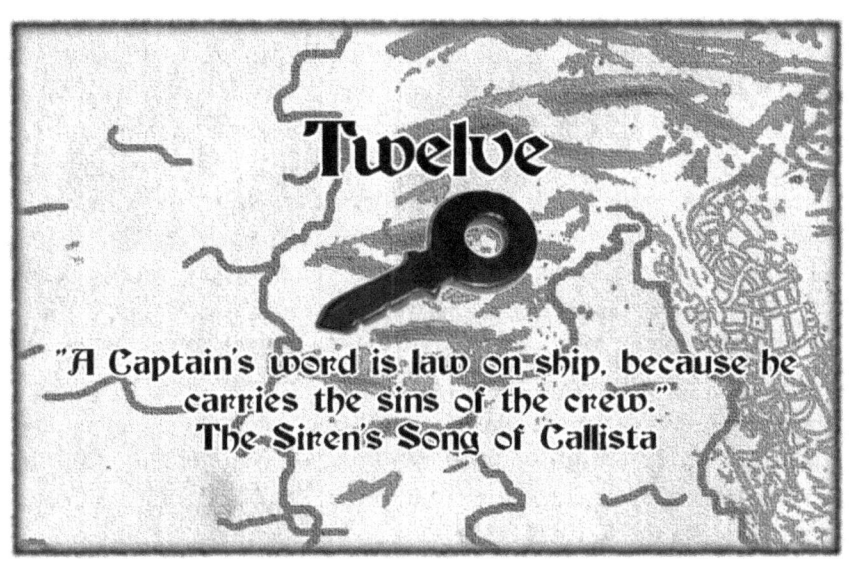

Twelve

"A Captain's word is law on ship, because he
carries the sins of the crew."
The Siren's Song of Callista

Catriona stepped away from the door and exhaled. She slipped into her aloof demeanor easier than she had thought she could after such a confrontation and stepped forward toward the end of the hall and the freedom of the deck. She was numb again, as she had been for so long, back when she had thought Nicolai was dead. Now, Myrgen needed to be dead to her, or rather, the part of her heart that cried out for him needed to be silenced. Her obligation was to this crew and to the Land.

She started braiding her hair again, the tie from when she had undone it moments ago tucked into the cuff of her glove. The door opened behind her and she stopped.

"Catriona."

She felt her heart race. Would he come up to her and kiss her? Would he reprimand her? Yell? Disintegrate? Or would he say nothing, and make her read him? She turned to glance back at him.

"Can you really do it? Can you really leave it like this?" Myrgen swallowed, waiting.

"Myrgen, you are a part of my crew, and my life. I need to get you all to safety and right now, that's a bit up in the air as to whether or not I can. There are shadows chasing us and the animosity of a king that I will gladly placate with my freedom if it saves the lives of my family. My home is in pieces at present and I have a hundred men counting on my leadership to keep her afloat. I hope you will forgive me if I am unable to devote the kind of time and attention our problem deserves at present."

He blinked and rubbed his head. She could see from his posture he was chastising himself for being so selfish at a time like this. "It is I who must ask your forgiveness, Captain. I was thinking of myself, and lost sight, for the moment, of the larger picture. It won't happen again."

"Thank you, Myrgen." She pulled the tie from her glove and bound her hair again, this time more securely than before the attack. She was stabilizing, equalizing back to center again and it felt comfortable to know what to do next. Myrgen nodded and stepped back into her chambers, the sound of boards being selected echoing down the hallway. She returned to the deck and crossed to the other passage where the spare cabins were. She knew the passenger cabin on that side was unoccupied and unlocked the door to see how it had fared in the attack.

There were no broken boards, water, or cooling artillery. That comforted her quite a bit. The damage reports would be ready in an hour and she wanted to give everyone time to see how bad things were. Truth be told, as Captain, she would be supervising the repairs but unless something unexpected happened, she would not be allowed to assist, so she stepped into the room and sat down on the bed.

There was a blood drop stain on the floor from where Myrgen had bled at the end of Alexander's sword, back when she had healed the wounded guardsman in this room. It had been cleaned, the bedding changed, but there was still that presence. He had bled for them, bled for her, for the crew, even for the ship, judging from the hint of a cut on his bare shoulder. He was a good man, but with some dirt on him from his decisions in life. That was more appealing than she could ever let on, especially if she wanted to stay the course in her obligations to the Land. She hoped he would find a home in the arms of her beloved Caratian mountains and the family awaiting them.

She closed her eyes and entered the state of mind where she could read the ship. The repairs in the hold were going well, but there was severe damage to the supplies. Ambrois was currently cataloguing the losses to the kitchen cupboards and Draethen was getting his orders from the Bo'sun. Thessius was amidst the rigging, tying a rope which had come loose. Lawrence was prying an axe from the wall where it went flying during the attack. Each and every crewmember was busying himself with the challenges of their duties and pulling through, more or less. Eventually, the Captain's cabin door opened and Myrgen stepped out, nails and hammer in the small bucket she had grabbed to carry them.

He stepped into his room, set the bucket down, and looked over the damage. He pulled on a drawer in the ravaged desk and it collapsed onto the floor. Luckily, there was very little in it, a quill and pen knife, but he ran his fingers through his hair then threw the remainder of the drawer. The once beautiful wood shattered against the now cold metal of the canon ball. She didn't need to read him to know it was not just the disrepair of the furniture that had him so flustered. She blinked away from him as he sat down on his bed and put his head in his hands.

The destruction of his desk was going to prove a problem. He needed that desk to feel like he belonged, like he was contributing. Having it destroyed was probably shaking his faith that he belonged here.

Perhaps it's better that way, though. If he feels like he can't stay, he'll be more inclined to move on, and that would be better all around. No further temptations.

She knelt, touching the blood stain on the floor. *This must be a test. It has to be. The dreams, the emotions, that comment by Alistair about a third kiss making me Myrgen's. I've connected with him in so many ways, felt comfortable and safe with him. Even if I take into account there may be a Fae spell at work on the two of us, he's won the approval of the crew. What more does he need to do to prove his worth?*

She didn't know, but wondering about it wasn't going to bring her the solution. The more he lingered in her thoughts, the more she wanted to be with him, and down that path lay madness.

She had always been certain about her courses of action. She couldn't let her desires cloud her judgment now. Regardless, she was glad Myrgen's blood had left a stain. It meant the ship felt he was too important to forget.

Her greatest fear was that she was turning away from the best thing she would ever have, a thought she dreaded, but Anika had the Heartstone, and she had never been wrong. The Land was guiding them and she needed to trust it. She felt her heart ripping apart, pulled to pieces by Duty and Desire. Her ship was wounded, her lover trucking with demons and this incredible man before her but out of reach. She felt razed.

Everything Myrgen had said before was true. She didn't want to believe it, but that was simply because she was afraid to believe she could have loved two men in her lifetime that were such poor matches. She knew Alexander was a good man, but like all men put in difficult circumstances, she also knew he had made a couple bad choices. She didn't begrudge him those mistakes, but now, for the first time in their relationship, it disturbed her that she couldn't read him. Her only venue was to trust in the man she knew.

But Myrgen knew a different side of Alexander, the side he was as a royal and a D'Medici. If she were to take him up on his proposal, she would be dealing with that side as often as she had dealt with the Healer. The two faces were too different to live in the same host in peace. When that inner war finally erupted and declared a victor, was she certain she could continue to live with the man left behind?

A knock at the door barely preceded Octavius' entry. "Captain, what the hell are you doing?"

"Transferring rooms for the time being. How is Estelle?"

"Limping along. I wish you could heal her like you can heal the rest of us."

She stood. "I know the feeling. If it were the same distance either way, I'd head to Galadorn and take her to her tree. I think she could heal there while we repaired the ship."

"I highly doubt her father would allow her to return if that happened. Not after this." He looked at her. "What did you say to Myrgen?"

"The truth."

"Did you *blame him* for this?"

Catriona stood, looking at her First Mate. "It *was* because of him that this happened, Octavius." She glanced down at her gloved hands, "But no, I did not blame him for this. He was doing that on his own." She stepped out of her door and walked toward her cabin. She was going to need a few things to stay in the other room.

Octavius followed. "Why would he think that? It was Alexander who wrote a decree that prevented an entire town from fighting a fire in order to stop him from getting away."

"Knowledge of the facts does not always change the way one feels, even though it should. I also believe there was a decree. I can see no other reason why the city watch would abandon a fire to shoot at a fleeing ship. That's why I'm getting Myrgen away from Mervolingia. After I drop him off in Caratia, I'll return here and get Alexander to lift any other decrees he decides to levy. Our trade will suffer though, as long as he is still on this ship."

Octavius folded his arms. "And it's not like he's crew, right?"

She met his gaze. "No. He's crew. He's just already paid his debt."

"Wait, doesn't the rescue in St. Marguerite count as saving his life?"

"It does. Believe me. But then he moved me out of the path of the artillery that did this." She opened the door to her cabin and gestured to the gaping hole that used to be the window.

"Callista's Fury…" He looked around at the damage done to the room, his shock dressing him head to toe. She was glad he had not seen it before they cleaned it up.

"Once again, we are square, neither of us owing the other."

Octavius looked at Catriona and then back at the room. He followed the path of the cannon ball and saw the patched hole in the wall between their rooms. "I had no idea."

"Estelle didn't tell you?"

"About this? No. But it explains a few things." He looked at Catriona again. "He took you out of the way of this havoc?"

"Yes."

"And you're not in his room with him right now 'thanking' him?"

"That would be incredibly inappropriate, Octavius."

His brow furrowed. "Pardon? How did you come to that conclusion?"

"Other people have saved my life before. I've not 'thanked' them either." She glanced over at her bed and saw Myrgen's robe he had given her to cover up laying across it. "Besides, I still have Alexander."

"*You* have Alexander, or he has you?"

She walked over to her bed and picked up the robe. "Either. The result is the same."

Octavius narrowed his eyes at her. "Captain," he said, his voice extremely controlled, "you are not telling me, in the heart of this ship that has been torn apart by Alexander's obvious jealousy, that you are contemplating favoring the company of the man who did this over the company of a man who saved you from this."

"Alexander has saved the lives of more than a few of this crew in the past few years."

"And I'm sure they will forgive you for leaving him after this. This," he gestured around the room, "this is unacceptable. It's a royal tantrum, brought about by you choosing a better man than him. This is not the actions of a man worthy of your affections and it damn certain isn't the actions of a friend of this ship. This is selfishness and rage, not love. Not what Myrgen has for you."

Catriona snapped a look at her friend. "You overstep your bounds, Octavius. It is not for you to decide how Myrgen feels about me."

"I'm not blind, Catriona! I know a man in love when I see one. I own a mirror."

"Your love for Estelle is different." She tossed the robe aside, emphasizing the temporary nature of Myrgen's attraction to her. "This is affection born of intense circumstances. There's *no way* to believe it would last once the waters settle."

"With you at the helm? If intense circumstances are required for his affection, then he's chosen the right woman! Your life has not 'settled' since I met you."

"If given a chance, it might."

Octavius shook his head. "No, it won't. You thrive on the challenge. You won't be able to breathe if you are settled into court. You'll die there. What in the great sea of Erasmus would make you think you need to be with…" He blinked, understanding flowing into his features. "By the Teeth, Alexander bedded you, didn't he? You finally gave in to his pressure and now he has claim to you, doesn't he? Are you pregnant?"

"He has no more claim to me than he ever has. It's not by his will that I am considering him."

"Then why? Why would you put the entire crew in jeopardy like this? Why would you deny Myrgen if not for that?"

Voices outside the door drew attention to the fact that Myrgen was returning to his room. Draethen was saying something about helping fix the window tomorrow and Myrgen was thanking him. She heard him close his door and move around in his room. *At least this conversation will end now.*

She felt rather than heard his comment. *"Answer the question, Captain."*

Her eyes grew wide as she scanned Octavius. He was communicating in her mind, nothing said aloud. She tried to reply soundlessly as well. *"You're using the ship to communicate with me? How long have you been able to do that?"*

It worked.

"Always. How do you think I've always known when to interrupt things between you and Alexander? Now answer the question, Captain."

She glanced at the door and the shuffling on the other side of the wall. *"Because Anika told me I was supposed to be with Alexander."*

"Did she use the stone?"

Catriona nodded.

Octavius closed his eyes and shook his head. *"No, no that can't be. The Land would never want you to be with someone who could do this."* He looked around at the carnage of the room and ran his fingers over his head.

"I can only hope there's been some misunderstanding on my part. However, I have to be prepared in case there hasn't. I can't let my emotions interfere, Octavius. If the Land wishes this of its Stâpâna, then I will serve where I'm asked, just as our soldiers

do." She looked over at the robe again and then picked it up. "Here, I need you to return this to him. Please tell him thank you for the loan."

Octavius walked over and took the robe. "I'll return it to him tomorrow. It sounds like he's trying to get some sleep."

"Thank you, my friend." She put her hand on his shoulder and he nodded.

He looked at her and spoke aloud this time. "I'm going to drop this off at my quarters, check on my wife."

"Please let me know if she needs anything."

"I will, Captain. You going to bed?"

"I'm not sure, at present. It seems wrong to do that with things in such a state. I need to gather a few things here for the other room, then I'll figure out what to do."

"You know where I'll be if you need me." He bowed to her and left the room.

Thirteen

"Rub some salt water on it and get back to work!"
The Siren's Song of Callista

Alexander walked into the room he was occupying at the Vicar's manor, closing the door behind him. The fire had not claimed any lives, but several businesses were destroyed. The guards had been on the verge of getting ahead of it when he had ordered them to stop the ship's escape. He had let his rage get the better of him, and, even now, when he was exhausted, he could still feel it fueling his movements. Myrgen had gotten away, and Catriona had gone with him. Moreover, she had helped him. Just when he thought he had finally received her oath to stay with him, she had slipped away in the night to go to the Traitor. *How dare she?* He threw an earthen basin across the room, shattering it.

It didn't help.

He sat on the bed, trying to figure out his next move. His eyes found her pillow and a strand of her hair decorated it, like the one in his room at the palace. He closed his eyes. *How could things have gone so wrong? What could have changed between then and now to make her leave him so easily?* She had committed to him in the garden. He knew it. The only thing that went awry was...

That couldn't be it.

Alexander folded his arms.

It couldn't be that he had fumbled so during their attempts at sex that she pulled her support. She wasn't like that. If she had stayed put, she would have had him bedding her now, as dawn broke. He had planned to make absolutely certain of where she was when the axe fell upon Myrgen's neck. With any encouragement, she would have been screaming in ecstasy as the traitor died. To hear her gasping as he impregnated her while his rival gasped as his head severed stimulated Alexander. Had she been there now, he would have easily delivered upon his promise.

But she wasn't. He grabbed the pillow and threw it across the room to the chunks of basin. He had even made sure that girl knew not to return Catriona's clothes to a place she could get to them. He wanted complete control over the situation and he'd *had* it, yet it had sifted away like sand through... his... fingers...

Alexander remembered Catriona's devotion to "the Land", a belief of which he knew very little outside of the fact it was heathen. He had hoped to get her allegiance, then her marriage vow, after which, he would have explained that her heathen religion could not be practiced in Mervolingia. If his mother were to come upon something like that, she would have his beloved executed in the name of Heaven. He had planned to get that vow from her to keep her safe. If they were to return to Caratia, he would let her worship there. He knew there was an Augustinian church in Zara, Caratia's capital. He would be completely comfortable there. But for her own safety, and the safety of Alan, she could never practice her barbaric faith again.

He frowned. She would be on her way there now, and would never stop in a Mervol port again, not this trip. She would have learned her lesson this time. By the time she returned for the winter, if she returned, she might be pregnant with the Traitor's child, probably taken against her will now that she knew of the spell. He had to get Myrgen away from her, and that meant finding Tanglwyst.

Tanglwyst de Sablonnieres de Holloway awoke, a pain stabbing in her heart. Her blood burned and sweat broke out on her skin. She sat up, the small cot where she slept creaking in both the canvas and the wood. The weather was warmer the closer they were to the Papal City, but nighttime still required being fully dressed. In the past ten-day, they had gotten to within sight of the splendid city and she could see the light of her grandfather's window high in the tower at the center. She was almost safe. Then, three nights ago, she had a dream. Alexander was in danger and needed her to come to him. Those holding him hostage would not keep him alive for long and she knew where he was. They had not hurt him yet, but they inferred they might. If Alexander died, the whole of Mervolingia would consume itself in religious civil war. She couldn't let that happen, not when she could save him.

Besides, he still owed her a dance.

She had awoken and realized it was a dream but the thought would not leave her. It dominated her dreams and walked through her mind all day. The closer she got to the Papal City, the more it became apparent to her she could not enter it. The Toledan bandits she traveled with, who claimed ownership of these woods as only outlaws could, had stopped where they were, waiting for her to be ready to go to her grandfather, and she had been unable to go another step closer.

Her host stirred but did not wake. She slipped on her boots. She planned to claim the need to relieve herself if stopped but she wasn't. She felt her pouch for her gold and held it quiet. They were immune to her touch that made men fall in love with her. Apparently, most women in Toledo had this ability and it was a smell. They figured she had Toledan blood. They might not be wrong. Her father had sons with two other women during his time with her mother. For all she knew, she was not her mother's child either. Regardless, the Toledans had accepted her as one of their own, especially upon hearing the tale of how she was likewise an outlaw.

Her head had been clear of the mind-muddying she had felt around Elizabeth, all the more apparent once she was no longer being drugged. After a ten-day of actual clear thinking, it was a nightmare to have her thoughts no longer her own again. She had fought it for days. But when a thug in her dream had kicked Alexander in the chest, she had awoken with the pain. Some connection was there and she could ignore it no longer. Tanglwyst stole over to the horses but they were being guarded. Ramón was a good man, but he was nodding off after an all-night shift. If she went near the horses, he'd wake and see her. She had to leave the horse behind. She knew there would be inns on the road to get another horse and decided to forgo the danger and get moving. Once she got to St. Giles, she could get a horse from her own stables.

She slipped through the woods into the dark.

The Sinister Glove of Embertwist watched Tanglwyst slip away through the woods. She could sense a compulsion upon the woman but couldn't interfere. It had a holy component as well as an arcane one. Mixing magical essences like this was dangerous, especially with the divine aspect. The magic of Heaven was a jealous force, and it demanded control over the subject. During the Inquisition following the Soulless War, the Church used its influence and money to make sure all the cities in the Saintlands were laid out to channel the flows of the Divine. It removed or inhibited any other force from acting within the cities.

Only two places on the continent escaped the revamping: Caratia and Toledo. As Land worshipping cultures, they did not allow the Church its will. Yokotama, Yndia, the Dark Continent and Glarren remained pristine by virtue of water. Separated from the Saintlands by seas and oceans, the Mandian Pope Innocent III was repelled. Calista the Sea Goddess did not like Heaven's plan and to this day, Mandians dominated the land trade, but had to hire Latians to fetch their slave quarries across the seas.

The Glove only knew one person who could deal with the mixing of magical energies of this nature and it had been one hundred and fifty years since she'd seen him. After his beloved

Wilgefortis had finally passed, Raven had decided to wander the world. The Fae Father only knew where he ended up.

The Fae Lord Embertwist was interested in this woman, as was the Glove. After all, it was the Glove's magic that enabled Tanglwyst to have the Love Touch. The Glove bestowed it upon the woman to help her survive a massacre and had never seen fit to end the spell. The woman was simply too entertaining to watch get into and out of trouble.

This, though? This was different. This was danger of a truly destructive nature. Having a holy compulsion on a Fae-touched individual could cause madness and death. This was unacceptable but without knowing the source, it couldn't be broken. Besides, Embertwist was very interested in this woman's dreams, for some reason. She had yet to find anything of note in them but that didn't mean she shouldn't keep watching.

The Glove decided to follow her.

Tanglwyst traveled through the rest of the night, her dream driving her despite the hour. She hadn't slept much in the past three days in her flight from Patras and she felt the adrenaline rush force her onward. There was an inn about seven miles away going back towards Bordeaux and St. Giles. If she could make it there, she could get a horse and make much better time.

Almost dead on her feet, she got to the Inn as dawn peeked over the distant cliffs of Caratia. She was exhausted, but each time her eyes closed, she saw Alexander being hurt and she could not stop. She went inside as the scent of fresh bread filled her nose. She leaned on the bar and rested her feet.

"Can I 'elp you, miss?"

Tanglwyst nodded. "Water, and some of that bread would be wonderful, and a horse, please."

The lady behind the bar frowned. "You look exhausted, miss. Would you like a room? You look like you've traveled all night."

"I'm afraid I have, but I must return to Patras. I have to hurry."

"Well, I can help you with the food and the water, miss, but we 'ave no 'orses to let right now. You could wait and rest. Someone will likely come along."

"I have a horse, my lady."

Tanglwyst turned to the figure at a booth beside the door. No one else was in the room and she could only barely make him out as a cowled figure. The light coming in from outside cast him into shadows. "You do?"

He nodded to her. "And I'm going to Patras."

She swallowed, unable to free herself from the visions of her King in danger. "When, may I ask?"

"As soon as you are refreshed, my lady."

Tanglwyst nodded to the woman, who went to get her food and drink. She limped over to the booth where the stranger sat. "May I join you?"

The man gestured to the table. A glint of metal at his throat caught her attention as his cloak parted from the movement of courtesy. She looked at it as she sat. "I've seen one of those before."

He glanced down at his amulet. "Have you?"

"Yes. It's a holy artifact. You work for the Pope."

"Do I?"

She leaned in. "And you can travel through shadows."

His eyes flicked to the woman coming over with Tanglwyst's food. Tanglwyst sat back and thanked the barmaid. The woman glanced at the hooded figure who didn't acknowledge her, and she nodded to Tanglwyst before leaving. The stranger nodded to his companion. "You know a lot about me, my lady, but I know nothing about you."

"That's best, I think. For all you know, I'm a wanted criminal."

He leaned into the light at last and Tanglwyst saw a long scar across his face. His eyes looked like ink in water. "I'll take my chances."

"Duncan, come to me."

Duncan awoke in the secret room at the sound of the king's voice. He was surprised he was asleep, but not surprised he woke easily. He had been waiting for the king's call. He looked around the cube in which he rested. There were no windows, no doors, no exits of any kind. The only way in was through the amulet he wore, an ancient artifact from a war fought hundreds of years before. There were only three left in the world, and the Pope had entrusted him with one of them. He thought they might have been used by messengers in that war to get important intelligence to the generals, or there would be no need for a room like this. He also thought it might have been used to get rid of prisoners, or keep hostages.

This room was well furnished, comfortable, and timeless, but the only food here was that which the occupant brought in. He'd never thought to check if food here was kept timeless as well. All he knew was that the last time he had come here, he had dumped a body, one Alistair Hapsburg, but when he had returned, the body had disappeared, leaving behind a pile of dust. He doubted the man had actually turned to dust. He must have found a way to escape. Duncan didn't know how, but had finally determined he would have to be careful out in the world now. Someone knew his hiding place, and his secret.

Duncan rose and checked himself. He needed to shave. His beard was starting to get scruffy and his head was starting to reveal the ring of hair he possessed. He found he looked a lot more timeless himself if his enemies and allies never knew he was practically bald and turning grey far too soon. The king was at a salon in St. Marguerite at present. He had requested Duncan show up at the salon and fetch clothes he had at the palace, then deliver them to a messenger. The gown for Catriona was one Alexander requested be made and he believed the Caratian colors would have delighted her. Duncan wondered if that had gone over as planned.

He also hoped he would be allowed to avail himself of the services of the salon.

He closed his eyes and the amulet glowed with a flash of light and the smell of lemons.

"Your Majesty?"

Alexander stepped over to the door and opened it to Lysette. She also looked like she hadn't slept much either.

"There is a man downstairs to see you."

"A man?"

"Yes." Lysette wrinkled her nose. "Smells a bit of... bad eggs."

"Ah. Please, send him up."

Lysette curtsied and started to walk away but Alexander got an idea. "Actually Lysette, send him to the baths. I think he would appreciate the chance to get rid of that smell."

"Of course, Your Majesty."

"And Lysette, I want the same arrangement regarding jewelry as before, with the Stâpâna."

"All jewelry must be removed in the baths. Yes, Your Majesty."

"And this time, make sure the necklace actually makes it to my hand."

Lysette nodded, swallowing. "Y...yes Your Majesty."

Alexander closed the door and waited.

The young woman walked into the parlor and curtsied. "Milord, His Majesty is occupied at the moment but he has offered for you to use the facilities, if you would like."

Duncan smiled. "He is a benevolent king. Lead the way."

She opened the door to the bathing salon and Duncan marveled at the luxury. He knew of only two places like this in the world: The Open Lotus, which was also by appointment only and he had yet to see the inside, and a room in Tanglwyst's vineyards in Bordeaux near St. Giles. Tanglwyst had used a wine vat as a bath. This was lavish, like he had heard some places in Yndia sported. Bathing was for those with money and he had only recently started earning enough to think of such things. Even the secret room had no bath. No way to empty the water.

"You can put your clothing in this room, if you like. The policy is that nothing go into the baths except that which we provide, and your own body. We can also provide clean clothes for your experience here and return your clothing cleaned and freshened."

"Ah." Duncan nodded, sniffing his shirt. "That would be very much appreciated." He went into the changing room which held a red chaise lounge, a large mirror and several hooks upon the wall. On an elaborate end table carved with flowers next to the lounge was a pile of towels. All the furniture and the mirror had the same five-petal flowers motif. The towels smelled of roses. A black silk robe hung on one of the hooks.

Duncan stripped and looked around for a place to put his weapons. There was a drawer in the table and it was empty so he fit his dagger and boot knife in there. He put on the robe and walked out. The woman who brought him here pointed to his neck.

"All items must be removed, sir."

Duncan felt the amulet and shook his head. "This doesn't leave my person."

"I understand your reluctance sir, but those are the rules his Majesty wants enforced."

Duncan rolled his eyes. Clearly, the King's D'Medici ancestry was surfacing. He wasn't really surprised. Those people were notorious in the underworld for their clever assassinations. "I see."

"Besides, we have found here that removing all trappings allows you to fully refresh your mind and spirit. It allows you to look at whatever you were grasping with new perspective having let it go for a short while."

He handed her the amulet and she glanced at his wrist. The dark threads were gone but the scar was still there, though a faded pink, like the wound was a decade old. He pulled the robe down to cover the scar. The woman curtsied and took the necklace and his clothes out of the bathing room. He walked over to one of the pools of water and shed the garment which smelled of roses as well. He stepped in, looking forward to a long soak.

Alexander opened the door to Lysette's knock. She held up the amulet and he took it. "Thank you," he murmured. "Make sure his clothes are cleaned and ready for him, but come by here before you take them to him."

"Yes, Your Majesty." Lysette curtsied again and left. Alexander closed the door and held the amulet up. It seemed to shimmer, like ink in water. He took a deep breath and put the thing on. He half expected the protective shield provided by the Power of Sovereignty to flare, repelling the thing from his skin. In the end, it just lay there, unchanged. He nodded and closed his eyes.

"Take me to the *Righteous*."

There was a flash of light and the strong smell of lemons. He saw the world become engulfed in darkness, then he was gone.

Fourteen

"Better happy and at sea than land-bound with a view."
The Siren's Song of Callista

Alexander stepped out of the shadows onto a ship. His brother and his family had boarded this ship a few ten-days ago. It was only that Alexander had been on the *Righteous* once before as a passenger that enabled him to go here now. He looked around, wondering what to do, should he be too late to catch them before they set sail. The Captain was one of Catriona's and had sworn to transport his brother to an island where he and his beloved Marie and their son could live out the rest of their days. It was the best Alexander could offer to save the life and the sanity of his brother and the whole of the kingdom.

Alexander stepped more fully into the cabin where his brother lay sleeping alongside his mistress. A cradle nearby swayed gently with the waves, their son deep asleep from the motion. He went to his brother's side, which gratefully was on the outside edge of the simple bed, and put his hand over the man's mouth. Charles woke, frightened, but then let his surprise and confusion take over.

Alexander put his finger to his lips, then pointed at the baby and Marie. Charles nodded and rose after Alexander retrieved his hand. He slipped on a simple robe of some incredibly fine fabric scraps, pieced together, then Charles gestured to the door.

The two brothers left the cabin with its sleeping inhabitants and Charles ran his fingers through his hair, thinking. "What is the hour?"

"Uh, almost dawn. The sky is just getting light." *Would have been perfect for a beheading.*

Charles nodded. "The galley should be deserted at this hour then. This way." He led his brother to the kitchen on this ship and Alexander was impressed at the size of the place. He had not realized how well equipped the *Righteous* was. Charles went immediately over to the raised fire pit and stoked the coals under a pot hanging from a large iron hook. The coals hissed at him over being roused from their slumber but turned over and woke up nonetheless. Soon, there was a small flame warming the contents of the pot. Charles checked the pot with a finger, then went to a nearby barrel and got a pan of water from it, which he added to the pot. Replacing the pan on its overhead hook, he turned to his brother. "You can speak here. No one is around."

Alexander raised his eyebrows and smiled. "Sorry. I was just so surprised to see you puttering around a kitchen like you know the place. This simple life looks good on you."

"Marie has been letting me help her do the cooking while we're waiting for permission to settle on the island about ten leagues from here. It is directly between Nubia and Yokotama in the Sea of Blood, about three days from Caratia. Thus, there are a lot of permissions to get. Catriona's letter has gone far in getting this going though."

"How are your supplies holding out?"

"Oh, we're allowed to trade with them, we just need clearance for the building of a house. Apparently, the discussion is not whether or not we are allowed to stay, but which section of the island we are to put our home. I guess there's a war coming or something and both countries are very much against Saintlanders settling on their shores. If this doesn't work, Tristram says there's an island where Catriona has sway near Latia. Someplace called Galadorn. This was the first choice because it had very little contact with the Saintlands and the chance of someone figuring out who we were was very minimal. The risk is greater in Latia."

"Galadorn is where Octavius came from, where Catriona got her financing to build the *Enigma*. It couldn't hurt to have such a positive influence when starting a new life. But tell me about this war that's coming. Is it with the Saintlands or Caratia or just between Nubia and Yokotama?"

Charles shook his head. "I don't know. They are adamant about not having our 'taint', as they called it. Something about a man from Yndia or something telling them to maintain balance. I don't actually understand the languages, but I'm told there's a man coming who is going to act as an interpreter. Mikaru." He waved a hand and returned to his puttering. "However, that has nothing to do with what in the world has brought my brother, the King of Mervolingia, the largest kingdom known to man, to drag me from my bed in the middle of the night. I take it Catriona is nearby?" He took a couple mugs from the cupboard and a container of tea from the counter.

"Er, no. I've hit a bit of a snag with that." He looked at his brother, who turned slowly towards him.

Charles' voice showed a big brother's authority. "Exactly what do you mean, you've hit a 'snag' with that?"

"Well, after Myrgen took you three to this ship, back in Rouen, Nicolai showed up."

"Oh no. So they are still together?"

"No, he actually attacked us. Elizabeth blurted out in front of him that I was the one Catriona had been with last summer and he decided to attack."

"Wait a minute? *Elizabeth* was there? I thought she was..."

"No, not then... I guess you haven't really been brought up on the details. No, Elizabeth *is* dead. She tried to use the fake Ritual of Sovereignty, and I ran her through myself. By the Saints though, she had gone quite mad at the end. Myrgen did what we have always had our Chancellors do: he gave her the fake Rite we leaked to him. No one knew only the actual Heir has the ability to take the Sovereignty from the current Sovereign."

"Good. So have you chosen an heir already?"

Alexander nodded. "Yes. Alan, Catriona's son. I haven't spoken to him yet but I designated him when I took it from you. He's the heir unless he dies before I do."

"Or you have another child."

Alexander shrugged. "That provision is always there by the nature of the title but I have already overridden it. I named Alan after our grandfather. I have no other child but him."

"I take it Mother doesn't know either, then."

"She never asked. I was surprised to see her kneel so readily before me when it was done. Why didn't she ever do that for you?"

Charles scooped the tea leaves into a couple metal tea balls and put them into the cups. "I was stupid. I sent out a Decision that she didn't have to. It compromised my authority with her and she rode that all the way through my reign. You and her have been estranged since the Massacre and as Sovereign, she has no authority over you. Make sure you keep it that way. I don't care who it is, Alex, never send out a Decision that someone doesn't need to kneel before you."

"Not even Catriona?"

Charles looked at his brother. "Have you already done that?"

"Not that I know of, but I still don't know the powers here. I'm discovering them as I go. I've learned about the protective aura I have on me. I can control it, bring it close or spread it out. I've sent out a Summons already and I've also sent out a Decision that declared Myrgen a Traitor to the Crown. I was actually a little surprised to see the effects of that."

"What happened?"

"Well, it turns out the Vicar of St. Marguerite is Myrgen and Tanglwyst's brother. It let him know that Myrgen was on Catriona's ship, under her protection. Without her noticing, he left us, got Myrgen to step off the ship and arrested him. They were going to kill him today at dawn."

"Were? So you stopped it?"

"Not exactly…" He ran his fingers through his hair. "It's gotten complicated. It's why I came here to talk to you. I'm in a real bind here."

"Why don't you start at the beginning and tell me what's happened since we left." He brought the cups over to the hearth and set them on a counter nearby.

"Well, while you and your family were being escorted to this ship, Nicolai attacked Catriona. We were on the streets of Rouen, near the dock where the *Enigma* was moored. Nicolai fought me while I tried to give her a chance to get to her ship. I knew she would be safe on board. He got a couple good cuts on me, but I wasn't his target, and once he had me disabled, he went after her and almost got to her. But Myrgen rode up and knocked him into the water with his horse. Catriona got to the ship and got her swords while the rest of the crew looked for him. He climbed up on the deck from the far side of the ship and attacked her. Of course, she knew he was there. No one can hope to defeat her on her own ship.

"She didn't kill him though. I didn't hear what they said, but he got off the ship and started walking away from the whole thing. Then, I swear, she changed her mind, Charles. She came off the ship, calling out to him. I was about to lose her forever, I know it. Then an assassin's poison dart flew from the darkness and he dropped on the spot. Her crew had to restrain her from going to him as the poison shattered his body but he was dead in moments. Had she but touched him during those convulsions, I know she would have died alongside him. She would have tried to take the poison from him and that would have killed her. We burned the body to stop the poison from getting anywhere else and she stayed right by his corpse while it burned. Only after it was nothing but ash did she finally leave him."

Charles sighed, shaking his head. "Lucky for you that assassin came along when he did. Why would an assassin kill Nicolai Moriarity?"

"The general consensus is that it was meant for me, from the Emilianites. It barely missed me."

"Did they catch the guy?"

Alexander shook his head, his eyes avoiding Charles'.

Charles seemed to catch the guilt and he put a hand on his brother's shoulder. "You put out a Writ on him, didn't you?"

"As you lay in your death bed, Charles, still covered in gore. It was the first thing I did after Marie told me what was going on. Once she had returned to the catacombs to go collect the things you would need for this endeavor, I wrote the Writ. I left it on the desk and turned back to seeing to your body for the funeral. When I looked again, it was gone."

"The Writ Executioner is subtle. I've never seen him."

"Well, I have. His name is Duncan. It's because of him that I was able to come here to talk to you." He lifted the amulet from his shirt. "This enabled him to travel through shadows to get to places he's been before." He thought of the strands and pulled one from the amulet. "There's another feature too. This is a connection to a person, so I can go to the person, no matter where they are, even if I've never been there before. I'd put one on you if I could."

Charles looked at the strand that looked like a small hair or piece of thread. He raised his eyes to Alexander. "If you could? Is it dangerous?"

"I don't think so. I think it's how Duncan knew to come to you when you wrote a Writ. He said he put one on me, but I never even knew. However, this amulet is his and he's got his strands in place already. He'd notice if I took them off and put them on someone else."

Charles frowned. "Does he know you have this thing of his?"

"Not really..." Alexander noticed there were two connections with the amulet. One was to him, or rather, to the Crown. The other was to the Palace. "Odd. There's one missing."

"One missing?"

Alexander looked at Charles. "Yeah. There are supposed to be three, I think. I can sense one's missing, or unavailable. Damn! I was going to put one on Catriona."

"I take it you're not planning on giving this back to the King's Assassin?"

Alexander blinked, then glanced down at the amulet. "I suppose it would be stupid to try and take it away from him. Though," Alexander released the amulet, "if I put one on Catriona, I can clear up another mess."

Charles slapped his brother on the shoulder. "Less than a month and you've already got major issues of national security. What will next month bring?" He leaned over the hissing pot of water and poured some into the two cups with the tea. "So, your competition for Catriona's heart is gone. All you have to do is wait a little while and she'll come to you."

"I wish. That's the snag I was talking about. Gwen…you remember Gwen, right?"

Charles shook his head.

"She's Catriona's Protégé. Blonde hair, Dominic's intended."

Charles frowned, thinking, but Alexander waved it away, moving on. "Anyway, she's Glarren, a Fae meddler to boot. She went and cast a Fae spell on the *Enigma* I guess, to dispel all heartbreak and make the broken hearts ready for new love."

"There's a spell that can do that?"

"I guess so because she didn't seem to realize that Myrgen's heart was also broken, by Elizabeth, I imagine."

"Oh no. Don't tell me…"

Alexander nodded. "Catriona rescued him from his brother's trap and they sped off to sea earlier tonight. What's worse is she left my bed to do it."

Charles pulled the tea ball from a cup and set it on the counter as he handed the tea to his brother. "I'm about to throw a wild theory out here, so brace yourself… Has it ever occurred to you that maybe Catriona isn't meant for you?"

"Bite your tongue."

Charles smiled and leaned against the counter he had just put his own tea ball on. "I know, I know, but with the Fates conspiring against you like this, maybe you should start looking at other prospects."

"How did you feel when you were told you would marry Elizabeth instead of Marie?"

Charles glanced away. "Point taken." He rubbed his nose and shrugged. "I don't know what to tell you, Brother. Unless there's a way for the spell to be broken, you've got a real fight on your hands."

"Well, I haven't investigated that yet."

"So, I have a question. Why are you here? Why haven't you gone to her with your fancy traveling amulet?"

"You want the truth? I'm afraid to. She left my side to rescue Myrgen. What if I go there and they're together?"

"Do you really think she would do that to you?"

Alexander moved a bit closer to the fire, the heat comforting in the early morning sea air. "I don't know. She's been very reluctant to be with me. I can't say as I blame her."

"Huh? What do you mean? Can she read you too? I thought it was just me."

Alexander looked at his brother. "You?"

"Yes. After she saved my life by exposing Myrgen and the assassination plot, all of a sudden, I knew I had no secrets from her anymore. Luckily, I've never really had any to keep, well, not that would matter to her, but if she could look at you now…"

Alexander let that thought permeate his mind and it ate through his soul like acid. "I have done far too many things that would destroy any semblance of love for me if she knew about them. The Writ alone…" He shook his head, relaxing a bit. "No, you're right. If it were, she would have thrown me out of her life, not practically accepted my proposal. No, that hasn't happened, and I need to make sure it never does."

"How do you plan to do that?" Charles took a sip of his cooled tea.

Alexander shook his head. "I don't know. You said she could read you after she revealed the assassination plot?"

"Yes. She saved my life."

"Ah yes. You saved her life years ago at that church when we came upon her after Giovanni-- after he left her for dead. She's always aware of life debts. It's how she decides who gets their own ship or who travels with her on the *Enigma*. She told me before that was why she can't see my secrets. I've saved her life a dozen times in the past several years. Until those debts are repaid, she can't see through me." Alexander leaned back against the counter where the loose tea was still out and exhaled.

Charles pursed his lips and cocked his head, a discerning eye surveying his brother. "I know this is none of my business, but maybe you need to stop doing things that would put her off if she ever discovered them. I love her too, but I would *never* want to get on her bad side and I would never want to assume our history together would be enough for her to forgive me. What's worse, you'd better hope she never comes here. If she sees me, she'll know your secrets. I'm afraid she's already seen what happened on St. Michael's Day."

"She did? How?"

"It was the first thing she did when the life debt was settled. I must say, having been scrutinized now, I definitely plan to stay on a righteous path."

Alexander nodded and sipped at his tea. It was very good tea. "So, other than marrying someone else, do you have any suggestions for, say, winning her to my side?"

Charles looked at the ceiling, his eyes squinting in thought. "Not really. Removing Myrgen from the picture seems to have done the opposite of your intent. Any further attacks on him will alienate you completely. I just don't know. Strategy has never been my strong suit. I don't even know who you could go to for guidance."

Alexander furrowed his brow. "You said there was a military something or other on this island. Maybe they have a strategist."

"Do you speak Yokotaman?"

"Uh, no."

"Well, ask around then. Maybe Tristram knows someone, or I suppose you could always take this to Mother."

"No. After seeing what she did to your life. Not a chance."

"Do you have *any* allies in this?"

"Well, Gwen… But she's the one that got us into this mess in the first place."

"Well, Rule Number One is that people who have failed you once will double their efforts to redeem themselves if given another chance. You said she cast this troublesome spell in the first place, right? So have her un-spell it. Catriona might throw the traitor off her ship if her vision is unclouded by this thing and she'll return to you of her own accord."

"I did leave rather suddenly. Saints, was it just yesterday afternoon?" Alexander raised his eyebrows.

"Well, if you just disappeared yesterday afternoon, you can return before Dom notices you're missing."

"I was in St. Andrew."

Charles furrowed his brow. "Why?"

"Chasing Catriona. Speaking of which, if I want to mend this problem, I need to get back to Duncan. He's still my best bet to find Tanglwyst."

"Wait, I thought you were chasing Catriona?"

"I'm trying to find Tanglwyst so Myrgen will return and I can put him to death for treason."

Charles shook his head and drained his tea. He hugged his brother. "Make sure you stop by next month. I can't wait to see what's next."

Alexander willed himself back to his room at the salon as his brother left the kitchen.

James turned the page on the journal and leaned forward. He felt his back scream as a cramp took it and he sat up, his breath hitching. Breathing through his teeth, he went over to the wall and grabbed the door handle, stretching his back. His Glarren gold hair framed his ice blue eyes in a slightly tousled mess, a cowlick at the back causing a halo. He was barely taller than his sister but just as sturdily built. He tried to pull the strain out but it failed.

"Gwen!"

The blond young woman fully dressed on the bed sprung up, her blond hair half her height thrown all over the pillows. "What?!"

"Cramp!"

She looked at him as he strained and he pointed his sister to the muscle that was refusing to relax. She pushed him against the wall and started pulling the muscles downward to get them to loosen. It took some kneading but she managed it. He shook out the strain and stretched his neck as well.

"Thanks."

"Have you been up all night reading that thing?" Gwen looked at the page he had just opened.

He nodded. He was really feeling the lost sleep now that the adrenaline kick of the cramp was passing. He pointed to the journal. "You should too. That's important stuff. Like, did you know there was a war three hundred years ago that almost destroyed the world? It took all the forces of Heaven, the Fae, the Land, the Arcane and the Infernal to create the mess and practically that number to put it down. One man, an arcane caster, drugged pregnant women and captured them, trying to get them to give birth to babies that would give their souls to these monsters."

He pointed to a drawing of a great symbol on monoliths set in a circle. Women with swollen bellies and agonized faces screamed as a dark robed man wearing the same symbol on his chest sent energy to them, his eyes black.

Gwen recoiled. "That's horrible."

"And a group of arcane casters freed the Fae Lords to help with the battle. Between the Lords and their lieutenants, they created a way to banish the monsters forever into the dark." He shifted forward a few pages. He found some drawings, one of a strong man in plated armor with long, flowing hair and a score of strong looking combatants supporting him. "See? That's Corrigan, the Midsummer King, the greatest of all Fae warriors. And that's Calpurnia Allegheri, the Autumn Mistress. She's apparently a gifted sorceress and helped capture the monsters." He navigated away form the tall, slender Fae woman with intense features and a great oak staff. The next page had a man who looked like a cross between smoke and willow branches, a very mischievous smile as he turned a pouch inside out. Next to him, grinning as well, holding a tree branch, was a stunning woman decked out in black leather with impossible suppleness.

"This is Embertwist, the Rogue of Spring and his favorite, the Sinister Glove. Uncle Alistair never calls her by a name. Just the Sinister Glove of Embertwist. Makes sense that a master rogue would have a sinister glove instead of a right hand man. And then you saw the picture of Gloriana, the Midwinter Queen." He looked at Gwen. "I'm not yet sure who Alistair was, outside of him being royalty. He didn't tell of himself in this first part of the book. Just of the other play…play..ers…" A yawn drew out his words and he delighted that Gwen got caught in it as well. *She yawns if you just say the word yawn. I love that.*

She hit him. "Stop that." But continued to yawn as well. "You need to sleep. I've been waking up at just about every noise just in case it's Alexander returning."

"Why not set a watcher? There's that black Fae cat downstairs." The name of this Inn was the Black Cat and Anchor and downstairs, on a wide mantle was a large anchor and an orange tabby cat named Anchor. Gwen and James had noticed the black Fae cat at the same time at dinner.

"Oh yeah. Okay." She went out of their room. The proprietress, Ce'Nedra van Oppal, had discovered to her great surprise that Gwen was traveling with the King of Mervolingia and had enjoyed a glut of business as many of the townsfolk had put on their best attire to catch a glimpse of the new monarch. James had found out over the course of the previous day that Alexander had been king less than a month, after his brother Charles was murdered by the Queen. A hunt was out for the former Kingdom Chancellor Myrgen de Sablonnieres, who just happened to be in the company of the woman the King loved.

James also knew Catriona from an encounter years before, and Gwen was her ward. Serendipity had brought them to this place, along with their uncle Alistair. Poor Ce'Nedra was worried sick about him since she had not seen him since yesterday. James was a little worried, but his uncle had regularly disappeared to conduct private business during the eight years James had sailed with or for him. He felt certain Alistair would turn up.

Until then, this stuff was fascinating. He sat down and, mindful of his sore muscle, and began reading about the Baroness Wilgefortis and her mage lover Raven Grasshair.

"That was subtle." Karma turned to Alistair. "The book."

"It seemed appropriate. I needed a way to impart the knowledge of the Ancients to him, arm him against what was coming, but I'm no longer there to guide him."

"Were you ever, really?"

Alistair winced at the barb. He had tried to be, later, after James turned sixteen, but he had let his "sister" raise the boy from infancy to save him from growing up with the boy's mother. It had been the right decision and limiting the contact between them had the best way to ensure that he grew up human.

"Besides, Raven and Wilge deserve to have their story known. It was a saga worth telling. All of those mages deserve to be remembered. They saved humankind from destruction, but the

106

Church stole their glory and sacrificed them instead of thanking them. It turned its greatest allies into enemies once the fighting was done, all to establish dominance over the people."

Karma held her forearm. "It was war. People wanted to feel safe from supernatural threats. The Church was available to them."

"And you don't need to be anything special to be a part of the Church. Magic, the Fae, even the Land seem to require some prerequisite, but the Church is all encompassing. It is their best weapon. Anyone can work for the Church."

Duncan woke up to the sound of footfalls on the marble. The room was bright but the water wasn't cold because of the heated area beneath, if his bottom's opinion could be trusted. At that moment, Duncan wasn't certain he could because it was asleep. He was surprised to see the person entering the salon was the King. He was carrying Duncan's clothing which was washed and folded. On the top was his amulet. Duncan leaned on the side of the tub, giving his buttocks time to regain feeling.

"Your Majesty, or have you taken a job here?"

"It would mean better food and quarters and probably more money. I ran into Lysette on my way here and she said she had not yet bothered you. Where did you want these?"

Duncan pointed. "Third from the door."

Alexander stepped into the changing room. Duncan leaned on the edge of the pool and was about to pull himself up when he noticed the scar on his wrist had turned red. *Probably the hot water.* He hoisted himself out of the water and grabbed a towel to dry off. He realized he still needed to shave. He looked around for those tools and found a basin area near a mirror. He dried off and put the robe on as he walked to the basin.

Alexander came over and Duncan immediately smelled rotten eggs. He looked at Alexander. "Were you assaulted?"

"No. Why?"

"Move through a chicken yard?"

"No."

"You might need to avail yourself of the facilities, sire. You must have gotten egg on you somehow."

Alexander smelled himself, then looked at Duncan, as if just now understanding what he meant. "Oh, yes. There's a sulfur spring nearby. I visited it this morning. That must be it. Perhaps I should take a bath and see if these can be aired out." He walked over to the hallway and pulled a cord. A few minutes later, a man came by and nodded. Alexander changed, bathed and perfumed while a young page took his clothes away.

Duncan donned his outfit as the page returned. A fresh set of clothes had apparently been purchased and the king got dressed. They weren't tailored, to be sure, but he had a shirt and breeches and seemed content. He finished getting dressed as Duncan pulled his belt through the loop on the leather. "Now what?"

Alexander smiled at Duncan. "I should get back to St. Andrew. What were you doing before I called you?"

Duncan shrugged. "Waiting."

"Still haven't heard from Tanglwyst yet, eh?"

"Not yet."

Alexander nodded, then looked at Duncan's amulet. "Why don't we get back to St. Andrew and see where we go from here?"

Duncan nodded and after signing a note for Dominic to pay the bill, they slipped into the shadows again.

Alexander and Duncan arrived in St. Andrew a few seconds later. He preferred traveling with Duncan at the helm because the Sovereign shield protected him from the swirling eyes and rancid egg smell. He looked at the surroundings and realized they were not in his room at the inn. The full daylight illuminated the front of the alley and there were throngs of people in the market place, hawking their livelihoods. Fish and sea air vied for control of his olfactory senses and gulls fought for his attention in the sky and road.

"Why did we land here? I was hoping for my room."

"I haven't been to your room."

Alexander pointed down the road to the Black Cat and Anchor Inn. "I'm staying there. Gwen accidentally revealed my identity to the proprietress and she rushed me into a room before I was mobbed. She's a nice lady."

Duncan looked uncomfortable. "Yeah, I don't really go there when I'm in town."

"Why not? It's the only stable in town."

"I don't exactly use a horse, Your Majesty."

Alexander glanced at Duncan and nodded, returning his gaze to the inn. "Right. There are a hundred people out side the doors, nearly all of them rich, court types who can't make it to a usual court. By the Saints."

Duncan scanned the crowd. "There are more parents with daughters present in nice clothes than sailors, which was pretty impressive for a port city at sailing season. I take it they don't know you're spoken for?"

Alexander shook his head. "It was Gomez' idea. Send out a decree saying I'll be out and about. It would set the nobility to putting on their finery rather than plotting against the Crown."

"Gomez. He's a crafty one."

Alexander looked back at his companion, aware of the well-deserved animosity between this assassin and Gomez, the king's Grand Guard. "Speaking of guards, there are at least five over there working crowd control, plus several personal guards. St. Andrew can't possibly have that much nobility. They must have shipped some in for the occasion." He stepped back into the alley shadows.

"Do you want to go somewhere else, Your Majesty?"

Alexander shook his head. "No. Gwen's in there. I need to at least tell her she can return home. Plus there's a man with a ship, James, who can get me to Caratia. Unless you've been there?"

Duncan shook his head. "You could go overland, you know. You might be able to meet her there that way."

Alexander nodded. That wasn't a bad idea. He wanted Gwen with him when he went to Catriona. Gwen could explain why they belonged together while also working those magicks of hers to make Catriona fall for him again. She had been so close yesterday. "Yeah, but that doesn't get me in the front door. And it doesn't get me private conversations at all." He looked at Duncan's amulet.

"Can I use that for a bit? Get to my room? I can return it after I speak to her."

Duncan looked at the amulet, fondling it with his wounded hand. "I'm not sure. It's an artifact from the church."

"And I'm the church's appointed sovereign for Mervolingia. My Power of Sovereignty proves that. It's from a holy source."

"I don't even know if you can use it."

Alexander knew to push this would result in Duncan clutching the amulet tighter. He needed to let it be left in Duncan's hands. "Good point. I'll see if there's another way." He walked to the end of the alley on the other side. "There might be a way to the back door."

Duncan looked at the crowd. "No, I know where the back door is. It's covered as well. You'll not be getting in there without being spotted." He looked at his amulet. "Okay, here's what you do."

Alexander smiled as Duncan took off the amulet. He didn't really listen to the instructions because he had already done the trip. Instead he made sure he was reassuring to Duncan. He handed Alexander the amulet and Alexander put it on.

"Where will you be?"

Duncan nodded to the red door nearby. "Working out some frustration."

Alexander nodded. "I'll see you in a while." He closed his eyes and willed himself into his room at the inn.

Fifteen

"He sets fire to you near the shore, then lets you become glass on the sand."
The Siren's Song of Callista

Tanglwyst stepped from the inn and looked towards the southwest. She could feel her king in that direction, the danger to him still there, but she knew she had time. This servant of the church would enable her to get to him well before the danger overtook him.

Hang on, Alexander. I'm coming.

The Scarred Man stepped out behind her, motioning her to the stables. She walked into the shelter, the musty scent of straw and hay blended with fur and sweat. The sun had crested the horizon and she could see sunlight starting to peek through the slats of wood at the fragments of dust and straw in the air. There were a couple horses in the stable, and they whinnied, eyes wide with distrust and fear. She frowned.

"If you have an amulet, why are you riding a horse or staying at an inn?"

"Ah, that's easy, my dear." He turned to face her, holding the amulet. "I use them to hunt."

He touched her shoulder and they disappeared, followed only faintly by the sound of panicked horses. They came out in a room ripe with the smell of death and iron. The smell of sulfur and lemons mixed with it and made her gag. When Duncan took her to the secret room, he said he smelled lemons but she had noticed a sulfur smell on him. This time, there was no mistaking it was from the Scarred Man.

She dropped to the floor, trying not to wretch. Her hands landed in something sticky and she lost the fight. The bread she had just eaten splashed on her hands, soaking her shirt sleeves and gloves. She barely had time to recover when she heard the sound of a blade being drawn from a sheath.

The Scarred Man grabbed her hair, pulling her to her feet. She felt cold metal against her throat. It was iron, not steel and for some reason, it burned a bit.

"Ah, as I thought. You have a little of the Fae in you, miss. I thought I smelled it."

He ran the point of the blade down her neck. She felt it burn and she threatened to wretch again at the smell of seared meat. She reached up to grab his shirt, then push him away. Her gloved hand closed on the amulet. Before she could think, she yanked on the amulet, drawing the leather thong around it against the blade edge.

The dagger was as sharp as she thought and cut the piece of leather holding it in his possession. She closed her eyes and thought of home.

The Sinister Glove dove into the stables and slammed into the stench of rotten eggs. The horses were rearing and crying out, causing shouts from the innkeeper to the stable hand. The Glove touched the nearest one, whispering. The horse calmed but its nostrils still flared. The back door of the inn slammed closed, a young man's voice breaking through the walls.

"You folks okay?"

He walked into the stable and a raven flew past him. He flailed his arms around, then looked in. He shouted at the wall.

"It's just a raven, Mother. Got into the stable and spooked the horses." He sniffed. "Smells like a weasel might have stolen its egg and one of the horses stomped on it."

"Are those folks still in there?"

He looked in the stalls. "No. His horse is still here too. Maybe they didn't come here yet."

The woman stepped out of the back door, wiping her hands on a towel. "Where else would they go? It's not like there's a town here to buy supplies. And that woman was quite anxious to get going."

"What do you want to do?"

She glanced around at the interior of the stable. "Let's give them a while. The Patrol comes by in a bit. If they haven't turned up by then, we'll tell them. Personally, I'm glad that man is gone. He made the brownies leave. I haven't seen a sign of a Fae since he arrived. Had to churn my own butter this morning."

The raven looked around. She saw no signs of any Fae either. This was bad. She flew off to find Embertwist.

Tanglwyst opened her eyes and staggered against the impact of actual light in the room. Her eyes, dilated with fear, were overwhelmed by the sudden brightness. Patras was closer to the sea and the uninterrupted horizon made day come hours earlier than in the mountains or forest. She blinked, expecting to see her stained glass window from her study.

Instead she found the light coming from under the door, the room actually without a window, being an interior one on the third floor of the palace in Patras. She looked around and saw the personal belongings she had kept here were gone. She realized the reason her thoughts of home brought her here. This was where she had fallen in love with Alexander.

Her knees started to buckle as the adrenaline faded so she sat on the bed. Her stomach was settling but she could feel it on the verge of heaving again when the thrumming in her nerves calmed, eventually. Right then, it felt like she would collapse if she wasn't careful. She hadn't slept well since the dreams started but she couldn't help but nod off as the crash came. In spite of the danger, exhaustion claimed her and she melted onto the bed.

The smell of a black smithy overwhelmed her, heat and ore combined with something else, something unidentifiable. She'd been in a smithy before and knew the smells but this other one was... sinister. Like burning sin. The fire was loud and close. She tried to see through the heat. A beautiful being with wings was sitting in a huge, ornate throne, larger than the Mervol throne and more gaudy than her Grandfather's in the Papal City.

He picked up a dainty cake and ate it in two delicate bites. A large tray of them was next to him. Tanglwyst's own dessert chef was adept at these. She called them petit fours and used them as a way to show off her cake decorating skills. The frostings on the things would melt in this heat though, but the cakes and the being seemed unaffected.

She looked beside her and all around. It was then that she realized why it was so hot where she was. As the being smiled at the next tiny cake, she grabbed the bars of the inside of the furnace and started to scream.

"My Lord."

The Sinister Glove nodded reverence to her Vernal Monarch.

Embertwist cocked his head at his lieutenant, then looked again at the hand of cards in front of him. He slipped a deuce from the deck and tucked it into the sleeve of the man upon who's shoulder he was sitting, leaving it out *just* enough that his rather rough looking opponent would see it when the gambler showed his hand.

"That should take care of him. Water down *my* ale, will you? Those Brownies worked hard on that you greedy filth." Embertwist stepped down from his perch to absolutely no one's attention, not even the gambler. No one seemed to have noticed a full grown man sitting on another man's shoulder like a parrot. He nodded to a small humanoid creature in a barkeep's outfit and the little Fae returned the nod.

"Sire, the woman has disappeared."

"Which one, Glove? I have so many to keep track of." He smiled and batted his eyes in an attempt to be charming.

"The one I gave the touch to."

His face darkened. "The one who traveled through the shadows with that pirate? Did you glean anything from her dreams?"

The Glove shook her head. "It might have helped, Sire, had I known what to look for."

"What's this? Are you *cheating?"* The table erupted in fists behind the pair and the Fae lord dodged a flying tooth.

"Well, Glove, here's the thing: That Tanglwhatever woman has been through the shadows with a 'Walker. She's seen a realm you and I can never see. Thus, there are secrets there we won't discover without her insight. So, tell me," he stepped aside as a mug of ale shattered and splashed on the tavern floor, "what was on her mind?"

"The king. She spoke of him the entire time, when she wasn't mummbling about grapes, or stained glass windows. Or stained glass grapes." She inhaled, shaking her head and rolling her eyes. She had no idea what detail might be the one her lord needed. "Mostly, it was him, dancing, tea, small delicate cakes. Typical rich human fare."

"Hm." He stroked his small, red beard. His green and brown finery shimmered in the now prominent light through the newly broken window. "Perhaps it was because she was not the one operating the amulet. Of course, if she were to be the one allowing the Shadows to ride her, that gift you gave her would be devoured. The Shadows were designed to destroy Fae on contact."

"Would it hurt?"

Embertwist sighed, his eyes sad. "Yes." He put his hand on her shoulder. "Your magic is great, Glove, made moreso because of the human connection. It wouldn't leave her without a fight."

She moved a step to the left to avoid a leaping city guard who was now handling the brawl. "I hope you're right, Sire. I worry about her."

"She's the granddaughter of the Pope. Her divine blood might throw off the Shadows for a bit. She'll be fine."

"And if she isn't?"

He took a deep breath and strolled with her out into the street, stepping over debris. He really didn't want to think of that possibility.

"So you think he'll find one?"

Tanglwyst's eyes shot open, her heart pounding in panic. It took a moment to settle from the dream, even though she couldn't remember anything except petit fours. She realized where she was and remembered she was a wanted traitor who'd escaped house arrest a tenday ago. If she were caught here…

"Who?"

"The *king*, silly. Do you think he'll find himself a wife?"

Tanglwyst stopped, looking at the door. The two women in the hallway were ones she remembered cleaning her room before. Maisaile and Marisa Kendric were sisters who always talked of opening a tavern and calling it the Two Spinsters Shore Side Inn. Tanglwyst stepped a little closer, listening.

"Oh, that nonsense. I thought he was pretty close to finding a good one in that Tanglwyst. Pity she was suspected of murdering King Charles."

"Do *you* believe she did it?"

"Peh," Mairsile sounded shocked at the thought. "I believe that Myrgen scoundrel acted alone, just like he told the guard. Implicating that nice young woman was just the queen being evil."

Marisa's voice lowered. "They say he cut her down without a lick of hesitation. Did you believe Alexander capable of that?"

Tanglwyst staggered, bumping the door.

"What was that?"

Marisa raised her voice. "Is someone in there?"

The door handle moved and Tanglwyst grabbed the amulet and disappeared.

She dropped to the floor of her bedroom in her home in Patras, coughing and gagging at the stench of sulfur. Her hands hurt, as did the mark on her neck from the Scarred Man's blade. Her mind went to him for a moment, pondering his fate. The rooms had no escape except the amulet. She didn't know if they preserved what was in them but she vowed never to return to find out.

The room was cold, the fireplace long dead. She crawled to her bed and pulled herself to her feet on the bedpost. Dust was on the bedding. It looked like no one had disturbed her room even to clean it. The door to her study lay open, the light from her beloved window cheering her heart.

She stepped into the room and heard people moving around downstairs. The heavy boots and deep voices told her they were guards, probably set here in case she returned. They never would have suspected she would appear out of the air, reeking like a sailor's fart. The top drawer of her desk was open and she reached into it, remembering the letter Catriona wrote to Charles, warning him of the attempt on his life. Myrgen had been smart and not shown his face at the original offer to hire her for the assassination so he would have been safe. No need for either of them to be charged with murder.

Tanglwyst, for some reason she now suspected was Elizabeth's fault, refused to allow anyone else to be the killer. She wanted Catriona to murder the king and for Nicolai to find out. That hadn't worked, but now that it was all done but the hangings, she regretted ever thinking the thought aloud. Nicolai was dead and she knew she needed to move on.

She needed to help Alexander, but apparently, he was off somewhere, looking for a wife. At least, that's what the staff believed. Tanglwyst wasn't certain there wasn't something else afoot. She changed clothes, mindful of the guards downstairs. She gathered a few more things to help her on her journey and held onto the amulet.

She closed her eyes. "Take me to Alexander."

She felt nothing and opened her eyes. She was still in her bedroom. She tried again. *"Take me to Alexander."*

Still no change. She heard footsteps near the stairway and poked her head around to see if someone was coming up. Her eyes caught on the open drawer. She realized she might need to go to the palace and see if there was an itinerary of where he was. Once she knew his route, she could go. She knew he had a secret passage to the catacombs in his room but she'd never been in there and never been through the catacombs unescorted. She didn't think she would know which room was his.

Elizabeth's was just down the hall from his though. She knew that room very well. She could teleport in and figure out the way to Alexander's room. Her stomach reeled at the idea of another use of the amulet but she forced it down. Alexander needed her. She couldn't be queasy.

She closed her eyes and thought of Elizabeth's room. Before she could say a word, her stomach revealed she had jumped again. Her hands burned like she was holding a hot stone and her vision refused to clear for several seconds. The stench around her was getting stronger and more nauseating. She was grateful there were no servants in this room, but she didn't expect there to be. There was no Queen yet.

She leaned against the wardrobe to catch her breath but the handle to the room moved and she heard the spinsters outside. Their discussion had been informative before. Maybe they knew where the king was.

She opened the wardrobe and stepped inside, closing the door. She felt a click in the floor beneath her feet and another door opened up behind her. She stepped into the secret room, closing the wardrobe wall behind her as the two servant ladies entered the Queen's bedroom.

Little sound at all filtered into the room through the thick wood and Tanglwyst realized she would not be able to discern any names or information through the furnishing. A torch flared to life behind her, startling her. She spun and saw two others light themselves. The room reeked of dark magic and she remembered the Fae tales Elizabeth used to tell.

Krakte has the Black Forest as its center, a place where every dark and dangerous Fae was imprisoned. Beth said sometimes humans went into the woods because they were the only ones who could. If anyone with any Fae blood entered the Forest, they were trapped. She also said that sometimes, women went into the woods and came out pregnant. Sometimes, this drove them mad. I wonder if this ever happened to Beth.

Large alembics and scales adorned the room, cluttering the tables alongside other items mechanical and alchemical.

Ingredients filled every available space between, some loose, some bottled. A couple of recipes seemed to be in mid-production. She walked over to one of these and saw an empty bottle marked "Herbspyce". Next to it was a recipe written in Dominic's hand. The paper was old and stained, but the detailed effects of the mixture cited its purpose: To cause a slow, painful death via headaches.

Beneath that card was another and Tanglwyst pulled it out. It was in Krakten but she could read it. It was an old family recipe, passed down from queen to queen. It was best served in wine of a certain vintage from a very specific vineyard near the Forest... to ensure the pliability of a subject to any suggested course of action.

She looked around. Another work area had a finished alembic housing a pink liquid. The recipe was inside a letter from Sovereigna, Elizabeth's mother. Also in Krakten, it showed more than Tanglwyst wanted to know.

My Dear,

I got this recipe from an old witch in the Forest. I included the ingredients so you could specialize it for your quarry. Catherine is a D'Medici. She undoubtedly has Cyprian Herb around. It will be a plant the Prince has watered and tended personally. This is specific to him. Find it and use it.

The effects are thus:

If the quarry for whom this has been made drinks this potion, then the next person he sees will be his true love, forsaking all others. If you prefer to use it on your faithless king, he will slay his own children and mistress at your request.

Happy hunting!

Tanglwyst set this aside. When she saw Alexander, she would tell him of this place and let him destroy it.

Alexander.

She looked around. She was wasting time here. She needed to find him. She closed her eyes and grasped the amulet. Dominic would know where Alexander was. As Acting Chancellor, he had to know for legal purposes. They had not parted company on the best terms before, but she couldn't let that sway her now. Alexander needed her.

Myrgen's secret room.

She opened her eyes on a darkened area and fell to the ground, grasping her hands as her unwilling cry bounced off the stone around her. The pain filled the room and she tried not to whimper as she waited for it to subside. It took much longer than she expected. It felt like it must be dark by the time she could bring herself to stand.

The stone hid her pain from Dominic's room and she felt around for a catch to the door. It opened and she stumbled into the catacombs. The expanse of space told her she had gone in the wrong direction. It was all she had to go on because the place was almost entirely dark. She could see a faint light ahead but she wanted to talk to Dominic. She turned back, bumping the stone door with her hands. The pain redoubled and she couldn't stand. She leaned against the door, pushing it closed before she could stop it.

She breathed through the pain until her mind cleared. She could feel Alexander to the south but the thought of using the amulet again was beyond repelling. She dropped the amulet on the floor of the catacombs and moved towards the light.

Dominic D'Medici closed the door to his chambers and looked at the hidden door to the secret prayer nave. He thought he heard something during the long report the Chatelaine was giving regarding the current state of the kitchen's spices. *Listening to that woman's voice is like chewing on iron.*

Now that he was free of her, he went to the secret latch and opened the prayer nave. The stench of sour eggs caused him to pull his sleeve to his nose. The gesture barely saved his eyes from watering. The nave was empty otherwise, though the dust on the floor was disturbed. Marks in the dirt led to the back door.

He took a candle from his desk and opened the door to the catacombs. He listened but the echoing passages revealed no source to the noises he could make out. He was about to return to his room when the light caught on something by the wall on the floor.

He picked up the amulet on the cut leather thong. The markings were divine, invoking St Giles against dark magic and the Archangel Michael in fighting evil. The composition was gold, but it looked odd. He sniffed the leather and caught sulfur. This had been in the cloud of foulness in the nave.

He walked into his room, closing the catacombs door before he could open the bedroom one. In the better light, he recognized the gold. It was Mandian. He gripped it in his fist. The maker's mark on the bottom revealed its manufacture: the Royal City of Roma. The King's foundry was the maker of this.

Dominic realized the danger of having a spy from his homeland hiding in the catacombs of the royal palace of Mervolingia. If they got word to their King that Alexander was gone, any number of horrors would become a way of life here.

He opened his door and called for the guards.

Tanglwyst heard the shouts of guards bounce off the catacomb walls. She wasn't sure she could get outside before she was discovered, especially since it came out by the kitchen. She grabbed the single torch in the hall and went to the area where her cell had been. The secret door closed just as the lights were starting to descend the stairs to the labyrinth's crossroads.

She remembered the burnt-out church near the cell where Alan was held during the kidnapping. The boards were old but sturdy and it was difficult to get through the space between. Myrgen said there was an escape out of there through the church that let out near the King's Woods. She scraped through and her hand brushed something fabric on the floor. She reached through the boards and retrieved the torch she leaned against the wall.

The firelight revealed the chemise she had worn when she discovered Charles in a spreading pool of blood. Brown blood still marred the hem. The more disturbing discovery was what lay beside it. A piece of beige silk subtly embroidered with tulips was the backdrop for a yawning purple lioness, stretching to the base. This was the favor she gave to Myrgen to show Catriona as proof of Tanglwyst's capture.

Its presence here meant Myrgen had found this chemise discarded and hidden. He must have come to the conclusion that she was willing to sacrifice him for Elizabeth. Although true at the time, she now knew that was not through her own volition. It hurt a bit to think Myrgen wouldn't have figured something was amiss. Tanglwyst's behavior was far from her normal fare.

Or was it? My actions have not always been rational when it comes to men. Look at my willingness to go with that scarred man.

She pushed the torch into a wedge in the boards and pulled off her gloves. There was still a red dent where the pain has caused her to clutch the amulet and they still throbbed, but the scarring she expected was not there. Her hands felt like they had all the skin removed through fire, yet they looked fine.

She picked up the favor and dusted it off. This represented so much of her life before this moment, and he brother had discarded it because of her actions. She felt tears streak through the filth on her face and she stood. She had lived a life that made her feel like she could manipulate any man she met. It never protected her against a woman bent on destroying her country.

She dropped the favor back into the ash and debris. None of that mattered anymore. All that mattered was Alexander. She'd ask forgiveness from her family after she returned, but the country needed its king. She took the torch and began picking her way across the skeleton of the old chapel.

Gwen woke up when the Fae cat leapt on her chest. She suspected Ce'Nedra was Fae touched. Why else name her inn after a black cat no one else could see? The thing was far heavier than she expected. "Is he back, Kitty?"

The black cat meowed and she moved him off her chest to get out of bed. The sun was up and the sound of carts and wheels over the cobble streets echoed around the room. She could smell bread and fish. She threw on her plaid Caratian coat and stepped out into the hallway. Sure enough, there was movement under Alexander's door. She glanced back in her room but it was empty. James must have decided to go to his own room and rest. *Probably asleep on that journal.* She walked over and knocked. "Grymalkin?"

Movement behind the door stopped and she heard him walk over to the door. "Yes Gwen. It's me."

"Are you all right?"

He opened the door. He was wearing nice dark blue breeches and a white shirt that looked new. He smelled of roses and sulfur.

"By the Fae…" She looked into his eyes and saw the irises were swirling like ink in water and he stank of rotten eggs. She clutched her robe at the neck, her panic coming forward as she took a step back. "Alexander, where did you go?"

He looked down at his fresh shirt. "What do you mean, where did I go?"

"James!"

James opened the door to his room on the other side of Alexander's and stepped out, mostly dressed. "Gwen, what's wrong?" As soon as he looked at Alexander's eyes, he stepped between his sister and her king. "What happened to your eyes?"

Alexander's eyes grew wide and he went to the small tin mirror in his room.

James came up behind Alexander who had paled as when he saw the swirls in his eyes. He never took his eyes off Alexander's. "Gwen, go back to your room and lock the door."

"I'm not leaving you alone, James." The eyes were frightening enough, and she was concerned Alexander had become possessed by a dark Fae, like a goblin. Dark Fae were mischievous and without caution or moral fiber. Most of the Fae avoided them. It was not unheard of for them to kidnap someone and impersonate them. It was also not unusual for them to rape young maidens.

Alexander made the mistake of moving towards Gwen and James put a dagger at his throat. She didn't even know he had been carrying one. And where was he keeping it until then?

"Try to touch her and your heir inherits." James looked at the amulet on Alexander's neck. "Gwen, get the book, the journal from my room. Now."

Gwen looked into her brother's room and saw the journal on the floor. He must have thought she was in trouble and dropped it. She picked it up and it was open to a drawing of an amulet. It was used by the church to travel to distant places during the Inquisition.

He suspected the amulets were touched by the infernal because all who wore them hunted and destroyed heathens and Fae across the Saintlands in the name of Heaven. Anyone not Augustinian fell before their blades. Its weakness was fire because the Church's mage who created them could not use fire magic at all.

She came back into the room with James. The amulet was the same. "That amulet is in here. It says it was used to destroy Fae."

"That's what I thought." James snatched the amulet off Alexander's neck, breaking the cord holding it there. "Where did you get this?"

Gwen had asked the inn Fae to keep the fire in Alexander's room going and to let her know when and if he returned. He apparently decided Alexander was taking too long to answer and James threw the amulet into the fire. The light exploded the amulet, and Alexander's eyes grew wide as fire burned through them. He fell to his knees, his hands to his eyes and smell of scorched flesh punctuated the room. James stood over him, the dagger ready to commit regicide if Alexander made the wrong move. Gwen prayed he wouldn't. The light in the fireplace threw out hideous toxic smoke, and Gwen ran to the window to open it and let it out.

People on the street looked up at the gesture and alarm at the potential fire at the Inn, moved them to the buckets and nearby troughs for dealing with a fire. Gwen waved them off. "Bad incense! Not a fire!"

The people on the street called up to her. "Is the inn alright? Is that the King's chamber?"

She glanced behind her as Alexander rested his hands on the ground, a trickle of blood dropping onto the floor. "The king is in this inn? By the Saints! I've been on my honeymoon for two days! Honey, the king's at this inn!" She turned from the window and then watched carefully to see if her ruse had worked. The people in the street set down the buckets and went on about their business.

Alexander glared at James and Gwen. "How dare you! That was..."

James was unimpressed by Alexander's wrath. He narrowed his eyes and held his ground. "I know what that was. The problem is you clearly don't."

"It was a traveling amulet. That's all."

"One that takes you through darkness, possibly even Hell." James motioned to Gwen to show Alexander the book. She saw that with the black swirls of ink were gone, but his eyes looked a little like he had cried blood. The waterline above his lower lashes were red.

She set the book on the ground in front of him. "Alexander, that was an artifact from a terrible war hundreds of years ago. Made by a very bad man."

James nodded, arms folded but still holding the dagger. "According to that account, it was made for the Church by their own mages, but it is suspected part of Hell crept into the process because it corrupted anyone who used it to commit atrocities."

Gwen thought about the trip with Alexander to get here, to see her friend. Had he become so obsessed with making Catriona his queen, he would try witchcraft and sacrifice his own soul to get to her? She remembered something Alexander had said. "Grymalkin, that man in St. Giles, the one who killed that woman. You and Myrgen both indicated I should not be sad I couldn't read what was written."

James looked at her. "You know about that? I found out about it yesterday while getting serviced at the Red Sky."

Alexander took a knee and tried to stand, but sat back on his heel instead. "That doesn't seem like appropriate business talk for a brothel."

"Some girls were whispering about it in the bath. They think a fabric screen is an actual wall but," he pulled his collar over his lips, "if you can hear me through my shirt, you can hear me through my tent," he dropped the collar, "or through a fabric screen in this case."

"Alexander," Gwen touched his arm, "Are you alright?"

She saw as much as felt James tense at the gesture, and realized the foolishness of being so close to someone who might have fallen to evil. Alexander wiped his eyes and looked at the blood tears, startled. "I see why you are asking. I thought my Power of Sovereignty was protecting me. That's why I smelled lemons instead of sulfur. I thought maybe Duncan might have detected the sulfur on me through another means."

James frowned. "Duncan? Duncan McVryce?

Alexander paled. "You know him?"

"Yes, and he's here in town. He gave this to you?"

Alexander looked at Gwen. "I've been getting a lot of gifts lately."

Gwen blushed, realizing that was her fault for revealing his Majesty's presence in the common room downstairs.

James was still hostile. "Where did he get it?"

"I didn't ask."

"But you asked enough to find out how to use it."

"I don't need to explain myself to you."

James set his jaw and nodded. He backed up a step, sheathing his dagger. "You're right. But I just destroyed your only other means of transportation and unless you tell me exactly what's going on, I'm not going to let you on my ship, or near my family."

"I don't need you or your ship. I can hire someone else."

"Yeah, good luck with that. Everyone in this town knows you're the King. Let's hope you get a reputable captain who won't hold you for ransom. Come on Gwen. You're not allowed around this man again."

"You can't order her around. She's *my* subject! I hold her fealty!"

"Better check that again, Alexander." Gwen's voice was quiet, but determined, and cut through the room like a sword. "I won't give myself to someone who can willingly use something that destroys Fae just to get around quicker. Especially if he's covering for a murderer."

"Duncan's not the murderer." Alexander ran his hands through his hair.

"How do you know?"

"Because he was rescuing Tanglwyst from house arrest that night. I doubt he left her side the entire night." Alexander motioned to the book. "What's this?"

James took it. "A personal journal we recently found. It has a lot of information in it about a war from around three hundred years ago. There were a dozen or so of those things." James nodded to the fire.

"I'm sorry. I didn't know."

Gwen looked at her brother. "I believe him. I know he wouldn't do anything to hurt Catriona, or her ship or crew. I'm going to help him."

126

James looked at her, holding her gaze. "This is foolish. We have better things to do."

She looked at Alexander. "If he's the right man for her, then no, I owe her too much to have her unhappy because I failed her."

James patted his sister's hand. "Fine. We'll use my ship. If you're traveling with him, I need to make sure you stay safe. Alistair would have wanted that."

Alexander straightened up. "Thank you."

James looked at Alexander. "Why her? Why Catriona?"

"I fell in love with her when I healed her through the power of my faith in Heaven. I gave her a part of my soul then. You just saved me from losing the rest of it. I owe you a debt, sir. But I could no more abandon her side than you could abandon Gwen's. She inspires that kind of loyalty. This kingdom has suffered at the hands of so much injustice. They deserve to be inspired."

James flicked his ice blue eyes at Gwen and she saw them sparkling at the thought of this devotion. "Gwen, do you trust him?"

Gwen looked him over and realized something. No. She didn't trust him. But she wasn't about to let him go after Catriona without being in a position to warn her. He used to be a good man, but this desperation to marry her friend was disturbing. She would stay with him and watch. She looked at James. "No. Alexander, you're not the man I knew. You're different, and you're not worthy of Catriona right now." She watched his eyes close and his soul sag. "However, I trust the man you used to be. I trusted him with my life. In fact, I trusted him with *her* life, more than anyone in the world. I'll help *that* man."

Alexander's eyes opened and he exhaled. "I will spend the rest of the day finding him again. You look me over and tell me when we're ready to go after her. Will you do that, Gwen?"

Gwen nodded. His ability to say just the right thing was very impressive. And definitely nothing to be trusted. "I'm going to rest a bit more. James, you should actually sleep. We'll see you this afternoon, Alex."

Alexander bowed to them both as they left the room. She turned to her brother as they closed the door. "Thank you for helping me."

"I promised Uncle Alistair I would." He glanced at Alexander's door. "If you're determined to help him, that's your choice, but I don't trust him and I'm not his servant. Don't expect me to bow before him or serve him because *you* do."

"He's really a good man, James. One of the best I've ever known. He never wanted to be king, but now he is and he's trying to secure the one thing that would make this bearable. We have to help him figure out how to do it, and if it can't be done, how to go on from there. But James, he's worth my trust. And he's worth her love. She knows it."

James glanced down and watched the floor a moment, then pointed to it. Gwen looked down and saw the shadow of Alexander near the door. He was listening to their conversation. She looked back at her brother.

He looked at her and shook his head, rolling his eyes. "Look, I'm not going to discuss this when he's sitting here on the other side of the door listening. So far, all he's shown me is an aptitude for being a really good orator and the only reason I'm interested in going along with this is to watch her see right through his crap and toss him to the ground. However, you have a very good point, I'm feeling tired now after that scuffle. I'm going to rest like you said." He turned away and went into his room, his disgust evident in his walk and breathing. She turned and went to her own room, hoping Alexander would wise up and start acting like himself. James was a very sharp individual and the smartest person she knew. If he wanted a strategy to win Catriona back, Alexander needed James on his team.

Sixteen

"The tide returns to me the things I love."
The Siren's Song of Callista

Myrgen opened his eyes and let out a sigh. He just wasn't sleepy, despite the trials of the past few hours. He had heard Octavius leave her quarters and then listened as she did likewise a few minutes later. She had slowed when she reached his door and he had sat up, hoping for a knock that never came. She moved on and he lay back down, more disturbed than before. His heart kept trying to convince him that she cared for him, but reason kept blocking the attempts. She believed the Land wanted her to marry Alexander. When one has direct experiences with one's deity, he couldn't imagine one saying no. His own experiences with his rescue in Patras and the Land's magic was enough to shake an already fractured faith in the Church.

Maybe she's right. Who am I to defy the wishes of the Land? It was its Will that I be freed from my prison in Patras. I owe the Land my life, and maybe it's about time I started acting like it.

Regardless, lying here isn't doing any good.

He reached down and grabbed his boots, putting them on. He would go on deck and walk around a bit. The night air might help settle his thoughts.

He stomped his boots on and grabbed his shirt, remembering the rip in the shoulder. Maybe he could talk to Octavius about where to find a sewing kit. He pulled a comb through his hair, then realized he was grooming for her, and put the comb down. He was tired of this. He was tired of questioning everything he was doing. He was tired of feeling things and not being able to touch her, to tell her he had fallen in love with her. As long as he didn't say anything, it could still be denied. The original plan was for him to take over her company duties in Caratia. He would be in Zara while she went back to sea. She would leave, and he would heal. He just had to make it to that day.

He tossed the shirt onto his bed and opened his door. He was surprised to find the night air uncharacteristically warm. They had been traveling south and the more temperate climate was revealing its charms. He walked over to Octavius up at the helm. "Hey, Octavius."

"Myrgen? What are you doing up at this hour? I thought we cut you loose a while ago."

"You did. It just didn't take."

Octavius glanced down at the helm. "Sorry about your... difficulties."

"You heard about that, huh?"

"From a couple different sources."

Myrgen glanced around the ship but no one was looking at him and he wondered who else had overheard their discussion. "I wasn't aware our conversations were so public."

"They aren't." Octavius smiled.

"You just know stuff?"

Octavius nodded, his smile fading a bit. "Still, I don't approve of her choice here. Luckily, I think she'll avoid it as long as she can. After what he did to the ship, she's disinclined to spend any further time in his company."

"That isn't going to stop her from marrying that D'Medici if it's the Land's will. She told me that herself. She's being directed to do this and the Land doesn't strike me as a fickle deity."

There was no moon, making the sea around a land mass dangerous to navigate. With the damage the ship had sustained in the attack, they could not afford to encounter ill winds or hidden reefs. They had anchored an hour out of sight of St. Marguerite and the Crow's Nest had been given orders to sound the alarm if anything came in sight. The *Enigma* was on high alert and running thin on tolerance for approaching ships at the moment. Myrgen hoped things went smoother tomorrow. He wasn't looking forward to another learning experience at the hands of the crew.

He looked up at the sparkling sky. Away from the city, the sky's charms were revealed. It was easy to see why a man would fall in love with the sea and this sky. The sounds of the sea were relaxing and soft, the lapping of the water against the hull and the cry of gulls diving for fish. It could be hypnotic, if he let it. He felt his mind come into focus. He blinked slowly, breathing in the sanity.

"So, Myrgen, is this your first time in love?"

"Saint's no. There was a period about four years ago where it seemed like I fell in love every month. I was surrounded by beautiful women adorned in billowing silks and intoxicating eyes. That Xannu reminds me of every one of them."

"Well, she's not married, you know."

"I think she would object to being a second choice. Besides, she's a bit too bright to truck with someone like me." He looked at Octavius. "What about you? You ever been in love?"

The First Mate got a very impressive smile on his face. "Oh yes."

"How did you know?" Myrgen turned to face the man he had come to consider a friend.

"Well, she wasn't subtle. I was living at Galadorn. This was after Catriona saved my life from that wolf attack. The Covenant at Galadorn had told Catriona she had their leave to build a ship of her own from the profits of the trade she had begun. She left to do so and I was saddened by that because, at that point, I was quite enamored of the Captain. I was lying awake in my room and I thought I heard a woman singing. I got up and went to my window and when I looked out, I thought I saw Catriona walking in the woods. I was a little concerned that she was walking through the woods at night when she was supposed to be in town, building a ship. I got dressed and went outside to see if there was a problem. I also thought to myself, 'Moonlight, woods, alone time with this woman. What an opportunity!'"

Myrgen smiled and nodded.

Octavius leaned his hands on the railing. "I ventured into the woods there. Now you have to understand, these are the Midsummer Woods and Corrigan Starshadow is the Fae ruler. Although he was actually not opposed to humans from Galadorn in his woods but it didn't mean there weren't more than a few creatures that did. I followed her through the trees until I saw her enter into a clearing. But when I got there, she was gone. I stood there a moment, looking for her, when suddenly, she was right behind me. She put her arms around me and said, 'I like you.'

"I turned to look at her and saw it wasn't the Captain, but an incredibly similar creature, with the most penetrating blue eyes I've ever seen. She was amazing. We talked in the clearing until dawn and she asked me to come back the next night, same place. I returned there every night for a month, falling more and more in love with her. I knew she was Fae. She just had to be. Then, one night, I came to the clearing and she wasn't there. Her father, Corrigan Starshadow, the Midsummer King himself, was though. He told me it was against the natural order of things for a Fae to love a human. He also told me that if I tried to see her again, he would lock her away until I died.

"I went to Catriona and begged her to help. She had been accepted by the Midsummer King as a friend and she promised she would talk to him. She went into the woods in the morning and came back out three days later. She told me she had convinced the King not to imprison his daughter and not to kill me, but because it would end the life of the Fae princess, she said he could not betroth her to me. When faced with the possibility of living without her but knowing she would live, or being with her and bringing on her death, I chose to live without her, because knowing she was in the world made it a world worth living in.

"Well, she didn't feel the same. Instead, she came to me, to my room. She tried to make love to me but, and I'll tell you this would never happen anywhere but on the edge of a Fae forest, I *refused* her."

"Liar." Myrgen smiled.

"I know your reasoning and I will say the second afterwards, I couldn't believe I had done so, but she ran crying back to the woods. I didn't sleep a wink that night, but I made a decision. I clearly couldn't stay so close to the place where she was. I had been strong in that moment, but I had no delusions I would not be so strong the next time. I decided right then to go on the ship with Catriona. I got up, packed my bag and cleaned out my room where I had lived for the previous five years. Catriona was in town, overseeing the building of the ship, *this* ship, and I told the Chancellor of the Covenant I would no longer be continuing my studies. He told me, 'Octavius, there's more than one way to study the world. Sometimes, you have to be out in it to do so.'"

"Very true." Myrgen nodded, looking back at the sea. "Very true."

"I agreed then and I still agree. Well, as I left the school, I walked past the woods for the last time, and I saw a white stag, a common Fae sign for seeking a meeting. I followed the stag and it took me to our clearing. Waiting for me there was Corrigan. He said he had a gift for Catriona, for her new ship. He handed me two buckets of black pitch. He said to make sure the pitch covered every timber, every surface. I looked at these two buckets and told him the ship was sizable, but he assured me there would be enough.

"I did as told and when the ship was completed, we christened her the *Enigma* and set sail. That first night, I went to my room and I felt someone put her arms around me. At first, I thought it might be the Captain, but when I turned to see who it was, I saw it was my beautiful lady. She told me she had spoken to Catriona during those three days and had chosen a life as a mortal to be with me. Her father had refused and said he would never let her go to me. She was heartbroken and was going to run away, but Catriona told her not to do that. Instead, to turn herself into a tree and Catriona would request sap from that tree to seal her ship. She put her essence into that sap, and joined with the ship when it was sealed."

"So this Fae woman is the reason why you and Catriona know what's going on here at all times?"

"Yes. The Captain married us that next day and we've been together ever since."

Myrgen nodded, smiling. "That is one hell of a story. So, has the rest of the crew met her?"

"Well, we don't go off the ship together or anything, but a few of them have seen her, yes. Most of them just see her as the spirit of the ship, and newcomers who first lay eyes on her, in the hold or walking the deck while they are in the Crow's Nest, just think it's the Captain. She speaks to the Captain as well, and Catriona has always been respectful of her existence. Does kind of stop us from having children though, because her physical body is a tree in the Galadorn Woods, but we're together every day, and her presence invigorates me so I don't have to sleep as much. I'm practically exhausted if I spend a night off the ship."

Myrgen smiled, then a thought crossed his mind. "So, your wife is a Fae? Does she know about spells, then?"

"Spells? What do you mean?"

"Alexander told us, when he was on board in St. Marguerite, that Gwen had cast a Fae spell on us. I wanted to know if it were true or just another lie in his repertoire."

Octavius looked at the helm. "Yes, but I don't think she's up to taking visitors right now."

Myrgen stood. "I didn't mean to imply I would request it now. I imagine she needs her rest, what with the attack…"

A wisp of breeze brought the smell of gardenias and jasmine to his nose and he turned as he saw someone had stepped onto the bridge. A beautiful woman with long hair and an ankle-length black coat stood behind them and Myrgen, at first look, thought it was Catriona. Then he realized she was bandaged about the arm and there was a bit of bulk from a similar bandage at her waist, peeking from under the coat she was wearing. Her eyes were blackened, like she had been hit in the face by a chair or fist. Her presence surprised him.

Octavius turned, concern in his voice. "Estelle? What are you doing up?"

Myrgen felt as much as heard the woman speak. "Bring him to me, Octavius."

Myrgen followed Octavius to the First Mate's cabin and marveled when he saw how lavish it was. Clearly, the Fae princess didn't approve of living in a small compartment because this room was considerably different on the inside than the outside. Across from the door was an arbor arch with a clearing on the other side. Mountains were decorated by fluttering trees with white trunks and a tall tower rose out of the leaves about a mile off. "This is the scene in Catriona's window, the stained glass one."

Octavius nodded. "Yes."

Myrgen gestured towards the clearing. "Is that a portal to the place?"

"No. You walk over there and you'll bump into the wall of the ship. Most Fae magic is illusion, and all of it is based on illusion."

"So none of it is real?"

"Oh, that doesn't make it innocuous, let me tell you. Think about it: The power to make someone or something seem different than it is. You can make a bridge complete when it is actually broken or a stream of snakes or spiders chase someone. You can make a person's greatest fear or greatest inspiration stand before them. It's very powerful stuff. People base a lot of their opinions upon what they perceive."

Myrgen nodded. "Does the knowledge of the illusion break it?"

"On the lower level magics? Yes. You can learn to see through them if you are exposed to them often enough. I know an illusion when I see it. So does the Captain."

"Can you tell if I'm under a spell now?"

Octavius let a beleaguered smile tint his eyes. "You're worried about the spell Gwen cast."

Myrgen nodded and walked over to the arbor. "If she truly is meant to be with Alexander, I don't want some illusion mucking up my perspective. I've made a lot of mistakes in my life, Octavius, but at least I knew they were *my* fault, *my* mistakes. I'll own that. If I blunder into a decision like this with a pretty view wrapped around my eyes, then the spell will break eventually anyway. I just don't want to look back and see thousands more problems that I caused that were out of my control because I didn't see them coming."

"What if removing the spell doesn't change the view?"

Myrgen turned back to his friend. "Well, that will be an entirely different problem. But I don't want this as an excuse."

"A wise choice." The woman's voice came from the four poster bed in another part of the room, the shimmering curtains concealing the speaker. Octavius led him over to the bedside and moved the curtain aside. She looked much better here than she had on deck and the light in the room made it easier to see the details of her appearance. She had long, dark hair, falling in waves and exotic eyes and lips. Her cheeks were carved and had a rich color to them, like iron nails left out in the weather. Her eyes were a rich, summertime sky blue. She reached out to Myrgen and took his hand. "Octavius was right about you."

Myrgen lowered his gaze in reverence. "My lady."

"I am Estelle Starshadow, Daughter of the Midsummer King. You are in need of my help?"

"I'm not so pressed to have you expend your energy away from healing."

"You are worried about the spell the girl cast."

"I don't even know if a spell was truly cast. I only have the word of a man who is a rival."

"And on the words of a rival alone, you think a spell exists?"

"I don't know, but if one is in place, then I will always question whether I loved her of my own will, or someone else's." He glanced down at the delicate hand in his. For a moment, he saw the bandages, the bruises, but she seemed to exert her will and the wholeness returned. His brow furrowed as he realized the pain he had caused this beautiful creature, whose only crime was giving him sanctuary. "I am so sorry for hurting you."

"Thank you." Estelle blinked slowly and Myrgen saw the reflection of Catriona's habits in the expression. It caused him to smile. "But you are right. Having an illusion cloud your judgment is not going to be helpful. Let's see what we can do about that."

She retrieved her hand and reached out for the arbor. A breeze sprung up and the leaves on the trees fluttered until one of them broke loose and flew over to her. She blew on it and it went through all four seasons in the space of a breath. Within seconds, it was dried to the consistency of paper. She crumbled it in her hand until it was fine powder then turned suddenly and blew it in Myrgen's face. He blinked as the dust went into his eyes and he turned away, wiping the dust from his face. Estelle voice took on a commanding tone, like she spoke with great authority.

"Spirits of illusion, you are released. Let this man see what has been hidden."

136

Red wisps of smoke rose from Myrgen's eyes, obscuring his view and suddenly, he saw many things. He saw the wall of the cabin. In fact the whole cabin was merely an officer's cabin on a ship. The bed was a simple double bed and the woman in it was almost translucent, a mere spirit. She did indeed have bandages on her arm and torso. The damage to her eyes was heavy and untreated. He blinked away from her and wiped some sudden tears from his face. Estelle and Octavius looked at each other, both a little puzzled.

"Thank you, my lady." She inclined her head and he stood and turned to his friend. "Octavius, I'll leave you and your wife to spend some time together. I have some things I need to see to."

Seventeen

"The Land has Fae, as does the Sea."
The Siren's Song of Callista

After Myrgen left, Octavius turned to Estelle. "Are you all right?"

Estelle lay back on the bed. "I'm just tired."

"You didn't need to do that. He said he would wait."

She looked up at her husband. "Yes, I did. Especially now. Besides, it wasn't that much work."

"That was some show you put on, though."

Estelle looked indignant. "What?"

He mimed pulling a leaf, crushing it and blowing it. "That."

"He wasn't going to just accept that it was as easy as me waving my hand in the air." She lay back on the pillows, closing her eyes. "Humans expect fantastic things from magic, flashy, elaborate shows. Otherwise, they don't feel like it's magic."

"So, did Gwen actually cast a spell on them?"

"Yes. I saw it a few ten-days ago. A whale spirit came by the ship and rose three times."

"So you knew about the spell?"

"Of course. That would be like asking if I could tell a fly was walking on my bare skin."

"But you let it come on board?"

"Yes. I knew it couldn't affect them."

Octavius arched an eyebrow. "Why not?"

"The spell was to relieve any suffering or broken hearts from grief. There wasn't any of that. Catriona had made her peace with Nicolai's passing years before it happened. It was enough to allow her to let him go when he did pass on. And Myrgen? Well, he was already right where he needed to be."

"Then what did you do just now?"

"A spell similar to an offensive spell we have. We can tell the person's mind to come up with its greatest fear. That way, we don't even need to know anything about the person. They do themselves in. This spell was the same principal, but I had him feel what he *believed* he should be feeling."

"And what was that?"

"Probably guilt. Humans seem to like guilt."

Octavius nodded. "What about the Captain? Should we tell her?"

"No. I rather like the idea of her finding that out for herself. She gets so few surprises in her life." She turned to her husband, opening her eyes and offering him a weak smile. "What I ought to do is cast a stronger spell on her and make her reveal her own feelings to him."

"What makes you think she won't do that on her own?"

Estelle rolled her eyes and winced at the effort. "Because... it would take an event of epic... romantic proportions to get her to admit her feelings, and frankly, I'm not sure we have that kind of ...time."

Octavius noticed the change in her voice and took her hand, concern etching his face. He was the only one on the ship who could actually touch her, not just imagine they could touch her. "Estelle? What's the matter?"

"Don't worry, Octavius. It's not what you think. I'm not going to die on you. My tree is being taken care of. I'll survive any physical damage done to me." She frowned, her eyebrows joining in the furrowing in worry. "That's not where I'm in danger, to be honest. When Myrgen was hurt, she couldn't tell he was carrying a parasite that would have destroyed me, something that destroyed thousands of Fae centuries ago. Someone sent an assassin my way and it's only because you and that young Myrgen man are vigilant that I'm safe. However, if a shadow gets on here, I'll be corrupted, and my tree will become a conveyance for the shadow into the heart of the forest. My entire family can be brought down if I fall and every Fae in Galadorn will turn or die. We need to warn my father, so he can do what must be done in that event."

"You mean kill you."

"Yes."

Octavius raised her hand to his lips, then leaned down to kiss her head. "I'll tell you what. I'll talk to the Captain about going to Galadorn. We can check on your tree, you can see your father and we'll talk to him about the danger we've been sensing." He looked at her. "In the meantime, we'll simply make sure shadow magic doesn't get near you. I'll tell the Captain to be more alert. How would that be?"

She touched his face. "Thank you."

He patted her hand and stood up. "I'm going to let you sleep now. I'll talk to you in the morning." He turned to look at her again as she closed her eyes and then left the room. The air outside still felt good and he looked around. He heard a little banging and followed the sound to the Captain's quarters. He opened the door and saw Myrgen with a load of lumber and a bucket of nails. He pulled a nail from the bucket and pounded it into the board on the floor until it was almost through. He looked up as Octavius came into the room.

He returned his attention to the board and Octavius furrowed his brow. "Myrgen? What are you doing?"

"I figured, since no one was trying to sleep on this end of the ship, now would be as good a time as any to get this patched up." He stopped hammering for a moment. "I had no idea how connected she was to this ship, Octavius. The story you told was... incredible, in every sense of the word. There was a part of me that didn't believe it, until I saw her. Such beauty, wrecked..." He returned to hammering and Octavius looked in the direction of his own cabin, then back at Myrgen.

"Wait a minute, Myrgen, what exactly did you see?"

"Bandages, and the marks across her eyes, like she had been hit in the face. She looked like I did after my initiation into the group here."

Octavius came over to him and knelt beside him. "You actually saw all that?"

"Yeah. Why?"

"Because Fae magic is illusionary. She lets you see what she wants you to see, and I'll tell you right now, she would never allow anyone to see what she really looked like there."

"So, that was another illusion?"

"Um, no. That's the problem. One thing about the Fae is their vanity. It's their universal weakness. Flatter them and you can get away with almost anything. Threaten them with scarring or maiming and you have the upper hand. Granted, keeping it is a challenge but you can count on it as sure as night follows day. If you can see through their illusions, then they lose their power over you and she would never voluntarily turn that over. Especially not to a stranger."

"Trust me, she could not have called up a more motivating image had she known me all my life. If that was what she truly looked like, then my work here is even more important." He returned to hammering and then walked over to a board that was nailed up haphazard on the wall he shared with Catriona. "I don't have the ability to heal like Catriona does. I can only heal myself. I can't repair the damage done to the people on this boat. But I can damned sure repair the damage to the ship. In fact, I think I might be able to fix her up pretty well. I won't be able to replace that beautiful window, but I can do nearly all else. And I'll do my best to repair that hurt as well, as soon as I'm able."

He returned his attention to his task of removing the sloppy repair and Octavius stepped up to take the board from him. Myrgen smiled and nodded his thanks, and then the two went to work.

Eighteen

"To know the nature of the water, taste it."
The Siren's Song of Callista

Catriona stepped out onto the deck of the ship and looked around. The sky was bright with impending dawn and she was glad the ship still managed to help her stay alert. She had been worried Estelle would not be able to maintain the energy of the ship, but today, the *Enigma* felt strong beneath Catriona's feet. She went to the helm and was surprised to find Octavius *not* manning it.

"Thessius, where's Octavius?"

"Aye aymayjin 'e's still 'elpin' Myrgen, Cap'n."

She was about to ask when she heard a hammer banging from behind her. She walked down the stairs and followed the noise to her cabin. She opened the door and found herself in a rare state of surprise. The large hole in the window was gone, boarded up tight. The room was lit by about five or so lanterns which were hanging from long nails on the new boards. Octavius was wiping his face with a cloth and looked over at the Captain as she entered. Myrgen looked up from putting the tools they had been using in the half keg. Octavius looked at Myrgen and then back at Catriona.

"Captain. Good morning."

"Octavius. Myrgen." She looked over the work they had done. It was nice. They hadn't simply slapped the boards onto the wall. The boards had been cut off even so the replacements were flush and smooth. Even the repair to the wall between her cabin and his was new and clean.

Octavius lifted the nearly empty half keg and nodded to Myrgen. "I'll get this down below."

"You need any help with it?"

Octavius shook his head. "Nah, I got this." He gave a nod to Catriona as he closed the door.

Catriona gestured to the work. "This looks good."

Myrgen grabbed the cloth Octavius had been using and looked around, snagging a couple more. "Well, after being the cause of all this, I needed to do something."

"This really wasn't your fault. It was Alexander's choice to fire upon us."

"Which he wouldn't have done if you had stayed and I had been properly executed like a good citizen."

"Somehow, I prefer having you be marked a traitor." She smiled, something she found more common with him around.

He looked directly at her. "Careful. Talk like that will keep me pinned to your side." He looked for a moment like he was going to come over to her, but then he returned his gaze to the rag in his hand. "Sorry. I suppose that sort of thing is 'inappropriate', huh?"

Catriona felt her face fall, regret joining the familiar paths of guilt. "Look, what I did last night…"

"Forget it. I deserved it."

"It was inappropriate and I shouldn't have done it."

"There's that lovely word again." He looked back at the window repair. "I hope this is all right."

She looked at the repair. "It's very impressive."

"I'll see about replacing the window once I have some money."

"Don't bother. It was a special type of window, actually. Irreplaceable by normal means, created in a Fae palace in Galadorn."

Myrgen looked back at Catriona. "Octavius said something about convincing you to take the ship there first instead of Caratia, to help her heal."

She looked at Myrgen, a little surprised by the comment. She scanned him quickly and saw that he knew about Estelle. "Octavius voiced concern that her father would never allow her to return if she showed up in such a state."

"Well, hopefully the damage won't be permanent and she'll be able to recover."

Catriona paused. "Hopefully, you'll stay and she'll be able to get your help recovering. You've done so much to help already."

Myrgen took a step closer to her. "Are you sure that wouldn't be inappropriate?"

She looked into his eyes and then averted them, landing on the chart table, which was not the right memory to keep her mind focused. She looked at him again, under control this time and he seemed to see her resolve. "Yes, you're right. But your efforts are appreciated, regardless."

Myrgen glanced at the rags in his hands and took a deep breath. "You're welcome, Captain." He nodded and turned to leave.

"Forgive me, but I need to ask: what prompted the meeting of Estelle?"

"I wanted to know if she could remove Gwen's spell on me. Turns out she could. It just wasn't proper for me to feel that way about you, not when you were destined to be with someone else."

"That was very selfless of you. The spell gave you a convenient excuse."

He turned partially towards her, looking over his shoulder at her. "I guess I found the state of affairs decidedly *in*convenient." He started towards the door again, still facing her. "And, as you said, inappropriate."

He stopped at the door. She could see he was hoping she would stop him. She didn't and he put his hand on the doorknob. "You know, from the moment I met you, one thing has been driving us, has been the momentum behind every step we took, every decision that crossed our path: Choosing who you want to be with. I wanted to be with Elizabeth and pined after her for two years, hoping for my chance. You spent all winter, wishing you could have what I tore you away from last night. Hell, Charles staged his own death to love the person he wished. The whole impetus behind this entire encounter has been to be free to love who you want to love." He glanced at the ceiling and bobbed his head a bit. "Well, that and a crazy person trying to steal the Sovereignty of Mervolingia…"

Catriona folded her arms. "I can only hope nothing pushes us to that length." A bit of humor stole into her voice, and Myrgen joined her in the smile.

He glanced at the new boards on the window, which seemed to sober him. "Well, I guess that's my point. That's why Gwen's spell was such a violation, but she hadn't meant for it to affect us like it did. She had only meant for the pain to go away. Trouble is, we are made and molded by our pain. It's what makes us who we are. The sum of our experiences. Your life seems to be moving toward a new chapter, one where you leave all this behind. Maybe you and I will just swap lives, with you moving into the palace in Patras and me taking my place among the ranks of random sailors on a restless sea. I'm lucky. I'm being allowed to acclimate to this life. I just don't know how prepared you'll be for my world. Nicolai was right, you know."

"Nicolai?"

"Yes. 'If you marry him, you'll never sail again.' Isn't that what he said after he attacked you on the ship?"

She blinked. "How did you know that?"

Myrgen shrugged. "I… heard it, somehow."

"How?" *He said that on my ship. After our fight. The shouts of the crew seeking him and the shrieking of gulls and the thrum of the city.* "You were on the other side of the street, tending to Alexander."

He raised his eyebrows and shook his head. "I honestly don't know. It was like it came through the ground, or something."

Through the ground? How? We were on the water. The Land doesn't communicate through water.

Myrgen shook his head, his lips pursing a bit. "Regardless, is the Land ready to prepare you for the life of rumor and intrigue? You saw what it was like for me. Is it anything like that in Caratia?"

She looked down at the flooring and shook her head, her own fears being presented to her like he was the one who could read souls. "No. Caratian life tends to be simpler. There are very few intrigues there. It is dangerous ground to tread and people know the penalty of their crimes. I pray you do not discover this fact for yourself."

"Don't worry. I don't intend to plot against anyone in the place giving me sanctuary." He opened the door. "You might say I've learned that lesson." He nodded and closed the door and she let him.

Octavius saw him come out and nodded. Myrgen walked over to him. "How did it go in there?"

"Awkward. It's tough to be near her, knowing her choice is someone else." He wiped his hands and tucked the rags into his belt. "However, she did say she preferred me alive to executed."

Octavius smiled. "Well, that's a positive sign."

"That's how I took it, but she closed up again after saying it, as seems to be her way."

Octavius shook his head. "Damn that woman."

"Well, I told her what an incredible fool she was being and how she'll never find someone who will love her more completely than I. That should teach her."

"No you didn't."

"No, I didn't." Myrgen pointed at Octavius. "But I should have!" He leaned on the railing. "That would have put a knot in her rope." Myrgen looked over the decks. "Anything else need a carpenter's hand?"

Octavius shook his head. "No, I think she's fine now." He tapped the deck of the ship with his heel. "She feels strong again. I think you might be a healer after all, just not of people."

"Well, I don't know how true that is. I just put up boards."

Octavius shook his head. "No, you didn't. That's what the others were doing. You made an effort to actually fix her beauty as well. That takes a special touch."

"Well, I've never actually looked into the eyes of a ship before. It makes a difference."

"So, you going to be okay?"

Myrgen shrugged. "Yeah. Just not right away. Hey, can I ask a favor? You think, once she's out of there, that I can take up that other passenger spot on the other side of the ship?"

Octavius took in a breath. "I don't know. Look, I don't really know how to tell you this, so I'm just going to say it straight. Right now, you've been up all night. You've clearly gotten your second wind, but still, you're tired. Don't make any decisions right now. Wait at least until you've had a chance to rest. And frankly, I personally don't want to see you move from that spot. Truth be told, if she's going to choose Grymalkin over you, I want you to make her work for it. Don't make it easy on her."

He shifted his eyes, then got a little smirk on his face. He looked over at a brass monkey holding some cannon balls and a half keg holding a few more. "Hey, would you mind loading that monkey real quick, then I'll send you away."

Myrgen got a suspicious look on his face. "Why?"

"Because it will wear you out quickly. Help you sleep. Right now, you don't look tired and Estelle says that will fatigue you. She apparently wants you to be able to rest when you go to bed."

Myrgen nodded and went over to the half keg tied to the rail. He took the half dozen cannon balls from the keg and stacked them in the brass monkey. The exertion reminded him quickly that he had not actually slept in over a day and he saw what Octavius meant. The stretching helped release his muscles and he stood up from the task and arched his back. He looked at Octavius and nodded. "Okay, you're right. I want to go to bed no…w…"

Catriona stood looking at him, eyebrow arched. She was standing at the top of the stairs, hands at her side, as a light breeze blew up the side of the ship, tossing Myrgen's hair across his eyes. He nodded to her and looked at Octavius. The First Mate covered his mouth, hiding a smile from the Captain, and gave Myrgen a wink. Myrgen sighed, realizing he had, once again, been set up. *The ship probably told him Catriona was coming out.* He took the other set of stairs down from the helm and walked across the decks without looking back. Once he got to the hallway, he hazarded a look from the concealment of the shadows.

Catriona turned towards the railing, and walked over to a bucket Draethen was hauling up onto the deck. She grabbed the thing and upended it over her head, much to the shock of *nearly* everyone on board. Octavius walked over and spoke to her like nothing was out of the ordinary. Myrgen ducked back into the hallway and returned to his room. Maybe Octavius was right. If she truly believed she was better off in Alexander's arms, then maybe she needed to be sorely tested beforehand, just to be sure.

Nineteen

"Be grateful when you run out of eggs, for then
the barracks will smell better."
The Siren's Song of Callista

Alexander sat in front of the fireplace, staring at the flames. He had not slept since the alarm had gone up of Myrgen's escape, and after lying in bed here through the morning, it seemed he was incapable of it. Instead, he had gone over the events of the night to try and make sense of things. He picked up the poker next to the hearth and poked through the wood and coals. There was no sign of the amulet. James was right; he had destroyed Alexander's only means of fast travel. He had always kept his identity a secret out in the world because he didn't want his status to prevent him from doing what he wanted. That had always been an abstract before now; a bit of hubris that he was so well-known and important that being recognized would inconvenience him.

But James knew exactly what he was saying. Before, Alexander had been important as the heir to the Mervol throne, but not that many would believe he spent time out in the world amongst the populace. His discovery here, now, coupled with his time in St. Marguerite, meant that every citizen of Mervolingia would be aware of his tendency to travel in their streets and his days of moving freely were over. It wouldn't even matter that he was simultaneously here and in another city several days' travel away.

Alexander snarled again at being thwarted by Myrgen's machinations. Damn that Traitor! He knew exactly what he was doing when he threw me into that tavern and revealed my identity to the barkeep. For all Alexander knew, he was currently bedding Catriona and having no trouble whatsoever pleasuring her or being a man. To be so embarrassed in front of this woman in particular was the sort of thing kings in the past had killed over. Kings were supposed to be virile and fertile. Having a performance failure like that in front of his future queen could jeopardize his status amongst his people. The sycophants at court could remove their fealty over such a failure, assuming he truly was inclined towards men as bed partners and incapable of siring an heir.

But that's not the real problem here, is it? The real problem is that I'm so desperate to win Catriona that I made allies she would have never accepted. Maybe Charles is right. Maybe I should be looking elsewhere. Perhaps Gwen? She's loyal.

Yes, but she's loyal to Catriona, and I would constantly be reminded of their bond, every time she came to visit. I would want to make love to Catriona and that would lead to a betrayal of her friend, something she would never tolerate. No, this won't do.

He stood up and walked around the room, trying to figure out a way through. He couldn't think right now. He was tired and sore and still quite angry. Figuring out a way to secure Catriona was why he needed a strategist in the first place. Best to focus upon securing Gwen's loyalty to him again. That path was the right one.

He walked over to the small table and picked up a sack he had received from Catriona that chinked of broken ceramic. He opened it and pulled out a piece of the rim. He imagined her lips upon this piece of ceramic, that maybe she imagined his lips as well, sharing the mug, kissing her every time she drank from it. It was shattered now, but he had hopes it could be repaired, somehow. He had come to associate it with their relationship, and it being in shards like this frightened him.

He set the pieces out on the table, puzzling out how they went together. Part of him thought, if he could just restore this, it would restore Catriona to him, but another part of him recognized this was merely a way to distract his hands while his heart sussed things out. He needed guidance, but he didn't know where to look.

He remembered the last time he was with Catriona in the palace back in Patras. She had come to him and he had managed to convince her to lie with him and sleep for a while, to give him a reprieve from all the chaos in the palace. She had stepped out of his prayer nave like a dream come true and for the first time in his life, he had felt that Heaven had heard his prayers.

He leaned on the table, closing his eyes against the feelings of defeat. Heaven seemed a long distance from there right then.

A knock on the door broke his thoughts and he opened it, expecting several people to be at the door with food or gifts or nobility. Saiban stood outside, displaying a worried look. "Sire, I'm terribly sorry to bother you but there's a man in the alley. He has a symbol on him of the church and of the Royal House, according to Lady Ce'Nedra. We don't quite know what to do with the body."

"Body?"

"He's been damaged. He can't be long for this world."

Alexander nodded. "Take me to him." He followed Saiban out the door and down the stairs. He expected the inn to be full and to have to fight through the main room but the place was blissfully empty. "Where is everyone?"

"Lady Ce'Nedra started to run out of food and patience with the people who were here. They were ordering her about like she was a slave and the quality of people went from folks to rich folks. When one of them came in and tried to set their own staff in her kitchen, she closed the doors. 'By Royal Decree'. She hopes you won't mind."

Alexander waved his hand in a dismissive gesture and made the command true in his mind. "Not at all. I shall have to reward her for her insight. Where is the man?"

Ce'Nedra looked up from the pile of black cloak ever so familiar to him. "We brought him in from the alley. People were starting to gather when I opened the back door, like they thought they might get a way in."

"Brilliant, my Lady." He knelt over Duncan and pulled aside the cloak front covering his hand. The thing was missing completely. He had more cuts and gashes, all looking fresh but Alexander recognized a few of them from when Duncan bathed in St. Andrew. These used to be his scars, but now they were burns, practically fresh, as if the original scars were reopened, then closed with fire. There were over a dozen and Duncan shifted, his head turning. His good eye opened and he looked at the King.

"What… did you do…?"

Alexander swallowed. The amulet was destroyed hours ago. How long was he out there, near death? Alone? Tears formed in his eyes as he looked at his servant, at Heaven's servant.

"I'm sorry I failed you. I'm sorry…" He looked at Ce'Nedra. "Make him comfortable, please. We'll need water and I'm going to get my healer's kit. Saiban," he turned to the young man, "his hand is missing. Will you go to where you found him and look for it? I don't want a dog running off with it or a child finding it. I'm sorry to ask this of you."

"It's fine, Your Majesty." Saiban stepped out the back door into the now empty alley.

"By the way, I confirmed your comment of it being my will to have the inn just for me and my companions. You will be compensated."

"Thank you, Your Majesty." Ce'Nedra bowed and went to get hot water and towels.

Alexander stood and left the kitchen.

Twenty

"The man marooned with his lover is a man in paradise."
The Siren's Song of Callista

Alistair pushed aside the bed curtains he had used for viewing and stepped into the room. The Realm of Karma, as he had decided to call it in his head, was a soft, scented place with décor of sand and coral, aquas, cobalt blues, rich purples and greens all decorated with gold. It smelled of cedar and sandalwood, Layers of wispy cloth hanging in sweeping drapes crossed the ceiling and dangled down to the floor. Cushions and low tables populated the floor, making it dangerous to traverse but cushy in the landing should one actually lose their balance. He stepped over to a sideboard with several decanters in jewel tones and poured a goblet of gold liquid from an orange bottle.

A large portrait of Shiva, pale and seated cross-legged and meditating, was a calming effect compared to the portrait of Kali across from it. Kali, the mother of the world as well as the destroyer, was blue, like the infinite sky. Her dark hair flowed violent and chaotic behind her ten arms and infinite forms. She wore a necklace of fifty heads which flowed across her full breasts, death and nourishment all in the same place. To Alistair, Kali was the true symbol of balance achieved through equal parts of extremes. Shiva was the center, the fulcrum upon which Karma was laid and if one aspect of Kali was allowed to flourish more than the other, the balance would shift. Too much destruction would end existence, but too much life would cause the same finale through disease and famine. For things to live, other things must die and, for some reason, this immense dynamic had decided upon *him* of all creatures, as their representative.

According to the entity that brought him to this place upon his death, he had died in exact balance. He was exactly as good as he was evil, arrogant as he was humble, worldly as well as naïve and had set foot in every continent in the world. He had followed as much as he'd lead, stolen as much as he'd given, been passionate and chaste, feared and kind and every other opposite one could drudge up to describe him. He had no idea such a possibility existed. It had only taken him a little over three hundred years to accomplish it, and even then, he did so accidentally. He died in an instant after living an eternity.

Alistair turned to the room, the luxury at times feeling like a prison. Movement on the pillows behind several sheer curtains called his attention. A voice came from inside that area.

"You seem troubled, my Champion."

The woman sat up, trailing silks from her head, shoulders and waist, her form enticing, and yet still frightening in its anonymity. Alistair took a deep breath to shake the troubled tone from his throat.

"I was just thinking about something a friend of mine told me. Raven said the Dûcesa is walking the earth, devoid of a Stapan. He thinks the time is right to find a new one for her."

He drank the liquid in his cup and set it down, the *ting* of the metal contact with the wood sideboard musical in the silken room. It echoed off the pillows in the exact opposite way that the laws of physics required. The tone rippled and rang throughout the room, tumbling into a faint, backdrop of harmony.

"And what do you think?" The silk-clad form rose from the bed in the curtained area, stepping onto the floor of pillows like stepping onto a floor of stone.

"I think if Raven feels the time is right, it probably is. Slade is not returning from where we sent him." He leaned on the sideboard and sighed, the weight of the subject feeding on his soul.

The woman slipped through the folds of fabric separating her and Alistair. "You did not choose his fate. He chose it to save her."

"Because he loved her. Did you know they were going to marry? She told the Land she wanted to have him by her side as her Duce. The Land granted him the ability to lay down the Stone Sword. He set it aside because he could not marry her if he was her protector. They had one night to belong to each other. Then the Soulless appeared and attacked their home. She fought them as did he, but she was being drained from the effort. He ran back into the room that had become their home and left it a room for only her.

He held in his hand the Stone Sword, his position restored. I got the impression that he believed he would never be able to lay it aside again. He chose to abandon a life with her to save her. He threw himself into that place where we sent the Last Child in order to take that monster away from this world, and away from her.

"He gave his soul to save her and he's never re-emerged from the ground." Alistair shook his head.

The Woman in Gold sighed. "It is the strength of love that unites all people, all creatures. Hate and fear can motivate them, but only love draws people together to become one."

He glared at the wall. "Is that what you're doing with Catriona? Putting love in her way to see if she unites with someone?"

"I supply all manner of challenges to help people become who they are. It is part of my duty. Look."

He straightened up and moved to a section of the room with a tall pillar of ice in it. Images floated around in it, chronicling the activities of a man with a long scar across one eye. The iris was black like the shadows he was battling at the moment, a sharp contrast to the pale violet of the other. He ran his sword through the monster he had discovered in Mande, his breathing heavy from the effort. His features were that carved Krakten that only comes from those with heritage from the royal line. His skin was a golden brown, like baked bread. His eyes were the wicked violet of Sovereigna herself.

"Who is this?"

"Lothric Berenger, the Black Prince of Krakte. His mother is the notorious Sovereigna Berenger, the Evil Queen of Legend."

Alistair's eyes narrowed. "And current ruler. Her daughter Elizabeth was married to Charles Maxamillian IX of Mervolingia. Alexander succeeded the throne from him upon his recent death."

The Woman smiled through her shroud of glistening gold silk. He heard it in her voice, mingled with admiration. "Oh yes. Lothric is perfect in his balance. Born of a human woman and a Fae king in the Black Forest, he can wield powerful magic from both parents, but is susceptible to neither. That which can destroy a Fae is the very thing he hunts."

Alistair looked at the Woman. "He can fight Shadows?"

"Chooses to. The scar across his face was from his first battle against them. He was to be married to a woman from a Glarren lineage, to bring strength back into the bloodline. Heinrich's line was too intermingled with his siblings, a fate which ultimately ended Elizabeth's life. So, Sovereigna encouraged Lothric to find his own wife.

"He fell in love with a simple goat herder he encountered in his travels. She got his help birthing a lamb in the field and he ended up staying with her to protect her against predators. She saw the Fae in him but did not turn away, unlike his cousins on his father's side. They engaged to marry, but an assault of shadows under the leadership of a demon slew her. He found out later, it was simply to spark his anger."

Alistair looked at the man. "It looks like they succeeded. I've never seen anyone be so brutal."

"Or balanced. He is almost perfect."

Alistair slowly turned to face her, leaning his shoulder on the pillar. "You sound quite whimsical over him. If he's so perfect, why did you choose me?"

"I didn't. You simply died first." She reached out and touched the pillar and it disappeared.

Alistair dropped to the floor, caught off guard. He was about to call her out on being so rude when he caught a glimpse of a tattoo on her right ankle, one he had seen before elsewhere.

An open lotus flower.

Karma.

It was mid-morning before Catriona realized she was hungry. She ducked her head into the galley to see if there was anything available. She grabbed a piece of fruit from a hanging basket and walked to her cabin to get some wine. The bottle was empty. She suspected Octavius of sharing it with Myrgen while they did their work. She still couldn't get over what a good job they had done, and in only about four hours. Clearly, there was some talent there. She decided not begrudge them the last of her wine and went over to a footlocker in the corner of her room near the foot of her bed.

It was filled with a few choice morsels, the Captain's Personal Stash, including a fine tea from York, bread from Xannu, spices, herbs and, most important at the moment, a couple bottles of fine Caratian wine. She smiled and stood as a knock came at the door. "Come in!"

Octavius poked is head in the door. "Captain, you free for a time?"

"Just gathering a little sustenance. What can I do for you, Octavius?"

"I have the preliminary damage reports."

Catriona took a deep breath. "Ah. I suppose it's about that time. Wine?"

"No thank you." He handed her the papers with the tally of destruction.

She glanced at the papers, leafing through them for a quick assessment of the gravity of their situation. "By the Stones, there were a lot of losses."

"Four casks of powder, two casks of nails, only one of which has been accounted for as being swept out a hole in the side. We've used all the extra wood and much of the canvas got soaked in the attack. A lot of things came loose from the deck and were lost overboard."

"Things like what?"

"Four barrels of fresh water and about a dozen cannon balls."

She looked at the papers. "The cannon balls we will hopefully survive without, provided there are no further attacks, but the water is a problem." She handed the papers back to Octavius. "How is Estelle doing?"

"Better. She looks good but she's still weak."

"Well, I would expect nothing less. The fine work you and Myrgen did last night has helped structurally, but with so many provisions missing, it's no wonder she's feeling weak. A hundred feet of rope?"

Octavius nodded. "And three grappling hooks."

"By the Land. We can't afford to get into any skirmishes, Octavius. Make sure whoever's on lookout knows this."

"They do, Captain." He nodded and left the room.

She went over to her desk and pulled the anchor-shaped corkscrew from her desk drawer. Voices outside her quarters told her Myrgen was in the hall talking to Octavius. She found herself wishing she had a reason to talk to him. A knock at the door made her heart leap and she consciously willed her breathing to slow before speaking.

"Come in."

Myrgen opened the door and nodded greeting. "Captain. I was just wondering how the repairs were holding up."

She looked over her shoulder at the new wall. "Fine, although it will be nice to get the window replaced. I fear I overslept this morning due to the darkness of the room."

"It could be you needed the rest."

She nodded, pouring the wine into her goblet. "That's very possible. How about you? Did you get some rest, finally?"

"Not really. Off and on. I kept having dreams pull me out of a deep sleep."

She looked at Myrgen. "Bad?"

"More, unhelpful than bad. I kept seeing Estelle so wounded."

Catriona frowned. "Estelle? You mean the ship?"

"No, I mean Estelle. I saw the wounds she suffered all over her face and arms. Her eyes were blackened and bruised and she wore bandages on her arms under her gown." He shook his head. "I'm afraid it rather unsettled me, knowing I was the cause of her pain. I saw it over and over again whenever I closed my eyes."

She blinked, confused. "You saw her wounded?"

Myrgen nodded. "Don't worry. Octavius told me that was unusual. I guess it means she was a bit weaker than we all thought. It's one of the reasons I came in here to fix this wall."

"Have you seen her today?"

"No, but if you see her, please tell her I asked after her, would you?"

Catriona nodded. "Of course."

Myrgen nodded and left the room, closing the door.

Catriona sat down and drank her wine, thinking and giving Myrgen time to get where he was going. She didn't like avoiding him and it was beginning to wear on her. Evading him made her not the person in charge, and she didn't like someone else being in charge on her ship. She hadn't let the near kiss on deck during the whale incident interfere with the running of her ship. She had decided to nip it immediately, to stop any awkwardness from showing its face. Besides, she missed him.

She looked into her goblet. That was probably the reason why she had not gone to him this time. Her desire to be with him was too powerful, as displayed by the slightest invitation from him the night before. She had dared him, right before the attack, to take her to bed and he had been willing to oblige. Then her foolish response last night proved she had very little judgment when it came to him. Such spontaneity was troublesome on a ship, and this crew was very protective. She might be setting Myrgen up for another beating at the hands of her men if she wasn't more careful.

She sighed and drained her cup. Sitting around her cabin wasn't helping matters and she was tired of being wary. If Myrgen wanted to risk flirting with her again after last night, then she needed to be enough in control of herself to let that not affect her. Better to be the fire than the moth, and frankly, she had things to do. She put her empty goblet in the holder and got up, making sure she had not spilled any on herself. She grabbed a small bottle from her desk and opened it, letting the scent of oil of clove decorate the area around her desk. A dab of the breath sweetener, which also served as a numbing agent for toothaches curiously enough, and she was ready to go.

She left her cabin and nodded to Octavius who was talking with Myrgen and Ambrois, probably about supplies. She was glad they were occupied and proceeded to Octavius and Estelle's quarters. She was surprised Estelle had let Myrgen see her so soon. There were men on this boat who had sailed for years before finally glimpsing her. She knocked and felt rather than heard the offer to enter. She opened the door and poked her head in the room. "Estelle?"

"Welcome, Captain." Her voice was faint, like effort was necessary to speak.

Catriona entered the cozy room, a bit surprised by what she was seeing. Gone were the elaborate illusions of a vast palace or expansive forest usually in place. Instead, the cabin looked like an officer's cabin. Quaint, but definitely a shipboard cabin. Catriona looked around for her friend. The bed had sheer curtains hanging from it, feathery weighted things that usually billowed like smoke, but not today. At present, they lay limp and stationary, save the movement caused by the sea. Catriona went over and sat on the chair nearby.

Estelle lay almost transparent on the bed, truly a ghost. Catriona was surprised the bedding was supported by her form, she looked so frail and insubstantial. She reached out and touched the edge of the bed, careful not to graze the ghostly form. Her heart broke at the sight of the soul of the ship being in such frail condition. "How are you feeling?"

Estelle breathed deep to prepare to speak. It appeared to take concentration to do so. "I am fine, Captain. Weak, but repaired, at least for the moment." She sighed. "Everyone has worked so hard to..."

Catriona almost reached out to touch her hand, but then set aside the urge of physical comforting. Octavius was the only one who could truly touch her, so Catriona never insulted her by pretending. One would destroy an illusion by touching it, especially if they knew it was an illusion. Those who did not know this could be tricked to believe they were actually being touched.

Catriona wished she could read the ship like she could read men, to keep her from needing to speak. "Would it be easier for you to communicate the other way?"

Estelle turned her head. "It is the same effort either way. Thank you for asking." She mustered a smile at Catriona. "I must thank you for bringing that Myrgen on board, however. It is because of his added efforts I have healed as much as I have."

160

"I will be sure to tell him."

Estelle arched an eyebrow. "Will you now? Because the things I have witnessed between you two have not shown cooperation of late."

Catriona glanced down at her friend's hand. "Things have gotten… complicated between us."

"Complicated…" Estelle moved her head slightly to look up at the ceiling and closed her eyes. "You humans always make things complicated. What could be so complicated about caring for one another?"

"Because my faith and my heart are at war over him."

"Faith? What does faith have to do with this?"

"Everything. I promised the Land I would serve it for the rest of my life if it saved my son the day he was born. The Land did so."

"I don't believe I have heard this tale."

Catriona exhaled, thinking about that day. "Well, I was captured by Marco Giovanni and held against my will. Then, on the day my son was born, Father Benjamin, the priest who delivered the baby, said he needed to get me away from there or Giovanni would slaughter the infant. He gave me an herb remedy which enabled me to ignore the pain and weakness until we could escape. We got to a small church on the end of town and sought sanctuary from the local priest, Draethen, inside. We were trying to determine where to go next when Giovanni's men arrived, having discovered my escape.

"Giovanni ordered the church burnt to make us flee into the open, then cut down Father Benjamin as he was trying to escape with the baby. Benjamin fell forward, holding my son and I knew he would smother before I could save him. I was held down and," she swallowed, afraid of the memory of the rape, "unable to get to him. I begged the earth to save my child and I discovered later than a large rock was found under Benjamin in the exact place it needed to be to make an air pocket for Alan and keep the blood and weight of the priest from smothering or drowning him."

Catriona raised her head. "I have been beholden to the Land ever since."

Estelle took a small breath, her eyes narrowing. "And what makes you believe the Land does not want what your heart wants?"

"After I got Alan out of the place where Myrgen had put him, my friend Anika told me the one I was supposed to be with was still trapped back at the palace in Patras. Anika is the Ducesâ of Caratia and holds a very important artifact of the Land: the Heartstone. It shows her ideal matches for the Land's people. She didn't know I had spent the entire winter wishing I could go to Alexander, and I had managed to see him for only a night when I had to leave him again." She looked down at her hand, holding Estelle's but her eyes were seeing Alexander's grateful smile when she had said she would stay by him and help him sleep. She took a deep breath. "But I failed to rescue him before he was trapped into being Sovereign. Now, the only thing I can do is get this ship home so I can return to him as his Queen, if he'll still have me."

Estelle frowned, her eyes sharp. "You plan to abandon me?"

"I don't wish to leave you, but I cannot sail and sit a throne at the same time. I will turn the Captaincy over to Octavius and he will take you wherever he wishes to go. You will still float, I just won't be on board."

"You'll die away from the sea, Catriona."

"No. I'll miss it. I'll miss *you*." She smiled. "But I'll not die. It is a different path I've chosen and I can't let my personal feelings get in the way of my duties. I've already failed Alexander once. I cannot fail him again."

"And you cannot be wrong?"

Catriona looked at her friend. "Wrong?" She shook her head, regretting the fact she needed to navigate this avenue aloud when she had avoided it in her mind since yesterday. "No, the Heartstone is never wrong."

Estelle started to say something but Catriona stood. "I should let you rest. You are still weak and you need to get your strength back before we hit the Fingers of Mande. The weather there is always tumultuous."

Estelle lay back on the pillows and Catriona nodded, then left the room.

Myrgen turned the corner into the hallway to Octavius' cabin and almost ran into Catriona, who pulled up short, keeping the papers from flying into an amusing mess. "Catriona!"

"Myrgen!"

It was unusual to him to see her surprised as well. He believed she always knew what was going on around her. "I'm sorry. I didn't mean to startle you."

She shook her head, getting under supreme control again and he found he was irritated by that. There was a time when he felt they were relaxed around each other, but now, it was ever the exertion of supreme control. He nodded and moved past her to Octavius' quarters. He went to knock and she stepped up next to him.

"Is there something I can help you with, Myrgen?"

He looked at her as she came back down the hallway towards him. He shook his head. "No. Octavius said I could use his desk to work on, since mine is a wreck."

"You're welcome to use mine." The words were out before she seemed to know it, and he smiled a tiny bit. *Perhaps she is not under rigid restraint after all.* He decided to save her from herself.

"Ah, no. That would be a bad idea."

She took the few steps toward him, glancing over her shoulder. "I was just in to see Estelle and she is still pretty weak. I left to let her get some rest."

"Ah, I see." Myrgen glanced down at the papers in his hands.

"I'd offer the other cabin, the one I stayed in while you repaired mine but it doesn't have a desk."

"Ah."

"Estelle said she really appreciates your efforts to heal her. She's just still weak from the attack."

"Again with the ah."

"So, as bad an idea as it may be, you're only choice seems to be to use mine."

He looked at her. "And where will you be? I don't want to run you out of your room."

"I have things to do on deck. I can give you the time that you need."

"I don't know," he looked down at his papers. "This could take a while."

She stepped over to him. "What is it?"

"A cataloguing of the supplies currently on board. I need to go over these records here and compare them to the original record from before the attack, to assess what we've got versus what we've lost. It could be important." He looked at her. She had stepped over to his left shoulder to look at the pages and her scent had just welcomed him into her presence.

"Yes, especially since it could be a while before we get to resupply. The trouble back in port will have traveled by pigeon within a few days. How are things looking?" She raised her eyes to his and he fought between Octavius' plan to make her think hard about her choice, and his own desires to kiss her and get it over with.

Instead, he looked back at the papers and took a step back to put some distance between them. "I have yet to make a proper assessment, Captain. I would not want to mislead you with unconfirmed information." He looked down the hallway to the corresponding one where his own cabin was housed. "I think I'll just take this back to my own room. I can spread this out on the bed as easily as a desk."

"If you're sure."

Myrgen looked into her eyes. *No sense in lying. She'll see the truth anyway.* "No, frankly I'm not sure. All I am sure of is that if I'm near you, I might make a mistake and I am trying to respect your decision. I just can't afford to be in that kind of an intimate setting. As long as I keep our contact strictly public, I figure we're both safe." He looked back at his papers then nodded to her. "I'm going to go work on these. Excuse me, Captain."

Catriona nodded and let him leave, much to his relief. This was going to be hard enough without complicating matters. He hated feeling like this, so he decided to ignore it and hoped it would go away. He went into his cabin and closed his door, then went about separating the pages of supply notes. The writing was easier on the original pages, measured and relaxed. The current tabulations were in hurried strokes, driven by panic and sleep deprivation. He wasn't even sure he'd be able to read some of them. He sighed and rubbed his eyes.

"Can I offer assistance, Myrgen?"

Myrgen snapped his eyes to the voice. "Estelle?" He turned to face the willowy form. "What are you doing out of bed? Catriona said…"

Estelle waved a translucent hand. "I told Octavius to let you use our room so I could speak with you. Catriona actually interfered with my plans."

"Oh." Myrgen stood and offered his seat.

"Please, Myrgen. I'm a spirit. I don't need to sit."

Myrgen nodded. "Of course." He glanced around the room. "Forgive me. I wasn't expecting visitors."

Again, Estelle waved her hand and all the broken furniture was gone, replaced by his study from Patras, complete with his bed and the stone door leading to his secret shrine. He looked at the ship's spirit. "How…?"

"It is something we Fae can do. You imagine the thing you most desire and we grant you the sight of it." She looked over at the stone wall and arched an eyebrow. "What is this?"

"An act of complete folly, my friend. My greatest masterpiece, and my greatest shame." He moved over and worked the catch that opened the door to the secret chamber. It surprised him that he could feel the stone, cool and hard beneath his fingers. The door swung open and the candles in the room illuminated a life-sized portrait of a beautiful woman. Her long black hair billowed in the wind that filled out her long coat, baring toned legs sheathed in black hose, a soft, silk shirt with a standing collar brushing her jawline. Her emerald eyes glittered like the sea as she pointed to something off the rail of the *Enigma* in the distance. It was so exact in detail, he felt he could touch her and she would step out of the picture.

Myrgen was speechless.

Estelle came over to him, looking at the portrait. "I don't know. I think it looks wonderful, a perfect likeness of the Captain. I wonder what she's looking at?"

"A whale…" He looked at Estelle. "Was this part of your spell?"

She looked full into his face. "Myrgen, this is all you. I'm just the canvas." She looked at the portrait. "You are the paint."

He stood looking at the portrait dancing in the firelight of the thirty candles around it, dumbfounded. The light caused the subtle tricks of a master painter to make the sea come alive, a trick with which he was very familiar. It had taken ten-days to get the paint to perform on Elizabeth's portrait, but this one seemed simple, like small flecks of glass dust were sprinkled in the paint to make the sea look alive. A similar effect enhanced Catriona's eyes and hair and he finally had to close his eyes against the beauty of a romantic memory made real.

"Remove it, please."

Estelle sounded puzzled. "Why?"

He opened his eyes to look at her. "Because it is not appropriate for this to be here." He left the room without looking at the portrait again. He stepped back into the bedroom and the vision of the palace study faded around him, returning him to reality. He exhaled. "Thank you, Estelle."

"You truly do care for her."

"Be that as it may, she has chosen to go to Alexander. I'll not dwell upon what cannot be." He turned to his papers, his heart heavy, like the stone wall he had touched. He turned to look at Estelle. "Is there anything I can help you with, Estelle?"

"I was coming to see you. I understand you are cataloguing the supplies left. I can help you with this."

"How?"

"I can feel into the areas and tell if what you are looking for is there. I know what is in most of my areas."

"Only most?"

"There are a few places I do not go, out of respect. If necessary, I can probably look there as well."

Myrgen looked away to his papers. "If you don't mind, doing this work by hand and alone will help me settle and organize my mind. It will keep me busy and I need to be busy right now."

Estelle nodded and her smile faded a bit. "Then I will leave you to it."

She disappeared as easily as she appeared and he was left alone in the room with his mind even more full of Catriona than it had been when she was standing next to him.

He tried to work for about a half an hour but found he was constantly looking at the wooden wall, wishing it were that stone one from moments before. He eventually got up and went outside to stretch his legs. The deck felt comfortable beneath his feet, like home to him now. There was the easy sway of the ship and the smell of the sea air to set him straight and ease his troubled mind. He went upstairs, across from the helm where Octavius and Catriona were talking and leaned on the railing, waiting for a chance to speak to him. Catriona glanced over at him a couple times, then nudged her chin in his direction to Octavius. The First Mate looked over at Myrgen and nodded, coming over.

She's reading me from that distance. Callista's Fury. He looked out onto the sea as Octavius climbed the stairs to the forecastle.

"You need something, Myrgen?"

"Damn that woman. Can't I keep a single thought to myself?"

Octavius looked over at the Captain and leaned on the railing next to the ship's Steward. "Um, no, not really. Job hazard. What's wrong?"

Myrgen sneered a bit. "Oh, I just had a little unsettling occurrence with your fine wife, Octavius."

"Do I need to get some swords and settle this as a point of honor?"

Myrgen looked at Octavius, realizing what he had just implied. "Would you, please? Could you just run me through and get this over with? That would be immensely helpful."

Octavius smiled. "What did she do?"

"She came to me in my chambers, just now. She... changed my room. Like the way she does yours, only not quite. This was stronger. You told me you would bump into the wall, that your room's dimensions stayed the same, but this was different. It was my room back in Patras. And there was a secret passage into the catacombs beneath the palace. I went to the secret wall and it was cold and stone, and it moved and there was a room as big as my cabin on the other side."

Octavius blinked, frowning. "Go on."

"Inside... Remember how I told you I fell for the Queen of Mervolingia?"

"Yes."

"Well, inside that room was a life-sized portrait of Elizabeth. I painted it and it was my masterpiece, but no one could ever see it. I eventually showed it to her and, well," he raised his eyebrows, "she responded quite pleasurably." He looked back out at the sea. "But this time, when I went in, it was different. Instead of the portrait of Elizabeth, it was Catriona. Right here." He patted the railing. "Right on this deck. A few ten-days ago, we were here and we saw a whale."

"The spell."

Myrgen looked at Octavius. "You're right. It was a portrait of the spell." He blinked, wondering if that was significant. "Anyway, I just couldn't have her leave it like that. I would have never been able to function again."

"And you say the room actually was bigger than your quarters?"

"Well, yeah, it seemed so. But so did yours."

"Except that it was all illusion."

"Yes," Myrgen nodded. "But didn't you say that was minor magic? Couldn't the same spell be used to actually make something bigger?"

"Um, Fae magic doesn't work like that, Myrgen."

"Then what?"

Octavius shook his head. "I'm not sure. But I can tell you this. Estelle has been in our room all day. I haven't felt her leave our cabin."

Myrgen blinked and glanced at Catriona, who looked away from the two men. "Excuse me, Octavius."

Myrgen left the First Mate's company and walked down the stairs and up the others across the deck faster than he thought he could. "Captain, can I speak with you?"

"Are you sure you want to?"

"Yes."

She seemed to see he was quite serious about this and her visage changed. "Of course."

"Come with me, please."

He took her back to his cabin and they went inside. He closed the door, causing her to turn toward him, a little uneasy. He looked around. "Do you sense anything unusual about this room?"

Catriona frowned and looked around the room, then shook her head. "No."

He frowned as well, a little disappointed. *Maybe I was wrong then.*

She put her hand on his arm. "What is it, Myrgen?"

"I just…" He shook his head. "I guess it was nothing."

"Clearly something has disturbed you. What was it?"

"Oh I probably fell asleep and dreamt the whole damned thing." He ran his hand through his hair, casting about the room for some sign the incident had really occurred, and finding nothing. "Look, I'm sorry. I didn't mean to alarm you." He lifted her hand absently to his lips and squeezed it.

They both realized what had just happened at the same moment, the instinctive movements they both experienced, and a heartbeat transpired between them. He carefully released her hand as she stepped back, opening the door from behind her back. Myrgen kept his eyes from hers with some effort.

"I'll leave you to your work then, Myrgen."

"Thank you, Captain."

She left and he looked over at the place where the wall had been to the portrait room, then shook his head and returned to his ledgers.

Catriona closed Myrgen's door behind her and exhaled slowly, trying desperately to regain control. When she had seen he was disturbed by something, she had been ready to be cold and unwavering, but the urgency in his body had changed when he had approached her. Her distance was closed almost immediately and her concern for him was the only thing she acknowledged. Something had happened and she couldn't brush it aside as quickly as he.

Something different about the room?

He had spoken to Octavius. He might know. She stepped away from the door, her heart moving her feet to the same beat. Octavius met her on the stairs.

"Captain!" He put his hand to his chest, shaking off the sudden surprise. "Forgive me. I got the impression that might take longer."

"He just asked me if there was something unusual about his room."

Octavius blinked. "Odd. Was there?"

"Not that I could see."

"Then who came to him?"

Catriona blinked, eyes narrowing and head tilting slightly. "Someone came to him?"

Octavius stood up straight. "Oh boy." He rubbed his face. "Um yeah. Someone who looked like Estelle came to him and changed his room to be the one he had in Patras, I guess. He said it was different because there was some portrait that had changed."

"His cabin *here* changed to his room in Patras?"

"Apparently so."

"His room in Patras was huge compared to that room. Bigger than both our cabins together."

His eyes widened. "*That* much bigger? What about the portrait room? He said he went in there."

"Octavius, there's no way that cabin would accommodate the illusion of his room and the prayer nave where he kept Elizabeth's portrait. The nave was the size of his cabin. Estelle's abilities can only cover what's there or not there, but she can't change the dimensions of the room. Something's happened here."

"Well, I think I know why he went to you then."

She looked at him, waiting and worried.

"He said he touched the stone door to the portrait room and it was cold stone."

Catriona blinked. "*Here? At sea?*"

"Yes."

"Excuse me, Octavius." She turned away and returned to her cabin, removing her gloves and tucking them into her belt. She closed her door and went to her chart table, unsheathing her sword. She placed her hand on the onyx key at her neck and her other hand on the pommel of her sword, the connections she always had to the Land.

I hear your call. I do your bidding.

Silence answered her and she squeezed the two stone elements of her office.

I hear your call. Please, tell me what to do.

Still no new sound came to her attention and she fell to her knees.

Do not forsake me now. You are putting signs in front of him but you are refusing to speak to me? I am doing everything I think you want. If this is not your desire, turn me from it before I can't go back. If it is his arms where I belong, I will claim him and let him claim me but do not tease me with signs and then ignore me.

Estelle asked if she might be wrong. Was that possible? Could it be that she misunderstood Anika? Her Dûcesa had said the one she was to be with was trapped within the palace. She had assumed the Heartstone meant Alexander, trapped by his brother's death into being king.

But he was not the only prisoner in that palace and she had freed that one.

She opened her eyes and saw her cabin had changed. Gone were the restored boards and the movement of the sea, replaced by stone walls with which she was familiar. Grey stones with red veins glistened in the afternoon light coming through the window overlooking the harbor at Zara. Multiple sizes and shapes of canvases, leaning one atop the other lined the walls. She saw her face over and over again, reflected in oil paint. A chest of paints and vials set open on a table next to a sizable easel and close at hand, small bottles had little piles of gemstone dust next to them.

On the easel itself was a portrait that captured her essence as surely as it did when it occurred in real life. Her hand was outstretched, pointing to something just off the canvas and she was absolutely certain, even in her finest days, she had never looked that beautiful. The sea sparkled as if alive and the moonlight on her hair shimmered as the wind blew it. She moved to see what her likeness was indicating and realized to her surprise that the image was two-dimensional. The painting has so consumed her, she had expected to shift and see the whale that caused all this unrequited angst.

Myrgen finished wiping the cleaning fluid from the brushes and stared out the window as he dropped them into the stone cup, handle down. He set the cloth on the table and walked over to the window. He leaned his shoulder against the window frame and looked out at the harbor. The light brown shock in his hair looked good, despite the circumstances that gave it to him and he was wearing a shirt she didn't recognize with the pants and boots he wore now.

He took a deep breath and let it out in a rush, then pushed away from the window.

"I miss you, Catriona."

His cheeks were damp and he turned to the room, gazing at the multiple sets of her eyes looking at him. A small bed against the wall had a dagger with a whale handle lying on it and his eyes found this detail as well. Finally, he turned to the latest work, still drying. Her portrait was life sized and he stepped up to it, touching the face. His hand dropped to his side and he closed his eyes, shaking his head.

"I can't do this anymore. This is madness."

He opened his eyes and went to the door, opening it slowly. He pulled a key from his pocket and without another glance at the room and its contents, closed the door and locked it.

Twenty-One

"The depth of the sea is only imagined."
The Siren's Song of Callista

James opened his eyes to the sound of a crackling fire. He felt warm and still sleepy and there was someone in his room. He looked over by the fire and saw a woman, sitting in the chair. It was his mother. A man was sitting in the chair across from her, his father. She was holding an infant which was cooing. His father reached out and touched the infant's tiny hand. "He's beautiful, Orabilia."

"Isn't he though?" She looked at her husband and smiled. "Are you sure you don't mind, Gavan?"

"No, dearest, I don't mind. Maybe the presence of a child here will encourage the Fae to gift us with one of our own."

She looked back down at the child. "My thoughts exactly."

"Have you figured out what to name him yet?"

She nodded. "James."

James awoke and sat up. He looked around the room for others, but he was alone. The fire in the hearth had burnt down and the rosy morning light of pre-dawn was everywhere from the open curtains. He rubbed his eyes, trying to figure out what the dream was. It almost seemed like a memory, but he was not in a position to know this information. It was almost like he was watching…

From the shadows.

A knock at his door got him out of bed and he opened it to find Alexander. He folded his arms across his chest. "What do *you* want?"

"I'm sorry to bother you, James. I have a problem."

"That's an understatement."

"May I come in? I don't want word of this to drift."

James glanced down the hall and stepped back. "Come in." Alexander stepped into the room and James closed the door. "So what's so pressing that it couldn't wait until later?"

The King took a deep breath. "How familiar are you with knife wounds?"

James looked at the monarch's empty hands. "Uh, well I've had a few, but I'm no healer. Gwen might have more…"

Alexander waved him off. "No, this isn't something I can go to Gwen with."

"Why? Does it involve those shadows?" James' look took on an intolerable nature.

"I suppose that's a fair question, but no. It would be better if you come and see what I mean. I'm not sure I can describe it."

James frowned and pulled on his boots and a shirt before leaving his room, all the while keeping track of Alexander. He glanced at Gwen's room but saw no movement under the door. He followed Alexander into his suite between the siblings.

Duncan McVryce lay on the King's bed, covered from the waist up with bandages and the waist down with the sheet from the bed. He was unconscious, a wine bottle on the end table and wine stains on the bed.

"Exactly how do you know this man?"

Alexander nodded towards Duncan. "He is a loyal servant of mine. He disappeared from Patras a few ten-days ago, rescuing the woman he loved. He returned to me last night, covered in wounds. I suspect he got them while wearing that amulet he gifted me. I have been able to tend all but one, but this remaining one is beyond my ability to heal."

Alexander pulled the sheet back and moved the gauze he had placed there to absorb the urine. His penis had been split down the center into four pieces, like a strange flower. James flinched immediately, backing away and grabbing his own crotch protectively. "Callista's Fury! What the hell happened to him?"

"It's from a weapon called a *dentate*. It means he met up with a Mandian woman and tried to force himself upon her, or met up with her husband after the fact."

James shrugged. "By the Fae, this is a nightmare."

"Any suggestions?"

James set aside his horror and looked at the wounds of his friend and shipmate. He pulled back the bandages to see the severity and noticed scars for the most part. Nothing bleeding. Nothing really fresh. "I have no workable idea. This is a dead man I'm looking at." He pointed to the wounds. "Every one of these wounds are healed in this state, and most of them are lethal. Any two of them would kill a man, yet Duncan breathes still. There's either fair or foul magic at work here."

"You know him?"

James nodded. "We sailed together for a few months when I was getting my sea legs."

James thought for a moment. He had spent time before doing triage on the ship. Before that, he had been an animal medic at the farm. He knew how to repair animals and make it so people would survive, if not be whole. He rubbed his neck and looked at Alexander. "I might be able to do something but if we want Duncan to be whole again, we need to take him somewhere else."

"Where?"

James paced a little, rubbing his palm with his thumb. "Well, I was just in Yndia. They have a way of healing there which might help. It's three ten-days travel though."

Alexander looked down at his charge. "He won't last that long, not without amputating. Can they reattach severed…"

James shook his head. "They don't do it. The individual does. They teach you how to heal yourself. I don't know anyone who can heal someone else."

"I know two people who have: Catriona can heal others, and I did it, once."

James stopped rubbing his hand and looked at Alexander. "You have? When? What were the circumstances?"

Alexander looked at James. "Well, there was a woman who had been chased by an evil man to a church. The priest had tried to get her and her newborn to safety but the villain caught up to them. He raped the woman and left her to die. My brother and I came upon her and the dead priest outside the church. I healed her through my will alone. That woman was Catriona."

"I take it you've tried it since. What happened?"

Alexander opened his Chirurgeon's kit and pulled out a small book, filled with notes, dates, circumstances, and handed it to James. "I've catalogued every attempt I've made to heal friends, family, even Catriona again, but with no successes. Not even a partial one. Nothing. Even under extreme circumstances, with the same woman. I've traveled quite a lot, learned techniques on medicines, retrieved herbs from foreign shores. No matter what I've tried, I have yet to do it again."

James handed the book back to Alexander and stroked his hand again, thinking. *Such an ability would be a gift from a spiritual source.* "So, the circumstances didn't matter?"

"No, apparently not. Catriona has been wounded worse than that day and it didn't matter, so I determined it wasn't the direness of the situation that caused it."

James went back to pacing, muttering to himself. "It isn't the woman, either. It must be reproducible. You just haven't hit upon the right formula." He looked over at Alexander, a small silver cross hanging from an earring in the king's ear. "Wait, you said it took place outside a church?"

"Yes."

"Have you tried reproducing that part?"

"No, not really. It was a church on fire and I can't desecrate holy ground to test a *theory.* "

"Understood, but have you tried it since then on consecrated ground?"

Alexander blinked, then consulted his log book, flipping through the pages with a hopeful light. "No. Do you think that might be the factor?"

"Maybe. I can't say for sure without a field test." James looked at Duncan. "Is he going to be out for a while?"

Alexander lifted the bottle next to Duncan, then nodded.

"Help me get him to the church."

"I'm not sure we should move him."

"Think about it. Would you want to live after that kind of injury?"

Alexander moved over to the bed and wrapped Duncan in the bedding. "This will keep him warm while we transport him."

"Actually, if we can, let's get him dressed. We don't need to call attention to the fact there's a practically dead man in the company of the King, especially not in his bed."

"Good point." He glanced at Duncan's unconscious form. "And I pray to the Saints this works."

Twenty-Two

"You spoke to me differently, Captain, before
your Letter of Marque."
The Siren's Song of Callista

Myrgen's door flung open and Octavius looked in, eyes panicked and searching. "Is the Captain in here?"

Myrgen got to his feet, his heart thumping at the ferocity and worry in the First Mate's voice. "Of course not. Why?"

"She's gone. Estelle said she was in her cabin and then, she couldn't feel her presence any longer."

"And you checked her chambers?"

Octavius nodded. "First place we looked. You're the second."

"How could she just disappear?"

"If I knew that, I wouldn't be explaining it to you, I'd be explaining it to my terrified wife. She thinks the Shadows got her. She said she felt a presence earlier but it went away before she could determine what it was."

Myrgen glanced at Octavius, his eyes guarded. "Earlier when?"

Octavius shrugged. "An hour? Maybe more?"

"When I had that incident with the room being bigger than it should have?"

"Callista's Fury." Octavius paled. "Yes."

A shower of sparks came from the darkness in Catriona's cabin and the men turned to see what it was. In the momentary light, they saw Catriona's form standing in the room, then the darkness enveloped her again.

Myrgen spurred to her side, ready to catch her if she collapsed, his own ordeal in the Shadow Realm foremost in his mind. "Catriona?"

She opened her eyes. "Myrgen?" She looked at the other man coming up to her. "Octavius? What's wrong?"

"Where were you just now?" Myrgen looked at her to make sure her eyes weren't swirling with blackness but he couldn't tell in the near dark.

"Elsewhere." She looked at Octavius. "Where's Estelle?"

"In our room, in a fright. She thought the Shadows got you."

"Don't be foolish, Octavius. If that had happened, we would have sunk. I need to speak to her. Excuse me." She shouldered between the two men, sheathing her sword and donning her gloves.

Myrgen watched her walk away, and realized he was actually quite put out that she would dismiss their concerns so quickly. He set his jaw, determined to read her out for it, but Octavius grabbed his arm.

"Don't."

"She can't just…"

"Yes she can. She's the Captain. It's not her job to inform us of every detail of her decision-making process." Myrgen started to protest but Octavius cut him off. "Think about it. Something just fetched her away from us, out here. Give her a few turns of the sandglass to do what she feels she must."

Myrgen looked after her, then nodded, retrieving his arm. He glanced around the room for signs of what could have happened and, finding none, he returned to his room and his tallies.

Catriona knocked on the door to Estelle's room and was greeted with acceptance immediately. Estelle was up and pacing and ran to Catriona as soon as she entered. "You're back!" She threw her arms around Catriona, which passed right through her.

"Yes, I'm back. I'm sorry I worried you, Estelle. I didn't realize I would be missing." Catriona never would have called attention to the fact Estelle was a spirit. Her state of being was painful enough to her.

"Where did you go?"

"Someplace painful. I need to know, am I under a spell? Myrgen and I, are we under a spell to have us feel this way?"

Estelle frowned. "What? Worried you could be deceived by a 'Fae spell cast by a human girl'? Yes, Captain. Of course I heard you calling Myrgen weak minded for succumbing to Fae illusions. And Gwen is not just some human girl, Catriona. She has a connection you wouldn't understand."

Catriona realized she was in trouble. When someone is missing, the first stage is worry and panic, fear-based emotions. After a bit of time, the fear turns to anger. It will, with the passage of time, switch back and forth between the two. Returning during a worried phase was good. Not so much the angry phase.

"I'm sorry to have bothered you, Estelle and very sorry I worried you. I'll let you sleep."

Myrgen sat down on his bed and looked over the paperwork he was doing. He was still annoyed at Catriona's dismissal. *I guess this is the way it's going to be between us now. I can't believe I cared so much for her! She was so....Augh! I can't think!*

He put his face in his hands and tried to calm down. This emotional storm she was putting him through was exhausting and he was starting to get a little seasick from it. One moment, she was kind and concerned, the next, cold and cruel. Was this just a trait of *all* women? He could barely breathe he was so angry.

And Octavius! Defending her like that, like she had the right to disappear and scare the life out of everyone!

He stood up again and started pacing. *How could she just... I was there because I cared and... And Estelle was worried too! To toss all that aside for her own selfish....SELFISHNESS! I ought to tell her I wouldn't work for her if she paid me ten times my salary at the palace! I can hardly wait to get off this boat!*

He kicked the bed, meaning to kick it near the base, but his foot hit the mattress instead and the papers he had organized puffed up in a hail of chaos and threw themselves around the room. Myrgen discovered his inner sailor and swore like he had never done in his life. He unconsciously experimented with different curses for the different languages he spoke and apparently settled upon a Krakte-Mervol blend with a Papal City decorative element which he favored the entire time he spent picking up the papers.

He grabbed one that had slid under the bed, one of the earlier catalogues of initial food stores. He blinked out of his tirade and looked the log over a bit more carefully. *Six cases of nails?*

He scrambled around looking for the newer tally and searched the information. *That can't be right.*

He looked at his door and stood, rushing over to it and outside. The hold was still a bit of a mess and he saw what he was looking for. When he had been down there before, he had noticed a few nails sticking out of a keg. He had forgotten in the rush to repair the ship to look closer at the situation, but he remembered assuming the large barrel was where they kept all the nails. He couldn't think of a reason to have a fifty-gallon barrel of nails, much less six of them, and this was definitely a barrel, not a case.

He went over to the barrel and its accompanying crates of foodstuffs, realizing it was in a different place from the other carpentry tools. As he approached, he caught a whiff of rotten eggs and vinegar. He saw several nails scattered around the floor behind the ropes between this barrel and the six behind it, but the shadows of the hold impaired his view. He went back by the stairs and grabbed a lantern, lighting it. He shined the light near the barrels, then set the lantern on top of one and got down on his hands and knees to look into the area between the barrels.

The floor was wet, but not as wet as he had remembered it being during the repairs. He had assumed the water was from the waves lapping into the hold as the ship made its escape but now he wasn't so sure. He could see a small glint of metal between the barrels of the crew's water and stood, breathing deep. He untied the rope holding the barrels, and grabbed the lantern. With one hand, he moved the empty water barrel aside to expose the carnage behind.

They had been looking for the offending cannonball but had not found it. There had been so may other things to do, he had simply given up and moved on. Now he had found it. An assessment of the scene indicated the cannonball must have hit the side, then slammed into a crate of nails, lending its momentum to the nails. The barrels were peppered with shards of metal and each one of them was low or empty from the leaks the nails caused. One barrel had a chunk out of it from the path of the cannonball and Myrgen followed the path to locate the offending ordinance.

He found the cannonball inside a crate at the bottom of a stack of crates. The final course of the thing had punched through the sides of three food crates, destroying the contents in its path. The tops of the crates were intact, and unless you were at the precise angle to look into the holes made by the ball, an onlooker would think the things in this area had escaped the damage of the attack.

This could not be further from the case.

The pickles, eggs and cheeses were all crushed into a paste along with the wood from the crates, and they had started to rot. The smell was more prominent with the barrels moved out of the way, and Myrgen pulled his neck scarf up over his nose to keep from vomiting. Nails had embedded in the food crates as well, adding to the damage, but the food was a loss, even without the added metal.

He put his hands to his eyes and ran his fingers through his hair. This was going to change everything.

Twenty-Three

"The monkey chatters on because it doesn't
know to fear the shark."
The Siren's Song of Callista

Myrgen came up the stairs from the hold as Catriona came out of the hallway from Octavius' quarters. She spoke his name, calling him from his inventory.

"Captain." He looked at the papers again, figuring she was going to go on with whatever she was doing.

"Myrgen, I need your help."

He blinked at her, actually a little surprised and still a bit caught up in his own problem. "Uh, sure. What did you need?"

She motioned to her hallway, apparently wanting a bit of privacy. He raised his eyebrows, now a bit more concerned about her interest. He led the way, stopping at his own cabin to put the papers in on his bed. He turned and she was in the room, closing the door. He swallowed, aware he was still a little annoyed at her for dismissing his concerns and more than a little worried she would read that in him. He took a deep breath and calmed down.

"What do you need, Captain?"

"First of all, let me apologize for being so abrupt before. I did not mean to dismiss your concerns. And before you become irritated at me for seeing this in you, let me assure you I did not read you. I overheard you as I was leaving, when Octavius was speaking to you. Unfortunately, what I needed to address was rather pressing at the time and I hoped you would understand."

Myrgen sighed, his ire fading as he accepted her apology before even voicing it. However, he wasn't quite ready to let it go just yet. "Well, in order to get my forgiveness, I'd like to know what the hell was so important."

She lowered her eyes, but not before he saw the slight smile in them as she turned away a bit to examine his room. *Damn! She already knows I forgive her.* He sat down on the bed, piling the papers into a stack and setting them on the footlocker he was using as a bedside table and impromptu desk surface, rescuing him from a repeat of the mattress fiasco.

Her eyes grew steady again and she looked at him. "I'm sorry, but I need to speak to my Dûcesa before I can answer that, I believe."

"I see." Myrgen became irritated again at her avoidance. *Perhaps my forgiveness is not nearly as cut and dried after all.* "Yes, well, I'm afraid I have a lot of things to focus upon right now." He stood again, gesturing for the door. "Thank you for stopping by, Captain."

"Myrgen."

"What?" He looked at her. "What, Catriona? Forgive me for being a bit preoccupied here and not interested in playing these dodging games with you. Come back when you're ready to actually talk to me and we'll talk, but I'm not going to be distracted from my current course because you want to feel desired." He picked up the tallies. "I have something a bit more important than your ego to deal with right now."

"My ego?"

"Yes. If you want it stroked, just go up on deck and look around at all the buckets for the Morning Ritual. You put it on deck every day so the entire crew can stroke it at once. Personally, I'm getting a little sick of the whole thing."

"How *dare* you? I can have you thrown overboard right now!"

He stepped up to get in her face. "Then do it. One less man on board to feed. That's rather important right now."

She started to say something else, but then he saw the look come on her face that indicated she had seen something in him. Her anger turned to concern in the blink of her eyes. "You've found something."

"More like I *didn't* find something." He looked back at his tallies. "More like several somethings."

Catriona put her hand on his upper arm. "Myrgen, I'm sorry."

He shrugged off her hand and stormed away from her. "You're sorry, but not sorry enough to *stop* this ship and deal with it! You're too much in a hurry to get home so you can dump this entire crew without even *telling them you're leaving!*" He was so angry and he suddenly put his finger upon why. He shook his head and turned to face her, jaw set in anger, pointing at her with the papers.

"You know, Alistair told me that you broke with him because he put hundreds of sailors out of work. You ended probably the best thing you had at that moment because you cared for men who weren't even your crew and now, you turn your back on these people, whose *lives* you've gone to the trouble to actually *save* at some point, and why? So you can run off and play queen, a job you are uniquely *not* suited to actually perform well. Your ambition disgusts me, Catriona, and you were someone I thought would be above that sort of thing."

Catriona blinked, stunned into silence and inactivity. "How… how…"

Myrgen rolled his eyes. "Yes, well, as thrilling as this conversation is, I'm afraid I'm going to have to ask you to leave." He flipped through the papers. "I have things to do that involve the survival of this ship and this crew. I'm sure you have some hairdressing and wardrobe planning to get on so, if you'll see your way out, I would appreciate it."

He put his full attention on his paperwork, flipping through it all. He had run out of paper to write upon and had scrounged several things so there was writing in the margins of manifests and on the backs of other documents he had deemed a bit more expendable. One of them was his contract as Acting Ship Steward, the seafaring term for Chancellor. He wondered if there were any extra pages Octavius had he could borrow and looked up as the door closed behind Catriona.

He closed his eyes and shook his head. *I'm pretty much going to be put to death any day now. Should have stayed in Mervolingia. Well, at least they won't have to feed me anymore.*

He looked over at the wine bottle he had picked up the last day they were in St. Andrew. He had bought a couple bottles specifically to share with Catriona. He set the papers down on the bed, then moved the drying socks he had washed himself off his footlocker and opened it. His stomach growled a bit as he rummaged through the contents to find the two bottles but he ignored the rumblings. He pulled the bottles from their wrapping in his soft clothing.

He stood and looked at the labels. Not too expensive, because he couldn't afford much at the time, but good years for that area. He tucked the bottles under his arm and opened his door, going to the galley. Ambrois, the assistant Cook was there and Myrgen pondered the point that, even though Ambrois was the *assistant* Cook, Myrgen wasn't certain he had ever seen a journeyman Cook in this kitchen. If someone was cooking, it was usually Ambrois. The man was talking to another man and they stopped as Myrgen entered.

"Ambrois… Oh, hi William."

The other man nodded. "Hullo Myrgen." William the Navigator had a Yorkish accent that, although distinctive, was in general very comprehensible and Myrgen rather liked speaking with the man. Interesting since the first encounter they had was when he entered a fighting ring in the hold with the wiry pugilist.

Ambrois wiped his hands on a rag on the counter. "What can I do for you, Myrgen?"

"I, uh, I picked up a few bottles of wine back in St. Andrew and I wanted to turn them over to the crew stores. I doubt I'm going to get the chance to drink them myself."

Ambrois took the bottles and both men looked at the labels. "Uh, thanks, Myrgen. I'll put them to good use."

Myrgen nodded and pointed to the man. "Make sure they get distributed amongst the crew, now. No keeping them to yourself."

"Course not."

Myrgen turned to leave and William followed him out. "Hey, Myrgen, you got a moment?"

"Sure. Whatcha need, William?"

William folded his arms and glanced around the area. A few men were in their hammocks, resting up for the night watches but they were pretty secluded here. "I feel a little odd asking you this, but are things okay between you and the Captain?"

Myrgen shuffled his feet and folded his arms as well. "You're right. That is an odd thing for you to be asking me."

"Well, it's just that, well, you were rather shouting a bit a few moments ago and, well, the sound carried to a few blokes. They started asking questions."

Myrgen shook his head and squinted a bit at the Yorkman. "No, I can't really say it's going well between us. I'm sorry to no longer be a player in the drama that goes on onboard this ship. Now, if you'll excuse me." He pushed off the wall they were leaning upon and started to walk away.

William wasn't quite done however. He raised his voice a bit when he asked, "What did you mean, she's leaving us?"

Myrgen turned and walked quickly back to the man, stepping up close to him to keep their conversation private. "Watch your voice. Look, I don't know what you heard or what you *think* you heard, but that was a private conversation and if the Captain has something to say to her crew, she will choose the proper time to say it. You can't question her judgment, William. That way lies madness, and as long as she's Captain, she'll have my full *public* support in her decisions on what she does with this ship and this crew. Understand?"

"Yeh, yeh. Sorry. Didn't mean to upset you."

Myrgen kept his eyes on the man a moment longer, then backed off. "Forgiven. Now, I'm sure you have something to get done."

William nodded and slipped past Myrgen as he got his breath back. The last thing he needed was to cause a mutiny based on a rant he decided to go on. He put his head back and took a deep breath.

He was hungry and he was getting cranky because of it. He went back toward his room, noting the men still sleeping in their bunks. At least he had managed to keep his voice under control this time. As he stepped onto the main deck, he saw more than a few men talking to others and glancing at the Captain, who was on the forecastle with Octavius.

He thought about warning her, but she was still looking a bit on the stunned side and he didn't want to give the crew more to talk about. Besides, he wasn't sure his anger was going to be any more controllable now than it was when they were alone. Better to focus upon the problem he could solve than to linger on the things over which he had no control.

He still had not figured out how to count the supplies like he needed. He was going to have to move everything in the hold to make sure there were no more surprises and in order to keep the crew from panicking, he would have to do it alone, which would take a long time, longer than he felt they had. He hoped there would be a better way to do it, but the only person he knew with the ability to know everything that was going on within these wooden walls was Catriona, and he was not certain he even wanted to try that course. *Better to do it myself.*

Catriona looked over at him and looked away, averting her eyes and excusing herself from Octavius' presence. She walked down the stairs and looked as though she might come over to him, so he looked away, walking to the railing to give her a chance to either talk to him in private or to leave without feeling his eyes upon her. He waited a few moments until he heard the door to her quarters close and then pushed off the railing and went up to Octavius.

"Hey, I had a question for you. Do you have any paper you aren't using?"

Octavius looked at him, thinking. "I think so. How much do you need?"

"I couldn't say. Quite a bit. I have a bloody meandering series of scrawled notes on every piece of parchment I could find in my quarters. I need to sort them out and any clean sheets will stop me from using my walls."

"Yes, I would prefer you didn't write on my wife's flesh. I'm sure I'd hear about that."

"Ah, she'd know, wouldn't she?" A light came to Myrgen's eyes as he found a way to deal with this situation. "*She* would know. Octavius, do you think she would help me?"

"Help you with what?"

Myrgen glanced around them and stepped a little closer. "I found one of the missing crates of nails. It was embedded in the water supply. I haven't yet determined the rest of the damage, but several crates of food were also lost and at least three barrels of fresh water that I originally thought were good, maybe more."

"Callista's Fury, Myrgen. That's more than half our remaining supplies."

"I'm well aware, Octavius. I'm more surprised that you aren't."

"I've been dealing with traveling problems. The ship has been listing to port, thanks to that injury she suffered."

Myrgen thought a moment. "The bandaged arm? I was wondering about that. I didn't think anything hit that side of us."

"We must have. There's no outside damage so I'm hoping you can tell me, since you've been down in the hold so much."

Myrgen glanced at his hands. "I'm still not done. I was hoping Estelle could tell me."

"She's been sleeping since Catriona saw her yesterday. I didn't want to wake her."

Myrgen inhaled, not relishing the idea of tackling the task alone, but now seeing no other way.

"There *is* another option, you know."

Myrgen looked at the First Mate, eyebrow arched. Octavius arched an eyebrow back and glanced at the hallway Myrgen shared with the Captain. Myrgen frowned. "Oh no. I'm pretty certain I wouldn't be welcomed right now. Besides, she's probably painting her nails or something, some queenly activity or another."

"What?" The quizzical look on Octavius' face made Myrgen shake his head.

"Sorry. I'm tired. And I'm hungry. And I'm a little bitter over the whole Alexander affair."

"Why would that stop her from wanting to see you?"

Myrgen rubbed the back of his neck. "I sort of *told* her that."

"You told her… what?"

"That she was being an ambitious, arrogant woman who didn't care about this crew. That her ego was so great, she demanded it was stroked in buckets every morning by every man on this ship and I was no longer susceptible to her petty machinations."

Octavius blinked. "You sleep pretty light, do you?"

Myrgen cracked a grin. "I'd better start." He glanced down at the deck for a second. "What's more, apparently, I was a bit vocal in my opinion and some of the crew overheard me. William just asked of Catriona was leaving the ship."

"Ah. So that's what all that chatting is about. What did you tell him?"

"I told him the Captain would tell her crew what she felt they needed to know and to not question her."

"You mean, like you just did?"

"Look, I don't need your logic muddying up my ranting."

Octavius put his hand on Myrgen's shoulder. "Myrgen, don't give up on her. We need you. *She* needs you, to free her from this. If she gives in to Alexander, we'll lose her. She's worth the trouble, I promise."

"Is she? Or is she just a spoiled brat who has let her power go to her head? She gets away with so much, she might as well be royalty. That attitude she threw at us when she disappeared? That's not acceptable behavior for someone in her position. These people care about her and the fact that..." Octavius glanced around, motioning for him to lower his voice. Myrgen did so. "The fact that she hasn't let this crew know that this may be her last voyage on this ship is unacceptable. Many of them might have gotten off at other ports near their homes rather than be stranded in Zara when she decides to reveal her intentions."

"Perhaps that means she hasn't made up her mind to go with him, yet, Myrgen. She needs a reason to say no. *Be that reason.*"

Myrgen thought about protesting but realized the desperation in Octavius' voice would preclude such reason. Instead, he nodded. "I'll try, but right now, I've got more pressing things to think about. If Catriona can't or won't help me, I'll need someone else to help me do the count. Alone, we'll be out of the supplies before I know what we're missing."

Octavius glanced around, then settled upon Thessius. "Wait, you just need someone who can count, right?"

"Well, I guess so."

"Thessius! Come here!"

The seasoned sailor nodded and finished tying off a line to a belaying pin. He came over to the pair. "Aye, 'Tavius. Whotcher naid?"

"Actually, it's Myrgen who needs you. He needs someone to help him get some inventory done in the hold. You can count so I'd like you to help him."

"Wail, eh'd love ta, 'Tavius, boot eh'm doo ta ralaive Ehmbroose ain th' naist. He woon soom taim froom meh ain eh gaim lest naight."

Myrgen blinked and wished he could see what Thessius just said written down. He figured it would be easier to understand that way.

"Hmm." Octavius looked up at the Lookout post. "Thanks, Thessius."

"Aye." Thessius strode over to the main mast and climbed.

Myrgen shook his head. "I like that man, but I doubt I would have been able to do this with him."

Octavius looked at his friend. "Personality conflicts?"

"Language barrier. I apparently don't speak," Myrgen waved his hand near the mast, "whatever he does. Damn! And I thought I was getting better too."

"It's not your fault, Myrgen. One of the dock workers was apparently fresh off the boat from the Highlands back in St. Marguerite. He was on the ship in the sloop next to us, and we could overhear him talking to someone. We were all hoping Thessius wouldn't hear the man because even the slightest contact with his homeland gets his accent back up to full illegibility. After picking her up in Glarren originally, we needed Gwen as an interpreter for two months."

"Oh no. So, when he went onto their ship to leap across that yard arm onto the *Enigma*, he heard the guy."

"Is that how he heard it? Amazing. We thought, since he escaped and we pulled out in such a hurry, he wouldn't have been able to come in contact with the man. And we'll be in Caratia a ten-day before we can understand him again."

Myrgen thought about what it would be like pulling into Catriona's homeland and the thought felt uncomfortable. He had not expected this, having been on course for Caratia for almost a month now. They would be there in a ten-day. *Why am I feeling the need to be off this ship before then?*

"Myrgen? You okay?"

"Yes. Yes, I'm fine. Just tired, I think. The stress is catching up with me. Look, about that paper?"

"Yes. I'll bring it to your room. Go talk to the Captain. See if she can help."

"Sure. Thanks."

He walked back over to the shared corridor and thumped on Catriona's door. Shuffling inside made his stomach turn a bit but he steadied himself as the handle moved and the door opened.

"Myrgen?"

Twenty-Four

"I love my wife the most when I am away at sea."
The Siren's Song of Callista

Catriona walked into her room and closed the door behind her. She had seen Myrgen turn his back on her on deck so she wouldn't have to deal with his eyes upon her, and she wasn't sure how she felt about that yet. She walked to the lanterns on the far side of the wall and turned one of them up, casting vague, blobby shadows in the rest of the room. Shapeless and illegible, they reflected her current thoughts with surgical precision.

Myrgen was right and she was at a loss about how to deal with the situation. Although the things Myrgen had said were, of course, incorrect, they hurt like the truth. She did not put her ego on deck for the entire crew to stroke. Truth be told, she noticed more the *lack* of emptied buckets on the *Enigma* compared to the wet decks constantly present on Alistair's ship. Sure, there were one or two every day, but they were rarely the same person two days in a row and if they were, it was never continued on the third day. Even Myrgen had only done a few times and nothing since the attack.

No, the part he was right about was the part regarding Alistair. She *had* broken with him because he had crippled Tanglwyst's shipping by seizing three of her ships. When he stole them, he had launched all life craft with the entire crew, crewing with his own sailors. Once the ships were gone, Tanglwyst did not have work for the sailors or the captains. Although Catriona was able to hire nearly a third of the displaced men, she did not have the ability to put to work more than that. She had already known of twenty men who had died because they signed on with a ship with an inexperienced captain and they were lost in a storm.

Alistair had claimed the idea was not his, nor was the fault, trying to push the incident off on his "protégé" but she still held him responsible because he let the man use his moniker so he could court Tanglwyst while Black Sparrow was off terrorizing the woman's business holdings. That woman seemed quite adept at making men do foolish things just to be with her.

She had gone to Estelle hoping to learn something. If this were a spell, she wanted it removed. If it wasn't, then everything she was feeling was real. His comments were terrible and could get him keel-hauled if overheard but she could not deny their honestly. Clearly, she was not the only one with a penetrating sight.

She *needed* that insight. Myrgen's point of view was invaluable to her, especially with his comment that she would make a very bad queen. She wanted to ask what he meant by that, but she knew the answer already. Patras courts were D'Medici territory, full of intrigues, poisonous people and plots and secrets everywhere she looked. Even glancing at Dominic made her eyes hurt with all the deceptions and the only reason she let him have them was because they didn't hurt Gwen. In fact, in some cases, they protected her, but Catriona knew Gwen would find out those things on her own and she would be irritated if Catriona tried to sway her opinions. Gwen was very strong willed, just like the rest of her family, and very capable of taking care of herself. If he were to lie to her about anything more important than her birthday gifts, Catriona knew she would have one less connection to Mande. Catriona needed Myrgen with her in that place and it was the one place under the sky that he could not tread.

His tirade on her made that even more evident. He could go places within her no one dared. To chide her like that, on her own ship? That took substance. And he cared about this crew. She could read that in him without even trying. It was prominent in his features these days, more than his affection for her had been of late. She seemed to be fading into the background in his priorities and she couldn't blame him. She had made a choice, and that choice was one she wished beyond wishing that she did not have to take. She did not want to return home so she could disband her crew. She wanted to return home to spend one last time with them in the happiest place she had ever been. If she were to go to Patras with Alexander, she wanted her crew nearby and she didn't know how to ask them to give up the sea and move to, what was for many, a foreign country so she would have people around her she knew she could trust.

Perhaps Myrgen was right though. She should probably give them time to think about this so they could be dropped off at their own homes before that final disembarkation into Patras. Even if they chose to come with her, Octavius never could and she would need to turn the *Enigma* over to him. He had always been well liked by the crew. They would surely rally under his banner.

A knock at the door brought her out of her thought process and she opened it. "Myrgen?"

"Captain." He was still brusque but she could hardly hold that against him. "I'm sorry to bother you but the crew needs your help."

"Of course. I am at your disposal, Myrgen, *and* the crew's. It is no bother at all. What do you need?"

Myrgen hesitated, then seemed to get past whatever he was about to think and moved on. "As I told you before, I have discovered several more casualties from the attack in St. Marguerite, but I was wondering if you can help me do the counting? I was going to ask Estelle, but she is not well and I don't want to task her."

"Count?"

"Well," He glanced down at the papers in his hands, "more like *confirm* a count. I need to do it quickly because if this is as bad as I think, we'll need to do something within the next two days."

Catriona took a deep breath and nodded. "What do you need from me?"

"Octavius says, outside of Estelle, you know this ship better than anyone, even him. Can you use your connection with the ship to help confirm some things for me, by *feeling* them?"

"*Feeling* them?" She shook her head. "No, I can't do that. Anything I know about this ship comes to me through Estelle. Since you're asking me and not her, she must not be capable of it either."

"She's still resting. There's an injury that is effecting the steering of the ship and I don't want to disturb her while she's trying to heal." He took a deep breath and looked at the sheaf of papers in his hands. "Well then, do you have any extra paper? I need to clarify some of my notes."

She saw a rather chaotic series of scribbles and illegible writing that had smudged and gotten wet. She could see why he needed to redo it all. She held up a finger, smiling.

"*That* I can help with." She went over to her desk and pulled out a book about twice the size of her hand. The paper had been printed with lines running across it on every page. "I've been meaning to give this to you."

He took it and leafed through it, aghast at the marvel in his hands. "Is this from one of those new printing presses from Krakte?" The glimmer in his eyes indicated he had forgotten all about their argument before.

She nodded, looking over his hand to see the workmanship. "It's a first run. I know the man who made the machine. You should have seen the size of the thing. A lot of machinery for such a simple thing, but he gave it to me. He plans to do a Book of the Saints now that he has the problems worked out."

"That's very ambitious." He shook his head and looked at her. "This is too precious. I can't use it." He held it out to her.

She put her hand on the book, folding her fingers across his. "This is precisely what this book was made for, and you need it. Please, for the sake of the ship."

"You really mean that, don't you?"

She held his gaze. "As much as you do."

A heartbeat passed between them, soft and powerful, but then she saw his resolve return. "Then *prove it*, Catriona. Warn your crew about your imminent dismissal of them."

She retrieved her hand. "You assume I plan to dismiss them." She turned from him and walked towards her chart table, glancing over her shoulder at him to encourage the conversation.

"You don't?" She could hear his disbelief in his voice, strong as ever.

"No. Never did."

"Then, what…?" He folded his arms. "Okay, you have my attention."

"I have no more intention of dismissing them as I have of dismissing you."

She glanced back at him to see his reaction. He remained unshakable.

"You assume I plan to stay."

Her heart stopped, fear drenching her as she did not hear the tell-tale hint of falsehood she expected from his voice. She turned to face him, scanning him to see if he meant that, wanting desperately to find that he did not. She did not get what she wanted.

"You're not joking."

"No."

"When did you come to this conclusion?"

Myrgen took his eyes off her as he thought for a moment. "Apparently just now." He held her gaze for a moment more, then he looked down at the book in his hand. "With that revealed, I think I need to finish the task I came here to do. Thank you for the book, Captain. I'll return it when I'm done."

He nodded to her and left the room.

Twenty-Five

"You cannot reason with a hungry belly. It has
no ears."
The Siren's Song of Callista

Octavius saw Myrgen emerge from the hallway holding an item, a book from the looks of it, and waved him over. The Ship's Steward climbed the steps to the aftcastle and nodded greeting.

Octavius stepped close. "How did it go?"

Myrgen shook his head. "She can't do it. It looks like I'm alone in this and I need to get started."

"Let me talk to her. I'll see if I can get some help for you."

Myrgen glanced sideways at the crew. "Are you sure that's wise? I don't want to cause a panic."

"It's not like they won't find out. It's a hundred foot boat made of wood. Word travels fast." He looked at the book in Myrgen's hand. "What's that you've got there?"

"Oh! It's amazing." Myrgen brightened, opening the book to show off the printed lines. "Look! The printer made it with lines all across every page."

Octavius looked at his friend and couldn't keep the grin from his face. "Did she tell you where she got it?"

"Yes. It's quite ambitious for the printer to try to do a bible next."

"Did you thank her?"

Myrgen looked up from the book. "Of course I did."

"How?" Octavius raised his eyebrows, giving the universal sign for intimate contact. He hoped the presence of the book meant the two were back on good terms.

Myrgen closed the book. "Not like that, that's for sure. Like she would let me do anything like that." He shook his head. "Look, Octavius, I've been down that road before. Clearly the Fates or the gods or something don't want us together because every intimate opportunity has ended with us being fired upon or my imprisonment. I'm not going to try and convince her to not go with Alexander. That's a choice she's already made." He glanced out to sea, like he was searching for answers or resolve in the waves. "Maybe I'll find a nice, unattached girl in the next port and set up shop there, or slip into Mande. I have a few contacts there."

He returned his gaze to Octavius. "But that's not what I need to focus upon right now. I've got to get to checking things down below."

Octavius nodded. "I'll tell you what. Go get something to eat, just to tide you over and I'll see about getting you some help. I'll meet you down in the hold at the next bell."

Myrgen looked about to object, but his stomach rumbled so loud in response to Octavius' orders, it seemed foolish to try. The First Mate decided not to trust him on this and gestured to the stairs. "After you, Myrgen. I will personally escort you to the galley, then, after being certain you have eaten at least something, I will speak to the Captain about how many hands to put on this."

After several complaints and objections, Myrgen was sitting at the counter in the galley, eating stew that was on the menu for the night meal and drinking some wine he had apparently given Ambrois not an hour before. With him out of the way, Octavius went to Catriona's cabin and knocked.

Her arrival at the door lost a bit of shine when she saw it wasn't who she hoped. "Octavius, come in. What can I do for you?"

"Myrgen is going to be inventorying the hold and needs help. I want to assign him some men to make sure it gets done quickly."

"Is that necessary? He hasn't told me anything about the problem, only that one exists."

"And you haven't *read him* for the information?"

She shook her head, not meeting his eyes.

"Catriona, the ship is at stake here, the lives of the crew, and you haven't read him to find out what's wrong?" He turned his head a bit, watching her for changes. "*Are* you planning on leaving us in Zara?"

"I don't know, Octavius. I…" She seemed lost, trying to figure out what to do. "I haven't read him because I don't want to see that I've lost him." Her voice was soft and clear, full of regret.

It was simple as that.

"You don't have to lose him. Be honest with him. Let him know what happened, what you're thinking. Before this, he has been unable to keep anything from you, and now, his only maintained secrets stem from fears you have imposed. It's time you had someone from whom you kept nothing."

"Would that really be enough?" Hope dared to creep back into her voice between heavily guarded gates.

"I'm not the person to ask that. But first, let's avert the current problem, yes?"

She took a deep breath, then nodded, her authority restored in her posture and visage. "Indeed."

The bell tolling the hour from the crow's nest penetrated the doorway as Octavius opened the door. *Right on time, too. Damn! I'm good.*

Myrgen finished washing the dishes he had used and put them in the cupboard and drawers. Ambrois smiled his gratitude and Myrgen gathered his papers. He had thought to look over the notes while he ate but the food took hold of his senses and he had thought of nothing else. Now, his imminent task loomed before him and he felt guilt over the full stomach.

Ambrois seemed to catch his guilt on his face. "You worried about eating too much, Myrgen? Well, you really shouldn't be. As Ship's Steward, you're an officer and entitled to the fuller menu."

"It's not that. I'm just," Myrgen shook his head and gathered his papers, "I'm just worried about the supplies."

"Myrgen, we are never more than two days from a port no matter where we are."

"That's what I'm afraid of, Ambrois."

Ambrois nodded as Octavius poked his head in the room. "Myrgen, you ready for your task?"

He looked at Octavius. "Yes." He turned to Ambrois. "Thank you." Gathering his papers, he walked out the door.

"I've spoken to the Captain. She said to use every available man to do your count."

Myrgen gave a slight nod. "Good. Thanks. I couldn't quite get the question out when I went to her."

Myrgen followed Octavius down the stairs into the hold. Several lanterns were lit around the hold areas and as they entered, two more on opposite sides flared to life. Myrgen looked around as every officer on board looked at him through the flickering illumination. They were all there and as he counted his assistants, Ambrois came down from behind them and nodded greeting.

Ambrois nodded to the area a few feet in front of Myrgen. "Reporting as ordered, Captain."

Myrgen looked over to the last bastion of shadow left in the hold and saw Catriona materialize as if being summoned from the darkness. "Thank you Ambrois," She turned to her other officers and men, "and thank all of you for coming as quickly as you did. We have a lot to do and a very short time to do it." She looked to Myrgen, nodding. "Chancellor, if you please."

Myrgen took a breath, surprised at how quickly and easily the help he needed had assembled. What was more, the officers would know best what they needed and what was missing from their own areas. He just needed to emphasize the importance of thorough checking.

I am really not alone in this community. I shall miss it.

"Gentlemen, as you know, we suffered an attack a little over a day ago. Due to the nature and timing of the attack, we were unable to do an accurate count of supplies until this time. Earlier today, I found that a box of nails which was missing and assumed swept overboard through a hole in the side was, in fact, propelled into the water supply, destroying over half the fresh water we had on board."

The crewmen exchanged worried looks and Ambrois' eyes grew wide with understanding.

Myrgen continued. "It is important that each area be re-inventoried, and it is vital that the items be moved to ensure that they are what they appear to be. The water barrels looked undisturbed in their placement, but when I pushed one, it moved with ease. Please, select an area and check each box, bottle and barrel until we can be sure we are completely accounted."

"Do you want us to write this down or..?"

"Actually Ambrois, I have a fresh book to catalog the remaining supplies where my original notes have gotten smudged and wet. They are no longer viable. As you count things, please let me know your totals. I'll stop what I'm doing to write it down."

The men got to work and it only took a few minutes for the first tallies to start coming in. Within the span of two bells on ship, roughly an hour, he had several counts coming to him at once and he started to panic that he was taking too long recording the information in order to keep it straight.

"What do we do with the broken stuff?" Ambrois had just discovered the mess with the eggs.

Myrgen pointed to the stairs. "Let's take it up on deck. If it can be salvaged, we'll have better light to figure that out." He turned back to his entries.

Catriona stepped up behind him. "Can I help?"

Myrgen darted a look over his shoulder. "I'm more efficient than I thought. I can't keep up and if I don't put things in the proper place, I'll be no better off than with my scribblings from before."

She put a hand on his shoulder and squeezed. "I think I have this." She walked over to Deitrich the Sail Master and spoke quietly to him. He felt around his pockets for a moment, then produced a large piece of chalk. She took it and smiled. "Gentlemen, if you would please, step over here and give your tallies to me." She moved a few items away from the hull and, as runners relayed their counts to her, Myrgen was able to go at a better pace, unconcerned he would not be able to organize things. He dared a smile of gratitude in her direction and she paid for his smile with one of her own making.

At the end of the Lookout shift two hours later, every officer had counted their area and assisted where they could with another until they were no longer needed and Octavius, Catriona and Myrgen were left alone in the hold. Myrgen continued to scritch his notes onto the pages, having sharpened his graphite no less than six times during the endeavor. The walls looked like something out of the Bible, white crisp lines denoting the future of the ship and her inhabitants sharp against the black boards. Myrgen's hands were grey with graphite and he imagined he had it on his face and forehead where he had scratched an itch or rubbed it in thought.

Octavius put out a few of the lanterns on the far ends as Catriona came over to Myrgen. "Well?"

"It doesn't look good, Captain." Myrgen showed her the tallies on food and she stepped back a pace to catch her breath. "I'm sorry."

Octavius blew out another lantern and came over to look at the afternoon's efforts, carrying a lantern to light his way. Myrgen handed the book over to the man and let him and Catriona examine the information while he turned out the remaining lanterns. As he blew out the last one, he plunged the hold into darkness save the light the First Mate carried. The sudden lack of light cause Myrgen to be night blinded and he stumbled against a low crate he had forgotten, hitting the deck with a most profound thump-slap.

"Myrgen?"

"I'm okay, Captain." *Just a bit of an idiot, that's all.* He went to stand and a small bit of light from ahead of him caught his eye. He waited until his vision adjusted to the dim and then stood again, using his hands to guide him through the obstacles while he kept his eye on the small light. It seemed to be an ember or something and he could hear sloshing of water and smell charcoal. As he grew closer, the sound of the sea was far too prominent and there was the faint shimmer of the lantern light reflecting off something.

"Octavius, can you bring that light over here?"

The area around him brightened as Octavius responded, and the three of them gathered near the area hidden by a series of weapon care supplies. Myrgen put his hands on a crate he had seen the Quartermaster Lawrence move earlier and was stopped as easily as if he had tried to move a mountain.

"What the?" He shoved it with his shoulder but it didn't move aside until Octavius lent his own shoulder to the effort.

"What did you find, Myrgen?" Catriona's voice sounded at home in the quiet of the hold and betrayed no concern.

"I think I see something here." He took Octavius' lantern and lifted it to dispel the shadows in back of the crates. Behind the boxes were the remains of a lantern, glass broken and embedded in a few places on the deck. Water sloshed in through a small hole in the hull where the bulk of the flame that had once burned contained had died after gaining its freedom. A small area was still smoldering, just out of reach of the incoming sea but not entirely protected from the occasional splash of the water on the deck.

"Callista's Fury, do you see that, Captain?" Octavius surprise seemed to echo that of the rest of the trio.

Myrgen reached down and splashed some water from the deck directly on the ember, dousing it for good. "We must have missed this when we were looking for damage. It's a miracle it stayed this contained."

Catriona stood. "It's no miracle." She turned to Octavius. "It's Estelle. She has been fighting this wound since the attack. That's why she's been so weak and tired."

"If you'll excuse me, Captain, I'd like to go check on my wife."

"Of course. I'll stay and help Myrgen fix this up."

"Thank you." Octavius left, taking the steps two at a time.

Catriona went over to the carpenter's supplies and got a hammer and a couple shorter planks that seemed to be from a broken crate. She put some nails between her lips and grabbed a sealed bucket that Myrgen recognized as holding the special pitch. He stood and took the bucket and the hammer, freeing her hand to better hold the boards. He looked at her heavily armed lips and smiled.

"Maybe I should try that look. Might keep me out of trouble."

"'Fraid not," she replied through gritted teeth. "It would just prompt different ways for people to take the nails from you."

He looked at her, surprised by her flirtation and she seemed to grow self-conscious under his scrutiny. He looked at the hole and walked over to the carpenter's supplies to find a plug and some cloths. "I can handle this, Captain. You don't need to stay."

"I'd like to help, if you don't mind."

He found a small piece of wood to use as a plug and cloths he could tear up to be the right size. He walked back over to the work area. "No, I don't mind." He nodded to the markings on the wall. "You've already helped a lot."

Catriona looked up at the wall. "Yes, I'll be scrubbing that off here once we get her fixed up."

"Well, provided any of the boards are still present. They may end up tearing them all out and replacing them."

"You know anything about ships, Myrgen?"

He looked at her. "Some."

"You respond to things here like you were born to them."

Myrgen focused upon putting the plug in the hole. It was too small but he hoped the rags would suffice to give it the right girth. "Well, I guess it's better than the stuff I was actually born to."

There was silence a moment, then Catriona broke it. "I've been thinking about what you said before."

He stopped, waiting.

"I'm not the person you think I am, Myrgen."

"No, I think you're not the person I *used to* think you were." He stared at the hole in the wall. "And honestly, neither am I."

Her voice was quiet, like she wanted to keep him talking. "What are you now, then?"

He leaned back, wrapping the cloth around the plug to test the size. The action kept his hands busy while is mind sorted things out.

"I'm not sure. I just know I'm not walking the same path I used to." He looked up at her. "I've walked the road you're looking at taking, Catriona, and it's not a road I... It's not a road you should want to take."

"It's not like I'm going to be alone, Myrgen. I plan on offering guard positions to anyone on the crew who would like to join me."

Myrgen went back to messing with the plug. "Well, they might follow you, but they won't be able to protect you. Those people there, they're unlike any foe you've ever faced."

"Gwen will be there. She knows her way around that life."

"Gwen is a sweet, naive girl. Look who she's engaged to." He tore the piece of cloth and wrapped the square around the plug.

"And I'll have Alexander."

The comment hung in the air like a thunderclap. He stopped for a moment. "Yes, you will. But that shouldn't comfort you."

Catriona swallowed. Her voice was guarded. "Why not?"

Myrgen exhaled and looked up at her. "Because as soon as you get close to anyone who isn't him, he'll get rid of them."

She blinked, watching him.

"It happens, Catriona. I've seen it happen. Hell, I've *made* it happen." He stood up, joining her at eye level. "And before you try to tell me Alexander isn't like that, I'd like to remind you why we're down here right now. This ship is something you love, something that will come between you and him, and he's done this to it."

"This ship wasn't his first target, Myrgen."

Myrgen blinked, her point hanging like a teetering lantern. "No, it wasn't. But I don't think it will be his last target either." He closed his eyes, gathering his thoughts. "I take no pleasure in knowing I've landed in his hunting range, Catriona, but it's not unfamiliar territory. I can take care of myself."

He looked around at the surveyed goods and the damaged ship. "But these people, they count on you to protect them from this, and you've brought it upon them."

She closed her eyes and sank a bit under the weight of his comment. He was glad to see she was taking this seriously, but he wished he didn't have to deliver the felling blow himself. Moreover, it bothered him that he still cared so much. He looked at the plug in his hand and knelt down to continue his work.

"Have I truly fallen so far in your eyes, Myrgen?"

Myrgen blinked, not wanting to tell her his thoughts. "Yes. I'm afraid you have." He put a hand on the floor to steady himself. "I seem to have a need for women I love to be so high above me, out of reach, out of range. But you," he looked at her again, "you came down here, to me. You came to me in the prison, in the caves, in the church. You even came to me in the darkness, that Shadow that sucked me in. You have been my rescuer time and again and, in a way, I feel inadequate that I'm now being asked to rescue you."

Catriona's eyes softened. "You don't need to rescue me, Myrgen. I'm not in danger."

"*Yes*, you are!" He threw the plug across the room, frustrated that it still was too small, despite repeated wrappings of the cloth. He leaned on the crate, facing her. "You are, and the fact that you don't know it just makes things harder. You don't see how bad it is but I know this world, Catriona. It will swallow you whole. It will take you in like that shadow stuff did to me, and you won't be able to escape and there won't be some rock just lying there, waiting for you to pick it up and fight your way out of this."

Catriona furrowed her brow. "Rock? What rock?"

"Just some rock. That's not my point."

"No, wait. What rock? Was there a rock in the Shadow?"

"Don't try to sidetrack me here." He shook his head, trying to regain his steam. The idea of the rock had just popped into the conversation and now it seemed to have completely stopped him cold. "What was I saying?"

"You were talking about a rock."

"No, before the rock. Ugh! Oh yes, you being in danger." He looked her in the eyes again. "Look, I don't want you to go with him because I can't protect you."

She blinked, apparently forgetting the discussion about the rock "And you want to protect me."

"Yes."

"Why?"

"Because I..." He watched her eyes, trying to figure out if he still felt like that.

Catriona blinked, her own gaze begging for him to continue. "What?"

He fought with himself, not wanting to betray his heart now that it had finally hardened enough to handle her leaving with Alexander. She frowned a moment, like she was fighting a thought of her own, but she maintained her eye contact. It mattered to her what he was saying and he knew, again, that he had not yet stopped loving her. He knew she could read that and he didn't understand why she hadn't yet. *Why isn't she reading me? Why doesn't she know?*

Then it occurred to him. She was afraid. She was afraid he no longer did. His mind did flips as he tried to figure out what to say to her. He cared about her, about this ship and this crew, about her family and what they would think of him, about her country and whether they would allow him to live there, even about her deity and if it would accept him. He even cared about Alexander, because he was the one thing that could take her away.

He looked down at her hand and reached out to take it. Suddenly, he heard Octavius' voice inside his head. *"Myrgen! Is something wrong?"*

Myrgen's eyes widened and he jerked his hand away from hers as if the touch had somehow brought on the mental invasion. He backed away, arms spread wide to catch himself. "What the hell?"

"I'm trying to reach the Captain, but she said not now! What's wrong? Is it a breach in the hull?"

Catriona rushed to him, her face frightened. "Myrgen, what is it?" She reached out to touch him.

He jerked away from her touch and put his hand against his head. "Octavius! He's talking to me inside my head!"

"By the *stones*!" She closed her eyes for a moment. "He's gone now."

"What the hell was that?" His eyes were wide and he felt like he was on the edge of madness. He sat on one of the crates out of pure luck. He was just as likely to have splashed his butt into the water near the leak.

"It's just a way Octavius and I can communicate with each other. Through the ship. I thought he could only contact me. He must be quite panicked to reach out to you."

Myrgen buried his face in his hands, trying to rub the mental invasion out of his eyes. He looked up at Catriona, dazed. "He does that with you?"

She knelt beside him, her knee on the repair boards. "Just every once in a while, when it's important. It's not like we use it to just chat where no one can overhear us."

He watched her now, like she was the unsafe one instead of Octavius. "Where no one can overhear you?"

"No, we... we *don't* use it... Myrgen, let me..." She reached out her hand to touch his shoulder and he stood up, turning away from her over the crate to put it between them.

"No, you just keep your mental voices to yourself."

"It's not spread like a disease. He contacted you directly. You didn't get it from me."

"Why would he do that? Why would he come into my head like that? Like it isn't bad enough you read my mind, now *anybody* can?"

"No, of course not! Myrgen, we have to fix the ship. If we don't hurry up, he might do it again."

"I can get that on my own. Why don't you just," he waved his hand at her, shooing her away without getting too close to actually touching her, "just... just g, go on up and tell him not to do that again."

"You need my help, don't you?"

He looked into her worried eyes but he had no comfort to offer. "No, I'll be fine. Just go. Please."

She stood and turned her back, measured steps carrying her away. She turned back to look at him at the foot of the stairs, then glared up the steps and spent her fury going up them. He heard the door slam as she left the hold and furious strides walking away on the main deck. Myrgen shook his head to get the sanity back and leaned forward, rubbing his face.

By the stones, what next?

Twenty-Six

"You stitch closed the cut on my toe but the sword pierced my arm."
The Siren's Song of Callista

Myrgen stood and walked to the carpenter's supplies to find a different plug. This officer's position was not dissimilar to the Barber-Surgeon's in that most of his time on the ship was spent in preparation for the emergencies. The Carpenter usually had several plugs pre-shaped to fill holes but the attack a few days ago used up several of the plugs and Eadric had yet to replace the ones used. Not to mention there had been no new wood brought on board because they had yet to pull into a new port since the attack.

He leaned on the crate and bowed his head, closing his eyes. *It's because of me. They can't pull into another port because of me. Their supplies are low, the ship is taking on water and they can't stop because of me. It keeps coming back to this and I can't come up with a good solution. I can't stay here. I can't stay here and I can't leave.*

"Myrgen?"

He looked behind him and saw he faint shimmer of a woman's form near the wall. Her features were watery and indistinct, but her voice was familiar. "Estelle. You shouldn't be up right now. You need to conserve your strength."

"For what? If I can't help you repair me, there won't be much to conserve my strength for."

"How can you help me?"

"For one, I can help you find what you need." She nodded to the crate he was looking through. "Check the one beneath it."

He looked back at the crate, then blinked back into clarity. He moved the top crate and used a pry bar from the other crate to open this one. As sure as stone, the plugs he needed were right there.

"Thank you!" He turned back to her but she faded from view as he did so. "Thank you." He returned to the plugs and pulled out three different sizes to try. "Now if you could just help me with my other situation."

With a new sense of hope, he moved with a purpose to do the repairs.

Catriona knocked on the door to Octavius' chambers and waited, her anger still prominent on her mind. Myrgen had been about to make a breakthrough and Octavius had interrupted it. Now, it was doubtful he would ever get to that stage again. She heard a call from inside and entered.

"Octavius!"

He looked up at her, worry in his eyes. The woman he loved was in very bad shape and it was only proper that he was desperate for news regarding the repairs being done to save her. He kissed her forehead and then came over to his Captain.

"Yes?"

Catriona blinked, dismissing her anger. She knew, were a member of her family in dire straits, she would be no less impatient. "How is she doing?"

"Better I think. Here, come look."

She followed him to the bedside and he moved the bandage from her left arm. "The redness is gone. She said it happened when he put out the fire. She's talking now, which means the thing that was keeping her weak is gone."

Octavius sat beside her again. Estelle moved a bit and mumbled something, but Catriona couldn't make it out. It sounded like she said "Myrgen," but that could just be because he was on Catriona's mind, not Estelle's. She shook off the thought of him. It was inappropriate right now.

"So, what was happening down there when I reached out to you?"

Catriona took a breath, pulling her eyes from Estelle. "Oh, just figuring out what to do. The plug he was using wasn't the right size."

"Did he find the right size?"

"I'm not sure. I'm afraid your contact with him rather, um, *surprised* him. He got a bit distracted after that."

"Oh." He looked down at the floor for a thought, found it and looked back at her. "You mean, he didn't know we did that?"

"Well, no. Why would he?"

"Well, because..." He made a vague gesture she couldn't interpret.

She furrowed her brow. "Because what?"

"Well, you two are so, you know, close."

Catriona looked away and wrapped her arms around her chest. "Not really. Not so much any more."

"What do you mean, 'not so much any more'?"

She just turned away.

Octavius stood up and walked her away from Estelle. "Catriona, what do you mean, 'not so much any more'?"

"We had a fight and he..." She shook her head. "Things are different between us now."

"Why? Because he told you you were being selfish and inconsiderate?"

She looked at him. "You listened?"

"He told me."

"Oh."

"He also told me he read William out for thinking you were going to desert the crew once we get to Caratia. And he's given his own supplies to Ambrois to supplement the crew's until we can dock. I saw the bottles of wine he bought in St. Andrew in the galley. Ones he told me he bought to share with you."

She closed her eyes against the onslaught of insight his information carried. "That doesn't help, Octavius."

"What do you mean, it doesn't help? He wants to share those things with *you.*"

"Not anymore!" She shook her head. "Don't you see? He *gave them away.*" She turned away from him, her voice quiet. "He gave them away."

Octavius sighed and she recovered some of her posture. Not enough to face him and not enough to deal with Myrgen, but enough to get her across the main deck to her chambers if she didn't meet up with anyone on the way. She didn't dare look for Myrgen for any number of reasons, not the least of which was Estelle's weakness so she needed to get out while she still could. He would be busy with the repairs for only so long.

"Please let me know if her condition changes, Octavius. I'll be in my quarters."

"Captain, you need to talk to him."

She didn't face him, but spoke over her shoulder, not looking at him. "And say what? At the end of the day, Octavius, nothing has changed. We still can't be together." She put her hand on the door. "Better to let him go."

She opened the door and left before Octavius could say anything else.

Myrgen finished the repairs halfway through the second hour of the new watch. He wiped his hands of the pitch, surprised that it actually came off. *This is definitely not the regular stuff.* The middle sized plug ended up being the correct size mainly because he needed to pound it in, breaking away much of the burnt wood. Now it seated up against solid wood and all the black material was gone. The Fae pitch sealed the wound like it never happened.

He gathered up the tools and put them back in their crates, returning everything to its inventoried state. That reminded him and he pulled out the ledger and recorded the use of material, including the loss of the lantern that started the entire thing. The end result was still no better. It was a very good thing the boards he used had been too small to do much else in the way of repairs. Nothing got wasted.

He wiped his brow with the back of his sleeve and looked around. He blew out the lantern he had been using and put it on the peg by the foot of the stairs before returning to the surface. He put his hand on the door, intending to visit Estelle and see if he had done it right when a thought stopped his progress.

What if Catriona is there?

He blinked, not certain what to do. He didn't need another dose of the intensity of their relationship, or *non*-relationship, as it were. He had been so close to throwing it all aside and telling her he loved her, kings and gods be damned. Had Octavius not popped into his head at that moment, he wasn't certain he wouldn't have grabbed and kissed her, hoping to bring about the prophecy Alistair had made.

He rolled his eyes. Yeah, that would be the height, breadth and depth of stupidity. Pinning my hopes, my future on the prediction of an ex-lover of this woman. It's not like he has some divine calling.

There was so much that was foreign about her. Her faith, her family, her relationships, her employment history, her hiring practices. Nothing he had come to consider common or normal seemed to be a part of this woman's life. Her ship was the body for a disembodied Fae, darkness came to life around her and poked holes in people, her primary suitor was the King of Mervolingia and her self-professed fiancé schemed to put her in bed with another man. What in the world would it truly be like to be intimate with such a bizarre creature?

Well, it damned sure wouldn't be boring.

Regardless, he wasn't feeling up to running into her right then. He needed some time, some sleep, the chance to recharge his body and settle his mind. He most decidedly *didn't* need a recap of the afternoon's near revelations. He opened the door a crack and let himself be blinded by the light. People were still moving about the broken supplies, but it looked like the majority of the salvageable goods were done being salvaged and just needed his count to let them be returned to the hold. That meant time on deck, quite a bit of it, too, and lots of chances for the Captain to see him. He would be ready later, but not now.

He closed the door and rubbed the backs of his teeth with his tongue, thinking. *I could do it. He probably knows right where she is.*

The thought of trying to contact Octavius' mind sent a shudder through his spine and he dismissed it before it could make his teeth itch again. He didn't feel comfortable contacting Octavius, despite their friendship, but he did feel comfortable contacting someone else. He lifted his head and looked down into the dark hold.

"Estelle."

His stage whisper echoed off the stairwell and down into the hold. He looked for her glowing form but saw nothing. He took a few steps down into the dark, courting the area of the steps where the light coming under the door to the main deck no longer cast its radiance, and called out again.

"Estelle."

"Yes, Myrgen?"

Her voice came from behind him and he spun around, losing his footing on the stairs and falling to the bottom. He flailed and grabbed the railing right before hitting the last stair with his lower back, softening the blow and probably stopping himself from getting killed.

"Oh no!" Estelle disappeared and reappeared next to Myrgen at the foot of the stairs. "Are you hurt?"

"Ow..."

"Oh dear! You're hurt! I'll go get the Captain!"

"No!" He reached out to stop her but his hand passed right through. She stopped and looked at him. "Please, don't."

He concentrated on the area in his back and focused his remaining energy on the pain. He felt the bruised muscles calm and the pain subsided. He opened his eyes and started to get up. "See? Perfectly fine. No need to fetch the Captain."

"Oh. I forgot you could do that."

"Luckily, I didn't." He pulled himself to his feet using the railing and rubbed the spot on his back. "Speaking of which, where is the Captain right now?"

"In her quarters, pacing."

"Good. Why is she pacing?"

"Because she can't sleep."

"Oh. How late is it? It looked bright outside."

"It's just about sundown. The crew has strung lanterns to continue work on the salvage."

"What do they have that's salvageable?"

"Most of the nails were recovered, the water barrels were plugged, ropes are being dried."

"No food though?"

"No, sir."

"Damn." He looked at her. "Can you tell me everything they've managed to keep?"

"Of course."

He took out his ledger and graphite and began to record her survey by the glow of her spiritual light.

Catriona sat down because her feet hurt from pacing. She had asked Octavius to let her know when Myrgen was finished with his repairs so she could return to her cabin, giving him the freedom to assess the salvage without her around and he had done so. She had laid down at first, trying to sleep until he came to give his report. She didn't know how long it would take for Myrgen to get that ready and she didn't want to be snippy because she was exhausted.

The idea of laying down had failed utterly. Instead, she found herself thinking of him over and over, different things he did or said, they way he held her, the way he kissed her. At one point, she started to drift off and the dream she had of them making love had started to coalesce behind her eyes, causing them to pop open as she forced the issue back into the dark.

Her feet were sore from stomping earlier and being on them all day, and she pulled off her boots to rub her soles. They smelled of sweaty leather and were dark where the leather stain had soaked through when they were wet in the hold. She opened her footlocker and pulled out a small glass bottle marked *foot soak* that Xannu had made. Like all her things, it had the exotic scent and she sprinkled a few of the granules into her hand. They were supposed to go into water but with the situation on board at present, she had no water to spare and the soak reacted poorly with salt water, creating a strong seaweed smell. As it stood, she had turned over the water she kept in here to Ambrois to add to the rations.

She rubbed the granules into her feet, letting the scent absorb and remove the smell of the hold. She glanced at her open footlocker and saw the two bottles of wine she had recently put there. Ambrois had given her the wine Myrgen had donated. Most of the spirits were kept in her cabin for rationing purposes and these were no different, but she had found she had a hard time putting these with the others. She hoped they would be able to do something about the situation with the supplies before these needed to be sacrificed as well.

She got up and walked over to the chart table and the map of the coast they were skirting. There were plenty of ports in the next day's travel but every one of them was Mervolingian and was undoubtedly aware of the outlaw status of this ship and her notorious passenger. Alexander had been so angry when they pulled away from the docks. She highly doubted he had cooled down before sending out a declaration of the whereabouts of Myrgen the Grey. Even if he had, the Captain of the Guard would have sent out pigeons by now. It was his duty to do so.

She picked up her other foot and absently rubbed the smoothed crystals on it while she scanned the coastline. She imagined they could beach between ports in a lagoon or something and harvest supplies instead of buy them but that would take even longer and with no supplies to spare while others were hunted, she could not ensure the delay would be worthwhile. Besides, a main road followed the coastline here. The patrols would just as likely find the crew and they might have orders to attack before questioning. If what Myrgen said before was true, who knew to what lengths Alexander was prepared to go?

She looked farther down the coast. Soon, they would be out of Mervol territory and into Mandian but the demarcation between the two governments was a series of reefs which forced ships further into deep water. It was especially treacherous because the natural shape of the land around them caught storms and held them. Catriona had heard tales of a pact made between the D'Medici founders of Mande and the Storm Lords of legend which kept their enemies at bay for a hundred years, after which, all

D'Medicis would then serve them. If the myths describing the Storm Lords were true, it would explain the greedy ferocity with which the prominent family governed. Their practices were, to say the least, extremely self-serving.

Catriona traced the coastline back from the reefs of Mande and her eye caught on a small, very well protected bay. She thought for a moment, trying to recall the name of the place. It was close enough to the Mandian coasts to have a Mandian name, she remembered that, but it was still in Mervol territory. She wracked her brain, trying to remember the place and why it was noteworthy. *Port of something.*

Then it hit her.

Portabella.

The pirate port. The terrain, both by land and by sea cut it off from all outside forces, protecting the inhabitants from raid by authorities. Landward, cliffs reached high with a single trail winding down its face, making it possible for an old woman with a broom to defend it. By sea, the famous reefs of Mande began their secret touch going into the bay. These threatened to beach a warship before it even got within firing range and only the bravest of merchant ships trucked with these demons. They made their way by sitting in wait and attacking ships too inexperienced to know to avoid the area. Had it not been for Thessius' experience, this ship would have fallen prey to them a few years back.

Catriona smiled.

Portabella. It was perfect.

Myrgen stepped out of the hold, putting away his graphite. William came over to him, gesturing to the salvaged goods on the deck. "We've done as you asked, Myrgen. Tossed the destroyed stuff overboard and kept the other goods here until you counted them."

"Thank you William." He stepped over to the items and glanced them over. Estelle had given him very accurate details. He nodded. "Thanks. Okay, you can put them in the hold now."

William nodded and the crew standing by set about getting the items below. Myrgen looked at his notes and nodded. He finally felt ready to give his report. He walked down the hallway and reached up to knock on the door. His cuff was filthy from the coal and the water and he realized he looked just as bad as the hold had the first time he cleaned it. He pulled back and sniffed his cuff and recoiled from the smell of sweat and rotten egg water.

He knew the water situation was not good and he could hardly expect to use water to bathe when people's lives depended on the small amount of water they currently had on board. He thought of the buckets on deck but the knowledge of the vermin he had picked from his hair before reminded him one did not use buckets pulled from the depths to clean oneself. He shrugged and shook his head. *It's not like she wasn't down there too, kneeling in the same water. She'll be just as rancid as I will, and just as unable to do anything about it.*

He stood up straight and knocked. Catriona called for him to enter and he stepped into a room fragrant as the incense house in Rouen. Catriona had her boots off and was walking around barefoot on a cloud of exotic spice and powder. He rolled his eyes at the impressive quantity of wrong he seemed capable of discovering when it came to this woman.

Catriona turned to see who it was and stopped pacing when he entered. She started to walk over to him but he held up his hand.

"You might want to keep your distance. The hold was not kind to me in terms of olfactory presence today."

"Understood." She backed up a bit and rested her butt on the edge of the chart table. "What have you got?"

He looked down at his notes. "Little in the way of good news, I'm afraid. As you might have guessed from the notes you transcribed on the wall below, we have less food than I thought. It's worse because apparently some of the stuff that was originally thought as salvageable turned out not to be so, according to what was left on deck."

"Is the hole in the ship repaired?"

Myrgen looked up from his notes. "Yes. Yes, I finally found a plug that fit. The damage was pretty severe though. I had to make the hole bigger in order to clear out the damaged area. It's practically right at the waterline too, so it will be difficult to repair without the ship being beached or in dry dock. The repair should hold though, provided we can steer clear of reefs and bad weather."

Catriona reached back and put her hands on the table behind her. "That's going to be decidedly difficult with the Fingers of Mande on the way."

"Is there any way to go around them, avoiding the Storm Catch?"

She turned to the map behind her. "Yes, but it's not a better choice. The Islands of Cyprus flank the sea across from the Storm Catch and they are rife with whirlpools and maelstroms. No ship has ever successfully sailed through there and returned to tell the tale."

She waved him over and he grimaced. "I don't have an entire incense house at my disposal. I'm not sure my manly scent can overpower the smell of the hold."

"I've been on this ship for five years, Myrgen. I doubt you have anything new to contribute that I haven't withstood before."

He pointed at her as he walked over to table. "Remember you said that."

"I promise, if I see or smell anything I don't recognize, I'll throw a rock at it."

"Where are you going to get a rock?"

"Where did you?"

He put his hands on the table and looked at the map. "I'm not having that conversation with you. What's the plan, then? We need to port to resupply."

"I know. I have a place in mind, but it's dangerous." She looked at him.

He returned her look. "How dangerous?"

"Well, of all our options, it's the safest, but that isn't saying much."

He straightened up and rubbed the back of his neck. "What do you have in mind?"

"I'll tell everyone at the meeting. Can you be ready to tell the crew what you've learned within the hour? If we are going to act on the idea I have, we'll need to make for it by morning or we'll miss it."

"Sure. I can do it now."

She put her sleeve to her nose. "No, feel free to take a few minutes, if you don't mind."

He looked at her, then smiled, putting his arm down. "I warned you."

From behind her sleeve, she nodded. "Yes, you did."

He stepped closer to her. "Are you sure you don't want to breathe in my sultry man-stink?"

She shook her head several times, keeping her sleeve up and backing away, but he could still hear the smile she was hiding. "No, not really."

"I'll bet my breath is just as impressive. Come, lover, give us a kiss." He reached out and grabbed her around the waist and she pushed his chest away, maintaining his distance forcibly, combining what sounded like a gag and a giggle.

"Mercy! Mercy, please. I'll never doubt you again."

She looked at him with smiling eyes and he realized again how much he loved her laugh. He remembered his place and let her go, the smile on his face fading a bit as he did so. "See that you don't."

She saw the change in him and sobered up as well. "You have my word."

"How long before the meeting?"

"In an hour, if you can, but we won't start without you. Take some time."

He glanced down at his filthy clothes and hands. "I'm sorry I don't have much that will help here. Water's kind of scarce right now."

"Didn't you get some oil from Xannu in your things from the incense house?"

"Um, yes, but I didn't cook anything so I didn't open it."

Catriona shook her head. "It's not for cooking. It's for bathing without water. We often go quite a while without being able to bathe and the oil has special cleansers that stop the skin from becoming chafed from the dirt. Rinse off with some sea water first, to get the big chunks off, then use the oil. Spread it on your skin, then wipe it off with one of the towels I gave you."

"How long do you leave it on?" This concept was very foreign to him because, in the times he had traveled with Tanglwyst, they had always had bath water. He wondered now if that was at the expense of the crew's rations.

"Start at the top and by the time you reach the bottom, it will be time to wipe it off."

He nodded and opened the door. "I'll give that a try then. Thank you."

She took her sleeve away from her nose and nodded. "Don't mention it. Please. Just go."

He smiled at her chiding and left.

Twenty-Seven

"The sea brings me to Yantap, that I may show
these silks your beauty."
The Siren's Song of Callista

Myrgen stepped out of his cabin feeling slick, but smelling far better than he thought possible. He had decided, since they were anchored until the next course of action was determined, to jump into the sea rather than draw water up from below. His actions panicked a few crewmen who thought he was trying to end it all but Thessius was kind enough to defray their suspicion by joining him. Granted, his comment about the sharks likely swimming below them did manage to end Myrgen's instinct for bathing, but the plunge did get the bulk of the smell and filth off him.

The oil thing was odd and a bit sensual and it was only the idea that Octavius could burst into his mind without warning that he managed to get through it as quickly as he did. It wouldn't have done to be walked in on at a crucial fantasy moment. Fresh clothes and a comb through his hair and beard made him almost presentable. His teeth still felt furry, so he swished some wine around in his mouth to get the bulk of it off. He was really looking forward to being in civilization again, where he could get a proper bath.

Many of the crew were already on deck, talking over coils of rope or leaning on railings. Octavius and Catriona were talking on the aftcastle near the helm and he nodded to her when he saw Myrgen. She motioned Myrgen to join them and he moved through the crowd as quick as possible. It was dark and already quite late and keeping the men up much later was only going to make matters worse. Octavius called the men to attention as Myrgen got to Catriona.

"Gentlemen," she began, her voice projecting better than Myrgen thought she could. "We have the final reports regarding the status of the ship since the attack. Mister Rhiann, would you mind?"

The Carpenter, a short man with long, thinning salt and pepper hair and beard stepped up to the edge of the aftcastle so he could address the crew. His loose shirt completely hid his extremely defined muscles and Myrgen knew from talking to him that he had recently proposed to his lady, Danielle, right before going off to sea for the season.

"We dealt with the damage to the ship that we could but she's going to need to go into dry dock once we get to Caratia. It also means we need to avoid any storms between here and there if possible."

A murmur slipped through the crowd as Rhiann stepped back to the other officers. Myrgen leaned in to Octavius. "Is it always like this? Divulging everything to the crew?"

"Yeah. Every man here has a say in what we do because their lives are on the line."

"What if Catriona suggests something they don't want to do, like stay in Caratia?"

"They tell her. But usually, they trust her."

"Myrgen?" Catriona looked at him. "You're next, please."

He nodded and stepped forward to the railing overlooking the main deck. "First of all, I'd like to apologize for causing so much trouble here. None of you people deserve to have to deal with this."

A voice from the crowd said, "Take it out of his pay!"

Everyone laughed, including Myrgen. "I've already offered, men. Why do you think I don't gamble with you guys?" He glanced around and took a breath as the laughter died down.

"But to the reason we're here. I've checked my figures and the stores in the hold and the attack has taken out over half the supplies, including the water. Now that means we're going to have to pull into port in the next day or so or we're not going to make it to Caratia."

He looked behind him and stepped aside as Catriona stepped forward.

"Men, I have a suggestion but it will be risky and dangerous, but it will get us the supplies we need. We can make our repairs on the way and prepare ourselves for skirting the Fingers of Mande and the Storm Catch." She stopped as she got the attention of every man on board. She looked at Thessius. "We're pulling into Portabella."

A whisper went through the crew, disgruntled and a little frightened. Thessius shook his head and swore under his breath.

"What's the plan, Captain?"

"We have the most unique ship on the sea, and the finest crew and I'll need every one of you to do your part if we are to pull this off. Now, here's the plan…"

The entire crew seemed lost in thought at the end of Catriona's explanation and she took this as a good sign. If they had objected immediately, the plan would have failed. One of the men shouted, "And you think this will get us in *and* out of a pirate port?"

"I do. But we have to make it convincing sounding."

Another man asked, "What about the appearance?"

"Octavius and I have that covered."

The men mulled this over but seemed disinclined to pursue the subject. They had learned to trust her.

Thessius lifted his head. "Ye 'ave m' seppurt."

Catriona scanned the rest of the crew and saw them nodding, following his lead. She knew that Thessius' support meant a lot because he was the one who stopped them from entering Portabella in the first place. She took a deep breath and straightened up. "Thank you all. Octavius, please set a course for Portabella. We need to arrive as close to sunset as possible."

"Aye Captain."

She nodded to the men and turned around as the officers left the aftcastle to perform their parts in the ruse. Myrgen came over to her.

"I know about this port, Captain. It's been a thorn in the kingdom's side for over a decade." He looked around to make sure no one else was within earshot and motioned her over to the rail away from any other crew. He glanced around and moved a little closer to her to keep their voices from carrying to the men working nearby. "So, have you ever been there before?"

Catriona shook her head as imperceptibly as possible. "We've managed to avoid it every time. The first time we encountered it, I would have had us pull in for supplies if Thessius hadn't stopped me. He said the inhabitants were ruthless about letting ships rip out their bottoms on the reefs at the neck of the bay and picking the bones. He also told me one other thing: they were very superstitious."

He arched an eyebrow. "There's a sailor who isn't?"

She smiled. "Well, pirates have their own brand of superstition. It's a higher grade, so to speak. Because they lure ships in and prey upon them after they've been crippled, damned near anything even remotely ghost-like will send them into a frenzy. They see it as retribution."

He glanced behind them as a couple deckhands brought out some chains from below and started tying them to ropes. Catriona scanned them and saw they were trying to listen in on what was being said between her and Myrgen.

He saw them and leaned a little closer. "Well, there's a reason why I'm so interested in this port. I think it might be a good place for me to leave the ship."

She looked at his eyes. "Are you serious?"

"Take a look." His gaze was soft but steady and she knew she didn't want to look any deeper. He glanced down at her hand and took it. "This place is perfect for me. It has no communication with the Mervol guard network and it is self-sustaining. I'm sure someone like me can go there and have no trouble blending in or finding work. It's not like I haven't walked Underground streets in my time."

She studied their hands, not wanting to look at him. "But we're almost out of Mervolingia. After Portabella is the Fingers of Mande. We're barely more than a ten-day away from home." She was keeping her voice quiet but she could feel it threatening to crack.

"And exactly what am I going to do there? You don't need me as a Ship's Steward, not when every Mervol port has been ordered not to trade with you if I'm on board."

"You don't have to set sail again. You can stay on in Zara, where it's safe. My family is there, my son…"

He gripped her hand, calling her attention to his eyes. "And exactly what was the last encounter I had with your son? Have you ever thought of that? I was responsible for his *kidnapping*, Catriona. Do you really think he'll forgive me for that?"

"Tangl was the one behind that and Elizabeth behind *that*."

"And I still didn't release him once he was taken, like I should have."

"If you tell him about it. If you take responsibility for it."

His expression pleaded with her to see reason. "And what about these friends of yours? What were their names?"

"Drake. And Anika."

"Yes, that's right. You know, I had heard their names before and I couldn't remember them, but last night, it came to me. They are the Duce and Ducesâ of Caratia, aren't they? When you said you needed to consult with your Dûcesa, it was this Anika person you meant."

She pulled her eyes from his. "It's not important."

"*Not important?* Catriona, I've heard the stories about *him*, how he's never been defeated in battle, how he leads with great strength and rules without mercy? You honestly think a man like that is going to let it slide that I let your son be taken from his home and locked him in a dungeon beneath the castle?" He turned back to face the sea, releasing her hand. "I'd kill someone who did that to a child."

Her eyes stuttered as she tried to form a coherent thought. "Is that what this is? A death wish?"

He turned a gaze of steel upon her. "If I had a death wish, I'd stay on the ship. If I leave, it will be better for everyone. Look, I know we're almost out of Mervol territory. I've been marking our progress since we left Rouen. But you're blind if you think that will stop the hunt. I used to employ that network of bounty hunters and assassins. I know how this works. Mervol operatives have already communicated to their Mandian counterparts that I'm coming their way. Now, instead of guards, we'll have bounty hunters and that's a much nastier bunch than our previous opponents. Not to mention I'm known in Mande. Believe me when I say you'll all be safer without me on board."

"Myrgen, don't…"

"I'm sorry, Captain. It's my only real chance." He looked in her eyes. "It's not like I'll be able to go with you after you leave Caratia. And I'm taking a big risk having the queen of a country where I'm wanted for treason knowing my whereabouts. Best to make sure the whereabouts are as protected as possible."

"I wouldn't give you up to him."

Myrgen nodded. "I know. I'd better go pack. Good night Captain."

He walked away and she turned to face the sea so she would not watch him go. She could already tell the deckhands had gotten the information they sought, but it didn't matter. Come nightfall, Myrgen would be gone and then, only the ever-widening tales of his time on board would be all she would have left of him.

It took a while for her to get her emotions under control and for the light breeze coming off the water to dry the few tears she had shed, but eventually, she recovered enough to walk across the deck and go to her cabin. Myrgen's light was out when she passed and she knew he wouldn't admit her, even if she knocked. She entertained, for a moment, what she would do if he did answer the door and decided that kissing him that third time would be the best thing to do to make him stay.

But then she realized she would be forsaking her faith, her family and her country if she did and she could not turn her back upon the duty with which she had been entrusted. She was the Stâpâna, the Protector of the Land and Her People. Her own desires were not a part of this.

She opened her door and went into her room. She was going to need to rest to make sure she could do what she planned to do tomorrow. She took off her coat and boots and lay in the bed and when the dream of Myrgen's kiss came to her, this time she crushed it out like a cinder.

Twenty-Eight

"Where there is a sea, there are pirates."
The Siren's Song of Callista

Signoria Xeno della Lama stepped out of the tavern and pulled his collar up on his doublet, shifting it off the embroidered, stained collar that had folded into his neck again. *I really need to get that crease pressed out. Stupid laundress.* His black velvet doublet had seen better days, no longer even having both sleeves to tie in place, and his striped pants never did get that waistband sewn on. He tightened his belt a notch to hold the pants up and noted with annoyance that he had lost more weight. He glanced at his appearance in the tavern window.

His Mervolingian style beardlette looked good on him, but his hair had thinned and gone white, against his will. He discovered his head did not actually look better shaved and now just kept to wearing a head cloth at all times, even under his hat. His headaches would hit him on occasion as if he were being mugged by his own skull and the strain of this daily concern had etched lines too deep into his skin. He was barely forty-five years and still one of the best swordsmen in Portabella. He didn't feel he deserved such bad advertising from his own body.

The sun was almost beyond the horizon but the towering cliffs that hid Portabella from the outside world tended to make the street's shadows ripen early. Cutthroats liked to harvest the fruits of this crop but Portabella was not the place for such people. For being a pirate haven, Xeno found it to be far more law-abiding than any other city he had roamed. He guessed it had something to do with the nature of the people who came here and a bit to do with the fact he didn't allow petty thievery in his city.

A couple of street walkers came out of a boarding house a few doors down and nodded greeting as they passed. The one on the left was looking especially fetching and he caught her around the waist as she tried to pass.

"Well, my precious Belladonna, how fares my favorite night flower?"

"Just as easily as ever, Signoria."

He ran his eyes down her green gown, faux-laced down the front. He knew from experience she wore nothing beneath the gown and the front was that in every sense. She didn't even bother to wear a chemise to give the hint of decorum. He preferred that, actually. He had gotten more than his fill of high-born ladies and their impairing attire when he had served the King of Mande. The fact that his own clothing still had pile in the velvet was testament to the quality of fabric in which his family had traded, but the wars and lies of the government had worn his patriotism as threadbare as his clothing. By the time he threw away his uniform, he was happy to leave his homeland for this place.

Fierrah, the other woman with Belladonna, flipped her henna-dyed red hair and slipped an arm around Xeno's. "I thought *I* was your favorite night flower? That's what you told me the other night."

He tucked his arm around the other woman's sculpted waist. "I'm certain I could find enough work for both of you ladies." He buried his bearded maw into Fierrah's neck, causing her to squeal with delight. Belladonna did likewise to him and he turned from his left hand's distraction to his right hand's. He put his face in Belladonna's cleavage and glanced up. His eyes glanced the harbor out of habit and caught on a fog rolling in from around the horn of the cape. It came fast, like it was a living thing moving across the water.

He pulled his head up and watched it move. The women turned in the direction of his newfound attention and he released them to their own feet.

"What the hell is that?" Belladonna took a step towards the docks but her companion did the opposite.

Fierrah's eyes glittered at the phenomenon. "The fog, it's racing in like a gull."

Xeno glanced at the creaking sign on the pub. "And counter to the breeze."

The trio watched as the fog filled the bay and then stopped, not touching the docks. A heavy creaking sound echoed around the cliff walls, walking in measured steps to the spectators' feet. The sounds on the street started to slow, then stop as onlookers realized something was out of place. Xeno felt a chill run through him and felt it mirrored in the two women. Fierrah's visage turned from excitement to agitation as she realized the impact of Xeno's comment. Xeno knew she was a study of the occult, based upon a Nubian housemother in the orphanage from which she came. As such, he knew she was well versed in the ways of ghosts and spirits and how to dispel them, but also feared the creatures.

"Ladies, go inside."

Fierrah nodded and stepped into the tavern behind them where Xeno noticed several onlookers had also noticed the occurrence, the bar's extreme stillness as bizarre as the fog that caused it. Xeno cast about, noting the multiple faces pressed against the glass in the area around him.

"Bella, go inside."

Belladonna's face pinched in irritation. "The hell I will. And leave you out here alone?" She stormed a look up and down his form and he decided not to push it.

"Fine. If something fires, I want you to remember I told you so."

"Yeah, like I'd be allowed to forget." She walked forward, focusing on the fog. "Is that a ship?"

A thick shadow haunted the swirling mists and the sound of heavy chains and creaking wood ricocheted off the buildings around the dock. The fog parted like cobwebs, stretching around

232

the bow of the ship before breaking in front of her black form and Xeno realized the ship was not just dark. It was pitch black. Not a light was on in the beast and seaweed hung from the tattered sails, clanking like chains. There were great holes in the sides and a sound like demons were using their voices as mortars and pestles emerged from the wounds in the wood.

The ship moved up to the empty dock at the end of the pier and sat there, creaking and clanking. The railing shot back by itself and the gangplank lowered onto the deck with no hands moving it. Steps came down the plank, deliberate and slow but still no person showed themselves. The steps came down the pier and then, at the edge of the dock, a boot emerged from nothing, followed by a person dressed all in black. Her white face was stretched thin over severe bones and her gloves hung impossibly upon her curled, skeletal hands. Seaweed was caught on her arms and legs, like she had succumbed to the depths only to fight her way back out. Even her hat was banded in seaweed, and as she turned, he saw a long strand entangled in thin ropes encircling her neck like a garrote. Her eyes were white and she turned to one of the men standing at the edge of the docks, riveted in fear.

She raised a hand and pointed at him, then moved her fingers along the watchful eyes of the frozen populace. "The blood of the fallen is on your hands." Then to woman. "You poisoned your brother to get with his wife." To another man. "You left your wife and children to become a whore to feed your carnal appetite."

The people she spoke to shied away from her as she revealed their sins to the open air and as she turned her attention upon Belladonna, Xeno stepped between the specter and the woman, letting her gesture fall upon him instead.

"What do you want?"

The creature cocked her head at Xeno, unblinking eyes watching his own green ones. Belladonna started to whisper something but he shushed her over his shoulder.

The monster came closer and he smelled death and algae. "You. You were a soldier. Fought the sand riders. You were betrayed by your own people. They sought you out, brought their cannons to bear. All they wanted was your death."

"They met their own. What do you want?"

"Not entirely by your hands. The shot from behind. The thunk of wet skull against your chest. Blood mingled with blood. Shot through for you. Life debt owed."

"Life debt paid, a few years later. I saved her First Mate. She called us even."

"Then why do you mark this as your sin?"

Xeno took a breath to answer but the smell of decay caught him off guard and he coughed and gagged. The spirit turned her milky gaze upon Belladonna, who gasped and backed up.

"Bella," Xeno coughed, "get away."

"Yes, Bella, get away. Get away from your sins before they are exposed to your lover." The creature turned her gaze back to Xeno and he stood, his chest heaving from the wracking cough. "You can't afford the penance."

"What penance?" Belladonna's voice didn't crack under the pressure of this encounter, which impressed Xeno. He was not so sure he was faring as well.

"Atonement for your sins, soldier. Atonement for theirs as well. You have chosen to own this place. Time to pay, if you want to keep your soul. Otherwise," the ghoulish figure cast her gaze upon the buildings, "perhaps it is time to collect these spirits for their final reward." She looked at him again. "You have until midnight to pay your soul's ransom."

The figure turned away and walked slowly towards the ship at the end. Belladonna stepped forward, her body shaking but her voice steady. "What if we don't have that much gold to pay?"

The ghost stopped and turned back towards her. "Foolish child. The soul is not weighed in ore. You must commit that which is important to life. Each person's ransom is different."

She turned back towards her ship and stepped onto the dock. Her boot disappeared, followed by the rest of her and the sound of footsteps echoed up the gangplank again.

Belladonna swallowed, pale and waxy. Xeno bent, leaning on his knees. The foul smell had overwhelmed his senses and he felt one of his devastating headaches threatening to add to the mix. He was starting to get sensitive to the light reflecting off the fog, a sure sign he needed to get into a dark room and lie down. He definitely didn't have time for this ailment. It took a moment for his will to finally take control of his breathing.

"Belladonna, get inside. Tell everyone to stay off the dock until this thing leaves."

"What are we going to do?"

Xeno swallowed the taste of death the specter left behind, recovering his posture, resisting the urge to sully his streets with spit. His eyes watched the ship, trying to figure out what was nagging at him, and he stroked his beard between his thumb and forefinger, pinching it at the end. "Nothing. This thing is bluffing. If it were going to make us atone for our sins, it would have just taken that retribution. This is a con."

Catriona walked back on board and looked out over the streets of the town. Octavius came up to her and folded his arms. "How do you think it went?"

"Not bad. People wear their sins on their faces when the supernatural shows up on their doorstep. We have one problem, however. Xeno della Lama is down there."

"Xeno? Here?"

"Apparently. Judging from his attitude and position, I think he might be the one in charge, in fact."

"Did he recognize you?"

"It didn't appear so." She looked at her First Mate. "He remembered you though."

"Why would he remember me and not you?"

"Maybe I didn't look like myself. Where's Myrgen?"

"In his room. Estelle says she thinks he's packing."

Catriona nodded, returning her gaze to the docks. "Really? I thought he would have been all packed by now."

Octavius stepped in front of her. "You mean you knew about this?"

"He told me last night."

"And you're letting him go?"

"It's his choice, Octavius. I can't make him stay."

"Yes, you can. Just say, 'Stay.' He wants to be here, Catriona."

"No, he doesn't. In fact, he knows he's causing us trouble by being here. He explained it to me last night, after the meeting. Just getting away from Mervolingia isn't enough. There will be bounty hunters and we won't be able to trade with any ports as long as he's on the ship. That's our livelihood, Octavius, for this entire crew."

"This ship is going to be in dry dock for the rest of the season, Catriona. We're not going to be trading again until after the winter."

Catriona let her ire show in her eyes. "Don't you think I know that? That *he* knows that? He wants away from here and I won't hold him against his will." She looked away again. "Like he said, it's not like he can go with me after the season is over."

"You're still going to Alexander? Didn't Myrgen," He stopped, frustrated. "Didn't he talk to you?"

"About what? Yes, he talked to me about a lot of things, like how arrogant I am and how stupid it is to marry Alexander, and how dangerous it is for me to be near him and a bunch of other things but he never said or did anything that would make it necessary for him to stay."

"Did you?"

She blinked. "No. It would have been inappropriate to do so."

Octavius shook his head and held up two fingers. "That's two now." He walked away.

Catriona nodded. "I know." *I know. First Alistair, now Myrgen. Believe me, Octavius, I'm getting as tired of it as you are.*

Myrgen heard a knock at the door and straightened up, trying to figure out what to do. If it was Octavius or Thessius or one of the other crewmen, he would have to explain why he was wearing all the clothes he owned. If it was Catriona, it meant it was time to leave. He relished neither prospect.

"Myrgen?"

Octavius' voice slipped through the door and Myrgen swallowed. "Come in."

Octavius opened the door and Myrgen went back to rummaging through the footlocker for any other souvenirs of his time here.

"What the hell are you doing?"

Myrgen didn't look up. "Making sure I have everything. And before you decide to have a stern talk with me about how wonderful she is or how much trouble she's worth, understand I'm not doing this because of her. I'm doing it because it's the right thing to do."

"How can you possibly think that?"

Myrgen looked up at his friend. "Because I've walked a pretty dark and unpleasant road for a very long time. She has given me the desire to be a better person than I was, to be worthy of someone like her. Prior to this, I just stole wives or lovers that I wanted, but she's better than that. She deserves someone better."

"And just how long do you plan on spending becoming a better person?"

Myrgen put both hands on the footlocker, exasperated. "*As long as it takes, man.*" He pushed off the locker. "If I can work this out in time to rescue her from herself, then the forces that are keeping us apart right now will step back and put us together. But everywhere I turn, we are both finding signs that this isn't the right thing to do right now. I'm trying to walk a different path, Octavius, a path that doesn't end in my soul being eaten like that man back in St. Andrew. I've been in the dark where he is, and I never want to be there again." He returned to his rummaging. "Not while I can stop it."

"And getting left behind at a pirate port is the means to your salvation?"

"It beats getting hunted down by bounty hunters in Mande."

Octavius looked about to object, but then he seemed to understand Myrgen's point. He dropped his hands to his sides. "So, is this where you'll be then?"

"Probably. It's a really safe port."

"You and I have whole different definitions of the word 'safe'."

Myrgen smiled and walked over to his friend. "Don't worry about me. I'll be fine."

"Yeah, where have I heard that before?" The two men embraced and Octavius left Myrgen to his packing.

Belladonna stumbled into the tavern in front of Xeno, the entire tavern populace scared or nervous. Their fear shone in their eyes, was etched onto their faces. She had been far closer to the monster, and they were more scared than she. Xeno walked over to the bar and asked for an ale. Belladonna went to the window to stand next to Fierrah.

"What did it say to you?" Fierrah's face was pale and the dirt on it stood out, black on white.

"It said I didn't want it to reveal my sins like it had the others, that I couldn't do the penance."

"By the Saints, what have you done in your life?" Fierrah's eyes were wide and she looked like she wanted to step away from her friend. Several other tavern patrons were near the window and they turned their attention on her.

"Nothing to warrant this. Regardless, the spirit told Xeno it would take his soul in payment for the sins of this town if he did not pay by midnight."

The Blacksmith glanced at Xeno, keeping his voice low. "What does he plan to do about it?"

Belladonna folded her arms across her chest. "Nothing."

The people around her grew quiet and she knew what they felt. He was saying he would give his soul so they did not have to pay with their lives. Maria, the barmaid, frowned. "Won't that mean he'll die?"

"Yes, I imagine it will."

They stood in silence a moment, watching the strange fog. Then Belladonna took in a breath. "I'm going to pay the ransom. I don't want to meet whatever is going to take this place over if he's gone."

Over the course of the next couple hours, every crewman came by to give his regards in private to Myrgen and it wasn't until nearly midnight that the visitor he dreaded the most knocked at last upon his door.

Catriona opened his door and poked her head in. "Myrgen, it's time."

"Thanks."

He wondered if she was going to say anything else but she didn't and he had a hard time thinking that was a bad thing. *Honestly, what's she really going to say?*

He slung his satchel across his chest and looked around one last time at the home he had grown to love. He stepped out and closed the door behind him. The crew was scurrying about, being very quiet and solemn. Myrgen looked out at the town and saw very little activity. He went over to Octavius.

"Is this plan of hers working? I don't see any supplies."

"It'll work. See?" Octavius pointed to a dark alley where a man poked his head out into the lamp light. He stepped out and blew out the lamp illuminating the area between his alley and the dock. Once the light was gone, he brought over a barrel he shimmied into place. He looked around again and then scurried off into the dark. Octavius nodded to the deckhands on the dock and they slipped out and retrieved the barrel back under the veil Estelle had laid down.

Myrgen was sad he was going to miss saying goodbye to Estelle but he knew she was concentrating on maintaining her illusion. The success here depended upon two things: This illusion and their guilt. Myrgen hoped there would be enough supplies to get them through.

His way was now opened thanks to the first donor. There was a clear, dark path to slip in to and no more excuses. He slapped Octavius on the shoulder and went slowly down the plank. The measured steps enhanced the illusion, according to Catriona, so everyone was to walk slow and scary. Myrgen felt a little foolish but if it meant the ship got restocked, then he wasn't about to argue. He walked to the edge of the illusion and looked back one last time, then moved on into the shadows.

He ducked into the alley and moved around behind the one of the buildings. Another man was on the other side of the alley with a crate marked "eggs". Myrgen could hear the tink of the glass jars inside.

"Hey, you see anyone else out there?" The man's eyes were wide with fear.

Myrgen glanced back down the alley to the dock, then shook his head. The guy stepped out and was shaking so badly, Myrgen felt sure he was going to drop the things. "Here, let me help you."

The man looked about to protest but then a moan came out from the ship and he turned back to accept Myrgen's offer. He set the crate on the ground and grabbed the rope handle on one side while Myrgen took the other. They walked to the dock and Myrgen saw at last exactly why the whole town was scared to death. He swallowed, impressed by the complexity of the illusion. He decided to help the men out a bit and when they put the crate down, he gave it a push with his foot into the illusion. The crate disappeared and the man fell backwards in his hurry to escape. Myrgen followed suit and took the opportunity to look down the street at what might be a good choice to stay for the rest of the night. He saw a full and bright tavern and a brothel, but no good choices.

He slipped back into the alley and glanced around. He was tempted to stake out this area and see what supplies they got but that was just begging for trouble. Instead, he looked around for a back entrance into one of the shops but everything was locked up tight. He walked behind the buildings, ducking into doorways or alleys when he heard the squeak of hinges and soon, he was on the outskirts of town, walking near the cliff wall. Cut into the rock was a series of stairs and he looked up to see how far they went. From the looks of it, they went all the way up, but he didn't dare try to scale them in the dark. He sat down at the foot of the stairs and leaned against the stone.

Okay, Land. I'm here. Now, tell me what I'm supposed to do again?

He looked up at the stairs again and thought about it. *If I am seen coming down these stairs, it won't be assumed I came in on the ship.* He stood and took his first step up the cliff face, slowly putting his faith in the stone beneath his feet. The higher he got, the more faith he had to have because he realized just how defensible these stairs really were. There was no place to rest, no landing, no railing and nothing to stop you from falling a hundred feet to the sandy beach. He paused at about halfway up and leaned on his knees to catch his breath. He looked out at the town and saw the ghostly spires of the *Enigma* swaying in the harbor.

He looked down at his hands and then up at the climb ahead of him. He moved on up the stairs, using his hand on the rock face. He realized there were handholds in the rock and that made him feel better. As late as it was, he was beginning to think climbing up here was a bad idea. He didn't need to discover his exhaustion at this level but when it came down to it, he was more than halfway up now. He dug into his seafaring muscles and moved on up the wall. It occurred to him that there might be guards at the top of this climb but he decided when he got up there, that would be a good time to deal with such things.

He stopped again and looked back at town. Climbing the stairs was starting to give him cramps in his calves but the view was such that he could now look down upon the entirety of the illusion Estelle was perpetrating. It was still a frightening sight, even from this distance, and he was in on the ruse. He looked back at the challenge before him and moved forward, wondering if being in on a con of this magnitude was risking his lighter pathway. He took reassurance from the fact he still kept finding hand holds in the rock face, as if they were put there for him and not carved alongside the stairs.

He wondered if he would ever be able to forget Catriona but then decided he never would. He wanted very much for what he had said to Octavius to be true, but he wasn't sure it was. He didn't know if he was going to be done in time to rescue Catriona from herself. It all depended upon the great forces at play. They had wanted him on his own, he was on his own. *Lead on, oh great overseers.*

He finally came to the top of the cliff and he crawled over and stretched out on the cool grass, giving his body a chance to rest. His calves were sore as hell and it hurt to breathe but he felt satisfied that he had made it. It was as if he had been given a challenge and he had not let that challenge get by him. Hell, it wasn't even that hard. He relaxed as he felt the grass under his back and listened to the sound of the waves crashing on the shore. He also figured he'd be able to watch the ship sail away from up here, possibly even see her to the Fingers of Mande. He might stay up here all day, watching her go.

The look of Catriona's hair tumbling in the breeze as they sailed on through the night washed over him like a wave. He had almost kissed her on deck, that night with the whale. It didn't matter that it was a spell. None of it mattered because the Powers That Be had put them in each other's way. She could have left him behind in Patras, but she hadn't. He could have stayed in St. Andrew or let them leave him in St. Marguerite but instead he fought to be with her. It seemed almost odd that, after all they'd been through to be together, here, in this black port, they had chosen to part ways.

In the shadows, behind a lie…

Book Two

"Observe your enemies, for they first find your faults."
The Siren's Song of Callista

Twenty-Nine

"The old sailor used the tool the old carpenter made."
The Siren's Song of Callista

Gwen awoke to the sound of shuffling outside her window, coupled with her brother's and Alexander's voices in the alley outside. She got out of bed, glancing around the room in the early morning light. She went over to her window and peeked through the curtains, not wanting to alert onlookers to the fact she was watching. She knew her brother well, and knew he would be on the lookout for watchers.

She saw James and Alexander carrying a limp man between them, like a friend who had drunk too much. He was wearing James' doublet and Alexander's pants and that seemed to be it. No shoes or stockings, no hat and, apparently, no shirt. She could see bandages across his shoulder when the morning light managed to spook the shadows away from the gaps where the sleeves tied on to the doublet. Sure enough, James was glancing around like they were doing something shifty.

She got dressed in her plaid coat, wishing for not the first time that she could wear the black coat like Catriona, to better hide in shadows. Plaid wasn't subtle. Her boots were on in seconds and she scurried out the door. She left through the kitchens in the back, with a passing nod to Ce'Nedra and Saiban. She ducked down the alleyway that bordered their rooms and cast about for where James and Alexander had been taking the body. She didn't know what had befallen the man, but she suspected her brother had something to do with it. Otherwise, why would he be helping Alexander when, the night before, he had been so adamantly against the man?

She caught sight of them turning a corner and followed at a distance, keeping to the alleys where possible. Catriona had taught her a great deal about shadowing someone. She employed everything she could remember since she was following her notoriously paranoid brother. She finally saw them going into a building and was surprised to find it was the local church. She knew James was not very religious by Mervol standards, his own beliefs in the Fae being superseded by a life chosen on the sea.

Alexander must have suggested it, but that doesn't explain why he asked James for help after last night. Why not ask Saiban?

James came back out a few minutes later and looked around, then came over to her.

"You saw me?" She was disappointed and it showed in her voice.

"Naturally. Listen," he glanced around a bit, "I think I want you to go home now."

"What? Why?"

"Because that man you saw us bringing here was severely… damaged. The sort of person that would do something like that is not someone I want you to run into. I want you safe."

Gwen bit her lip and frowned. "James, I'm quite capable of taking care of myself."

"Undoubtedly, as adept as you are at not being seen when following someone." He put his hands on her shoulders. "Look, I've got this. You have a fiancé and a life to return to. Let me handle this and I'll let you know what happens." He raised his finger and pointed it at her. "I'll be back for you. Go home."

He kissed her forehead, then turned her on her heel and pushed her toward the inn before turning back to the church. He never even looked back at her indignant face she put on just for him. Nevertheless, she still felt sure he knew she was displaying it. She shook her head and stormed back towards the inn. She was going to have to travel overland to Caratia, apparently. James wouldn't allow her on the ship now that he had told her to go home and he would be on the lookout for stowaways, having talked extensively about doing it when they were growing up. It was annoying having a brother who knew her every move.

She stomped up the stairs and grabbed the knob on her door, ready to start banging things about in her anger, when she saw Alexander's door was not quite shut. Apparently, the man they were taking to the church had come from Alexander's room. James would have closed his door if his arms had been free. In fact, he probably thought he had. She slipped over to the door and went inside like it was found treasure.

The room showed signs of several activities. The fire was fading but had been tended all night, judging from the lack of wood by the hearth now. Grymalkin's medical kit was out and open, next to the bed, many of its supplies diminished. He was completely out of bandages. She was quite familiar with his kit, having watched him care for Catriona for years. It would take a lot of wounds to bleed out his supplies this thoroughly. For all those wounds though, there was no blood. Nary a drop, even on the bed. There was urine smell, but no blood. She glanced through the kit. Alexander's burn salve was missing. She looked around and saw it on the side table.

Maybe the wounds were all burns? That would explain James' over- protectiveness. There were no flakes of burnt skin and no smell of burnt flesh, so it must have been acid burns or something toxic. She shuddered, unable to repel the image of a man, scarred by acid, stumbling into this room and falling to the floor. No wonder James had wanted her to leave. She glanced around for the man's clothes. He had been wearing borrowed things, so the damage to his own clothing must have been extensive. If she could see the burns, she might be able to tell what acid made them. When no extraneous clothing sprung immediately to view, she dropped to the floor to look under the furniture.get the church

Under the bed, she found a long Mervol coat of black and grabbed it. She had never seen Grymalkin wear black so she figured it must be the coat of the injured man. She picked it up but it was completely undamaged. Now she was *very* confused. The man seemed to be bandaged and James had said he was burned, but there was no blood, no smell and no damage to his clothing. She frowned.

James was lying to get rid of her, and she wasn't about to stand for it.

James went back into the small church, looking for Alexander. The priest they had encountered had offered to help them get Duncan to a room with a bed where people seeking sanctuary were taken. James had been certain he had seen Gwen's golden hair darting between alleyways, her blue plaid coat dress all but shouting her whereabouts. The girl had no talent at all for subterfuge. Now that she was on her way, he had a few minutes to devote to his friend's condition. He was still going to have to pack her things personally, put her physically on a horse and check his ship from top to bottom before sailing to make sure she was on her way home. At least, right then, he knew her pattern was still in sorting out the details of how precisely to defy him.

He had no idea if his suggestion about the holy ground would work, but with the contact with an Infernal object a few hours ago, James wanted to know if the man could still go into a Church. If his dealings with the demons had ruined his chances with Heaven, James wanted proof to give to Gwen. He couldn't afford to have her inevitable defiance result in her injury or death. Mervolingia was strongly Augustinian with a secret population of Emilianites. There had been a civil war here a few years back, but James didn't really know the details behind it. Seemed to be done now, so he paid it no mind. Wasn't really his religion anyway.

He went to the alcove he had seen the priest and Alexander enter and hoped to find the room they had taken Duncan. Instead, he found a stairway. There was no other place to go this direction so he made his way up the stairs and listened for voices. He heard men talking down the hallway and saw a light coming from under one mostly closed door. He pushed it open and stopped, shielding his eyes with his hand.

Duncan was laid out on a small pallet with a thin straw mattress. The bandage on his arm had been removed and James could see Duncan's fire-ravaged flesh. The skin was warped and red, pocked with holes where the fat had boiled away beneath the skin, causing it to burn through, consuming flesh and hair to leave a desecrated wasteland where nothing would grow again. It looked like he had blocked a burning stick with his arm which had then lit him on fire for his efforts.

Alexander was on his knees beside the bed, holding the damaged arm, his eyes closed. The light in the room was not from a lantern or fireplace or window, but from Alexander himself. A holy mark on the wall in a sunbeam seemed to be directing the flow of light into the King, and he seemed to be directing that flow into the arm he was holding. The light played across the skin and where it touched, it smoothed away the damage, causing the arm to become whole again. The light dimmed and James looked at the King with new eyes.

Alexander looked up and saw him in the doorway. "James, you were right."

The priest rocked back and forth a moment, praising the Saints for their intervention, then stood and went to the doorway, swapping places with James.

"How did you do it?" James looked carefully at Duncan's arm but could find no trace of the injury that had dominated his appearance moments before.

"As soon as I set foot in the church, I felt stronger, like an infinite energy was available for me to use." Alexander looked down at Duncan's intact arm and smiled. "It was incredible. This wound looked like the worst, so I tried it first."

James, remembering the flayed genitals, silently disagreed. "Have you tried the others yet?"

Alexander shook his head. "No, but I'm not tired. I think I can do it all at once."

James glanced at Duncan's face. "You might want to do so before he wakes up then. Leave all this as a nightmare."

"Good idea."

Alexander placed his hands upon Duncan's chest and closed his eyes again. Light filled the room as feet ran down the hallway towards them. James figured it was the priest returning with other priests. This was not the sort of thing they would want to miss. Light flowed into Duncan's body, leaking through the bandages and moving throughout the man. James looked away and saw two priests, an altar boy and a cleaning lady in the hallway, looking into the room. If Alexander had been worried he was recognizable as King, he was going to be doubly so as the King Touched by the Saints to Heal.

James rubbed the back of his head. *Provided, of course, they don't burn him as a witch.*

Duncan gasped and sat up, his eyes bright with golden light. Alexander took his hands from the man and fell backward. James reached out and caught his shirt at the collar before he hit the stone floor. Duncan blinked and looked at the people in the room. "Where am I?"

The priest who had brought them here spoke up. "You are in St. Andrew's church."

Duncan looked around the room and saw Alexander unconscious, James supporting him. He looked down at his arm and saw the damage was gone, then looked quickly into the pants he was wearing and smiled. He turned to Alexander. "He healed me? He really healed me?"

James nodded.

The woman in the doorway muttered to herself out loud. "It's a miracle."

James looked around and saw the chair in the room, a simple armless number that had no padding. He tried to get Alexander's dead weight into it but couldn't get the leverage. "Could someone… help…"

Duncan leapt out of the bed and took Alexander's arm, helping James get to his feet. Duncan scooped Alexander up and put him on the bed instead, then knelt beside him. Alexander's eyes fluttered a bit and he opened them, looking around.

"What happened?"

James smiled. "You passed out."

"Ah. I must have been wrong about… it not… tiring me." He closed his eyes and fell back into unconsciousness.

James stood and looked at Duncan. "Can you stay with him?"

Duncan nodded. "I'll not leave his side."

"Thanks." He brushed past the crowd gathering in the doorway and left for the Inn.

"You lied to me."

Gwen folded her arms and frowned as her brother returned to the room. He looked at her, unconcerned about her wrath.

"Okay. About what?"

"About that man being burned. He wasn't burned. There's no smell of burnt flesh, by fire *or* acid, no blood, no anything. Even his *clothes* are intact. So you just want to get rid of me so you can get rid of Alexander. And I'm not going to let you. He's not a monster."

"Yeah, I know." He looked at the coat, picking it up to inspect it.

Gwen worked her mouth for a second, but her voice was apparently doing other things at the moment. "Huh?"

"I just watched him heal Duncan through the power of Heaven."

Gwen noticed the change in her brother's voice. There was curiosity as well as concern. "Is this the same Duncan who gave Alex the amulet?"

"That's what I'm looking for." He turned the coat inside out and saw something. "Here, there's a symbol sewn into the lining, near the heart."

Gwen came over and looked. "I don't know what that is."

James turned the symbol more to the light to get a better look. It was subtle, black embroidery on black material. "It looks Augustinian." He looked outside. "Duncan was a sailor. I would have sworn he worshiped Callista." He looked back at the symbol. "I saw a symbol like that in the room where Alexander healed Duncan. Get packed. You're still going home." He left the room with the coat before she could recover.

James walked into the church as three other people he didn't recognize ran past him. He went up the stairs and saw four more people in the hallway outside the room. He went over to the priest.

"Father, what's happening?"

The priest looked at James and beamed. "His Majesty is resting and his patient has taken up guard by his bedside, as is fitting of a man whose life was just saved. The word of this is spreading throughout the town."

James frowned. This was definitely going to impair Alexander's attempts to leave. He nodded to the room. "That symbol on the wall was glowing when he was healing. What is it?"

"That is the symbol of St. Brigit, patron saint of healers. A woven square with four limbs, symbolizing how everything is connected within the body. It is only appropriate that she would smile upon our King."

"Uh, yeah. Very. So, there's a symbol sewn into this coat. Can you tell me whose it is?"

The priest took the coat and looked at the symbol. "It's probably St. Christopher, the patron of travelers." He walked over to a lantern on the wall, its scant light still chasing away a few shadows. "Many people put his symbol in their traveling clothes…" He furrowed his brow, confused. "That's odd." He looked at James. "This is the symbol of St. Giles."

"Who's he the patron of?"

"Well, he's invoked against night terrors and the supernatural. Monsters." He raised his eyebrows and handed the coat back to James. "That sheds a different light upon that man's injuries, I believe. Those burns were more likely to be of an infernal nature. He must have encountered those foul Fae on his travels as well. St. Giles would be the only protection against such unholy magic."

"I see." James looked at Duncan. Alexander wasn't a Shadowalker.

Duncan was.

Thirty

"Better to hear the order from the Captain than the cook."
The Siren's Song of Callista

Alexander opened his eyes and looked around the barely lit room. He was in the prayer nave in his room at the palace in Patras, a dozen or so votives flickering in the darkness. The blue glass holders were set in filigreed gold casings which allowed the tiny flames to be patriotic as well as holy. He did not remember returning to the capital city, but he did remember passing out in the small room at the church in St. Andrew. Perhaps he had been returned home?

He raised his head and looked at the small, sparse room he used daily at the palace. He had always come in here to pray that he would be reunited with Catriona and, until recently, had believed the prayers were a futile habit. But then she had walked out of this very darkness at a time when he had truly needed her.

That was a few ten-days ago, having just spent time talking with Charles before his planned "death". Charles had asked her to come to Alexander, to explain why she could not accept his marriage proposal, but it was unnecessary. Alexander had been told by Catriona herself when Nicolai returned to their lives. Her sense of nostalgia had made her return to his arms.

Alexander's sense of nostalgia drove him to have Nicolai slain via Writ of Destruction at Duncan's hands. He had called it a matter of national security but Alexander knew the truth. Unfortunately, so did Duncan.

It occurred to Alexander he had yet to confess this sin and seek forgiveness. Perhaps that was why he was here.

He wished, at that moment, he had a priest or confessor in the palace, but he knew of no one he trusted enough to confess such a dire transgression. In all his years as a Prince, he had never done anything he felt the need to confess or be forgiven for, and thus, was actually at a loss for the next step. The Archbishop of Patras was the King's Confessor by law and custom. It was assumed only one of such high status in the Church could know the trials a King went through on a daily basis, and could offer proper counsel. As Prince, he had never seen the man. He imagined, if the first month of his reign were any indication, that he had better get familiar with the process.

He breathed in, hoping to catch a hint of Catriona's exotic scent still lingering in the air but instead smelled stone. He had never been one for burning incense at his prayer altar, but he didn't recall the smell of stone despite the room being made of it. An echo behind him caught his attention and he felt his heart leap.

"Catriona?"

He turned to look behind him and realized he was not where he thought he was. A large chamber was on the other side of an open archway, small candles flickering in smaller numbers just enough to show Alexander he was not in the palace as he believed. Shadows dominated the room, the votives in the stands merely illustrating the vastness of the chamber. There were hundreds of stands, each with a single candle lit in the grouping. *Is this the church in St. Andrew?*

"Is anybody there?"

He stood from the small prayer altar where he had been kneeling and walked over to the archway to look beyond. He realized the shadows were interfering with his vision, keeping the truth from his eyes. The echo indicated the room was huge and the line of candles indicated it was circular. There was something familiar about the room, but it flitted away from his grasp, leaving it undefined. He stepped forward and encountered a gate of iron bars which clanged as he bumped into them. The surprise presence of the bars startled him and he walked over to the votives and fetched one to examine the gate.

Ornate yet substantial, the bars were wrought iron, twisting decoratively while sporting the great fleur-de-lis of Mervolingia in the center. He looked carefully but there was no catch or hinge. He looked behind him and saw no way out of the prayer nave at all, except through this archway. A light wind rustled the candle flames in the main chamber, bringing with it the smell of rain. Alexander fought the urge to be afraid.

"Hello?"

He reached for his dagger to tap on the bars but he was not wearing it. In fact, he was surprised to find he was without all his accoutrements, clad only in a simple shirt without so much as laces at the neck, breeches without a codpiece, hose or stockings, and simple shoes instead of the boots he preferred. He was even denied gloves. He used the metal case of the votive to tap the bars.

"Is anybody there?"

The breeze picked up, and he noticed the smell of a coming storm. Shadows danced around the room, mocking him in his captivity. He raised the votive in his hand to inspect the tops of the bars. They went into the air about ten feet and then bent, attaching to the wall. No way out there. The swirling shadows made him uncomfortable, so he went over to the bank of votives and looked around. A box of long thin sticks for lighting the candles was sitting on the shelf. He pulled one out and used the light from the one in his hand to light the rest of the bank.

The extra light filled the room and banished the shadows from his immediate area. The lack of darkness in the nave made him feel better immediately, and he drew the parallel between this situation and the one with the amulet. His desire for Catriona had caused him to abandon reason in light of an easy fix, but he now knew he was deluded into thinking he would be immune. Power was dangerous and this sort of thing was the very reason he never wanted it. He knew his heart. He knew what he would do for her, what he would do to gain her, and in the light of this prayer nave, how deep his obsession ran.

He looked around and noticed the lights in the next room had brightened as well. Someone had lit several other candles in the next room from the look of it. Closer inspection revealed the chamber to be decorated with dozens of statues. Each one seemed to be different, like it represented a specific individual. Most of them were still hidden in shadow, their identities remaining obscure, but he could almost make out several of the statues. He felt as if he should know these people, like they were important. He needed more light.

He walked over to the box of sticks and grabbed several, lighting them off a votive. He reached through the bars and flicked his wrist, scattering the sticks across the floor towards the closer effigies. One of the sticks managed to land in a votive in the bank in front of a statue and lit the candle. Alexander was surprised to see that the additional light was enough to make out the features of the woman represented.

Saint Bridget, patron saint of healers.

Alexander blinked. *Is this a dream?*

No. This was a chance for forgiveness. Who better to hear his confession than his own patron Saint?

"Saint Brigit, I…" He looked down at his hands, humbled and without shielding, without the trappings of regality. "I don't know how to begin. I killed a man, one whose wife I coveted. I know I'm not supposed to covet another man's wife, but she was mine first! He stole her from me." His anger, his feeling of injustice blocked his vision for a moment and he noticed one of the votives faded and flickered out.

"What? I'm not wrong. He left, he went to another woman. Am I not entitled to fight for that which matters to me? Am I not allowed to be happy?"

The statue lost a couple more votives, giving the shadows purchase again in the alcove. Adrenaline shot through his trunk, triggering his flight response but he was trapped in this place. The demons of James' warnings started to slink around the edges of the statues.

"No! Wait! Don't leave me."

The flames continued to snuff, one by one and Alexander panicked.

"I'm sorry! I was wrong! I repent!" He dropped to his knees. "I repent. I killed him, I killed Nicolai to get his wife, and continuing to pursue her is just as wrong." He looked at his bare hands. "But I love her. I have always loved her."

The failing flame flared for a moment, not yet extinguishing.

"I am lost, St. Brigit. I need your guidance. I need Heaven to help my path. On my own, I have gone so far away, I will never redeem myself. What can I do?"

Her votives flickered, dancing, waiting.

"I fear so much, St. Brigit. I killed Elizabeth and although I was entitled to do so for the sake of the kingdom, Krakte will go to war. My people will die without the armies of Caratia to come to our aid. She's more than just the woman I love, she's a strategic stronghold. With her at my side, Caratia would…"

Another candle snuffed.

"What?" He looked out at the statues. "What? I cannot even have her as an ally?"

Snuff.

"Why? It's not like she's the enemy."

A candle, burning very low, flared to life.

Alexander blinked. "She's the enemy?"

Flare.

Alexander rolled his eyes. "Of course. Land-worshippers. You fear if she were around, more of Heaven's subjects would go to the Land."

Flare.

"But that's ridiculous. The people of Mervolingia are loyal to the Church."

Flicker.

Another light came up, showing the features of St. Michael. Alexander held the bars. "St. Michael?" The sound of it aloud reminded him of his part in the massacre years before. He and his mother brow-beat Charles into declaring war upon the Emilianites, manipulated by Catherine to believe they were responsible for hurting Catriona. The truth was revealed too late and thousands were slaughtered.

"What does that have to do with her? If anything, had she been by my side, Mother never could have tricked us."

The votives on St. Michael went out, leaving just Brigit alight. Then other votives brightened, illuminating St. Marguerite.

He winced, his most recent folly all too fresh in his mind. "Yes, yes. I understand. I handled that wrong." He lifted his head, his voice a bit desperate. "But I've learned what I did wrong. I know I can't trick her or force her. But, you see, I don't need to. She gave herself to me."

The votives on St. Marguerite flared.

"*She did!* It was that thief Myrgen who tricked her away from me. Had he not…"

All the votives around St. Marguerite flared, looking like a bonfire. He released the bars, shielding his eyes and face from the heat and light. He cried out as the flames grew closer and everything around him seemed to catch fire. He fled from the bars, hiding to the side. The votives in this room flared as well, catching fire and he curled into a ball as the flames licked the ground.

James returned to Gwen's room and she stood, rubbing her hand. "Well, what's the story?"

"It turns out the symbol is one invoked against monsters. Alexander wasn't the one who might be a Shadowalker. It was Duncan."

"Duncan? Who's Duncan?"

"An old shipmate of mine. He was on the *Raven* when I took on Catriona a couple years back."

"What's he doing in St. Andrew?"

James knitted his brow. "It's a sea port, Gwen. I saw him yesterday and we chatted. He might have been trying to find me when he was hurt and found Alexander instead. I'm not sure what he was doing but it seems as though Duncan was trying to get away from the influence of the amulet. Alexander mentioned a 'Power of Somethingorother' that protected him, or he thought protected him. Maybe Duncan knew about this and gave it to him, thinking he would be safe from the corruptive influence. I gotta admit a gift that would allow uninhibited travel would really benefit a man like that king."

Gwen noticed a change in her brother. "So, do you like him now or something?"

Let's just say Duncan's faith in him was not unwarranted. The fact is that Duncan was a dead man from those injuries. I don't know how he survived them, but I have a greater respect for his strength. Strangely, all of his wounds were in stages of healing." He shrugged, glancing out the window. "Hardly matters now. Alexander healed him at the church right before I came here."

Gwen looked at him, brow furrowing. "He treated him? Why did you take him to the church? What was wrong with here?"

"No, he didn't *treat* him. He did that here. He *healed* him. Completely." He looked out the window again. "Believe me, you have no idea just how impressive that truly is. You didn't see the man's injuries."

Gwen refused to be sidetracked, a common tactic of her brother's. "No, tell me what you mean by 'healed him'."

James shrugged. "There were injuries, the king touched them and glowed, then the injuries were gone and Duncan was awake." He snapped his fingers. "Just like that." He looked back at his sister, turning to lean on the window sill. "So, though I have no real loyalty to her myself, you are a good friend of Catriona's, right?"

Gwen nodded.

"What's the story with these two? He was desperate to be with her last night and just as desperate not to lose you from his group. I think he plans to use you to get to her."

"Well, he said he wanted my help to get her to listen to him. He can persuade her if she'll talk to him."

"Yeah, he seemed to know just what to say to me. Got my suspicious nature out of bed when he did."

"It has me nervous as well. I don't like the thought of him winning her. I'm beginning to think that having Myrgen around her is a benefit instead of the nightmare I used to think." She hugged herself against the thought of shadows getting to Catriona. "I don't think I trust him anymore, James."

"Luckily, I never did." He looked out the window. "At least, not yet. What he did at the church though, it changes a man's mind."

"So what's your plan?"

"I'm not sure yet. It's still forming. Look," he turned his attention back to her, "why don't you take off and get on back home? The presence of that amulet means Shadowwalkers and I want you as far away from that as possible. With the king performing healing miracles in front of Augustinian witnesses, word is spreading throughout town and that's the sort of zealotry that causes an Inquisition."

Gwen didn't like the fact he was trying to get rid of her, though she very much understood the danger he feared. She had heard of the Inquisition and its intolerance of other beliefs, but its reign had ended a hundred years ago. Was it really possible it could be restored? "What are you going to do?"

"I don't know, and although I'm not her friend or family or courting her, I have respect for your Captain. I'm not going to let this plot just happen. Not if I can interfere. With any luck, I'll be able to stop it in time." He leaned over and gave his sister a pat on the back. "But that means I need to be a part of this conspiracy, not babysitting you so get out of here. I want you gone by the time he comes back. Even if the amulet belonged to Duncan and not your illustrious regent, there's still shadowy dealings going on. You need to be not here."

Gwen looked at the church outside and nodded. "Be careful, all right?"

"Like I'm dancing on the head of a pin."

"And I don't need babysitting."

"Of course not."

Gwen thought about the way Catriona had felt all winter and her heart felt heavier from the worry settling there. She had wanted so much to be by his side, to go to him, and she had restrained herself. Though that was probably for the best now, Alexander was a very convincing orator. "He's going to want to go to Caratia, to follow her, especially now that the amulet's gone. James, I need to ask a favor of you. Don't go fast. Give me time to get there overland. Please."

"Why?"

She glanced down at her hands. "Because she deserves to know what he's done and that he's coming for her. I don't want to endanger her or the *Enigma* by letting him surprise her. I owe it to her not to let that happen."

"What are you going to do?"

"I don't know."

James tilted his head. "You could send a Fae to warn her."

Gwen covered her teeth with her lips, embarrassed. "Well, that didn't go so well the last time. I think I may just ride overland to see her."

"Oh no. What happened?"

Gwen shook her head, dismissing the subject. "Nothing I can't fix. But I need to be there to do so. I've done enough long distance. I need to be up close now, to make sure things go like I want for a change."

James frowned and folded his arms, cocking a hip out in practiced disgust. "Are you meddling again?"

"No."

"You *have been*? What did you do?"

"Nothing."

"You cast a spell on her?"

"Don't be stupid James. She's my mentor. She would never fall prey to a spell of mine."

James' eyes grew wide and his mouth fell open. "You cast a spell on your mentor and you think something has happened because of it!"

Gwen spread her arms and growled at the heavens. "I *hate it* when you do that!" She stormed out of the room to go pack her things.

Duncan looked at the people watching from the hall. "Excuse me? Could we get some wine and food, please? For when His Majesty awakens?"

The priest nodded, the awe on his face shaking loose. "Of... of course, Sir." He shook his head, snapping out of the wonderment that was ruling him. "Yes, of course. Yannic, go get His Majesty some food and wine. Caria, return to your duties and get the church cleaned up. We should leave His Majesty to rest. The congregants will be arriving soon for noon mass and we need to be ready for them."

Duncan nodded. "Thank you, Father." He eased the door closed as the altar boy ran off down the hall and the other onlookers started to mill away from the door, whispering their shared excitement.

A sharp intake behind him snatched his attention. Alexander's eyes were open, and he looked for a second like he was both surprised and glad that he was awake.

"Bad dream?" Duncan asked. The king looked like he saw something horrible for a second, making Duncan wonder if the Shadows that haunted him for years had come to attack his rescuer.

Alexander's brow bounced into concern, but then came right back out. "Yeah, I guess so." He looked at Duncan. "How are you feeling?"

He turned to face his sovereign. "Solid as a mizzen mast, Sire, thanks to you." He smiled at his own innuendo. "Question is how are *you* feeling?"

Alexander rubbed his eyes with the heels of his hands. "Exhausted, but undamaged."

"Saints be praised then, Sire." Duncan sat and leaned on his forearms.

"If I may ask, what happened? How did you suddenly have all those injuries?"

Duncan glanced at the floor, preparing for a long story. "Well…"

A knock interrupted them and Duncan stood to answer the door, silently grateful. He still wasn't certain how to tell the King about the will of the Church regarding Catriona, nor even if he should. He opened the door to see James. "Ah, you've returned."

"Yes. We had a shadow on our tail. I wanted to make sure it was dealt with before we did any planning." James looked at Duncan and Alexander. "I see my idea worked."

Duncan patted his chest with both hands. "Yep! I'm a new man!"

James stepped into the room, focused upon Alexander. "Yes, but he isn't. Are you all right, Your Majesty?"

Alexander waved his hand. "Yes, yes. Just tired is all. He was very wounded." He looked up at James. "A shadow, you say?"

James waved his hand. "Figurative, not literal. Gwen was following us. This isn't something I want her any more involved with so I sent her home."

"But she was helping me with..." Alexander paused, remembering the dream.

"I know what you told her she was going to help you with but that was before you decided to step into the Black. Now you're working with me until I decide you ain't worth helping. I'll not jeopardize my family by allowing a crusading Church access to them. Gwen is especially gifted when it comes to Fae dealings. She's been touched since birth. For her to be even in proximity to dealings with these creatures will kill her. They are unscrupulous and will take her when you aren't looking. I'll not have her involved."

Alexander nodded, a resigned sigh revealing his acceptance of the situation and he lay back on the sparse bed. Duncan was actually glad Gwen was going away. He was a pirate, yes, but women were distractions and he didn't want the distraction of James protecting his sister to interfere with whatever the King needed doing.

Duncan said, "Sire, I need to talk plainly with you. Do you want to rest or do you feel up to talking right now?"

A small snore escaped Alexander's lips and both James and Duncan smiled. James nodded to Duncan. "I think you have your answer."

"Hm. Yes, I suppose so."

"Anything you can talk to me about?"

Duncan glanced at the sleeping king, then nodded. "Actually, this might be better. I doubt he'll want to do what I'm about to suggest and I might need your help to pull a strategy together. Let's step into the hall."

They moved away from the monarch and closed the door behind them. The hall was empty at present, but there were whispers funneling up the stairs. James walked over and glanced down to see if anyone was coming up. No one seemed to be and James came back over to the door. "I think this may end up being problematic." His voice was low, barely audible to Duncan standing right next to him. "The healing he did on you could be construed as witchcraft. That will make him vulnerable, giving unsavory types the chance to take advantage of his desperation again."

"What do we do?"

James gave a smile of conspiracy. "We need to make sure we give people the right impression. He needs to be seen as a Holy King, touched by the Saints, or he'll lose his populace, and possibly his higher power."

Duncan rubbed his head. "I don't know how to do that, make people think what I want them to."

"Yeah, well, I *do*. Follow my lead." He moved towards the staircase and spoke in a normal but animated voice. "It was *amazing*, Duncan. You were *so utterly* wounded when the King and I brought you here. That man healed your wounds *completely* without using herbs or medicines." He nodded to Duncan, encouraging him with his eyes.

"Yeah, amazing." Duncan realized what James was doing. The voices whispering near the stairs stopped talking, and he realized their conversation was carrying down the stairs to the waiting ears of the faceless populace discussing the morning's activities. "Yes, I thought I was going to die, but he healed me."

"But it didn't work when he tried at the inn? It only worked on Holy Ground?"

"Yes. He's always been a gifted healer, I understand and he's used his healer's herbs to heal all manner of wounds on me before, but those ones…"

"Well, you did defend him against those assassins. He said he would trade his own life for any member of his populace."

Duncan arched an eyebrow, confused. James seemed to be going somewhere with this and he didn't know what to say next. "Well, thank the Saints he didn't have to."

"Actually, since it only worked on Holy Ground, I think it was another sign from Heaven. That makes three now."

Duncan blinked, swallowing. He shrugged as James looked down the staircase. "I guess it does…"

"Look, we need to abide by his wishes though. He doesn't want the populace to know about these. We need to do whatever we can to dismiss this one, though I don't know how we can do it with so many witnesses this time. Heaven seems to be wanting people to know he is its Chosen Sovereign. This goes well beyond what will happen at his coronation when the Pope crowns him. If those visions he's received are a sign of things to come, the Saints themselves will descend from Heaven to bestow his kingdom to him."

"So, what do we do?" Duncan was asking this as much for himself as for the ruse.

"We'll tell people the stories are exaggerated regarding your wounds, that they only looked bad but they weren't as lethal as people claimed. These stories always grow in the telling. It should be fairly easy to keep these miracles from getting out."

A hiss of whispers suddenly broke out beneath them, echoing the word *miracles,* and James smiled. "Quiet! Someone's coming. Let's get back to guard the door."

The whispers stopped momentarily, then started again as the two men moved away. When they got back by the door, James nodded towards the stairs. "People love to gossip. If they think they've stumbled across a secret, especially one this significant, they'll have his fame covering the country in a few ten-days. By the time his coronation arrives, he'll have the entire kingdom supporting him."

"That's important to your plans?"

James pulled a pair of chairs from down the hall and set them to either side of the door. "Well, it couldn't hurt. That massacre a few years back threatened this country with civil war, if I recall correctly, and he was a major player. With him becoming king, there will be people hurt by that choice who will rise against him. War is always a bad idea and I won't risk my family if I can prevent it. So, may I ask, what did you need to talk to him about?"

"Oh, well, I have a few things, actually. Are you sure this is a good place to be talking?" He glanced back at the stairs.

James nodded. "Can you hear the whispering?"

Duncan listened. "No."

"This area is pretty open. Sound gets distorted and muffled, lost in the contours of the stone. Plus, I'm watching this way and you're facing the other end of the hallway. We'll know if anyone arrives. What's on your mind?"

Duncan weighed the things he knew against telling James. His request by the Pope to save Tanglwyst was somewhat botched and he didn't want to likewise fail with the other task of preventing Alexander's marriage to Catriona. "I'm concerned about his obsession with the pirate woman."

James took a deep breath. "Yeah." He nodded. "Talk about civil war. You didn't hear the priest earlier but the way he talked about," James searched for the right word, "'monsters' made me think that the Church is still holding a grudge. If this priest is so indoctrinated against non-Augustinian beliefs, having a Land Worshiper on the throne won't make a good mark. I don't think the Pope would be allowed to bless a union like that."

Duncan thought about this. It was probably the truth, and why the Church wanted the courtship stopped. He was glad James figured it out. It saved Duncan from revealing too much.

James glanced past Duncan to the stairway. "So, speaking of monsters, the king said you gave him an amulet."

Duncan closed his eyes and sighed. "Yes. I'm afraid so. But I think something must have happened to it."

James took a deep breath. "Is that why you were so damaged all of a sudden, why your wounds were partially healed?"

Duncan sat back, realizing James knew more than he thought. "Yes. It had a healing aspect to it. I didn't realize it being destroyed would return the wounds."

"Duncan, I need to ask you something. How do you feel right now?"

Duncan glanced himself over. "Fine. Better than fine."

"No dark thoughts?"

Duncan blinked. "How did…"

"That amulet was an artifact from the Soulless War three hundred years ago. They were destroyed when discovered because they corrupted the people wearing them." He pointed at the King's door. "That man had clouds of blackness swirling in his eyes and he stank of sulfur from using the thing, and he thought he was protected."

"Sulfur?"

"Yes. It's the infernal element warning others of its presence."

"Oh no." Duncan leaned on his knees, looking at James. "I think he stole it from me before I loaned it to him. He came in stinking of rancid eggs when I was out of contact with it. I noticed myself feeling sick and having a few scars flare up, but at the time, I just thought it was the hot water of the bath."

"So, you only loaned it? You didn't gift it to him?"

Duncan took a deep breath, glancing at the door again. "I'm afraid that thing is addicting. The more you use it, the more you want to use it. Such ease of movement, to be anywhere you've ever been before..."He sat back, blowing out his breath. "Although I am not feeling that need for it right now, it's possible he will and him being able to go anywhere he wants, any time he wants, will put him in a lot of danger."

James smiled that conspiratorial smile again. "Don't worry about that. I destroyed that thing and frankly, had I known you had it, I would have done the same for you. My sister says Catriona is on her way to Caratia now and if we use my ship, we can control his comings and goings, keeping him safe, so he'll be stuck going where we go. My sister cares about him but his recent lapses in judgment has her worried. She doesn't think he's worthy of Catriona."

Duncan sat back. "Well, I'm not so sure she's worthy of him either."

James looked at Duncan with a penetrating gaze. "Why do you say that?"

"After what she did to us in the Firth of Mirth? How can *you* say she's worthy?"

"It's precisely *because* of what she did there that makes her worthy. She could have killed us, but she didn't. She just neutralized us. It was as stroke of strategic genius. She makes an interesting foe."

Duncan realized something of his own. "And your sister knows her."

James nodded. "Prizes their friendship highly. And I'm not about to do a disservice to either lady because some accident of birth makes a man think he's entitled to something, or someone."

A sound behind James called their attention as the altar boy entered the hallway from the back, bearing a tray of food. They stood as he approached.

"Here is the food you requested for His Majesty."

"Thank you, son," James said, taking the tray.

"Is he all right? The priest wanted me to ask."

Duncan opened the door a little. "He's sleeping right now but he'll hungry when he wakes."

The young boy craned his neck to look in the room and Duncan pulled up short to find the morning sun was streaming through the window, casting a glow upon his monarch. The sunlight made him look radiant, blessed by Heaven. The boy gasped and ran off down the closest set of stairs. Duncan looked back at James who was standing there, a plotter's smile murmuring victory.

The bald pirate smiled. Of course. When this boy tells of this sight, there will be no doubt it was divine intervention and not witchcraft. Good work, James.

Thirty-One

"A goddess who answers no prayers will lose all
her followers."
The Siren's Song of Callista

Gwen tightened the strap closing her saddlebag and stood,
looking around the room to make sure she hadn't forgotten
anything. She got down on her hands and knees and checked under
the bed and chairs, then almost screamed when she turned and her
brother was standing behind her.

She put her hand on her chest. "By the Fae, James! Don't
sneak up on me like that!"

He looked at her, his expression a bit numb. "How would you
prefer I sneak up on you?"

"James? Are you all right?"

He blinked at her and rubbed his face with his hand. "Yeah,
I'm fine. Tired. Looking forward to you going on your way so I
can go back to bed for a while."

"No, something's wrong. I know your look."

He rubbed his palm with his thumb. "Well, let's just say that Heaven is going out of its way to let people know your King is its chosen monarch."

He finally told her the details of the morning's activities, including the sunlight streaming in on the sleeping king. "We need to get you out of town before people start setting up shrines to you as the Holy Traveling Companion."

"I'm ready to go."

"What? No fighting? No tantrums?"

Gwen bent over and picked up her saddlebags. "Not this time. I need to get to Catriona to warn her about Alexander's trucking with demons. I can't afford for you to get there first. I need to figure out a way to help her."

"Well, she's pretty capable. I'm sure she'll survive without your help, if necessary."

"James, Alexander's greatest power is the ability to say just the right thing. Catriona is not immune to that."

James took the saddlebags from her, nodding and opened the door. "It is an impressive ability. Has this been a recent development or has he always been able to do that?" He closed the door behind them and they started down the stairs. The sounds of people talking in low murmurs over their boiled eggs met them on the stairs.

"As far as I know, he's always had it."

James frowned and navigated to the bar where he set Gwen's key for Ce'Nedra. She poked her head around the corner and saw the siblings.

"Was everything all right?" One of the innkeeper's honey locks of hair was insisting on being noticed hanging in front of her right eye. She puffed it out of her way as she brought a basket of rolls off a sideboard in the back. They were still warm, a shimmer of heat and the smell of fresh bread causing Gwen's stomach to growl.

She nodded. "Yes, it was wonderful, but I need to be returning home. His Majesty has things to do and I need to get home to my fiancé." She tried to ignore her stomach as it protested getting on the road empty handed.

Ce'Nedra seemed to hear Gwen's stomach and handed her a napkin with three rolls in it. "Well, I actually made this for your brother and his companions, but it seems you need them more. I put a surprise into the center to make them taste better on the road."

Gwen breathed a sigh, sniffing deeply the scent of the bread. She could smell the sweet blending of honey and butter seeping from the pores of the bread. "Thank you. You have no idea what this means to me."

"I can guess. I've had to be on the road at dawn once or twice m'self." She patted Gwen on the shoulder, smiling. "Keep your dagger sharp and your wits sharper."

"I will. Thanks again."

Ce'Nedra brought the rolls in turn to each table as James shuffled his sister out the kitchen door to the stables. Gwen unwrapped a roll as he saddled her horse, eating quickly to quiet her stomach. The center of the bread was indeed flavored with honey butter, like it had been injected somehow into every open area. She wiped a trickle of liquid butter from her chin as she finished her breakfast.

James seemed intense, like he wanted to get her on her way before it was discovered she was missing. It made her nervous. *Had someone said something to make him think she was in danger?*

"What's wrong?"

Her brother looked over the saddle as he put the tang into the hole on the cinch strap. Glancing back down, he shook his head. "Nothing. Some things I thought I had figured out last night are returning in the light of day and they aren't meshing with what I saw today. Last night, he was a shadow servant, but I feel *certain* he couldn't have done what he did for Duncan if he was partnered with the Infernal. Too much light involved. By the Fae, if he were to use that power *on* a demon, he'd destroy it. I think he could even take down the Last Child with it." He dropped the stirrup down and checked the bridle to make sure the bit was in the horse's mouth properly.

"The Last Child?"

"The last creature from the Soulless War Alistair fought in. Apparently, they were decidedly difficult to destroy, according to his journal. Those monsters were vanquished though, so all we have now are just plain, ol' minions of Hell."

"What are you going to do?"

"I'm going to watch this guy close. I'm going to travel at a safe pace to Caratia to give you time to arrive for your own insidious purposes. After that, I'm taking it a day at a time."

Gwen bundled up the remaining two rolls and tucked them in a pocket before going over to pat her brother on the shoulder. "He's a good man, James. He's just in unfamiliar waters right now. You need to help him get back on course. The man he used to be was one I would fight day and night to have at Catriona's side. This man? Not on your life."

James gave his sister a hug and walked her over to the mounting side of the horse. "Well, maybe Catriona will know what to say or do to save him here. I'm hoping this morning's activities will emphasize the dangers of dealing with Shadows. Duncan's injuries…" He exhaled and shook the image off. "I doubt he'll go that way again. I'm sure it wouldn't play to Alexander's plans to not be able to perform with Catriona once he actually got her in bed."

Gwen put her foot in the stirrup and threw her leg over the saddle. "Let's hope your right. Get some rest. You're no good to anyone if you're not sharp."

He nodded and slapped the horse on the rump to get it out the open stable doors.

Alexander woke up at the sound of the bells in the church and sat up, giving his equilibrium time to adjust to the change in position. The door was closed, as was the window, but the church was designed to carry the sound of the bells to let the inhabitant know which prayers were due. He rubbed his head, realizing he would have undoubtedly awakened on his own because nearly every part of his body was sore from the bed. His right shoulder felt moderately out of place and his fingers tingled from the lack of circulation. He flexed his hand as he sat on the edge of the bed, rubbing it with his good hand. He needed very much to urinate and looked around in vain for a chamber pot.

He stood and opened the door. Duncan was napping in a chair across from the door to the room and the sound of the creaking hinges started him awake. Apparently he had been there long enough to not be disturbed by the bells anymore, but the foreign sound of the hinges had drawn him from sleep. He spread his arms to the side as if to stop from falling, which he wasn't, and Alexander nodded greeting.

"Your Majesty, you're awake."

"Yes, and so are you now." Alexander glanced down the hall. "Privy?"

"Outside. I'll show you."

Duncan got up from the chair and walked down the hallway to the small staircase that led outdoors to the privy. Alexander made quick work of the facilities and was relieved to find he had managed not to get any on him in his rush. He met Duncan on the stairs.

"So, it's been pretty quiet, has it?"

Duncan nodded. "Yeah, James managed to get the populace talking about you in a positive way. We'll see if it takes."

Alexander wrinkled his brow. "How did he do that, exactly?"

Duncan opened his mouth but the sound of footsteps up the far staircase from the chapel interrupted them. James ascended the stairs and saw the two men standing at the end of the hall. He glanced over his shoulder then moved with a brisk step to the pair.

"Gentlemen."

Duncan nudged his chin toward the stairs James had just scaled. "How does it look down there?"

"Oh, there's a few more people than I think usually attend in this area, but not an unmanageable number, yet." James looked at Alexander. "That doesn't mean we're clear though. We should probably discuss our next move."

Alexander leaned against the wall. "Well, I want to go after Catriona. I have some things that have come up, things I want to discuss in person. I need to see her if only to apologize."

Duncan raised an eyebrow. "Why would you need to apologize?"

James also turned his eyes on Alexander and the young king realized Duncan was probably thinking of his part in the murder of Catriona's husband. He wasn't quite sure how to reassure him without revealing to James the details of the deed. Instead, he decided to downplay the incident in St. Marguerite.

"I had an indiscretion with her recently and she found out."

James blinked, a little of the shock he was feeling actually getting through to his face. "You had an affair on this woman?"

"No. That would be incredibly stupid." Alexander took a deep breath and rolled his eyes. "I sort of put out a decree to hunt down one of her passengers."

James cocked his head. "A decree?"

Duncan shifted his weight. "Was it an official decree?"

Alexander nodded.

Duncan rolled his eyes to James. "That means it can't be ignored. The Power of Sovereignty enforces compliance from anyone with an Oath of Fealty."

"Wait, even if they don't know about it?"

Alexander and Duncan both nodded.

James whistled his surprise. "That's some pretty heady power you wield, man."

"Yes, but all a person has to do to break the Oath is to decide they won't follow you anymore. The Power is useless if there's no trust or faith."

James nodded his understanding. "So you must balance your desires with what the people will tolerate. Interesting. Where did this power come from?"

Alexander glanced down at the ground, tapping the tip of his boot on the stones as he remembered the tales from his history lessons. "About three centuries ago, when the Church first gave its blessing upon my household to govern the country."

James blinked. "So your power has always come from the Church?"

"Yes. The endorsement of the Pope and the Papal City is key to the inheritance of the crown. Although I wield this power at present, I need to reinforce it by gaining the blessing of the Church at my Coronation."

"What happens if they don't?"

Alexander swallowed. "Then I imagine I lose the power. I become a citizen of the country and make way for the true sovereign to arrive. To be honest, I don't know. It's never happened."

Duncan shrugged. "It isn't going to happen now either. You're a good man, Your Majesty, and there isn't a person out there who doesn't know that. And if there is, we'll change their mind."

James got a smirk on his face and glanced back over his shoulder. "Speaking of which, we might want to get downstairs for mass."

Alexander ran his fingers through his hair and straightened his doublet. He nodded and led the way toward the far stairs. He noticed a hum in the air as he got closer to them and he glanced over at James. James nodded in the direction of the stairs and Alexander descended them. The hum in the air became tinged with the smell of sweat and breath from a steady diet of fish. He turned the corner to the chapel and saw that nearly every person in town was sitting in the sanctuary. Several people were standing at the back and most of the pews were crammed to an uncomfortable level. He even saw Ce'Nedra sitting about four rows back with Saiban next to her.

Alexander smiled as the pastor brightened at his arrival.

"Your Majesty! Please, we have waited for you."

"Ah, yes, Father. I am honored, but it appears you have a full capacity today."

"We have saved you a seat, Your Majesty." The pastor turned to his altar keepers and nodded. They brought out an ornate chair and a pillow for him to kneel on during prayers. They were set directly to the side of the dais for Mass, facing the profile of the priest while still in full view of the populace of the town. Additional pillows were brought in for James and Duncan with simple stools for the sitting parts of the Mass. Alexander smiled and bowed to the congregation, who had all risen as he entered the room. He moved over to the impromptu throne and sat, nodding to the priest to carry on as he did so. The pastor smiled and nodded to the townspeople. "You may be seated."

As the priest proceeded with Mass, Alexander leaned over to James. "I am impressed with your gift for understatement. I hope you are a better judge of troop numbers than you are of additional parishioners."

The smile on James' face translated into his voice. "Me too, Sire." He sat back a bit and Alexander heard the mirth drain away in a fast trickle. "Me too."

Alexander was about to question him when the priest stood. "Please rise."

When the mass had finished, Alexander had forgotten James' hesitant remark in the impressive aerobics of the service. He hoped the congregation didn't have to endure this every day but it might explain why living by the sea was supposedly so healthy. He stood at the end of service and the priest bowed to him, rushing over to him before he could slip back into the sanctuary of the room upstairs.

"Your Majesty!"

"Yes, Father. How may I help you?"

"A few of the congregants were wondering about seeking an audience with you. I told them I would ask."

Alexander wrinkled his forehead. "An audience? En masse?"

"No, no. Singly, if possible, Sire."

Alexander sighed and glanced at his attendants. "Well, that's part and parcel to being the King. Do you have a place for me to hold these audiences?"

"The Saint's chapel is always available for you, Sire. Please sit. I shall bring in the first congregants."

"Yes, thank you, Father. Before you go, I need some way to record the chronicle of the business brought before me. If there's a property dispute or something…"

"Pardon my interruption, Your Majesty, but that is not the business these people have."

Alexander eased himself back into the large chair and looked at Duncan and James, who stepped forward a bit. The priest went to the front door of the chapel and waved in someone. James leaned down, keeping his voice low. "Brace yourself, Your Majesty."

"Wha…"

A woman came in carrying a small child, barely out of toddling clothes who was wrapped in bandages across her eye. Alexander's eyes grew wide and he leapt from the chair, rushing over to the woman.

Alexander looked at the woman. "What happened to her?"

"She was taken into the woods by her father's uncle. When he tried to hurt her, he did this to her to make her submit. I believe it worked."

Alexander swallowed the lump in his throat, but the tears came anyway. He put his hands on the child and prayed for the healing powers to flow into her.

He was met with nothing.

He glanced up at James and Duncan, then back down at the child and tried again.

Again, nothing.

He closed his eyes. *It's gone.*

He looked up at the woman, her worried eyes upon her child. *What did I do?* He glanced around the chapel. "Here, let's get her off the ground." He reached out to pick her up but she grabbed her mother, a scream piercing the air.

"Marguerite, stop. He's here to help you, honey."

"Her name is Marguerite?"

The woman nodded, picking up the girl.

"Is your name Brigit then?"

She frowned. "No. Evelyn."

He looked at the frightened child before him, eyes dampening as he realized what was happening. "Marguerite, I'm sorry for what happened to you, for the damage lust and pride have done. I'm sorry for the terrible crime committed upon you. I promise, if you'll let me, that the things that happened to you will be undone. I'll do as Heaven commands."

He reached over and kissed the girl's forehead.

She quieted and he felt the energy of Heaven flow through him again, stronger than ever. It filled the room and when he stepped back, he could feel that the girl was whole again, head to toe. Even her memory of the horror was gone.

He opened his eyes to smile at her as the light faded. "You'll be fine now, sweetheart." He reached down and pushed the bandages away from her head, revealing a fresh, undamaged eye glittering like a robin's egg in the sunlight. The little girl wrapped her arms around his neck and he held her close. His heart filled, as did his eyes, mirroring the look of her mother's. He sniffed back the tears and handed the girl back to her.

"Are you certain the uncle did this?"

The woman nodded.

The priest said, "I'm afraid it has happened before. With other children."

"Why hasn't he been brought to justice?"

"He is the brother of a noble in Patras. He uses this to scare the townsfolk into silence. But I hear the confessions of the victims' families."

Alexander touched the child's hair, who smiled at her healer, revealing a couple of new teeth.

"Well, you might say I don't scare so easily. My lady, I need to ask you about the incident that caused this injury. Will you please stay?"

"Of course, Sire."

"Sire." James nodded to the slightly open door to the church. Through the crack, several people were visible, milling about or staring at the doors.

Alexander stood and stepped outside. At least half the people that had been in the church during services had brought people from their sickbeds and were waiting outside for help. There was no one in the street who was not maimed, or coughing or otherwise terribly sick. He was actually glad for this. What he had seen and felt in that child would have been unbearable if rich women had come before him demanding he fix their backs from wearing the latest fashion.

This, however, did not appear to be the case. The injuries he saw before him were severe and crippling. James noticed the same thing. "Why are there so many people with injuries?"

The priest sighed. "The area here has many useful trades. There is the fishing industry, of course, but we also have a lumber mill and the flour mill as well. Though profitable, both are dangerous professions."

James shook his head. "This is an inordinate amount of injuries, even for such industry. There's something wrong."

"Well, the industry is owned by the same family that did that to that child."

James and Alexander looked at the priest, then at each other as Duncan scanned the crowd, shaking his head. Alexander turned to go back inside. "Please bring them in one at a time, children first.

No nobles. Duncan, please help carry those who cannot walk on their own. James, I'm going to need you to take some notes. Can you write?"

"Better than I speak, in fact."

"Then please talk to that woman and write down what she says about the incident with her daughter. As I send other people to you, please do likewise."

James looked at the number of injured villagers. "Father, I'm going to need some help."

Thirty-Two

"Beware the sandy bottom that hides the stingray."
The Siren's Song of Callista

Gwen rode through the day, going over her plans for the trip. She knew she needed to get to Caratia and that going overland could get her there quicker than by ship if she was riding alone. It did put her in danger of bandits and that thought made her decide early in the journey to take the criminal element out of the equation. When it was starting to dim towards dinnertime, she moved her horse through the woods to a place where she could no longer see the road, then went about half a mile further, just to be sure. She came to a wide spot between trees and got off her horse.

In the woods and other natural places, even here in Mervolingia, the barrier between the Fae world and the human world was thinner, and Gwen felt herself relax as she attuned herself to her surroundings. She pulled out a small pouch of items she had assembled for a ritual and placed the cloth bag on the ground while she prepared the area. She cleared away the ground cover to get to the soil, then drew a wavy line in the dirt. Then she took some of the dried leaves from the ground and crushed them to a pulp. She sprinkled the leaves on either side of the line in the dirt. She then got a few rocks from around the area and put them on either side of the line. Last, she took out her water skin and poured water in the line, careful not to splash over into the leaves or stones.

She then opened the cloth bag and pulled out some gold powder. She closed her eyes and spread the powder over the small map as she muttered, "Spirits of Wayfinding, guide me to the place I'm seeking. Protect my path and carry me swiftly through thy realm. Accept this sacrifice and show me the way."

As the last of the dust fell to the ground, a small dust devil formed from the small breeze fluttering the ground brush. It caught the dust and blew it up around Gwen, then over to the horse, whose ears went back and he backed away from the phenomenon. The dust devil overtook him and blew dust into his eyes. The horse shook its head and stomped his hoof, then blinked, showing shimmering golden eyes.

Gwen smiled and went over to her mount. "Thank you."

The horse nodded and nuzzled her hand.

"Are you ready to go or do you need to rest?"

The horse looked back at the saddle. Gwen nodded.

"An all-nighter then. So be it." She climbed into the saddle and took the reins. The horse's eyes glowed for a moment, then the two rode off to into the trees. Gwen looked around when she could, trying to see the moon or the stars to give her some idea which direction they were heading but a few close calls with branches and her cheekbones taught her to keep her eye on the direction she was going. She heard a scream up ahead and leaned down close to the horse's ears.

"Did you hear that?"

The horse nodded and picked up speed. The moved easily between the trees and Gwen saw moonlight pooling up ahead of her. She reined in the horse and dismounted, walking carefully to see if the scream came from bandits. She saw a creature collapsed on the grass of the clearing near a large log. A woman's leg was draped over the log. Gwen went over to the creature and saw it was a goblin, a dark Fae which sometimes frequented the deep woods. She had forgotten there were any in this country, but knew she would be safe on her horse. The woman by the log must not have known this.

She drew her dagger, prepared to fight the goblin if it rose, but it lay motionless on the ground and Gwen now saw blood pooling in the grass. She nudged the thing with her hilt, then stood when the creature failed to respond. She walked over to the woman, expecting her to likewise be dead or badly injured. She had managed to take out a dark Fae but could hardly be unscathed. Gwen saw an obscene amount of blood on the grass near the woman's legs with a trail leading to the goblin, which was already fading into the moonlight.

She knelt down beside the woman and raised her head, then almost dropped it when she saw who it was.

"By the Fae! *Tanglwyst?*"

The door to Alexander's room at the Black Cat and Anchor opened, admitting the exhausted king and his two companions. They had taken statements from every injured person or accompanying family member regarding their injuries. Many were simple accidents but a few of the injuries were the product of neglect or abuse. Most of the abusers had fallen prey to the fates and passed on by divine justice, but a few working conditions put the laborers at risk every day. Alexander had told James and Duncan that he wanted to deal with the matter before they left and James had mentioned the ship could be ready to go in a day when he decided to head to Caratia.

Duncan watched Alexander flop into the hearth chair and James settle into the other one. A third had been brought in at some point and Duncan claimed it for his own. The king looked a bit spent, but not on the brink of collapse this time.

James glanced at the king and leaned his head back against the seat. "You look better today. Nothing like you did after you healed Duncan."

"I was just thinking the same thing, Your Majesty. You must be getting better at this."

Alexander let out a deep breath. "Well, I got a lot of practice today. I figured out how to channel the energy without giving up my own. It's rather like being able to gather the healing energy into me, then pour it forth into them, like pouring wine. Ooh, speaking of wine!" He popped out of the chair and went to the sideboard where Ce'Nedra had brought a fresh bottle and three glasses. Alexander turned back and gestured to his friends. "You want some?"

Duncan nodded and apparently James did as well because Alexander poured three glasses. He handed Duncan one, then grabbed the other two and brought them back to the circle.

"So, what do you plan to do with the notes James took?" Duncan sipped the wine, a pleasant little house wine that was good but had nothing special going for it. Good for conversation because it didn't distract the drinker.

Alexander leaned forward. "I plan to investigate the mills and bring a bit of order to their business. If it is a matter of little revenue not being able to make the mill safer, then I might invest a bit of money in them to improve the conditions. However, if it is a matter of corruption and avarice, I won't be quite so lenient."

James cradled the wine glass in his fingers. "What are you going to do about the man who did that to the little girl?"

Alexander sniffed, a cold look entering his eyes. "I'll do the right thing there. I'll kill him."

"Are you sure that's wise?"

Duncan watched James closely. *He's got something in mind.*

Alexander turned the gaze on James. "Excuse me? Did you see what he did to that girl? She was barely no longer a baby. "

"Yes, but the problem I have is going on hearsay for this. How do we know the woman wasn't simply trying to get rid of her uncle for inheritance purposes?"

"Well, I would say because her child wasn't the only one I treated today. I healed more than one maidenhead in a young one, among other injuries. Didn't their statements implicate the same man?"

"No. In fact, most of the people seemed afraid to speak about the incidents. They merely said they don't let their children play outside anymore. A couple blamed animal attacks in the woods when the children wandered off."

Duncan took a deep breath. "Your Majesty, we can find out the truth here, or rather, I think *you* can, specifically."

The other two men looked at him. Alexander said, "Yes?"

"Bring this man before you and ask for his Oath of Fealty."

Alexander blinked, his mouth opening as if to say something, but his mind working faster than his tongue would have. He let the thought race around his intellect for a moment and nodded. "I see. I think I will do exactly that. Make sure we handle that first thing in the morning." He turned to James. "Anything of note from the statements?"

James pulled the stack of pages from the back band of his trousers. "Yeah, there was one incident... let me find it... Here. This one was from the man with the crushed left side. His wife was very adamant about the conditions of the flour mill. She said she had found blood or parts in her flour from time to time. She also claimed most people would not say what needed to be said but she was not like them. She said the miller was an evil man who killed people and made them into bone meal."

"Do you believe her?"

"I don't know, but apparently the miller's wife has a lovely garden."

"Well, we can't arrest him for that. Perhaps I will ask for his fealty as well."

James twirled the wine around in his glass. "How will that help?"

"Once I have a person's fealty, I can make a request of them, such as tell the truth about the incident."

"Ah. That makes sense, then. You can find out the truth and make sure you're prosecuting the real bandit." He tipped his glass toward his lips. "Handy power, that." He sipped his wine.

Duncan leaned forward. "What do you plan to do if it turns out he's guilty?"

Alexander blinked slowly, the cold returning to his eyes. "I'm thinking of taking a lesson from Mandian women and their husbands." He finished the wine and set his glass aside. "I'm afraid I need to get some rest now, gentlemen. Thank you again for your help."

The two companions drained their glasses and retired for the night.

Thirty-Three

"He did not know he loved her until he saw her injured."
The Siren's Song of Callista

Gwen pulled into St. Andrew as the sun was lightening the sky. The speed spell she put upon the horse helped to cover the ground between the place where Tanglwyst had fallen and the seaside village and Gwen hoped her brother would be able to help her. She had dared to inspect the damage directly and had seen the glint of some metal in a place where nothing metal should ever be. It had frightened her enough to stop looking. She did not know the extent of what the goblin had done to the woman, but she did not find it necessarily unreasonable to believe he had stabbed her there for hurting his own privates.

She rode up to the Black Cat and Anchor, pulling the horse to the stables and tying it to the stall gate with a slap of the reins, the motion causing the leather strips to wrap around the post. She grabbed Tanglwyst from her position of being slung over the saddle and lay her down in the fresh hay in the empty stall. She knew she couldn't haul the noblewoman up to the room on her own and ran up the stairs to get James. It occurred to her after she pounded on the door that she hoped the group had not set sail already and she was disturbing some stranger.

Shuffling in the room and the door was cracked, a shadow peering into the hallway.

"Gwen?" The door opened further and James stepped back, a dagger in his hand. He glanced around the corner behind her and then stepped back into the room to admit her.

Gwen shook her head. "I can't come in, I need you to help me. I found someone in the woods and she's really hurt. I can't carry her up here alone."

James put the dagger in his waistband. "Where is she?"

"In the stables."

"How badly is she hurt?"

Gwen shied away from the subject by turning to head out to the stables. "Bad enough to bring her here instead of treating her myself. She was attacked by a goblin."

"By the Fae…" He followed his sister down the stairs, taking the lead when they got to the kitchen. It was still too early for Ce'Nedra to be banging around the stoves just yet, but Gwen could see it would not be much longer before the innkeeper would be up. She didn't want to have that discussion. She followed James out the back door to the stables, then pointed to the pile of hay where Tanglwyst lie.

James saw the body and the blood and stopped. He glanced outside for witnesses, then stepped around behind the woman, lifting her under the arms. "Here, help me get her up." He knelt down and Gwen helped balance her onto his shoulder. He rose, lifting her weight with his legs and Gwen scurried before him, making sure there were no obstacles in his way as he brought her upstairs in the twilight. Gwen opened doors for him and when he started up the stairs, she ran ahead to make sure there was no one else in his bed.

Luckily, it was empty and she moved the covers back to give a clear path. James came in a few moments later and gently put the lady on the bed. "Gwen, get that basin and pour some water on that towel over there to clean her wounds. I'm going to get a bit of help."

He was out the door before she could react and she walked over to the sideboard to do as he asked. She brought both over to the bedside, then went to the door when she heard voices in the hall.

"Your Majesty, I need your help. Gwen just brought in an injured woman she found in the woods."

"Gwen? I thought she left?"

"She did, but she was closer here than to anywhere else."

A door down the hall opened and Gwen heard another man ask, "Is everything all right, Your Majesty?"

"James has a patient in his room, a girl his sister found in the woods." The king's voice faded a moment as he went back into his room.

The other man asked, "Are you sure you are up to this, Majesty? Yesterday's healings…"

"I'll be fine, Duncan. I'm not going to neglect a woman in pain because I'm tired."

Footsteps in the hall brought them to the cracked door and into the room. Alexander nodded greeting to Gwen, then went over to the bedside. He looked around for a light and James grabbed the sulfur sticks from the sideboard and lit the lantern next to the bed. Alexander glanced down at the bloody area and James moved to block the delicate area from onlookers. The other man, a tall bald fellow who was obviously this Duncan person, moved into the room completely to close the door behind him. Gwen was certain she had seen him before somewhere.

Alexander moved the woman's dress to examine her wound. James hovered, holding the lantern. "By Callista, what happened to her?"

Alexander shook his head. "I'm not sure. There's something here…"

Gwen was about to tell the about the metal object but they seemed to find it.

"What the hell is that?"

"Remember that Mandian device I mentioned before?"

A pause, and James and Alexander looked at the object Alexander held up, which seemed almost like an arrowhead set into a piece of wood with a leather sheaf over the blade. Duncan gasped at the sight of the thing and Gwen looked up to find his eyes were wide. "By the Saints! Tanglwyst."

James stepped forward, putting his hand on Duncan's chest. "Maybe you should go back to your room, Duncan."

"What? Why would I do that?" He looked over at the woman on the bed.

Alexander looked back at Duncan and James, then at the woman on the bed. He moved her hair aside to get a better look at her face.

Saint's Blood. It is her. Alexander looked over at the two men. "Duncan, go back to your room."

"She's hurt? How did she get hurt? Is she going to be all right?" He pushed against James and Gwen stepped in to help her brother.

"Duncan, right? Look, His Majesty needs you to go back to your room so he can work on healing her."

Alexander turned to look at the others. "She's right, Duncan. James, you go with him. Gwen is more than capable of helping me."

Gwen looked at her brother, who nodded and pushed Duncan towards the door. "Yes, let's let the man work. C'mon Duncan."

Duncan seemed reluctant to leave, but eventually, he deigned to go as directed, and James closed the door behind them. Gwen walked over to the king and tucked her gloves into her belt. "What can I do?"

"I need to have you clean the blood away. Can you do that for me, Gwen?"

"Sure Grymalkin, but why don't you want to do it yourself?"

Alexander looked at Tanglwyst, shaking his hands and watching her for movement. "It's just unwise for me to do so. Violation of her privacy."

Gwen blinked, confused. "Didn't you treat her injuries at the palace when she was returned from her captivity?"

"Yes. However, I have reason to believe she might have been brutalized," he swallowed back the lump of anger, fear and memories. "I wouldn't want to have her wake up and find a man in that area."

"That's pretty unlikely, Alex. She never stirred the entire way here slung over my horse. I think she might be suffering from a goblin bite. It puts a victim to sleep so they can…"

Alexander leaned on the chest of drawers. *"Please."*

Gwen stopped.

Calmer, Alexander managed to hide the shaking in his voice. "I don't need to hear the details. Just, take care of her. I'll be back in a bit to give you time."

"Sure."

Alexander moved away from the furnishing, his eyes straying to his friend on the bed.

James took Duncan into his room and closed the door behind them. Duncan paced back and forth, rubbing his head. "Do you think she's all right?"

"Yes, I think the King will be able to heal her."

"Maybe I should go see her."

"Duncan, this woman used that device on your *dick*. It was splayed apart like a posy. How can you want to be anywhere *near* her right now?"

"What? What are you talking about?"

"Your manhood was split into quarters, Duncan, by a device that looked exactly like that one."

The door burst open and Alexander entered, his body glowing. His eyes didn't say healer this time. He grabbed Duncan and slammed him against the wall. "What did you do to her, you son of a *bitch?"*

"Nothing! I swear!"

"You recognized that device! I hadn't even identified her yet and you knew her from the dentate.*"*

James put his hand on Alexander's shoulder, then yanked it back, his hand burning form the contact. "Alexander, you need to calm down. Let him speak."

Alexander glanced at James, then let Duncan go.

James rubbed his hand. "We were just discussing this."

Duncan blinked, shaking his head and rubbing his neck. "I wouldn't hurt her. I couldn't. I don't remember anything like that happening."

James scowled. "I'm not surprised. My mind would break to survive that sort of thing."

Duncan looked at the floor, searching his memory. "I had used the amulet to take her to my ship. She had readied herself for travel with me but I don't think she expected the shadow travel. She passed out in my cabin and… I…"

"She wore that traveling?" Alexander's glow slowly thinned, but failed to disappear.

James nodded. "I can understand that. A woman on the road? It's not surprising, especially since she was a fugitive."

"If she put it in to travel with you, Duncan, then she *knew you were a threat.*" Alexander moved toward him and Duncan flinched.

James folded his arms. "I think the shadows took you, Duncan, and tried to rape her."

Alexander growled. "For all I know, they succeeded."

James shook his head and rubbed the back of his neck. "You saw that injury. He couldn't have performed after that. There would have been a lot more pieces and cuts. No, that knife did exactly what it was supposed to." He sighed. "Okay, get your things. We're leaving."

Duncan looked worried. "What? Where?"

"My ship. We'll get you away from her and that way, you won't hurt her again."

"Don't be stupid! I wouldn't hurt her now. It was *different* before."

James grabbed Duncan by the arm. "What makes you think *she's* going to know the difference? You saw where that knife was kept! It wasn't something she did with her hands. She defended herself from being *raped* by you!" Duncan tried to pull away but James gripped tighter. "Why would you think for a moment that she would want to see you again?"

"Because that was after she broke with Nicolai, when I took her to a ship. We were together after that. I don't think she knows that happened. No, she's more likely to be angry that I abandoned her recently."

Alexander couldn't believe what he was hearing. "You abandoned her?"

"Yes, while fleeing to the Papal City. *You* summoned me away from her side. I could simply appear beside you and I did, but your summons overrides any other activity outside of being knocked out. It even roused me from sleep. I was beside you before I knew it and when I returned to her, she was gone."

Alexander looked away.

James shifted his weight. "You couldn't find her?"

Duncan shook his head. "She had disappeared. I called out but I never heard anything. The road indicated the guard had been by and I feared she may have been arrested. I went to the towns nearby, but she was nowhere I looked." He looked at James with begging eyes. "I need to be here when she wakes to tell her what happened. She needs to know what happened."

James frowned. "Did you talk to Alexander about it?"

Alexander nodded. "Yes, but I couldn't help him because she was no longer a subject. Treason revokes that."

"So, her face is known to the guards and she's here now, and you want to wake her? Alexander, won't you be obligated by law to have her hung for treason?"

Alexander looked at Duncan. "Yes. If we're discovered here together, or if the guards see her, yes. The most I can give her if she is found is a trial."

James glanced back and forth between the two men. "Your Majesty, can I speak with you in the other room a moment?"

Alexander let his glare down. "Yeah, but stay away from her, Duncan."

The two men walked out of the room and over to the far end of the rooms. They had turned in Gwen's key but Cenedra had cleared the inn of other patrons at the King's request. They could hear people outside in the streets already but none in the common room.

"Your Majesty, you seem concerned about this woman. If you believed her guilty, you would have simply let her bleed to death. What's going on?"

Alexander folded his arms, finally getting his ire and holy aura under control. "This winter, when Catriona returned to her husband, it left two people bereft. Tanglwyst was Nicolai's lover."

"Oh geesh…"

Alexander waved his hand. "It wasn't like that, for either of us. Catriona and Nicolai both thought the other was dead. Seven years alone and a month after we finally… He showed up, as Tangl's lover. Tangl and I were left alone as the two decided to try again."

"Why? After seven years, why?"

"They have a son."

James rolled his eyes. "Ah. Yes. I can see that."

"It was horrible. Nicolai didn't even know it was me she was with, but Catriona didn't have the same luxury. Tangl got Nicolai a job at the palace. She visited Elizabeth, the queen, often enough to have the room two doors down from mine.

"We met when she was playing with Emmy, my niece. Emmy was into cookie and tea parties with her toys at the time. We… had tea. Every day. We helped each other get through the winter.

"When I heard she was part of the plot to kill Charles, I couldn't believe it. I believe she isn't like that. I… don't know what to think now. I just want to talk to her and see if she's alright."

James nodded. "Why don't you head back in to her then. I'll see about getting Duncan out of here." He took Alexander's shoulder in his hand, giving a concerned squeeze. He moved to look in the king's eyes. "Hey, you going to be able to treat her?"

Alexander looked at James and nodded. "Yeah. Yeah, I'll take care of her."

"Okay. Head on in."

Alexander took a deep breath and knocked on the door to see if Gwen was finished.

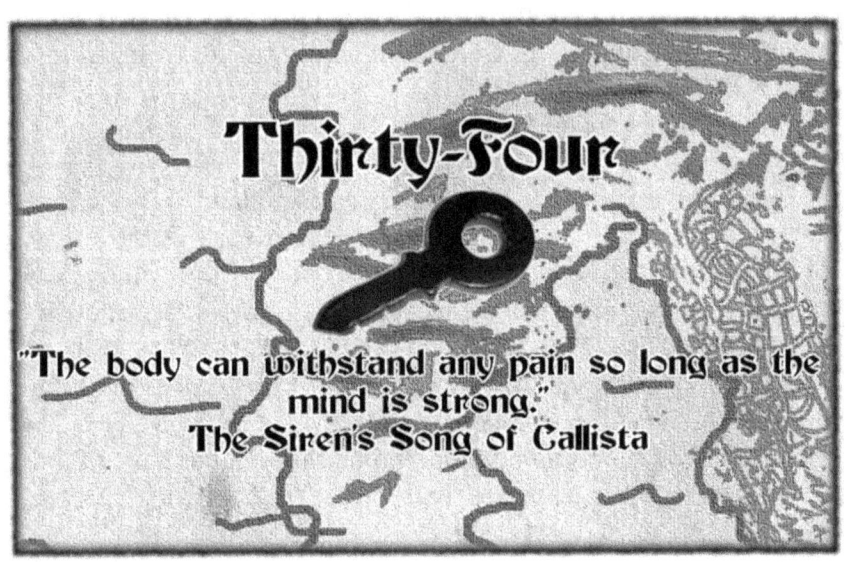

Thirty-Four

"The body can withstand any pain so long as the
mind is strong."
The Siren's Song of Callista

"Is she going to be alright? He's not going to kill her, is he?"
Duncan stared at James when he returned, his heart displayed upon
his chest.

"No, but he's not in an easy position with her."

The two men stood in silence as Duncan sussed out what he
was feeling. In the end, he closed his eyes and nodded his head.

James relaxed a bit. "As long as she stays anonymous and
asleep, she'll be no threat to him and she's safe. Once we leave
with him, Gwen will wake her and get her away, but I don't think
it's wise for an enemy of the state to travel with the king as his
guard's lover. Besides, isn't she married?"

Duncan nodded. "Yes. An old business rival named Urien
Atreides. I don't know if he's still alive or even around though. His
home port was near St. Giles."

"Then that's even worse. If he *witnesses* that, it's adultery and
that's against Church law here. Duncan, you have to leave her."

Duncan glanced at the shirt and coat he had draped over the chair in the room. He walked over and put on his shirt and coat, then pulled on his stockings and shoes.

James opened the door. "Ready?"

Duncan nodded.

The two men left the room and James knocked on the door to his room. Alexander answered the door. "How's it going in there?"

"Gwen says she's fine. She's not hurt. The blood is most likely from her attacker." Alexander looked at Duncan and James glanced over his shoulder.

"She was attacked?" Duncan's voice held a rising rage.

Alexander straightened, stepping towards Duncan. "Want to compare handiwork?"

Gwen came over to the door. "Could you please take this elsewhere? You're going to wake her."

Duncan pressed forward to the door but Alexander stepped in his way. "Gwen, was she attacked? Did someone hurt her?"

Gwen looked up at the tall pirate. "I think so."

Duncan exhaled, his rage evident now. "Where did you find her?"

"In the woods, but he's dead."

The rage seemed to drain away. He swallowed. "Dead?"

"Yes, he died from the wounds she inflicted."

"Oh. Can I see her?"

Alexander stepped out into the hallway, closing the door behind him. "That's unwise on several levels."

"Your Majesty, need I remind you that I was *with* her, keeping her safe from *your justice.* I rescued her from house arrest. She was with me willingly." Duncan calmed down. "I may have done something before, when I was under the influence of that amulet. But you look at me now. Am I still tainted?"

Alexander's gaze held Duncan's for a few seconds. He relaxed and they both backed down. "No. Not after yesterday."

James relaxed as well. "Good. I'm glad we've actually settled that."

Duncan looked at his companions. "Look, I understand your concern. But she and I were together and she got hurt because I was not there for her." He looked at Alexander. "You *owe* me this. I have to tell her what happened."

Alexander closed his eyes and nodded. "Fine. But you need to understand, I haven't healed her yet. She's still got some cuts and bruises from when he forced himself on her."

"He?" Duncan shook his head. "No man can lay rough hands upon her."

James sniffed. "It wasn't a man who did this to her. It was a Fae."

Duncan stared at James.

"Gwen told me. It was a goblin."

Alexander furrowed his brow. "Yeah, that's right. She said something about it to me too, but I'm afraid I was," he glanced at Duncan, "distracted." He looked at James.

Duncan looked at the two men. "I don't really know what that means. You mean, like an ugly man, or are you thinking the story book kind?"

James glanced at the common room below and kept his voice low. Alexander also leaned into the confidence circle. James said, "It's a more insidious kind of Fae."

"Here?" Alexander's voice betrayed more than just childhood fear. "I didn't realize there were evil Fae. I mean, I had heard of mischievous ones, but one that could do something like this?"

"Unseely Fae favor the unsavory side of things. They can be quite dark and cruel. Most of their pranks are benign or at least not like this. One good thing, they tend to shy away from evil folk so we can rest a little easier in regards to the Lady's guilt or innocence." James felt better as Alexander's expression relaxed to be more like the holy man he met the day before. "The worst of them, ones capable of this brutality, live in Krakte."

Alexander shook his head. "Krakte? They have monsters that can do this in Krakte?"

"Well, yes, but they are trapped in the Black Forest. It's a prison. That's my point. I would never expect to see something like this here. Mervolingia is notoriously inhospitable."

"Can they get out? Could this have been a spy from Krakte?"

"No Fae that enters the forest, Seely or Unseely, can leave. But that doesn't stop humans from going in and out, or for them to birth a child from an encounter outside the prison." James rubbed his palm with his thumb. "What are you thinking?"

Alexander's gaze steadied with the seriousness of the discussion. "The former queen, the one I executed for treason, was from Krakte. My mother suspects that will cause problems. It's one of the reasons for the marriage to Catriona, an alliance with Caratia's army, should the need arise."

Duncan closed his eyes. "The only undefeated army in the world."

Alexander nodded. "And not through lack of attempts. When they take the field, weapons can't hit them, not matter who wields them or for what cause. Even Krakte would back down from that fight."

"Unless they side with them."

Alexander's eyes showed his confusion. "Ally? With Krakte?"

"Krakte is a Fae-prominent nation, like Glarren. The Land has always allied with the Fae against the Church."

Alexander looked at Duncan. "James, you said those Shadow things were dangerous to Fae." He looked back at Gwen's brother. "Why? What are they?"

James shook his head. "Honestly, this might be better if you read it yourself. As much as I may not necessarily think Catriona is a good idea for a queen, I think she is a very *good* idea for an ally, especially if Unseely are getting this far south."

James stepped over to the door. "I need to get my things, then I'm taking Duncan to the ship. Less temptation." He turned to the king. "Your Majesty, I know we have some unfinished business here, but with this development, we need to leave."

Alexander nodded. "Yes. How long before we can sail?"

"We can be on the sea before Fourth Watch, Sire."

"Good, let's do that then. I'll go get my things. Duncan, help me, please?"

Duncan nodded and went in the king's room. James didn't want the man in the room with the woman who had such power over him and helping the king might distract the tall pirate. Alistair had told him tales of Tanglwyst's ability and but he had never experienced it first hand. The legends made him very cautious. He stepped into his own room, calling Gwen's attention. She was sitting near the bed, checking Tanglwyst for other injuries. "Did you get him calmed down?"

James shook his head. "Not quite, but I told him he needed to leave her be. She used that device on him at some point."

Gwen looked at the knife on the end table, horror coating her face like a flash storm. "How did he survive?"

"The amulet apparently healed him. He had no knowledge of it so he may have been more under their influence that we feared. Luckily, that no longer presents a danger so we may be safe again."

"So the Shadows are no longer influencing any of them?"

James shook his head, gathering his clothes and putting them on the back of the chair by the hearth. "Not that I can tell. The amount of healing energy he was channeling yesterday would not have been possible if there was a Shadow connection."

"How did it go yesterday?"

He grabbed his shirt and pulled it on over his bare chest. "Amazingly well. He spent all day yesterday at the church, healing people of their wounds. There are a couple mills and the local fishing industry, not to mention a vile man who hurts children. Lots of injuries." He glanced at the wall separating the king's room from this one. "You were right, Gwen. I hate to admit it, but he really is a good man, and worth serving. I saw that yesterday. He healed a little girl who had lost her eye because of this bastard deciding to hurt her in order to stop her struggling as he raped her. Gwen, the child was barely old enough to walk."

Gwen put her hands to her mouth, then leaned on the chair by the bed, her complexion paling. James didn't blame her. He had felt the same way, followed quickly by a near-violent rage.

"What did Alexander do to the man?"

"Nothing yet. Need to confirm he did it first. But Alexander said he might take a lesson from this device regarding disciplinary measures."

She glanced at Tanglwyst's sleeping form and straightened up, her own anger filling her eyes. "I don't know if that would be enough."

"Oh trust me. After seeing what she did to Duncan, yes, that would be enough. The man would likely die, but not before going through something as traumatic as what he put those children through."

Gwen's eyes snapped to her brother's again. "There was more than one?"

James closed his eyes and nodded. "Oh yes. What's more, he's the brother of a noble in Patras and thinks he's invulnerable. Alexander made it clear that this monster was not going to continue to terrorize this town." He shrugged into his doublet Duncan had worn the day before "Of course, with *her* around, I don't think we'll be able to stay."

"What do you mean 'with her around'?"

He tucked his shirt into his breeches. "Let me put it to you like this: Duncan would have broken down the door to be with her. We had to explain to him that he had clearly been on the receiving end of that thing at some point. Despite this, he thought she'd still want to see him."

He shook his head, his eyes reflecting the distaste he felt. "His crotch was split into four pieces from that device, and I can't bear to look at it. I can't even imagine what it would be like to have a memory of it being used on me. And yet, his first and only thoughts for her are that he loves her." He sat down and pulled on his socks. He nudged his chin over towards Tanglwyst. "How's she faring?"

"She's still sleeping."

Gwen turned towards her patient and her sleeve caught the tip of Tanglwyst's device. It spun off the table and clattered to the floor, a loud ping ringing off the clay walls. Gwen and James both watched Tanglwyst for a reaction, but when she continued sleeping peacefully, they looked at each other. Gwen sighed.

"I was afraid of this."

Duncan arched their eyebrows. "A what?"

"A goblin bite. It equates to a Fae sleeping spell. The kind they tell stories about. Usually, you get the Fae itself to wake the person but Gwen said the thing was dead."

Duncan raised his eyes to the ceiling, worry filling his features.

Alexander folded his arms across his chest. "How do we break it?"

James narrowed his eyes and scratched his cheek. "Well, I'm kind of wondering if we *want* to break it. I mean, she's neutralized and she is a traitor to the State."

"She's also a citizen, with fealty or she wouldn't be here now."

Duncan looked at Alexander. "What do you mean?"

Alexander thought about explaining the Summoning aspect of the Power of Sovereignty he had used but stopped himself. Tanglwyst had been missing for a couple ten-days thanks to Alexander's paranoia. Duncan was distracted from this with Tanglwyst here but to find out she was here because Alexander put a *geas* on her? He just might rebel against Alexander and turn back to the Shadows.

"I can feel her Oath still in place if I concentrate on it. Sorry, Duncan. I didn't know that before. I'm afraid I'm still new to all this." He looked at the wall between his room and the one housing the woman in question. "It's possible she restored it on her travels. It truly is simply choosing to do so at this stage."

James raised his eyebrows. "Interesting. So, the classic way to break these spells is, well, rather complicated in this case."

Alexander furrowed his brow a bit. "How so?"

"Well, the way to wake someone from this sort of thing is to kiss her."

Alexander raised his eyebrows and breathed deep. "Yeah, I see the problem."

Duncan spread his hands. "What? What problem? I'll go in and do it right now."

Alexander put his arm out to stop Duncan's progress at the same time James put his hand on the pirate's chest for the same reason, both of them saying in unison, "No."

Alexander looked at his subject. "The same problem still applies, Duncan. She's still an enemy of the state and suspected of treason and regicide. She escaped from house arrest before her trial, thanks to you. Like James said, she's neutralized right now. I can walk away if we leave her like this. You don't want to hurt her anymore than you already have. And vice versa." He looked at James. "What about you?"

James cringed a bit at the topic. "I don't know. I can't focus on strategy if I'm fawning over some woman."

"That's the same reason why I don't dare do it."

Duncan's gaze flipped back and forth between the two men. "Um, I'm pretty sure I've missed something important here. Why are you afraid to kiss her?"

Alexander put up his hand. "I'll handle this one, James. Duncan, Tanglwyst has an ability to… *bewitch* a man into falling in love with her. According to people who have seen it happen, she does it with a touch."

"Yeah, I know that."

Alexander blinked. "You… you do?"

"Hell yes! It's helped us escape more than one situation. She saved my life by doing that when we were breaking her out of her house arrest in Patras. But she has to choose to do it. It's not just any contact."

James and Alexander blinked.

Alexander nodded.

"Oh, well then I think I can handle this task."

"No, Your Majesty, that's still a bit dangerous."

"I've faced danger before, James. I'm certain I can handle this."

"But what about this Catriona woman of yours? Would she be so understanding?"

"Well what about you? I wouldn't want to put my strategist in danger in case she wakes up like she's supposed to."

"Well, I can hardly put my patron in danger for the same reason."

Both men stopped for a moment, thinking about this point. Alexander folded his arms and stroked his chin. "That actually does present a problem."

James took a deep breath, his face showing the inner struggle. "Maybe Gwen can give her a potion or something. Keep her asleep."

Alexander stopped stroking his chin. "How would we get her to drink it?"

"Maybe an infusion then? Something on the skin?"

"We'd have to be careful. Anything we give her needs to not knock us out too."

James nodded. "Good point. Anything on her lips or in her mouth would be just as likely to drug us as her."

Duncan cleared his throat. "Standing right here, gentlemen."

The two men started at Duncan's comment. Alexander had forgotten in the discussion that this was still the woman Duncan loved. Both men muttered an apology and James got a revelation to dance across his face. "Wait, I have an idea."

He turned and left the room, his two companions on his heels. He went into his room where the womenfolk were.

"Gwen, do you know a sleeping spell?"

Gwen blinked a few times, her brow furrowing. "For who?"

"For her." He nodded towards Tanglwyst.

"She's already asleep."

"Yes, but from a Fae *spell*. One cued to be broken with a kiss. *Your* spell can be cued to end when you want it to end."

Gwen looked at Alexander and Duncan, nervous. "Well, dealing with sleep spells itself is dangerous since the divine magic of sleep is very closely related to death. My spell would also be Fae-like. It's not demonic or anything…"

Alexander realized she was afraid of being labeled a witch, and glanced behind him. He nodded towards the door and Duncan closed it.

Alexander touched her shoulder. "Don't worry, Gwen. I'm well aware of the tricks of the forces of Evil. You don't qualify."

She smiled, glancing down at her hands. "Thank you."

He bowed in reply and she looked around the room

"Well, yes, I can do that, but I'll need to gather a few things."

James nodded. "What do you need?"

"Rain water, nightshade seeds, a mortar and pestle to grind the seeds."

Alexander raised his hand. "I have the mortar and pestle. There's a special lining I can put in it to make it useable in the future."

James nodded. "There's a rain barrel outside."

Gwen thought for a second. "I'm sure I saw nightshade in the forest when I was riding through the first time. I almost stopped to pick some but I decided not to, silly me."

Duncan folded his arms. "I'll come with you to protect you in the woods."

Gwen smiled back her surprise. "Uh, thank you."

"You're helping Tangl, and frankly, I'm not certain it would be a good idea for me to stay here." He glanced over at his sleeping beauty. "Might be tempted to wake her early."

Alexander nodded. "I'll go get that mortar and pestle."

"I'll grab the rain water." James walked over and grabbed the basin Gwen had been using to clean Tanglwyst's wounds. He looked at the sleeping lady a moment, then threw the towel over his shoulder and took the basin out the door. Gwen followed him out along with Duncan and Alexander closed the door behind him.

Thirty-Five

"If she comes to you as you slip into death and kisses you, she is taking you become a merfolk. But beware if she hugs you instead."
The Siren's Song of Callista

Gwen and Duncan went down to the stables and got the other horse James negotiated from Ce'Nedra. Gwen's was still saddled but the other one was bare. Duncan approached the animal he was to ride with his hands out in front of him, ready if the animal reared. He had often had trouble with securing a horse since he'd started using the amulet, the instinctive response of such creatures being to flee or fight if trapped. When the animal swiveled its ears at his approach, but then relaxed, his confusion must have shown on his face because Gwen asked, "Is there something wrong, Duncan?"

"Huh?" He glanced at her, then back at the horse. "Oh, uh, no. I just have had trouble with riding horses before. I'm afraid I haven't ridden in a while."

Gwen grabbed the saddle blanket near the saddle, unfolding it with a shake to put it on the horse. "I find the camaraderie with an animal for a journey, no matter how short or long, to be worth the time. I actually avoided riding for many years, sticking close to whatever town I was in. However, my recent experiences have truly shown me the value of a speedier method of travel. Tanglwyst probably would have died in the woods if I had not been able to return here as quickly." She walked over to the saddle on the stand next to his mount.

Duncan walked over and put his hand on the saddle before she could pick it up. "Please, allow me."

"I can get it. I've saddled my own horses before."

"Let's just say it's a thank you for helping the woman I love." He hefted the saddle and took it over to the horse, putting it on the saddle blanket on her back.

Gwen folded her arms. "You're welcome, but forgive me if I feel the need to assist. I'm not accustomed to standing idly by. Not to mention, you aren't skilled at riding horses."

Duncan lifted the stirrup and reached underneath to the cinch. "I said I haven't ridden much of late. I didn't say I was inexperienced at riding. My family raised horses growing up."

"Oh. Why haven't you ridden much recently?"

Duncan focused upon the buckle to avoid looking at her as he figured out what to say. "No need." He put the tongue into the hole and slipped the free end into the holding loop.

"The amulet."

He was surprised she knew about the artifact, but sighed, grateful that he did not need to deceive her. Since being healed, he had lost the addiction to the amulet as well as felt his soul cleansed. Hiding his connection to the thing that almost destroyed him seemed foolish. "I'm afraid so."

"I'm glad Alexander healed you. I hope you stay that way."

He stood and looked at her. "My lady, I will endeavor to do so."

She hesitated for a moment, then cleared her throat. "How did you get the wounds Alexander healed?"

He sighed. "Line of duty, in service to the Crown."

Gwen nodded and smiled. He could see the family resemblance to his friend. "Well, I expect *this* Crown won't let you get hurt like that."

She climbed into her saddle and turned to him. He stepped into the stirrup, following her lead and nodded to the entrance, allowing her to lead the way.

They rode into the woods a ways before she slowed her horse to a walk. "I'm pretty sure they were around here somewhere."

Duncan glanced down at the ground, looking for the poisonous plant and saw a strange drawing in the dirt, like a map. She dismounted, her feet landing squarely on it, obliterating it before he got a good look at it.

"Wait! There was something…"

Gwen looked up at him. "What?"

Duncan pointed to her feet. "There was something there."

She looked down and moved her feet, scuffing the thing beyond recognition. "Where?"

"Never mind. It's gone now. It looked like a small map."

"Oh." She dusted off the horse hair from her rear and looked around. "I think I saw the herb over this way." She pointed off to the side of the area and started walking. The underbrush was quite thick in some of the areas around them and she walked near one of these areas. "Yes, here it is!"

"What can I do to help?"

"Just keep an eye out for anything unusual." She knelt and began to inspect the plants, looking for something specific. "Tangl was attacked by an Unseely Fae. There may be more of them."

"Sure. I have no idea what one of those looks like."

She looked up just as a shadowy figure dropped from the tree onto him, pulling him from his horse. The animal bolted and Gwen stood, her dagger in her hand. The man bore Duncan to the ground far too quick for him to respond. Before, no one could have gotten the drop on him, literally or figuratively, but since Alexander healed him, he realized how much of himself had been controlled by the darkness within him. Gone were his fighting reflexes because he had used the Amulet to move quickly. Gone were his danger senses because he could disappear in the face of overwhelming odds. His sword lay useless at his hip, undrawn even to protect his charge.

A heavy boot stepped on his throat and a sword, thick with dark blood poked his chest. Dark eyes, swirling with hate looked at her protector, an evil humor at Duncan's inadequate security dancing upon his face. There was something monstrous about the man, though neither his size nor his build betrayed it. His ears and teeth looked slightly pointed but that could have been a trick of the dappled light.

"What a luscious thing to be wandering around *unescorted.*"

Gwen brandished her dagger at the creature. "Let him go."

The man looked at her, his smile curious at her threat. "That makes no sense, my dear. Why would you protect one of these?"

Duncan struggled under his foot, grabbing it and pushing but he seemed unable to move it. "Get off me!"

The man pressed harder into his throat and pushed the blade into his flesh. Duncan tried to scream but a weight like a horse pressed down upon him. Spots flared before his vision as he felt his life crush out of him. The man's voice sounded very far away.

"Why would you let one of these things live? They hunted our kind for *centuries* and still seek our destruction."

Duncan gasped and looked at Gwen with pleading eyes. He felt his sword trapped in his scabbard, then realized his boot knife was within reach. Gwen was talking to the man, something about her refusal that she was like him. He called her princess, like a term of endearment, then the conversation was lost in the sound of the blood in his head. His hand wrapped around the hilt and he plunged the blade into the man's upper thigh.

He screamed, turning his attention to Duncan again and the last thing he saw before he blacked out was a bright blast of color as the blood hit is face.

Gwen dropped to a knee, letting the adrenaline quiet in her ears. The half-goblin lay on the grass near Duncan, its muscles twitching in the death throws. She went to Duncan's side and pulled him from the villain's vicinity, keeping him from getting accidentally kicked or poked. She retrieved his dagger from the half-Fae's leg and wiped it off on the man's doublet. She noticed a ring on his finger with some sort of crest on it and took it for identification. She felt a bit weak from the exertion of the spell and sat next to Duncan, checking him for damage. His throat was darkening from the bruise forming but he was breathing so she sat back and waited, keeping an eye out for more monsters.

She was glad Duncan was alright, but just as glad he passed out before he saw the fight. There were some things she didn't want to explain to an Augustinian agent.

"What the hell happened to you?" James helped Duncan off his sister's shoulder and over to a chair.

Gwen looked at her brother and Alexander. "We were attacked by a half-Fae man. He was wearing this." She dug in her pocket for the ring and tossed it to Alexander.

"De Rochefort?" Alexander frowned. "I thought they all lived in Bordeaux, up north."

Gwen looked at the ring. "Near the Krakten border? That would explain it. How's our other patient? Any change?"

Alexander set the ring aside and looked at Tanglwyst. "None. What about you? Were you hurt?"

"Maybe a pulled muscle. That's all."

"Then I'll see to Duncan." Gwen went over to Tanglwyst's bedside while Alexander went to Duncan's.

Duncan rolled his eyes to look at James. "Did we get the seeds?"

James looked at Gwen, who nodded. "We'll do the spell tomorrow morning."

Gwen leaned over to look at them. "I can do it tonight."

"It's more risky at night. Besides, since it's really an awakening spell, isn't dawn a better choice?"

Gwen sighed. "Good point."

Alexander stood. "Let's get him to his room. He'll need to lie down anyway. Come on, Duncan."

"Ugh… And I was just getting less uncomfortable." The three men left the room and went to Duncan's.

The sound of gathering patrons in the main room of the inn filtered up the stairs. James threw a glance over his shoulder. "What's going on? I thought CeNedra closed the Inn."

Duncan closed his eyes, nodding. "She said people were starting to sleep in the street outside with their injured. Apparently, not everyone could get to the church the other morning." He looked at Alexander. "She said to tell you she hasn't rented any rooms though."

Alexander shook his head. "Another reason to be on our way soon. Although the Kingdom will reimburse her for the time, her good heart won't let people suffer when there are beds and comfort available."

James opened the door to Duncan's room. "How did you get through the throngs of pilgrims?"

Alexander looked at James. "Throngs?"

"Stories grow in the telling, Sire. I expect there will be a hundred people in the streets for you."

Duncan nodded confirmation. "CeNedra led us up. Said we were the King's men because I doubt we would have gotten through otherwise. After all, I just look like someone else needing to be healed." He sat on the bed and pulled at his boots. "I think I got touched by a few folks in reverence as we put the horses away. They're everywhere."

Alexander rolled his eyes. "This is ridiculous. We'll never leave here at this rate."

James waited at Duncan's door, looking over the railing. "It's not like you don't know where she's going. You can set up a meeting, maybe get her to come halfway to you."

Alexander eased Duncan onto the bed and knelt down to pull off his boots. "Well, she's in the company of a man that could endanger everything. He's already put her entire crew in danger by not allowing them safe port anywhere in Mervolingia. Her men can't survive on fish and salt water."

Duncan put his feet on the bed and stretched out, a grateful sigh escaping his raspy throat.

"Is there anything your Power thing can do?"

Alexander looked at James. "It was the Power of Sovereignty that put their ship in this position in the first place. Besides, they'd be in Mandian territory by now and I have no power over those ports. But with the knowledge of Myrgen's escape throughout the land, there will be bounty hunters after them now. She may be able to hold her own, but they will have to put into port somewhere and I fear for her safety."

Alexander moved Duncan's boots to the side of his night stand, frowning at something and James looked him over. "What else is wrong?"

Alexander looked at the young captain and sighed. "Gwen said she cast a spell on Catriona, a spell to heal her heart and make way for new love."

"Why did her heart need healing?"

"Because she got it broken recently."

"By you?"

Alexander shook his head. "By the woman in that room." He glanced at Duncan, who was sleeping now. He motioned James over to the other side of the room and they sat in the hearth chairs, not really having any other course with the common room filling.

"Catriona and I decided to join our lives last autumn, a month before the sailing season ended. I had said my goodbyes and prepared my life for being at her side for the rest of it. But Lady de Holloway called her for a meeting before the end of the season regarding refitting the ships during the winter. When Catriona walked into the meeting, Nicolai Moriarity was there. Her husband."

"Right, you mentioned that before. They went back together for the sake of their son."

Alexander nodded. "Well, apparently, it didn't take. Over the winter, Nicolai started seeing Tanglwyst at the palace, then *outside* the palace. She found out as she was bound to do, but being the sort of woman she is, refused to come to me simply because Nicolai was going to Tanglwyst. She was going to leave him, James. Then this whole mess with my brother happened and I landed in the throne with a war with Krakte on the edge of my vision. Add that to the possibility of a religious civil war and my whole kingdom is in great danger."

"Forgive me, Your Majesty, but if a united kingdom is your goal, the best way to achieve that is to stay right here and heal these people, and anyone else who comes here. Spend your summer touring your kingdom and healing their pain. You'll have a strong base and soldiers by the score to fight Krakte."

Alexander leaned on his knees, his face emphasizing his need to be understood. "How long do you figure that will take? Think about it, James. You said yourself they will be a hundred wounded in the streets by morning. They're pressing into this place in the middle of the night. It's not like the roads are closed or snowed in."

"I understand the need to heal this kingdom and I shall. First, I secure the protection of Caratia to guard our borders. I can't risk staying here while Krakte gathers her forces. Especially if their forces are comprised of creatures capable of doing that." He looked at Duncan.

James nodded. "Duncan is no inexperienced fighter, it's true. Half-Fae can be worse than their Unseely parent because a Fae's nature never changes, but humans can hide their nature, and change it. It's smart to fear an Unseely half-Fae army."

"Now, if what you say is true, I am even *more* pressed to get the backing of the Undefeated Army. See why I need to go there, to be there before she falls for... Someone else?" Alexander put his face in his hands, shaking his head.

"Let me ask you this: does she love you?"

Alexander looked at him. "I... I don't know. I know she did but I might have made a mistake recently, while under the influence of that amulet."

"What kind of mistake?"

Alexander took a deep breath. "The Firing-on-her-ship-as-she-fled-with-the-traitor-after-I-tricked-him-into-getting-arrested kind."

James blinked. "Oh, that one. Yeah, who hasn't made that mistake with a girl?" James shook his head. "Wow. So, yeah, a bit of urgency might go a long way with her. Well, my sister can send a Fae messenger to her..."

Alexander raised his hands, leaning back. "Oh no. She's done enough meddling with this. She put Passion Sap in Catriona's drink here in St. Andrew."

James frowned. "She's really putting the screws to you. Are you sure my sister is in support of this?"

Alexander smiled. "Well, your sister has no malice in her heart. She's just trying to help." He sighed, all his paths returning to the same road. "No, I need to make this right in person. I'd still like to send Gwen overland to talk to her. I think she's still got the best hope of convincing Catriona I'm worth keeping."

James leaned on his knees. "Well, we aren't going anywhere until that spell is done, but that does bring up a challenge: Rooms. I can sleep on the ship, no problem, but Duncan is not in any shape and Tangl's in my room. Gwen needs to rest in order to perform the spell. Although Gwen says she wasn't hurt in the attack, she seems a bit overtired from it nonetheless."

"I can watch Tanglwyst and Gwen can take my room. Probably should be me in case any injuries are present. This way, I can make sure Duncan doesn't awake in the night and wake her before we're ready. I know if my love were lying in that bed, you couldn't pry me from her side."

James nodded. "I'll get my things. This will give me the chance to prep the ship and get crew signed on for when we do leave."

Thirty-Six

"The sound of water will guide you to the spring."
The Siren's Song of Callista

Alexander closed the door behind him and set the lock. He was grateful that he wasn't going to spend the night awake, making sure Duncan didn't deliver the storybook kiss. He checked on her slumber but it was unchanged. He eyed the bed, but decided not to take any chances and sat in the chair anyway.

The fact that he had spent far too much time in the chairs made itself known through a series of grouchy complaints by his muscles and bones. His aches got worse as soon as he sat but he refused to fall prey to comfort's call. He shifted around and found a mostly comfortable position and tried to think of something pleasant.

His mind wandered to Catriona, the way she felt, the way she sounded. He loved her perfumes and soaps, her voice, the sound of the sea against her ship. He could feel the touch of her flesh beneath his fingers, smell her hair and her skin. He remembered being with her in the garden in St. Marguerite, how willingly she spread her legs for him. She had been so ready and he had wanted her so much. He hated the fact that he finished before he had the chance to enter her.

His dreams beckoned him to try again, to bring her forth in his mind to pleasure himself within her.

He reached out and touched her hair, her black silk trussed up for his edification. The golden dress was different on her, devoid of all the corsetry and hoops, but still flowing onto her in a glorious way. She shook her head and the black curls tumbled down, freed from their prison. He reached over to her and stroked her face and neck. Her cleavage summoned him, begging for his explorations. He took her into his arms, his mouth kissing his way down her neck to her breasts. He pulled them free, lips devouring her dark nipples. She arched, crying out in pleasure and he knew he had another chance to plunge into her depths.

He pulled her skirt up, feeling the richness of her skin, her thighs together but easily spread. He lay her down and was on top of her, her welcoming embrace making him so rigid, he felt he would burst. He freed himself as she writhed beneath him, her waiting femininity glinting in the night. He pressed against her and pushed, his heart set on pleasure.

What he got was severe pain as his penis was flayed apart into four pieces by the device embedded in her privates. He looked down upon his beloved and saw her eyes change. St. Marguerite's face looked back at him and she thrust her hips, driving him deeper. Flames grew around them, closing in.

Alexander started awake, looking around. The world was not on fire as he feared. He closed his eyes and took a few deep breaths to steady his pulse. He was fine. The dream was already fading but he knew he needed to make amends in St. Marguerite. He said a silent prayer, thanking her for the reminder, then settled again to try and sleep.

His mind shied away from thoughts of making love and he instead decided to enjoy thoughts of being at sea. He missed that and was glad they would be going forth on the morrow to follow his beloved to her homeland. He had never been to Caratia before. The closest he had ever gotten was York, which was technically one country-sized port city. There was a reef which ripped out even the shallowest boats but was irregular and, apparently, capable of changing. When he had been recalled from his meeting with the Queen of York, he had planned to return overland. The Wastland beyond the wall was too hostile and no ships would take him to Caratia. That was whe he heard of the *Enigma*.

That was when he discovered Catriona was *alive*.

It was also where he discovered something called *lutefisk* and it had ruined his bowels, a couple outfits, and any chance of catching the ship that cold travel to her home port. It also was where he started seeking ports that she might frequent. Rumor said she went north at the beginning of the sailing season, to Glarren, but there was never any set route. He now realized that was because of Tanglwyst's orders. She had no set schedule because she was too busy doing "pre-emptive salvage" upon Tanglwyst's targets. Still, it she would go to York, Mande, and Glarren, she might go to Patras as well.

He opened a door in a castle and saw Catriona sitting before a mirror, brushing her hair. She was nude, clad only in her hair which was longer than he remembered. Myrgen walked over to her, wearing the blue robe and dignified clothing from his capture, complete with the ragged edges of wear and tear, but clean and still stylish. He put his hands upon her shoulders and leaned down to kiss her.

Alexander was about to rage against him when he felt a cool hand upon his own shoulder. "This is not for you, my King. Your path lies elsewhere."

He turned to look at who was speaking and saw he was now in his room at the palace in Patras. He was holding a small vial of shiny pink liquid and was standing before his mirror. Beautiful hands slipped from his shoulders, the voice saying "You'll know what to do."

He looked in the mirror, searching his features to see why he needed this potion but there was nothing to indicate a use for it. He heard the stone on stone sound of the secret door closing in his prayer nave and he turned to the darkness to see a figure escaping into the black of the catacombs. He felt a fear of loss, of foolishness and need. Something important was leaving him and he needed to get it back. He ran after the figure in the darkness but she was gone and he knew he had lost the only thing that mattered.

Alexander opened his eyes, his heart aching from the loss he had just suffered. He rolled to his side, as best as he could. He knew he was just dreaming and that he was getting tired of such restless sleep. It was still dark and he was filled with neck cramps and sore places marking the bones of the furniture. He wanted to get some rest in case he was needed during the day and this simply was not working. Every time he closed his eyes, his mind shifted around, not going anywhere in particular except that he was aware he was wandering. He was trying to find his way, but all around him were flashes and images with no coherency. He opened his eyes as a single thought echoed through his mind, using James' voice:

You realize she hasn't moved at all in her spell.

Alexander looked over at Tanglwyst and saw that the voice was right. Not a muscle had moved. She was not aware in any way.

He pulled himself up from the chair and walked over to the bed, his aching body protesting while his mind celebrated the thought of lying down. He stepped over to the bed but realized Tanglwyst was right in the center and he was going to have to move her. He knelt on the bed and picked her up, shifting her to the right side of the bed. Space availed itself and he fell into the bed, grateful for the way the mattress felt and the pillow smelled.

He nestled in and found a relaxing sleep immediately. He found his dreams far more gentle, more of a caress than an assault. Soft pillows, crisp sheets, new flowers and the smell of the sea. He breathed deep this dream and before he knew it, he was safe and comfortable.

A knock at the door broke the hold of rest from him and he breathed deep a scent, peaceful and calm. His concerns were gone, as were his doubts. Instead, he felt rested and his head clear. His mind went to tea and tea parties and he smiled. He opened his eyes, hoping to see Tanglwyst's pale green ones smiling at him. His hand was holding hers, but she was still and quiet as he had left her. She had not disturbed him in his slumber as his fears insisted. Instead, the opposite had occurred.

He closed his eyes again, not quite ready to be awake, but the knocking insisted. He lifted his head to look at the offending door. He sighed and lifted her hand to his lips. He rose and smoothed the pillow and bedding beside her so Duncan would not be offended.

"Yes, yes, I'm coming."

He noticed first thing the taste like offal in his mouth. *When the hell did I eat that?* He opened the door to all three of his companions, then walked over to the wine and cleansed his mouth and throat with the liquid. "How is she, Gwen?"

Gwen examined her with a quick glance, then turned her attention to the items for the ritual. "She's fine. No difference." She looked at Alexander. "Did you move her?"

"Uh, yes. I thought you might need the room."

James picked up the basin of water, carefully bringing it to the bedside so as not to spill it. Duncan looked Tanglwyst over, then to Gwen. "What can I do to help?"

"Honestly, if you can leave, that would be best."

"Leave? Who's going to kiss her then? Wake her up?"

James raised his chin. "I got it."

Alexander furrowed his brow. "Are you sure that's wise, James?"

"Well, let's look at our alternatives. If the go-back-to-sleep spell doesn't work, having her wake up and find Duncan will be a problem. You fear for your royal life from this diabolical creature, so that leaves me."

Duncan shook his head. "You're the captain of the ship we're leaving on. If she entangles you, she's coming with us. Besides, she can only be awakened by True Love's kiss, right? That's the story."

"That will disappoint those ladies at the Red Sky Brothel."

Gwen rolled her eyes. "By the Fae, I can't *believe* you're tossing through this argument again! Look, you both leave and I'll get Saiban to kiss her when I'm ready! Go! Leave!"

Alexander folded his arms as the two men got indignant and looked about to argue. "Actually, I've got this one. James, I need the ship prepped and all our things on the way to it. Duncan, I can't leave this building if there are throngs of pilgrims waiting down there for me. I need you to clear a path or find a new one. I can help Gwen if anything goes wrong. Please, that's my Will."

"How will you protect yourself if she wakes up first?"

"I have my ways. Right, Duncan?"

Duncan blinked, then nodded, remembering. "Yes, Sire, I believe you do." He nodded to the door, guiding James away from the bed. "I'll explain later, on the ship."

James frowned. "But Gwen needs me for the ritual."

Gwen didn't even look up from her preparations. "No, I don't."

James seemed to concede defeat and Duncan closed the door with finality.

Gwen exhaled. "Finally, peace."

Alexander smiled at Gwen's exclamation and nodded. "They do seem to be fighting quite a bit for this."

"I can't figure out why. I mean, I guess I understand Duncan's point of view, but James?" She shook her head. "He can kiss a dozen pretty girls if he just walked down the street. Why is he so fixed upon this one?"

"Well, Tanglwyst is legendary. Her ability is known and feared among the members of my gender, Gwen. Escaping her is like escaping a kraken. Legend has it she leaves no survivors."

"You're joking."

Alexander shook his head and drained his wine. "Not a bit. Gomez told me."

"So why are you so ready to risk *your* soul?"

He swallowed. "Because, in the cold light of day, I know such talk is nonsense. No one has power that isn't given to them. This lady is no different. I was around her all winter. Catriona is still the only woman I love." He exhaled, looking away from the lady's sleeping form, where his eyes had settled. "Now, what can I do to help?"

"Mostly, just keep the room quiet. I'll need to concentrate."

"Okay."

She mixed some herbs in with the nightshade seeds and began chanting some words to herself under her breath. Alexander decided to clean his teeth and wipe his face to freshen up. He took the cloth by the pitcher of water and got it wet. Gwen was using the basin with the rain water so a quick wipe down was all he could muster. It felt like enough to freshen the ripe places. It wasn't like he was going to get a chance to bathe again once they were on the ship.

Gwen poured the contents of the mortar into the basin of rain water and a small puff of green powder bounced off the surface of the bowl. She dipped the pestle into the water and used the stone grinder to paint a couple symbols upon Tanglwyst's clothes.

Alexander watched with interest. "Why are you putting it on her clothes?"

Gwen kept writing. "Nightshade is a deadly poison, even this diluted. If it gets on her skin, it can kill her. Not to mention that you're going to have to kiss her soon. I don't want this stuff where it will put you to sleep as well."

"Thank you for that."

"Besides, this way, when the time comes to wake her, all I have to do is rip her shirt and the spell is broken."

"You have all the fun."

She stood. "Okay. We're ready. Wake her up."

Alexander wiped his mouth and tested his breath, which was fairly clear from its earlier foul scent. He realized he had just done this and was glad Gwen was looking over her handiwork so he would not have been embarrassed. He covered his awkwardness by bringing up the protection aura his Sovereignty afforded him and stepped over to sit on the bed. Gwen moved to get in a better position to watch the process, which made Alexander feel more self-conscious.

"Would you mind giving us a little privacy here?"

Gwen looked at Alexander. "Why? If the spell doesn't work, I need to be here to hold her while you get away."

Alexander scattered through several responses, but decided the best one was to just kiss the woman and get it over with. He was protected. He leaned down and kissed Tanglwyst's lips, a quick peck that barely touched.

He sat up and exhaled. "There."

"It didn't work."

Alexander's eyes went wide and he started shaking. "What? You mean she's..."

"Still under the first spell, yes."

"Oh, I thought you meant she was awake and in control of me."

Gwen furrowed her brow. "No. When my spell comes into effect, the symbols here will glow." She pointed to the symbols. "They aren't glowing."

"Oh." He looked back at Tanglwyst. "Should I try it again?"

"Yes, and maybe you should actually make contact with her. I think that last one went too quick."

Alexander swallowed. "Well, I don't want *that* kind of reputation." This time he leaned down and made sure he actually contacted her lips. He could feel the aura strong and firm between them but he figured the aura was part of him too so it still counted. He glanced down at the symbols, but there was still no glow.

Gwen frowned. "I must have done something wrong."

Alexander looked down at the powerful woman on the bed and took a deep breath. It wasn't Gwen's fault. "No, I think *I'm* the one doing something wrong. This is a Fae spell, right, like the ones in the stories."

"Yes."

"Well, those are broken by a more specific type of kiss, I'm afraid. I think we might need to go get Duncan after all. He loves her."

"We'll need to hurry. It's almost too late."

"Go then. I'll wait here."

Gwen left in a hurry and Alexander was finally alone with this woman. He couldn't have done this with Gwen in the room, or anyone else. He wasn't a public sort of person when it came to this. The kiss on Catriona's ship was the first time he had ever been so bold as to be affectionate like that in front of people. This was more his style.

He touched Tanglwyst's cheek and moved her hair from her neck. It was quite soft, James having washed her hair the day before so she would not wake up bloody and disheveled. Her hair was brushed, which Alexander had thought was a very tender gesture. Now, he was reaping the benefits of that kindness and he was grateful. He leaned down and smelled her neck. She had an amazing scent, truly her own and immensely powerful, and he drank it deeply, reveling in it. He brushed his lips across her skin, touching her like a suitor, finally able to express his desire. He looked at her peaceful expression and his heart reminded him of the promise of a dance which he never fulfilled. He had been lying before when he said Tanglwyst had never tempted him. In truth, she had almost saved him.

Yes, I could fall in love with her.

He lowered his protective aura and kissed her with his bare lips. Hers were cold, like she were outside in winter, but as he continued to kiss her, he warmed her with his own. He felt her body temperature rise and she began to kiss him back, a small moan escaping her lips. Alexander felt his protective aura come up, but instead of allowing it to separate them, he made it encompass them, joining them in a holy bond.

His hand draped across her shoulder, his thumb stroking bare skin on the edge of her shirt and she raised her hand to touch his face. Suddenly, the symbol on her chest flared and Alexander found he was saddened a little by the presence of the other spell. But this sadness came from within, not from an external source, and he didn't think it was because she started to wake. Her hand dropped inches from his skin and her breathing became deep and regular, different from the other sleep. He watched her again, tracing her lips with his fingers, before pulling away from her to let the spell do its work.

He went to the door and left, returning to his own room. He drew a few breaths to shake of the desire to return to her and try again to awaken her. He knew that would be counterproductive. Gwen had set the spell to end when *she* chose, not from any other interference. Best to ready his gear for the trip. He changed clothes and returned for his Chirurgeon's kit.

Gwen and Duncan were in the room as expected and Gwen turned to see him enter. "You did it?"

He bent down and closed up the kit, rearranging things so the lid would close. He would have to tidy it up when he got on board. "You might say I had my self well-defended and love isn't about that. Love is about letting your defenses down and running the risk of getting hurt. It's a dangerous endeavor, Gwen. If you're not willing to put yourself in danger, then you can't do what needs to be done." He nodded towards the glowing Tanglwyst. "Obviously."

He left the room and finished packing his things. Duncan came in and leaned against the doorjamb, folding his arms. "That was rather insightful."

"Thank you." He lifted the small pack he carried onto his shoulder, reaching in and finding a small pouch of gold he had set aside the day before. He dropped it on the vanity as a bonus for Ce'Nedra and all her patience. "Did you clear the way for me to get to the ship?"

"Yes, we found a way through. This way, Your Majesty."

"Again, thank you." Alexander took one last look around the room and closed the door behind him.

Thirty-Seven

"Excuses are the crutch of the cowardly. A truly
lazy person does it right the first time to avoid
the extra work."
The Siren's Song of Callista

"*This* is your way out?"

"It's the only thing I could think of."

Alexander looked down at the large carpet toward which
Duncan was gesturing. The tall bald man's plan was at least
unorthodox and probably wouldn't work but Alexander wasn't
sure how else to get through the throngs of sick and infirm pilgrims
who had turned up in St. Andrew to see him. The number had
doubled, at least since he had checked last night. James looked at
the carpet, then at Duncan, knitting his brow and rubbing the back
of his head. He seemed to be trying to figure out how to explain to
Duncan the breadth and depth of stupidity this plan exercised.
Alexander ran his hand through his hair and turned skeptical blue
eyes upon Duncan.

"What makes you think for a second that rolling me up in a
carpet and carrying me on your shoulder is going to work?"

Duncan shrugged. The bald man was over six feet tall, and wearing a white linen shirt he had borrowed from James. James was *not* over six feet tall, joining Alexander in being about a head shorter, and the outfit choice made Duncan look a bit silly in this early morning light. His arms stuck out below the wrists and his tummy kept peeking out when he raised his arms.

"Look, most of the pilgrims are asleep at this point. It's still early. We can do this. We can make it look like you're someone who didn't make it through the night, waiting for you to heal them."

James darted a look at Alexander and apparently his guilt showed on his face. The people assembled below were here because they needed healing, they needed help and Alexander was abandoning his people. No matter what, it seemed pretty selfish and petty when the light was shined upon it. His rash actions with Elizabeth has brought them to this end. Had he controlled himself at any time in the past month, this wouldn't be so urgent.

James cleared his throat. "Look, we can't stay. My sister put that sleep spell upon Tangl in order for us to escape. If we stay, the damage Duncan sustained in the attack yesterday will have been for naught. Forgive me for saying so, Sire, but I won't tolerate you taking these people for granted. You hold her fealty as well."

Alexander looked down at the carpet again. Duncan looked at the carpet, then at Tanglwyst, sleeping and glowing on the bed. Alexander knew he had to do something.

"Duncan, as much as I hate the idea of leaving, James is right. If we stay, Tangl might wake up and that puts her in danger. Think about the number of people who are here on blind faith right now. If they heard an escaped traitor was here, who had a hand in the killing of the king..." This idea seemed to hit the mark and Alexander put a hand on Duncan's shoulder. "Besides, I still don't think she'll receive you like you're hoping and I'd rather you leave here with hope than stay and be defeated. You can compose a letter on the ship for her, apologizing. I'll even help you write it."

"Actually," Duncan reached into his doublet, "that reminds me. I'm staying here."

James shook his head, chastising. "Duncan, you can't."

Alexander folded his arms. "It actually might be a good idea."

They all looked at Alexander.

"She trusts you, despite whatever happened before. She let you travel with her before and you protected Gwen in the woods. Get her home, put her back under house arrest. There, she'll await trial by me, but frankly, I plan to pardon her. After all this, to still have her fealty..." He shook his head. "She's no traitor. She's probably our greatest patriot." He looked at Gwen. "I hope you won't mind."

Gwen took it. "Not at all, of course not."

Alexander took a deep breath. He had donned the clothes he had worn for years looking for Catriona. "I'll just wear my hood up. I've managed to travel the length and breadth of the coastline for years without being identified. We should be able to leave unmolested and not rely upon deceptions wrapped in carpets. Luckily for this endeavor, I'm not well known to my people yet. My coronation has not yet been held and my brother's death is still on the wind in messenger birds to many provinces and villages. None will know it's me they seek."

"Should I accompany you to the ship?" Duncan's face was the pillar of grateful soldier.

"No. This place might be swarmed by the time we set sail. You two need to get Tangl out of here before it's discovered who she is."

The two men walked towards the stairs and Alexander saw with great trepidation the magnitude of pilgrims amassed on the floor of Ce'Nedra's fine inn. Several people had lain in rows, all but blocking the stairs to the door. Family members and friends were propped sitting, asleep, or kneeling in prayer beside their charges. The smell of sweat and pus was overwhelming.

"By the Saints..." James scanned the floor of the inn, his voice low. No one below seemed to notice them in the pre-dawn hour.

Alexander shook his head, overwhelmed by the task before him. He couldn't leave with all these people sick and hurt. "Are you changing your mind, James?"

James rubbed his palm, concerned. "Will you lose some of that fealty power you hold by not healing these people?"

"I don't know. I'd rather not test it but I've got to get to Caratia before it's too late. I can feel things slipping away with each passing hour."

323

James took a deep breath and nodded. "Okay."

Alexander nodded and James said, "Why don't you return that rug to my room so Ce'Nedra lets us come back here, okay?"

Duncan picked up the rug and walked into the other room. James waited until he was out of earshot. "So, are you really that concerned about Tanglwyst's fate, or are you just trying to get to your intended before someone else beds her?"

"To be honest, a bit of both, but also a dose of duty to the kingdom. I had my healing power held hostage when I started the other day after mass. I've been getting signs and dreams for days now about St. Marguerite. I know I made a huge mistake there. But I made a bigger one a few years ago. There's a lot of things to confess."

He looked at James. "That's going to be where I'll need a strategist the most. Mother was right. Krakte's armies are formidable, especially if populated with a few shock troops of half fae. I need Caratia to protect my country. Otherwise, we'll lose this war and all that healing will be lost on the dead."

James nodded at Alexander's reaction but didn't say anything more. It gave him a moment of pause, though. James was eerie in his accurate assessment of Alexander's fears. "I need to do something before I leave. I'll be right back." The king turned and went back into the room where Gwen was watching over Tanglwyst and closed the door behind him.

"Gwen, I need you to accompany Tanglwyst to Caratia."

Gwen stood from the chair in which she had been resting, her excessively long blonde hair shifting in the dawning daylight like heavy brocade.

"What?"

"She's going to want to follow me to Caratia. Take her overland to Zara."

Gwen looked back at the woman asleep in the bed and Alexander followed her gaze. Tanglwyst's auburn hair flowed onto the pillow like a satin cover and her delicate lips even now called to him, begging for a replay of his kiss to break this spell too. She was designed and built for sex, from the rise and fall of an ample chest, to the nature of the pheromones from behind her ears. Even her feet, small and with very high, graceful arches, begged to be touched. She hadn't laid a hand upon him, not awakened or been aware of him, and he caught himself feeling like this. *Would I still be on this trip if Alan had never shown up at the palace?*

"Why is she going to want to follow you to Caratia?"

Alexander tore his eyes from the sleeping woman. "Because she won't have a choice. I need her there, to deal with Myrgen."

"Deal with Myrgen?" Gwen's eyes started to grow wide, understanding what he had in mind.

Alexander knew he needed to act fast while her Oath of Fealty was still intact. "Gwen, I command it."

A pulse of energy flew from Alexander and hit the two women. Gwen turned to him, giving him a bow. "As you command, Your Majesty."

"Thank you Gwen. I promise, you'll be rewarded."

"Only your praise is necessary, Your Majesty. I am your servant."

Alexander left the room, settling his thoughts so he could face Gwen's brother and Tanglwyst's lover. He exhaled and walked back over to his companion, standing next to Duncan. James glanced at his sister's room. "What did you do?"

Alexander turned his thoughts away from the woman in the bed. He knew if he dwelt upon her too long, he might be turned from this course. *Catriona is my destiny, not Tangl.* "I told Gwen to keep an eye on Duncan here. I don't know if the Shadows will try and reclaim him without me around."

Duncan looked at the door behind which his beloved lay sleeping. "I'll stay vigilant as well. I won't let them take me without a fight."

"Thank you. James, let's get to your ship."

Alexander brought his sleeve to his nose, the early morning silence peppered with coughing and snores. This action served both to shield him from the smell of illness and hide his features. He started to descend the stairs and one of the propped watchers opened his eyes fully as Alexander entered his notice. The man moved to a kneeling position, moving out of the way of Alexander's progress.

"Your Majesty."

With this utterance, the other vigil holders turned to see their savior entering their midst, their eyes alight with hope.

"I thought you said they wouldn't know... you..."

"What?" Alexander looked down but saw nothing unusual about his appearance.

"You're, uh, glowing."

The vigil holder looked up, nodding at the conversation. "Yes sire. You emit a regal light. I knew instantly you were my king. It is why I have come to you, to seek your mercy for my family."

Alexander felt the tug of sorrow towards his people and he reached out and touched the man who first showed him homage.

"Please, be comfortable."

The man stood from his kneeling position, as inferred by his king. "Sire, my brother is sick. Help him."

Another citizen lifted his head. "Sire, my wife, she has been injured and lost her hand. Can you heal her?"

"Sire, my son is crippled…"

"My sister is blind…"

"Sire…"

Alexander reeled from the bombard of requirements.

Duncan's voice boomed in the early morning light from the balcony. "*Silence.*" He looked at Alexander.

Alexander opened his eyes. *Saint Brigit, help me now or I'll walk away.* "Please. Take your sick and injured outside. I shall heal them on the way to my ship. But there are others in my kingdom who are needy. I must attend them as well." He looked at Ce'Nedra. "My lady, can you find me an honest city official?"

Ce'Nedra smiled at the jest. "I think I know one or two."

"Then have them meet me on the docks. I have instructions for them." He looked over the nearest pilgrim and knelt beside her. He touched her, hoping the glow was for healing.

It was.

Her hand regenerated before his and the onlookers' eyes and he again was hailed as a miracle worker. He stood and turned to her family. "She is whole again. Go now and help the others be in my path."

Her husband nodded and his wife bowed before her king and then scurried off to move someone out of the doorway. The next person in his way was a man with miner's lung. Alexander could hear it in his cough. He touched the man and he was cured. Alexander sent him on the same task as the couple. With each person cleared from his path, he sent them on to aid those outside

326

and by the time he got out the door, there was a path lining the street but clearing of bodies. He saw a rich woman lying next to the road, lamenting her failing health but behind her, denied access to the street by her husband was a young sailor without a leg. Alexander reached out to the sailor and healed him in passing, ignoring the woman's imagined ailments.

This was the case all the way to the docks, where the phenomenon was finally explained. The priest stood on the docks, sprinkling holy water from a near-empty basin held by Antony the choir boy. The entire area had been blessed, enabling Alexander to extend his holy ground limitation, at least temporarily. At the docks, Saiban stood with a short, bespectacled man in a dressing robe holding a journal and graphite. "Your Majesty? I'm Henri de Porthos. I was told you needed me?"

Alexander smiled. "Yes. I have something I need you to investigate regarding the local mills."

Gwen watched the door close and let out a sigh. The man who had fallen in love with her friend and Mistress had just broken her heart. His obsession with Gwen's captain had gone past simple adoration. He was dangerous. He had just tried to use her oath of fealty against her, to make her take Tanglwyst to Zara. Who knew what he would do to Catriona? Gwen felt her oath lose ground and drop and suddenly, she could see Alexander for what he was: a liar and a cheat. She shook her head, amazed she had once thought this man was the one for Catriona. She was more embarrassed she once had a crush on him.

She rested her eyes and when she opened them again, she realized she had nodded off, as had Duncan. She went over to the window and saw James' ship on the horizon, barely visible. She felt comfortable now for herself and apprehensive for her brother. Regardless, it was time to wake her charge.

She shook Duncan awake. "We nodded off. We need to make sure we aren't seen leaving with Tangl. Would you go check the streets and figure out the best way out of here?"

He nodded, stretching. "Of course."

She walked over to Tanglwyst after her closed the door behind him, and took out her dagger. She ripped her shirt down the front, destroying the symbol keeping her asleep. Tanglwyst arched her back and gasped breath like she had been underwater. Her eyes flew open and Gwen moved back, sheathing her dagger to keep from frightening the lady.

"Hey. Are you all right?"

Tanglwyst looked around the room, fright prickling her eyes and movements. "Where am I?"

"St. Andrew. You were attacked in the woods by a goblin. You killed it," she pointed to an instrument on the nightstand, "with that."

Tanglwyst picked up the vaginal knife, turning it over in her hands. "Oh. Yes, that's right." She looked at Gwen. "A goblin?"

"Yes. It's what is called an Unseely Fae, a dark, unpleasant creature that preys upon the unsuspecting. It probably attacked you because you were wandering lost in the woods at night."

"I... I wasn't lost... I was..." Tanglwyst's brow furrowed, trying to get..." Her eyes widened. "Oh! Alexander! I need to help him." She started looking around, frantic. "I need to get to him. He's in danger but he's not... here now."

Gwen wrinkled her brow. "How did you know where he was?"

Her movements were frenetic and Gwen grabbed her hands. "Tangl, he's fine. He's been fine this whole time. He was here, in this room beside you. He helped heal you."

She seemed to calm down. "I don't know. I realized in the woods I could tell where he is anytime."

"Where is he now?"

Tanglwyst pointed in the direction the ship went. "About an hour's journey that way."

"You realize that's at sea."

"You realize I own a shipping company."

Gwen nodded. "Yes, I do." She looked down at her hands. "You know, you don't have to go."

"No, I do. He's..." She frowned as she searched her feelings. "He must have touched me or something."

"Yes. He kissed you. You were under a spell."

Tanglwyst looked at Gwen. "He... kissed me?"

"Yes, though I'll tell you now, I suspect you're still under one." Gwen shifted, knowing they didn't have much time to talk in private. "Tangl, why did you feel you needed to rescue him?"

"I kept dreaming he was being hurt, held by bandits. They were going to kill him if I didn't make it. I felt my strength draining every day."

Gwen stood up. It was a compulsion, and it would kill her if Gwen didn't break it. "Tangl, you're under a spell. He's not in danger. He never was. You are though. I can break it, I think. I know some…"

Tanglwyst touched Gwen's hand. "No."

Gwen turned and saw that this woman knew full well into what she was walking. "You *want* to stay under this compulsion?"

"Yes, I do. Look Gwen, what I did was wrong. I can't even tell you why I did it. It wouldn't matter. I know I'll be executed for treason. But he broke a spell upon me, saving my life. He doesn't want me to die. I feel better, like when I first started this journey but back in the woods, I was almost dead already. It really wouldn't have mattered if the goblin had finished the job."

Gwen found herself even angrier with Alexander for this. He apparently could have stopped the summons if he wasn't planning on killing her. He *chose* not to end it. "Tangl, he plans to use you to get to Myrgen."

Tanglwyst stood up, worried. "Myrgen? How?"

"If he has you, he can make Myrgen come to him."

"By the Saints." Tanglwyst swallowed the fear in her throat, but it migrated to her eyes. "Gwen, I can't stop it."

Gwen went over to her fiancé's employer and knelt beside her, looking up at her eyes. "Yes, you can. Forego your Oath of Fealty and you'll be free."

Tanglwyst drew back from Gwen, horrified. "No. Never. I'm a citizen of Mervolingia, Gwen. This is my home. I would not sooner renounce my Oath than cut out my own heart."

"But he's abusing it! He's using that Oath to torture you and plot against your brother!"

Tanglwyst grabbed Gwen's arms. "That's his right. He's allowed to punish those who threaten his populace. He has a responsibility to us. Myrgen and I made a mistake by trusting

Elizabeth. She knew exactly how to play me to get what she wanted. Between the drug and her suggestions…"

"Wait, what drug?"

Tanglwyst shook her head and got up, clutching her torn shirt closed. "Nothing. Forget I said anything." She looked around for the basin.

Gwen wanted to press the issue but she didn't feel it would end up well. She went over to some saddlebags in the corner of the room. She opened the flaps and pulled out a spare shirt. "This should fit."

"I can buy something in town."

"As a well-known wanted criminal?"

Tanglwyst opened her mouth, then closed it.

"Thank you. So, where is he going?" Tanglwyst took off her doublet and torn shirt. She fetched the basin and poured some water from the pitcher to wash up.

"Caratia. He is chasing his future queen."

Tanglwyst paled. "Out of the frying pan, it seems. You're supposed to bring me to him, right? How?"

"It's faster to go overland than by sea. Especially the way I do it."

"How's that?"

"I employ a Fae sprite to show me the way that will be the least trouble, the least distance."

"A Fae? You mean like that thing that attacked me?"

Gwen repacked her saddlebag. "Sort of. I attract a friendly sprite, not a creature like a goblin. Unseely Fae are very unhelpful."

"So, I gather from your comments that your Oath is not intact?"

Gwen took a deep breath. "No. He just tried to force me to obey his whim and make you to come with me to your death so he could use you to get rid of his rival in love. I don't take well to that sort of thing."

Tanglwyst blinked, wiping her face dry with a towel. "A rival in love?"

"Yes," Gwen closed her saddlebag and stood up. "Catrion…a." She looked over at Tanglwyst who was stunned, eyes wide. Gwen gulped. Oh no.

"*Catriona?*" Tanglwyst screeched. "The-woman-who-tried-to-kill-me *Catriona*? That one? Because I just want to be sure before I overreact."

Gwen winced. "Yes?"

"Oh I can't *believe* this! First Nicolai, now my own brother? This is a nightmare."

"If it helps, Alexander is trying to stop him from getting together with her."

"Like anything Alexander does is going to stop my brother and his charms."

"Are you sure?" Gwen felt the worry rise in her eyes. Myrgen was still a traitor, but when Gwen thought about it, having Myrgen win Catriona away from Alexander would be some pretty tasty revenge. He already had the upper edge with the charm Gwen had cast.

Tanglwyst leaned on the bureau next to the basin. "Think about it. He's my *brother*." She turned back to folding the towel and wiping the bureau down from the sprinkled water. "We're cut from the same cloth." She waggled her head. "Mostly."

"Mostly?"

"We have different mothers. I'm the only product from my parent's union. My brothers were from trysts when my father was at war. My brother Caiaphas is part York and Myrgen is part Toledan, near the Caratian border. My other brother Morgan was adopted."

"Really? I never would have guessed he was from there. I never knew you two were brother and sister until you invited Dom and me over for Twelfth Night."

Tanglwyst smiled. "That was a fun party. We were pulling that colored straw from places all year." She looked at Gwen. "I'm glad you came to that."

"Why?"

"Because I wanted to see what Dominic saw in you and I saw it that day. You were amazing."

Gwen blushed a little and swallowed the guilt in her throat for all the snide remarks she had made about this woman. "Thank you."

"You're welcome. We should get on the road. Although I feel good now, by the time I travel for two ten-days, I'll be pretty weak."

"So you're going to do it? You're really going to go to Caratia and help Alexander take her from Myrgen?"

Tanglwyst shook her head. "No. Part of my Oath is to protect him from all dangers to person and country. Catriona is a danger to his person, and a threat to our country. He will lose most of the support of the nobility and half the populace if he marries outside his faith, not to mention the support of the Church, something he can't afford to lose. This is very much a case of saving him from himself."

Gwen nodded and Tanglwyst got dressed. Suited up and ready to go, they stepped out of the Inn room and went to the stairs. Inside were several sick and injured people. They were coughing or moaning and Gwen descended the stairs with great sorrow. Duncan stood at the bottom of the stairs, looking over the crowd.

Tanglwyst looked into the faces of the infirm. "Where did all these people come from?"

"They came to see Alexander. He can heal people by touching them now, apparently."

Tanglwyst's horror showed in her face. "And he just left them like this?"

Gwen nodded. "Looks like it."

"Duncan?" Tanglwyst leaned over to confirm his identity as he turned to look at her.

His face and body were stricken, like what he was seeing was changing him somehow. "My Angel."

"What are you doing here?" She put her hand on Gwen's arm for a moment, like she wanted Gwen to stop moving toward the tall man.

He looked at a small child who was hugging her father. The child had vivid blue eyes like the older man at their feet who had a nasty cough. He sniffed. "Finishing the King's work."

He turned to Gwen and Tanglwyst. "Gwen, I'm sorry. I can't go with you on your journey. I think I know why His Majesty left me here. It was not to protect the two of you from molesters."

His eyes and voice turned cold and deadly. "It was to handle another matter." He took a deep breath and did not look at them again. "I hope you will forgive me."

He then strode through the crowds to the door and out into the light.

Gwen looked at the old man with his family and realized she could probably help with that cough if she had the right ingredients. She turned to talk to Tanglwyst and she was stooping over an injured woman, looking at her bandages. They were hastily done and she began unwrapping them, speaking to her in a low, soothing voice. Gwen smiled and nodded to Tanglwyst when she looked up. They would stay and help.

Thirty-Eight

"Tears and blood are a memory's physical form,
for they both leave stains."
The Siren's Song of Callista

Catriona picked up the report regarding the influx of supplies from Portabella and frowned. They were able to resupply many of their stores, enough to get them to Pardua at least, but she hated the cost. She stood and paced again, her boots wearing the finish off the boards in her cabin. She had neglected herself and the room was devoid of her usual scent of spice and sandalwood and reeked of seared lumber and sea salt.

Her ruse had worked, and her plan as well. The citizens of the pirate port had fallen for the illusion Estelle wove, and her own ability to read the sins of people had put the fear of damnation in the people. They had paid with supplies, food, even wood and nails and the crew had two more barrels of fresh water to get them to the next port. Catriona planned to send a note with proper compensation to Xeno when they stopped in Pardua. She had not known he was in charge of the place when she pulled in, or the ruse would not have been necessary. Once it was begun, it would have been a problem to change the plan.

Besides, if she had, Myrgen might have stayed on board.

She closed her eyes and furrowed her brow, then opened them and threw the report across the room. She had stayed inside her First Mate's cabin, watching over Estelle and waited until Myrgen left the ship and she had somehow managed to stay away from the rail to watch him go. If she had been in her own cabin, she might have been tempted to tear the boards from the windows to watch him go. With the illusion up, he never would have known unless he had ventured back into the illusion. If he had done that, she would have run to him and kissed him for the third time, sealing their lives together.

She had not even told him goodbye when she had the chance. Part of her never believed he would actually leave. Now, it was as if she had been told he had died and been buried somewhere unknown. Her heart had trouble believing they would never see each other again. Hourly, it was a fight to keep from telling Octavius to turn the ship around and retrieve him. She had not slept since they had left him there and dawn was overtaking them quickly. By afternoon, they would be in the Storm Catch, a treacherous area of land that held the turbulent maelstroms from the first peninsula of the Fingers of Mande. The smell of rain was already threatening and she knew, as soon as the storms actually hit, there could be no turning back.

He left me on purpose. It's my fault he's gone. If I turn back, I'll just be taunting him. I've already made my decision to be with Alexander. Don't make his gesture futile. She stopped and leaned on the chart table, her heart was aching and her eyes threatening to tear up again. She had fought her tears all night and she wasn't about to let them win.

She looked at the table, then at the boards across the walls where there used to be her beautiful stained glass window. She used to look out and watch the shore as they left it behind, or count the knots on the boards that checked their speed. Now, they were just boards across the hole from the attack in St. Marguerite, but those boards meant as much to her as the window right now, because Myrgen had put them there. His hands had placed them evenly, but his heart had built them, and she regretted with all she was that she had not kissed him at any of the opportunities presented. When he had her against this very table, her legs parted as he let his lips taunt her skin, refusing to actually kiss her until he had entered her, insuring she was his. She should have grabbed him and thrown *him* to the ground, taking the kiss.

Instead, they had fought before he left and her pride and anger had held her back when she should have begged him to stay. He had been the best thing to happen to her and she could not believe she had let him slip away. Her shoulders started to shake from the pain in her heart and she pounded on the table, her fists taking out on the wood what they could not take from her any other way. The tears beat against her eyes and with a scream of frustration, she fell before them, collapsing on the floor. Cascades of burning regret scored her cheeks, splashing onto the boards as her whole body shook from grief. She felt sick and she laid her head upon her arms in the floor.

Why? Why did you do this to me? Was this a test? You make me your defender, protector of your people. You throw my lost husband at me, then rip him from me again. You return to me a man I loved before he became King and then, when I am poised to do all you have asked, by the Stones, you bring this man before me as well? I have felt within my soul the very definition of love but I have denied it because it did not fit your plans! I am willing to leave my home, my ship and my crew to do as you have bidden. Must you pull this last joy from my life as well?

She raised up, her hair hanging to the floor in places. Strings of saliva connected her to the floorboards and she could feel her face was red and puffy. She opened her eyes, the swaying lanterns casting indifferent shadows around the room. She wiped her mouth and eyes with her sleeve and sat back on her heels, still staring at the floor. It was beyond effort to lift her head or even her eyes to look around the room. There was nothing here, nothing of him. He was gone and she had let him go. Soon, there would be nothing left of her.

His room.

Her head snapped up. *His room!* It had been barely eight hours since he had left the ship. She stood and opened her door, not caring if anyone saw her anymore. She went next door to his cabin and stepped in, closing the door behind her. His room still held the destruction from the cannonball, scars from the ordinance scuffing the floor after it hit the desk, destroying the top and drawers. The wall between their rooms had an expert patch where Myrgen had closed the wound the cannonball left behind. She lay down upon his bed and buried her face in his pillow, breathing in his scent. The smell brought the tears again and she closed her eyes against the onslaught.

Please, please, let us be together again. I'll do anything. Whatever it takes. Just don't let anything happen to him before I see him again. Please, let us be together again and I'll devote my life to your will.

The scent of his hair reminded her of the night he slept beside her, guarding her. She had awoken lying on his chest, his arms wrapped around her, the scent of the linen from his shirt surrounding her. She had felt so safe there and had forgotten all about being angry at her ex-lover, Alistair, for setting them up. Now, she would give anything to have those arms around her. Her loss started to sink in again and she felt her heart aching, she missed him so much.

She felt someone sit next to her on the bed and she opened her eyes to see Myrgen beside her. His brown hair had some streaks where his time in the shadow realm has sucked the life from the strands, and he looked upon her with grey eyes the color of storm clouds. His skin was tanned from working on the ship and his arms muscular, accenting his toned chest. He was wearing the beautiful clothes he had been in when he was arrested, a dark blue doublet and breeches with a long robe over the top. The collar of his eggshell linen shirt was embroidered with grapes and grape leaves. His hair was as unbound and free as her own, but he did not look like he had been crying. He reached out and smoothed a stray hair from her cheek.

"Hi there."

"Myrgen?" She threw her arms around him and he held her close, hand buried in her hair.

"What's going on here? I thought this would be easier for both of us."

Catriona shook her head. "No. It's horrible. I don't know what to do without you."

"You'll do what you always do. You'll survive. I'm not dead, Catriona. We'll see each other again."

She pulled back to look at him. "When? When will I see you again?"

He smiled. "Probably when you least expect it."

"I never got to say good bye. There's so much I wanted to tell you and I never... I never..."

He put his fingers on her lips. "I know. I feel the same way. But this needed to be done. The crew is safe because I'm not there and I won't put them in danger like I did in St. Marguerite. I won't let them be hurt because of me." He looked down at their entwined hands. "Never again."

"We're doing better. Estelle should be strong and surefooted soon. We got re-supplied in Portabella like we needed. We're going to be okay."

"Then the price I paid was worth it. Just as the price you pay now is worth the debt incurred. The Land saved the life of your son. You vowed at the time to serve its will until you died. Even I came to realize you could not turn your back upon that debt. That's why it won't return me to you for the same oath. It already possesses that."

Catriona let her eyes drop. "Octavius said the Land would not require me to leave everything I loved to serve it. He doesn't understand the prices it extracts of the servants it takes, the trial it puts us through. The Rite of Succession alone demonstrates the lengths to which the Land will go to make certain the right person is on the governing seat. Those candidates must let go of everything they know and love in order to have the chance to serve. The Land extracts a price in blood, because it gives blood to the people every day. This is not so different a price."

Myrgen squeezed her hand. "You know your god, Catriona. You have faith and do not doubt. Don't start now. Now, it's time for you to rest. You'll need your strength. There's a storm coming."

He kissed her forehead and smiled into her eyes. She closed them as he came in to kiss her and then smelled rain.

She opened her eyes and realized the smell of rain was powerful. The ship was rocking in the swells of waves and she heard the sound of rain hitting the deck above her. She looked around for signs it had been other than a dream but found nothing. She looked down at his pillow and picked it up, holding it to her face. She stood, holding it and then opened the door, ducking into her room before anyone called out to her. She put his pillow on her bed and then pulled her gloves from her belt and put them on. She left her room and looked into the dawn.

Red sky at morning, sailor, take warning. Time to get to work.

Thirty-Nine

"The healing comes from the Barber-Surgeon,
the sword from the Quartmaster."
The Siren's Song of Callista

Alexander opened his eyes, stray images from the lingering dream fresh in his mind. He felt confused by the images and, as he sat up, he tried to put them into some perspective.

He saw Catriona, as he did almost every night, but this time, the dream echoed of Tanglwyst and the ones he had back at the inn when he was guarding her sleeping form. He kept getting the impression the dreams were pushing him away from Catriona and toward Tanglwyst, but that didn't make any sense. Why would he turn away from stopping this war before it even starts, in favor of a traitor he'd have to execute?

He reached down and pulled on his boots, then rose and retrieved a clean shirt from the foot locker at the end of the bed. He wanted to talk to someone about the dreams but he wasn't sure who would be best. The images, the emotions, the settings all seemed to be inferring a connection or desire he was loathe to entertain. Tanglwyst's "love touch" was too dangerous and

Alexander could ill afford to lose himself in anyone but Catriona at this time. Besides, he knew his feelings for Catriona were real. There was no way to be sure with Tanglwyst.

He tucked his shirt into his breeches and walked outside. His restless sleep had kept him in bed for hours after dawn and he felt embarrassed as he saw the rest of the ship up and active. He sought out James and greeted him.

"Hey." James looked non-committal when it came to Alexander. He was reading a manifest and didn't stop looking at it when he spoke to the king. "Decided to sleep in, eh?"

"More like I couldn't wake up. Restless dreams."

"My sister says dreams are the mind telling us what we want. What did you dream about?"

Alexander glanced around. "Tanglwyst."

James looked up, arched an eyebrow and smiled. "Really?"

"Do you think she could have used her spell on me?"

"When? At the Inn?" James shook his head. "Doubtful. Not enough time."

"Duncan said it was instantaneous, that she just chooses to do it."

"Well yeah, but she didn't wake up, did she?"

Alexander looked at his hands folded in front of him. "Well, not exactly. She started to respond to my kiss, but then the spell went off and she dropped back into slumber."

James nodded, his brow furrowing in concern. "I see. So, she started responding, huh?"

Alexander nodded.

"Well, then maybe she did bewitch you. Do we need to turn around?"

"What?"

"Turn around? So you can be with her?"

Alexander shook his head, his eyes widening. "Uh, no, I…" he stammered, not really understanding what James was trying to say.

"You sure? I can chart a course back. I'm sure Gwen's awakened her by now. She'll be up and functioning." James looked up. "Granted, you might have to fight Duncan for her, but, well…"

Alexander held up his hands. "Okay, okay. I get your point." He snorted a small laugh. "You're right. There's no compulsion."

James nodded. "Good." He returned to looking at his manifests. "That means your interest in her is valid." He turned to the main deck. "Hey Mitchell! Where did that crate of eggs end up?"

As James walked away, Alexander's expression dropped a little. *Valid?*

He watched James talk to his First Mate for a moment before turning and going over to the railing. He knew he and Tanglwyst had grown close over the winter. He began to look forward to their visits. Emmy's little parties were uplifting in a time when it was hard to smile. She got him through a very difficult time.

Of course, all that changed when I saw Alan at the palace. Once I knew I could see a part of Catriona, I no longer cared about anyone else.

He realized that was no different from what Duncan was going through. Catriona had escaped with a traitor he was bent on executing, one who kidnapped her son. This was easily as powerful a betrayal as the one Duncan experienced from Tanglwyst and her *dentate*.

Except that he tried to rape her.

Which is different from what I did to Catriona how?

He imagined Catriona would see it no different. Her ship was damaged, her trust violated and she had to flee for her life. He still hadn't figured out how to apologize for that. He hoped it would come to him while they were at sea.

James leaned on the railing next to him. "Thinking about your lady?"

Alexander nodded. "Yeah. Trying to figure things out. I have no idea how to apologize for what happened between us."

"Which part? The firing on her ship or the making deals with demons to pursue her?"

"That was harsh."

James shook his head. "Was it? Do you really think she'll go with you when you get to her?"

Alexander glanced at the deck. "You don't know her like I do. She spent all winter looking out her window at my room. I have come to her side and saved her life at least twice a season for the past several years. I spent almost a decade looking in every port and every harbor for her until I found her. We belong together, James."

"Well, it sounds like you believe that. I'm just asking if *she* does."

"Why? Why would you ask me that now, here?" Alexander gestured to the ship. "We're already on our way. I left possibly a hundred people in pain back there to go after her."

"And you seem to think that will impress her." James shook his head and rolled his eyes. "How can it be that I know her better than you?"

"You can't."

"But you know this isn't right, at least on some level."

Alexander folded his arms. "Is that why you consented to take me to Caratia, so you could lecture me?"

James looked nonplussed. "You're not going to intimidate me here, Alexander. You put your friend through something you're unwilling to endure yourself: waiting. You did the same thing to those people you left behind. I don't know Catriona like you do, but I'll tell you this: She has a lot more substance than to put up with a self-centered son of a bitch like you."

"How can you say that to me?"

"Because I'm not your friend. I don't give a damn about your ego or your money or your position. So I don't have to make it palatable. All I have to do is speak my mind. Your own guilt at your actions is haunting your sleep. You endangered my sister for this endeavor, abandoned hundreds of people who came there to be healed by you. From a strategic point of view, *that* was a mistake. You had the chance to bring Catriona to you by helping *your own people*, yet you walked away to chase her. If I were a woman, I'd never look back if I managed to get away from you."

Alexander's mind tried to formulate the right thing to say and it came to him in an instant. "Well, if you were a woman, I might be dissuaded. You sure you don't want to put on a dress and give it a try, James?" He winked at the young ship captain, who shook his head, smiling despite himself.

"So, you feel better about your dream then?"

Alexander's smile relaxed. "Yeah. It's probably just because it was all so recent. I'm sure it will shake out the further I get from her and the whole mess."

"I hope so. I don't need some tragic creature weighing down my ship and depressing my crew."

Alexander nodded. James was right. He could go back to St. Andrew, heal those people and, when word spread to Caratia that he was working miracles, she would come. Of course she would. She'd be happy to see what he could do.

And she'd bring her new lover Myrgen!

The thought stopped his heart. He couldn't turn back. He didn't know what Myrgen had in mind, but she had rescued the man in St. Marguerite. Whatever his plan, it seemed to be working. Alexander's heart started to ache and he felt his brow become damp. He stumbled into his cabin and sat on his bed, breathing deep until the pain subsided. He couldn't turn back. Not if he expected to regain her, and stop Myrgen from getting her.

He closed his eyes and put his face in his hands. No matter the course, he felt defeated.

"That James guy is harsh. You going to do anything about him?" Saint Giles looked at Saint Brigit, who was watching Alexander on James' ship.

Brigit shook her head. "No. He isn't a player in this game. He's one of those Fae creatures. His faith is false."

"Unfortunately, his opinion is true, and accurate. Why did you push the Champion into this? You, of all people, hear the suffering of others."

It was true. Usually, as a Saint, they could listen for prayers or not listen as the occasion demanded. Being brought into Heaven to help the Angels did mean they had certain duties. Although none of them were bombarded with a cacophony of prayers every day, this luxury was denied during each Saint's personal feast day. On that day, the Saint began at sunrise and any prayers offered them came unfiltered until the next sunrise. It was on her feast day ten years ago that she had heard Alexander Angloume's prayer to save the life of the young woman with whom he was now obsessed.

"I wanted him to be more than he was, more than they wanted for him. None of the reigning royalty had an understanding of the suffering of their people, but *this* man did. He *cared* about someone he had never met, cared enough to save her. I gave him the ability to do it."

"But then you took it away. He went for years healing people without your direct intervention. Why do this now?"

"Because *now,* he's Heaven's Champion. The forces of evil in the world are growing bolder. If he is shown to be a holy man, he will bring the fallen to Heaven."

"The Angels do seem very interested in getting more souls up here. Any idea why?"

Brigit shook her head. "They guard the Well room constantly though. I fear the Well may be running dry."

Giles nodded. "That was my fear as well. I am being called upon lately as often as I am on my feast day. The activity of the monsters is beginning to impact humans on a regular basis."

Brigit turned from the viewing area. "Have you got a Champion selected as well? Just in case?"

He nodded. "I have. Just in case. George and I are planning to join forces. There is a Crusader from the Soulless Wars that has been trapped in a tempest for three centuries. He fights a beast from the desert Fae, one of fire. George says he has left him there to make him undefeatable against the Land's minions. He should be immune to magic by the time he is needed."

Brigit breathed deep, trying to relax. She knew the man to which Giles referred. Someone who had known only war, set to the task during the years following the near-destruction of the world by demons. She feared he would be ill-suited to rule the throne of Mervolingia. When one has known only war, peace was not possible.

She returned to her vigilant watch of Alexander.

Gwen and Tanglwyst rode into the forest just as the sun was setting. Gwen turned back to look, saddened by the fact she was not as helpful as she wanted to be. She and her companion were able to administer the poultices and things she'd made, rewrap bandages and set breaks, but when it came to healing the people, she felt lost. The more she heard about Alexander's miraculous healing, the more angry she became that he had left to pursue Catriona. These people needed his help and he left them.

What kind of king is he going to be?

She shook her head and turned back to Tanglwyst, who was looking at her.

"Thinking about Alexander leaving those people?"

Gwen nodded. "I just can't believe he ignored their pain, their suffering to pursue a woman."

"He didn't, Gwen. He healed many of them. There were more who arrived after he sailed away. He *told* them he had others to heal in other towns."

"But that's *not* why he left. He left to chase Catriona. It really burns me that he may actually get her."

"Well, I really hope he doesn't." Tanglwyst sat high in her saddle. "That woman will not be the right choice for him. I can't believe he's pursuing her."

"If it helps, he's been pursuing her for years."

Tanglwyst's brow furrowed. "Years?"

"Honestly, since he met her, the day her son was born. She disappeared for a few years and then they ran into each other at an inn in Cheryb. This was after she had heard Nicolai had died, when she got her black wardrobe. Hasn't worn any other color since."

"Even after she and Nicolai found each other again?"

"Not even then, though for a more practical reason. She didn't have time to get a new wardrobe this winter. Now, of course, it doesn't matter. He died in Rouen a month ago, according to Alexander."

Tanglwyst's gaze slipped to the neck of the horse. "Yes, I heard that."

Gwen swallowed, remembering now that Tanglwyst and Nicolai had been a couple while Alexander and Catriona were getting together. "I'm sorry. I didn't mean to…"

Tanglwyst looked up. "I know. It's just… this winter was difficult for all of us."

Gwen looked around and nodded into the woods. "We need to get moving. Are you sure you're up for this? You worked hard all day. We're still pretty close if you want to go back and rest."

Tanglwyst shook her head. Bringing up Nicolai's death stung and she realized she was the fault of that death. More blood on her hands. "No, we will never get out of there, and Alexander isn't coming back in time. There were cartloads of sick and infirm on the main road coming into town as we left. News of his ability has spread farther than even he can reach through a Royal Decree. I only have two ten-days before I can't function anymore. I need to get as close to him as possible by then." She looked Gwen over. "Do you need to rest?"

Gwen shook her head. "No. I took some tea earlier, when I was starting to feel worn out and it refreshed me. I'll need to get some sleep later though, but for now, let's put some distance between that place and us, shall we?"

Tanglwyst nodded. Gwen had cast the way-finding spell in the stables and the horses already had golden eyes and a spirited step. They nodded to the woods and Tanglwyst thought she could see a thin gold strip in the air before the horse, like a scent made visible. It went off in the direction of the deep woods and both horses bolted when the women spurred them.

Tanglwyst worried about little else than staying in the saddle while the horses ran through the night. She kept herself low to the horse's neck, as she saw Gwen doing and when the horses stopped running, the familiar signs of Patras were all around them. It looked for a moment like they weren't going to stop but then Gwen steered the animals around the back side of the capital city and they came out of the woods near her house. Tanglwyst felt a ping of fear as the thought hit her that maybe she was going to be turned in, but Gwen looked around carefully before they left the concealment of the woods. It was breaking dawn and Tanglwyst knew they had covered far more ground in a single night than was possible any other way.

They put the horses in the stable and went into the house from the back door. Gwen looked around, confused. "There's wood by the fireplace."

"Isn't that normally where you keep it?"

"No. Not when I'm leaving town for an indeterminate amount of time." She went over to the kitchen area. "Someone has been here."

Tanglwyst felt the fear return. "We should go, Gwen."

"What? I'm not going to leave my home. If thieves or worse have set up here…"

A creak behind her from the bedroom drew their attention. A tall, slender man with soft, doe-like eyes, brown hair cut in a bowl shape and Mandian skin stepped into the doorway, scratching his head. His hair was mussed and he had a bit of drool trace on his skin by his mouth. "I don't think I actually qualify as a thief since I'm engaged to you."

"Dominic!" Both women spoke in chorus, and then ran to the current Kingdom Chancellor to hug him. He returned their embrace.

He looked at Gwen. "Where have you *been*?" He looked at Tanglwyst. "And where have *you* been?"

Tanglwyst waved her hand. "That's a very long story."

Gwen started to answer, but instead she just nodded, jerking a thumb in Tanglwyst's direction. "What she said." She hugged her man. "What are you doing here?"

"Taking care of the place. Your animals needed feeding and your house needed to be kept up or someone might come in and squat here. I didn't want your home violated, so I stayed here last night."

"And you cleaned and took care of my animals?"

"Please, Gwen. Don't be silly. I hired some people to do it. Well, one person."

A tall Nubian man came out of the bedroom as well, built like he was carved from onyx, wearing work breeches and pulling on a shirt. He had long hair braided into tubes that he had tied back in a tail, which had the effect of looking like a faggot of willow branches tied with a ribbon. He had been bald when Myrgen had purchased him from the auction block in Veniche a couple years ago, the slavers having cut his hair to make him manageable. It hadn't worked.

"Michael."

He looked at Tanglwyst and nodded respectfully to his employer's sister. "Your Honor."

His Nubian accent was all but lost as he perfected his hold on the Mervol language, and she had been told Myrgen had taught him other languages as they traveled together. Her brother felt people would say things in front of a servant, especially a foreign one like a Nubian, because Occidental arrogance decreed no one of a servant class could possibly be literate or speak the native tongue. Often, they thought slaves only understood beatings.

Unfortunately, Tanglwyst was in an even more awkward place than most people when it came to Michael. While she was under the influence of the drug from Elizabeth, she had pushed herself sexually on Michael and he had only barely escaped. She had yet to get the chance to apologize for that. Gwen released Dominic and ran over to hug Michael. "Thank you for taking care of my home."

"I am grateful you have let me stay."

"Here, let me get some tea going and we'll sit and chat." Gwen went to the fireplace and pulled the kettle from the hook.

Michael went behind her and started stacking wood on the hearth.

"I need to speak to you, Tangl." Dominic motioned to her and Tanglwyst followed him into the bedroom. He glanced around the corner of the room to ensure they weren't being overheard, but lowered his voice to a whisper anyway. Tanglwyst looked around the room. Gwen had a small bed, built for one and Tanglwyst looked around.

"Where was Michael sleeping?"

"On the floor, where slaves belong. He tidies up the blanket every morning, and puts it in the basket by the bed." He turned back to face her. "What the hell are you doing back in Patras?"

"Just passing through, I'm sure. I'm heading back out tomorrow. I have to get to the King."

"Why?"

Tanglwyst shook her head. "I don't know. I felt like he was in danger but he wasn't. Now, I only know I need to be where he is."

Dominic frowned. "And if you aren't, do you get sick?"

"Yes."

Dominic rubbed his forehead, pulling his hand down his face. "A Royal Summons. Of course. Commanding a citizen to come to the King or die trying. That explains why there's been no Decree involving your death, like there was for Myrgen a few days ago."

"What? What decree?"

"You didn't feel it?"

"I was unconscious for several days. Gwen pulled me out of it."

"Were you hurt?"

Tanglwyst looked into Dominic's eyes. They had always been able to be very honest with one another, the kind of honest they couldn't be with anyone else. "Yes."

"What happened?"

"I was attacked in the woods by an animal and Gwen found me. She took me to Alexander, who healed me." She looked out into the area where Gwen was puttering and Michael was telling her about the activities of her chickens. "Gwen told me he can heal by laying his hands on people, if he's on holy ground. It's a miracle."

"A real miracle? Not some kind of witchcraft?"

"No, this is the real thing." She looked at her friend again. "He must have touched me because otherwise, I'd be dead by now, if not from the Summons, then from the animal attack. My clothes were ruined from all the blood on them. We're here to rest and re-supply, then we're back on the road."

"Wait, both of you?"

"Yes. Gwen has the ability to get us there. She knows the way overland to Caratia."

"Well, I'm sure there's someone else who can get that information. She should be here, where I expect her."

"Well, I'm sorry to inconvenience you, Dominic. She's offered to help me and I need it. I'll die if I don't get to him in time."

He folded his arms, pouting. "I guess she's just another resource to be used, right?"

Tanglwyst closed her eyes, remembering the details of their last conversation. She was still under the influence of the drug Elizabeth had administered and had said some terrible things, things she didn't believe were really true but she said them anyway. "Dominic, that wasn't me saying that. Elizabeth drugged me."

"How convenient."

Tanglwyst grabbed Dominic by the wrist. "It was decidedly *not* convenient when I finally came out of it. Knowing all the horrible things I had said and done? Kidnapping Catriona's child to get her to implicate herself in the murder of the king? No, I'm not that kind of person."

"Or maybe you are and you just never knew it. Maybe the drug didn't change you, it just destroyed your inhibitions against your true self."

Tanglwyst turned away from him and took a few steps away. She wanted very much for Dominic to be wrong but then she saw something that made her think he might be right after all: A kinky black hair on the pillow, next to a wet spot of drool. Dominic had been in here sleeping with Michael. *That's why my touch never worked on either of them.*

She felt very sorry for Gwen. She didn't deserve to commit herself to someone who would not do likewise. "I'll tell you what, Dom. You let Gwen go with me, and I'll let Michael stay." She turned to face him. "How's that?"

Dominic looked at the pillow and realized what she had just figured out. He paled a bit and then nodded.

"Get dressed. I'm sure you have to get to work soon." Tanglwyst turned away and went back into the main room. She went over to Gwen and whispered in her ear, "Problem solved. He won't give you any trouble about leaving."

Gwen looked at Dominic as he came out of the bedroom, his foul attitude obvious on his face. "What did you say?"

"Let's just say the drug that Elizabeth gave me apparently didn't give me traits I didn't have. It just revealed them." She held Gwen's eyes a moment as understanding passed between them. "I'm sorry. I guess it means I really am this cruel."

Gwen watched Dominic nod to her and pat Michael on the back as he left for the palace, then brought her eyes to the floor at the women's feet. "Well, we might need that cruelty before this journey's over. At least it has managed to get it started."

"Yes. Now, do you want to sleep first or second?"

"I'm not really tired yet and I want to do some baking for the trip. You go ahead and sleep now. I'll come in after a while and kick you out."

"See that you do." She walked over to Michael. "Will you be here when I wake?"

"I don't know."

Tanglwyst took a deep breath. "Then I'll say this now. There's no excuse for what I did. Not to you, to Alan, or to Myrgen. I wanted to apologize. I don't know how to make it up to you other than to tell you I'm going to see Catriona, and possibly Myrgen, if he's still with her. Did you want to come with us?"

Gwen looked up from her dishes.

"If you come with us, Michael," Tanglwyst continued, "You won't be coming back here. You're a criminal and a slave here, but there, you'll be reunited with my brother. It's up to you. You don't have to decide now, but think about it." She looked at Gwen. "I'll see you in a few hours."

She walked into the room and turned the pillow over. She didn't want Gwen to see this and figure out what she had. Tanglwyst wasn't even certain Michael was willing in all this or if Dominic was forcing himself on the man. Michael was a fugitive, a known accomplice of Myrgen's. All Dominic had to do was alert Gomez to this hiding place and Michael would be executed as a traitor. Michael was in danger here, as long as he was under Dominic's influence, and Tanglwyst had a bit of a problem with that. Besides, something in her instincts told her to lie to Dominic before, when he asked about how she was hurt. She knew the man was a Saint worshipper, like herself, but the things that Tanglwyst had seen of late meant she needed to have faith of a different sort.

And she was learning to trust her instincts.

Forty

"Don't follow a bad map twice."
The Siren's Song of Callista

Alexander awoke, the scent of fresh spring flowers flowing into his open window. He got out of bed and walked over to the window, looking out onto the rooftops of Patras. A single light was on in a window half a mile away and he could swear he saw the woman he loved sitting there. Had he only known at the time this was where she lived, he would have bought a spyglass to watch her. He decided to get dressed and walk over to her, to see if he could persuade her to leave with him and return here. He left the window and pulled on his boots, surprised to see he had fallen asleep in his clothes again. He brushed his hair in the mirror and left the room.

He walked until he found her house, the light in the upper window a backdrop for her silhouette. He was about to throw a pebble up to catch her attention when movement inside the house caught his. He looked through the window but did not see what was happening. Fearing a burglar, he went to the front door and *went inside. A cat ran from the room with a mouse in its mouth. He looked up the stairs and decided he couldn't wait. He had waited all winter.*

He went up the stairs two at a time and opened the door. She turned from her perch at the window, her auburn hair glinting in the sunlight.

"Alexander?"

"I'm sorry. I couldn't wait any more." He walked over to her. She stood, confusion playing upon her lips. Her lips parted to speak, but he silenced her with a kiss. She fell limp in his arms and he panicked. He heard someone enter the room.

Gwen stood in the doorway.

"How did that happen? I was supposed to wake her."

Gwen walked over and touched her. "You were lying to her. So now she's dead."

Alexander looked at the woman in his arms and felt her grow cold...

Alexander sat up, his heart pounding. This dream was only slightly different from the others he had for the past several days, but the same theme seemed to permeate them: infidelity with Tanglwyst, resulting in death. He knew Catriona couldn't read him but it was no comfort when he kept dreaming about a woman who would destroy him and his plans. She would be responsible for the destruction of thousands of lives if this war was fought. He had to find a way to put her from his mind.

He got out of bed and knelt, closing his eyes in prayer. His fingers gripped the blanket on the bed and the stag at his neck, an artifact one of the crew had given him after Alexander had healed him from a broken finger a few days ago. Alexander had donned the pendant to help ward off the dreams but he couldn't tell if it was working. This was the first dream since he put it on, but he could only hope the last few nights' dreamless sleep was due to this and not sheer exhaustion.

He prayed a generic prayer to the Saints, asking for help with the dilemma before him. He could not figure out why he was dreaming of Tanglwyst. He was starting to really worry that James was wrong and that Tanglwyst *had* delivered her bewitching touch. He could think of nothing else to cause them. He had requested

James avoid St. Marguerite because he felt they were still too close to put onto the shore. He believed Tanglwyst would feel him touch Mervol soil and she might turn away from her path. He *needed* her in Zara, usable against Myrgen. Having her come here would simply muddy the waters.

St. Marguerite was across from them on the shore. It looked no different from here than it had when he last visited on Catriona's ship. Her touch, the feel of her next to him, all this drove him now, but he realized it also drove him to something else far more sinister. His guilt over the way he left things in this village haunted him. He would probably have a city against him if he returned.

Alexander had decided to help out on the ship, doing barber-surgeon duty for the crew. Little daily issues kept him from dwelling overly on how much longer they would be at sea, such as the broken finger a few days back, or the sprained ankle yesterday. One of the men on board was a priest and had blessed the deck so Alexander could heal, and once that occurred, every man on the ship had come by to be repaired. He determined at least half the crew to have been infected with syphilis. None of the victims had started having brain damage yet, but it was in their future. Now, with a crew as fit as their first time on board, everyone seemed to have higher energy levels and be faster on their work. He expected this to slow down soon enough.

But these constant nocturnal visits with Tanglwyst were a problem. He would need to touch her as soon as he saw her to keep her alive, provided she survived the trip overland. The trouble would come if she was coherent and had decided to bewitch him for his negligence. The more he thought about it, the worse became this idea of having her around to control Myrgen. He felt certain she could get Myrgen to come to her, and if he could get Myrgen away, he could...

What? Have Duncan kill him like he did my last rival for Catriona's affections? How will that jeopardize my soul? Brigit wants me to stop the deaths, not add to them.

Then again, who knows how many have died because I left St. Andrew?

He had a hard time telling if he was on a path of salvation or damnation. At present, they both felt the same. He looked around and saw it was still dark. It had been a few days since he had left St. Andrew and he felt no less aware of Tanglwyst than he had when he leaned down and kissed her. All expectations of time and distance causing the emotions to fade had been proven false. He wondered how Duncan could stand it, having actually experienced her. All Alexander had done was kiss her.

He closed his eyes and put his head on the bed. He wished he had the shadow amulet now more than ever. To be free of this ship and next to Catriona would end this whole thing. If he could just talk to her, he could convince her to be with him. He felt the strength in this belief, this one recurring thought. It had worked in St. Marguerite. She had not only changed to accommodate him, but had gone with him to the garden and then to bed. If he had been able to perform with her, she would be his now. He was certain of it. She would probably be pregnant, in fact, with his child, thereby *ensuring* she had no choice but to be his Queen. This familiar mantra comforted him and he felt his tension release.

He lifted his head and movement caught his eye near his footlocker. It glinted in the faint illumination his own night vision provided. He leaned over and reached for the item and when he did, he realized what it was: An amulet. He stopped his hand in mid-reach, then pulled back slowly, like it was a dangerous animal and sudden movements might cause it to attack. He didn't know how it could have gotten on the ship but he didn't dare alert James. He'd probably accuse Alexander of bringing it on board or summoning another demon. He needed to get rid of it.

Alexander took his hand into his shirt sleeve and picked the amulet up with the cuff. He had been right, it *was* an amulet similar to the traveling amulet James destroyed. He had done it by fire, but Alexander knew from Catriona's ship that fires were not just left going on a ship. Everything was covered in flammables, including the clothing of the sailors. A fire was devastating to a ship. Instead, he opened the door and walked outside to the deck. He went to the side and threw it as far as he could into the sea. It disappeared beneath the water's surface and he exhaled, relieved.

"Killed a rat, eh?"

Mitchell's voice almost caused him to scream in surprise, but he managed to calm himself before turning. "Yeah. I woke up and it was practically sitting on my chest."

Mitchell smiled, his light brown curls tight enough to resist the sea-faring life. They bounced defiant, challenging Calista to do her worst. "Those things frighten the hell out of me. Never liked rats."

"I hear you. What are you doing up, Mitchell?"

"Couldn't sleep. Dark dreams."

Alexander frowned. Did the amulet cause nightmares in anyone nearby? "Dark dreams?"

"Danger, mostly. Storms, raiders, sharks. Nothing consistent. After a while, I just can't settle my mind."

"I see."

Mitchell frowned, crossing his arms. "Except tonight. Lately, it's been, I don't know. What do you call it when you keep dreaming the same thing?"

"Recurring?"

Mitchell's curls danced as he nodded. "That's it. I keep dreaming something's on the ship and is going to burn it. I've been going around every hour, making sure there are no fires on board."

Alexander glanced at the sea where he threw the amulet. "Really?"

"Yeah. It's odd. I've never been afraid of a fire on board before." Mitchell nodded. "Well, I'm back to bed. If you're still when I get up again to check for fires, just ignore me."

"I'll do that."

As the young man left the area, Alexander looked around. He would have to be very careful going forward. He didn't dare summon that thing again.

Forty-One

"The Water does not take what is not hers."
The Siren's Song of Callista

In the shadows, behind a lie…

Something about that felt sinister and Myrgen shook his head, trying to escape it. He tried to open his eyes but they wouldn't do it. Either that, or he was surrounded by a deep darkness. He tried to move, tried to breathe but everything failed. He opened his mouth to scream and felt oil flow into it, filling his body with darkness. A briar of shadows gripped him, tearing at his clothes and flesh. Myrgen sent forth his mind, lashing out. He searched around for a rock and this time, there was nothing there to save him. Jagged arms wrapped around him and he was dragged into the depths.

He started awake, sitting up and almost screaming. It took a few moments for his heart to slow down and he felt like vomiting. *Was that a dream?* He looked around, not sure where he was and came upon the eyes of a young woman with reddish-brown hair and eyes the light grey of altar marble. Her green dress had laces that went down the front but the laces seemed stitched in place, not really holding the dress closed as much as looking like it was. Colored heavy thread seemed to be woven into her hair in a brilliant trio and each was festooned with charms and beads that tinkled when she moved. She had her hand to her chest and her eyes were wide.

"You scared me to death!" She sat forward a bit, shaking her head. The charms caught the sunlight sprinkles and she smoothed her skirt into a more demure state with brisk strokes.

Myrgen rubbed his face with his hand. "Where am I?"

"On the cliffs outside Portabella. It seems the Fae folk decided to make a plaything of you. I wonder what you did to get them to cast a sleep spell on you like that."

"What? A sleep spell? How long have I been asleep?"

"Well, knowing the way these things work, I'd say no less than a hundred years."

"What?" He scrambled to get his feet under him but his trip up the cliff face took its price right then and only let him take a knee.

No. Nonono, please tell me I didn't miss her.

The leaves above danced happy shadows in the afternoon light as he scanned the harbor and then the sea for signs of the *Enigma*. There was nothing. He sat back on his heel and closed his eyes, dropping his head. She was gone.

"I'm just teasing you. You weren't up here two days ago when I was here last so it was probably just a little while."

"The Fae folk put me to sleep?"

"From the looks of it. We had a powerful spirit come through here two nights ago and something like that always attracts the Fae in the area."

"Two" he looked over at the woman. "Two nights ago?"

"Yes, a big ghost ship pulled right into harbor down there." She pointed to the bay. "A spirit called for ransom from one of our townsfolk. The mayor said no one was supposed to pay," she toyed with a blade of grass, snorting under her statement, like the direction was a foolish one. "Of course, they did anyway. I think everyone did who sets out milk or wine for the Fae behind a box in his kitchen, and probably several who don't even do that. People do odd things when they think it will save them from their prior transgressions."

"You know a lot about these things?"

"I know enough to kiss a sleeping man when I see him in the woods. I must say, I'm a little disappointed in the response. You're supposed to be grateful and fall in love with me for saving your life. You must learn to be more polite to women who rescue you." She tucked her legs under her and came up on her knees, extending her hand to him in greeting. "My name is Belladonna."

"Myrgen the Grey, ma'am." He took her hand, a moment's brush of his lips upon her skin.

She smiled and sat back. "Did you want to go into town?"

"Actually, I think I would like to sit here for a while, first, if you don't mind." Myrgen looked out over the sea of which he was no longer a part and felt his heart sink. *She's gone. I didn't even say goodbye.* He closed his eyes and let his breath go, wishing it would take this pain away but he knew it wouldn't. He was ready to stay up here and watch her go, to *let* her go, so he could leave and not dwell upon the absence of her. But the Fae took his closure away from him and the void left threatened to consume him. His soul ached like she had died and been buried without his knowledge and his heart rejected the belief they were separated forever.

He watched the sea move, the sounds of town filtering up the cliffs to his ears. He was surprised he had acclimated so easily to being on land again, but then he had just spent two days sleeping. As noble as his idea had been to save the crew from being attacked by bounty hunters, he now realized he missed them more than he thought he could.

"You seem to be lost in thought? Are you such a rare visitor?" Belladonna sat beside him, watching his face.

"Huh?" He looked at her. "No. No, I'm afraid I spend a lot of time lost in thought."

"Tell me what it's like where you are."

He blinked away from her. "Lonely."

She touched his hand. "Can I ease that loneliness?"

"I don't think so. It's self-imposed."

"Self-imposed? Why would you do that?"

He looked down at the ground, then got to his feet. "Because it was appropriate."

Belladonna narrowed her eyes. "You loved her."

"Yes, but it wouldn't have worked out between us."

She shrugged. "She was dead. What did you expect?"

He looked at her. "Dead?"

"The way you're looking at the harbor, it looks like you missed the ship you came here to meet, or you miss the one you were on. There's only been one ship come through recently, and your reactions indicate a connection with that particular ship." She leaned back, studying him. "I think you came in on the death ship."

He looked out over the harbor again and hung his hand on the strap of his satchel. *So much for people thinking I've come from this direction.* "Well, she's gone now. I guess that's what I should be doing as well."

"You're not staying?"

"No. I have things to do, Belladonna. Things I've put off while I was," he hesitated, not knowing what to say next. He couldn't put this woman in danger by telling her he was wanted by the Mervol government. He had given his name so automatically and now he regretted even that. He ran his hands through his hair.

"Falling in love?"

Such sweet naïveté. Catriona was right. This girl believes in magic, just like the rest of her town. She has no way of knowing that my days of pushing myself to exhaustion are what robbed me of my closure. Should I break her illusion? Tell her that the only beings that ever showed me what true magic was have left me? That I have abandoned such nonsense to memory alone?

He set down his satchel and took a knee beside her. He reached out and slipped his fingers into her hair, pulling her in for a kiss. A little flutter of surprise shot through her, eliciting a favorable response as their lips met. He let the kiss be solid and deep but he felt the difference between who he was kissing and who he wanted to be kissing.

She didn't deserve to live like he was going to. She didn't deserve to lose her fantasy to his bitterness. "Thank you for rescuing me, Belladonna."

She kept her eyes closed a bit longer, catching her breath. "Oh, anytime. Really."

He stood, gathering up his satchel, and looked once more at the sea, then turned away and began his trek to the mountains.

Xeno lowered the spyglass as Myrgen walked away from Belladonna, his irritation seething on the edge of his migraine. He didn't know who that man was but Belladonna clearly did. She had gone up there to meet with him and from what it looked like, they had met before. Her first response had been to kiss him and the way they had just parted, he was incredibly familiar with her. She had never reacted like that when Xeno kissed her.

He watched her descend the stairs of the cliff, trying to fight past the pain in his skull. The incident with the ghost ship two days prior had warned of one of these headaches encroaching, but it had waited until last night to actually hit. He wanted to go talk with her, but he feared his pain would give him a foul mood and push her away. He looked down on the street and saw Fierrah leaving their apartment. He tapped on the glass of his window, catching her attention, and waved her up.

He looked in his mirror in hopes that he was not too un-presentable and opened the door before Fierrah's knock could send throbs of searing fire cascading through his body. She stepped in, squinting into the dim room. "Signoria? Did you need something?"

"I have been thinking about asking Belladonna something and, well, I want to know if she's being courted by anyone else."

Fierrah arched an eyebrow. "Courted?"

"Yeah. If she's seeing anyone else."

"You mean other than our regulars?"

He rubbed his neck. "Yes."

"Not that I know of."

"Well, could you check, please? I don't want to make a mistake. How about you? You seeing anyone new?"

She smiled, her hazel eyes daring him to inquire further. "No, no one new. You planning on courting me as well?"

He smiled, pain splitting his eyes. "I haven't decided between the two of you yet. Thank you for your time."

She glanced him over, then left. He turned to his left and nodded to a shadowy corner. "Does that suffice, Ma'am?"

Movement from the area heralded the presence of its inhabitant. A black, heavily embroidered knee high boot emerged from the darkness, followed by matching breeches and bodice of dark blue brocade flattered by an indigo silk shirt. Dark brown hair flowed around blue eyes, striking features in the olive skin common in Mande. Lying just above her breasts, an amulet with an Augustinian symbol failed to shimmer in the low light, despite its appearance to be made of gold. Her gaze and movement reeked of a familiarity with the business of death dealing, and just a hint of sulfur.

"If this person ends up being Myrgen the Grey, you'll be well rewarded, *Signoria*." She spoke his title with the practiced ease of a native speaker of the language.

"How did you know he was here?"

She fondled the amulet, and Xeno saw what seemed to be two strands of black thread woven into the design on the medallion. "You might say, I play the odds very well, and it helps to know my quarry. Myrgen the Grey has been someone of interest for me for a month now. A parting gift from a now-deceased queen." She opened the door. "I'll be in touch," and closed the door behind her.

Xeno looked back out the window. The dark woman had come to town a ten-day ago on the last ship through, looking for this Myrgen person. Two nights ago, when the ghost ship had made its idle threat, she said she thought she saw the man in the back alleys but the shop proprietor she was patronizing at the time had locked the doors to keep the monsters out. Since then, she had been watching everyone and Xeno had noticed that Belladonna had not called on him since the arrival and departure of the ghost ship. Now, he knew why. She had a new lover.

And he was going to be tossed aside.

He found himself unwilling to interfere with that Malatesta woman in the pursuit of her prey.

Boots Malatesta barely stopped long enough to orient herself on her direction. She hated waiting and the leader of this scum city seemed obsessed with gazing through his spyglass out the window. She figured it must be because that cliff was the town's most vulnerable area for attack from the Mervol guards. A snort of disgust punctuated her travel. She knew from experience the Mervols rarely traveled this far south. Portabella was a hidden city, ignored by both Mervolingia and Mande.

It was why she figured Myrgen the Grey would end up here. Clearly this governor was inept. If she didn't have places to be, she would kill him and take over running of this town. He was far too open far too often. She could have bedded him when she arrived in town and done away with the deserter in less than an hour. She wasn't sure yet if she regretted not doing this.

She leaned up against the wall to the building and put herself in a spot where she could see most of the street unobserved, including Xeno's door and window. She saw Belladonna coming down the street and Boots realized she was coming from the direction holding Xeno's fascination. The girl looked a bit exercised too, something which now explained the governor's surly manner more than the excuse of a headache. Boots waited until Belladonna was past the point where Xeno could see them, leaning against the wall of the alley.

"Now, where have you been?"

Belladonna stopped, shocked at being spoken to from the shadows. "Sorry. I didn't see you there."

"I believe that was the point." Boots stepped out of the alley, still keeping her placement where Xeno would be unable to see her, but could probably still see Belladonna. "So, you look disheveled. I hope you got paid for your services."

Belladonna looked down at her clothes, then at Boots, a little more than wary. "I don't see how that's any of your business."

Boots inspected her manicure. "My business or not, the governor sure seemed to make it *his* business to know your whereabouts. He's been asking around about where you're going, what you're doing and with whom. Offering a pretty sum for information, too."

Belladonna frowned, irritation creeping into her features. She looked up at the window in Xeno's quarters and Boots smiled as the woman apparently saw what Boots wanted her to see. The young woman threw a glance at Boots. "Thank you for the tip."

"Anytime. You might say I'm disinclined to let any man think he has the upper hand on a woman." Boots peeled back into the shadows as her new attack dog went over to Xeno's door and stormed up the stairs. She knew the woman would not reveal anything the governor wanted so she did not eavesdrop. The place for confidences was not there, but in the company of the girl Xeno sent after Belladonna. Boots slipped into the tavern down the street and looked around for the other girl.

Fierrah was flirting with a potential client and Boots settled into a convenient area nearby. It took only a few minutes before Belladonna stormed into the tavern, her eyes set upon Fierrah. Several brisk steps covered the distance between them and Belladonna was speaking quickly and harshly at Fierrah. Boots watched carefully and saw Fierrah cringe at being caught. Belladonna's body language indicated she was informing Fierrah not to do Xeno's bidding anymore. Fierrah nodded, hands raised in surrender and Belladonna nodded, satisfied. Fierrah leaned in confidentially and Belladonna glanced around, nodding. She motioned for them to go outside.

Boots slipped tidily out the back and into the alley to listen in on the conversation.

"Yes, I did." Belladonna's voice betrayed an excitement, causing her voice to pitch just a tiny bit higher than usual. "He was up on the cliff, asleep. I tried to wake him but it didn't work. That's when I hit upon the idea that he might be caught in a Fae spell. I kissed him and he started awake! Scared me half to death."

"What was his name?"

"Myrgen the Grey."

Fierrah gasped. "The former Kingdom Chancellor?"

"What do you mean?"

"There was a woman here from that other ship looking for that man. The Blacksmith said he was the Kingdom Chancellor for Mervolingia and the woman said not any more."

"That dark woman? From Mande? She's the one who told me about Xeno's inquiries. By the Saints, I have to warn him."

"I'll tell Xeno. He'll do something abou…" Fierrah's comment was cut off as Boots ran her sword through the girl's heart.

Belladonna's eyes grew wide as she saw the sword tip protruding through her friend and she backed up. Boots put her foot in the middle of Fierrah's back and pushed her off the sword. Belladonna turned and ran down the street.

That's it, girl. Take me to him. Boots slipped back into the shadows, keeping Belladonna in view. Running towards the stairs, she kept looking behind her, searching in vain for Boots. Boots looked up the wall and realized Myrgen was one the girl was with. Belladonna caught her mistake, stopped, then turned back and went into her apartment, casting left and right for followers.

The damage was already done. Boots looked up the cliff and ran to the stairs. She needed to be careful. The stairs did not allow for false steps. She felt along the wall face but there were no hand holds of any kind. She twirled her teleportation pendant, walking with purpose up the stairs. Lack of foreknowledge about the location kept her from simply using it to reach the top in an instant, a problem she would not have again after this. At present, all she could see was the top of the cliff, and that was suicide. If Myrgen was really up there, he could kick her off, ending this mission.

Soon she reached the top, winded but safe. She looked around, then knelt down, looking at the long grass. There were slight depressions where someone had lay, then footprints going off to the northeast. She stood and felt something hit her from behind.

Belladonna was standing behind her, a large branch in her hand. "I'll not let you find him."

Did this little alley cat have a necklace? How did she get up here so fast? "Aw, what's the matter, little Nightshade? Afraid I'll kill your lover?"

"He's not my lover, but he doesn't deserve to be your prey."

"How do you know? He might be a murderer or worse."

Belladonna shook her head. "Unseely Fae don't mess with evil people."

Boots arched her eyebrows. "Really? I guess that's why I've slept so safe at night."

Belladonna took a swing at Boots, her improvised club actually connecting with Boots' face. She spun away from the attack, clutching her cheek. Blood oozed from a cut there and Boots narrowed her eyes at the humble streetwalker. She drew her sword, countering Belladonna's attacks as she figured out what to do. *Every moment I waste here puts Myrgen further away.*

Belladonna thrust again and Boots barely countered it, trying to stay away from the edge of the cliff. Belladonna was trying to circle around to put Boots between herself and the cliff and Boots was trying not to let that happen. Then Belladonna managed a good series of attacks and Boots realized the girl had pushed her too near the edge. Then she heard something that made the whole thing worthwhile.

Xeno, out of breath, crested the stairs. *"Belladonna!"*

Boots turned, her thrust going directly into Xeno's throat, and pushed. He grabbed his neck and fell backwards. Belladonna screamed Xeno's name and ran for him, forgetting for a moment her real enemy. Boots, however, did not, and ran Belladonna through the leg, making her stumble. Belladonna fell forward and hit the ground, sprawling to the edge. Boots was immediately at her side, bringing her sword down across Belladonna's spine, severing the cord with a surgeon's precision.

Blood and spinal fluid seeped from the wound and Belladonna tried to move but couldn't. Boots sheathed her sword, then stepped around and picked up Belladonna's legs. "Well, my dear. You wanted to save your men, and you have ended up saving neither of them. What a nightmare to be you." She walked forward, pushing Belladonna to the edge. The girl fought against it, grasping around her but the long grass ripped from the ground against the onslaught. Boots walked over to dangle Belladonna off the cliff, blood from her injury dripping onto Xeno's broken body at the bottom.

Boots held Belladonna for a moment, waiting to see what her final words would be, but then she decided she didn't really care after all and let go. The girl plummeted and hit her lover head first, making her body lay in a very unhealthy position, draped, more or less, across his.

"Nightmare over."

Boots wiped her hands on her breeches. She knelt on one knee in the ravaged grass and gripped the ancient gold amulet beneath her shirt. A flash of lemons later, light bled away and she was in a lavish gold and red room. A man with dark hair and a large mole at the side of his nose turned to look at his intruder. His face turned sour.

"Malatesta." The tone of the King of Mande showed blatant disgust, either at the thought of the traitor, or the messenger. "You have word of the traitor?"

"I do, Your Majesty. Xeno della Lama is dead."

He smiled. "You are certain?"

She nodded.

"Where did you find him?"

"Portabella, Your Majesty."

The King sneered. "A pox on the face of my beloved country. Filled with thieves and traitors." His eyes sharpened. "You have been there now? Walked its streets?"

"I have, Your Majesty."

"Excellent. I want it to burn." He turned his back to Boots. "No survivors."

She swallowed, her eyes fluttering. "There is more, Your Majesty. Myrgen the Grey was there."

He turned back to her. "Was he?" He smiled, walking to a desk in the room. He picked up a letter with an official seal of Mervolingia. "The Mervol Traitor. Of course he would find his own kind. This is quite serendipitous."

He dropped the letter on his desk but it fluttered to the ground. Boots saw the seal was done in Mandian wax. The King employed a Mervol national sworn to that crown for the purpose of getting official decrees and declarations. The letter said the traitor Myrgen was in the company of the Captain and Crew of the *Enigma,* a Caratian ship she knew of. Her eyes narrowed at the name.

Catriona's ship.

She looked again at her sovereign, who noticed the letter and her interest. He bent over and picked it up, placing it on the desk for certain this time. He looked back at her, cocking his head.

"You have your orders."

She blinked, recovering. "Yes, Your Majesty."

She grasped the amulet and disappeared.

Darkness failed to leave the burning port, the light from the fires of her handiwork reaching even up to the cliff. The stairs had been her first target, then the docks, blocking anyone from ending up in the sea to extinguish the flames from the alchemist fire. She had spread the compound far enough to stop anyone from so much as crossing a street, even if they ran. The most they could hope for was Callista's embrace as they died of flame and were put out in the sea.

Not many of them got that far.

The fires had erupted in sequence, the ability of the amulet coupled with the hundred balls of chemical destruction she had thrown against every surface. The inhabitants had been trapped inside. The few who tried to escape failed in death as they had in life. She glanced down to the couple still in a heap at the foot of the cliff beneath her. Xeno and Belladonna's bodies were the only ones not charred in the whole town. She dropped the last ball from the cliff's edge, obliterating the final memories of this place.

Now for the real work.

She turned to the woods in the direction Myrgen had gone.

Appendices

Appendix A: Characters of the Saintlands

Alan Moriarity: Catriona's son.

Alexander Angloume (ANG-loo-may): Prince of Mervolingia, Alexander is heir to the Throne after Charles. Alexander is also the Duke of Anjou, the family lands of the Angloume house.

Anika Heartholder: Ducêsa of Caratia and adopted mother of Catriona.

Antoinette: Cook in the mornings at the Patras Royal Palace.

Archbishop Alonzo de Patrone: Archbishop of Patras.

Armand de Mortes: Poison-maker employed by Catriona for making pest remedies for her ships. Roommate and companion of Captain Tristram Wulfschlager.

Arnold: Servant of the Royal Family in Patras.

Artemisia: Mythical name of the Moon and mother of the Sea Goddess Calista.

Black Sparrow: Notorious pirate who attacked the Tanglwyst Trading Company. Taken out by Catriona Moriarity.

Caiaphas de Sablonnieres: Tanglwyst's younger brother.

Catriona Moriarity (CAT-tree-OH-nah MORE-ee-AR-it-tee): Stâpâna of Caratia. The Stâpâna is the Protector of the Land's People in the country of Caratia, the second highest rank in the country. The Stâpâna is chosen through a secret ritual known only to those in Caratia.

Cecilia: Cook in the Patras Royal Palace.

Charles Maxamillian IX: King of Mervolingia, ruler and instigator of the St. Michael's Day Massacre.

Count Gabriel Plantyn: General in the Emilianite army and good friend to King Charles of Mervolingia. Murdered in the St. Michael's Day Massacre.

Dominic D'Medici (DOM-uh-nik dee MED-ee-chee): Assistant Chancellor of Mervolingia and fiancé of Gwen.

Drake Zapolya: Duce of Caratia. The ruler of Caratia can be either male or female and is chosen directly by the Land through a ritual involving several trials and finally culminating in a ceremony in the town square of Zara.

Duncan McVryce: A notable member of the Back Streets of Patras, Duncan has played a role in several events involving members of the Royal family, the Augustinian church and Tanglwyst's interests.

Evelyn: Arnold's wife.

Fallon: Princess Marie Elizabeth's nursemaid.

Father Benjamin: A priest in service to Marco Giovanni, he was killed helping Catriona escape her captivity in the breeding pans of the Giovanni estate.

Francois Angloume: Bastard son of King Charles, named after Charles' older brother.

Gomez de Santander: Head of Alexander's personal guard, Gomez began as a guard at the Giovanni estate.

Grand Guard Marcel: Head of the Gendarme police force in Patras.

Grymalkin: Prince Alexander's traveling identity.

Guillaume de la Rapiere: A big player in the Back Streets of Patras, Guillaume killed Richard de Holloway, Tanglwyst's first husband.

Gweneviere "Gwen" Douglas (GWEN-eh-veer DUG-lus): Handmaiden of Catriona, Gwen has the distinction of being her most trusted companion.

Henry of Vitus: Husband to Princess Margaret of Mervolingia and third in line for the Mervol throne. Member of the House of Guise, a financially powerful house in Mervolingia.

King Henry II: Father of Francois I, Charles, Alexander and Margaret, husband of Catherine, Deceased.

Lawrence: First shift baker at the Patras Royal Palace, Lawrence has been with the Royal family for over twenty years.

Lord of Kilmory: Yorkish landholder of the capital of Glarren, Kilmory is the trade face of Glarren on the continent side and still under the direct control of the Queen of York.

Marco Giovanni: Mandian Count and head of the Apolodorus family, Giovanni almost married his cousin to secure a large financial conglomerate but murdered his son and then committed suicide the tenday before his wedding, leaving the Apolodorus fortune to his oldest child.

Margaret - Sister to Charles and Alexander. Married to Henry of Vitus.

Marie Touchet - King Charles's mistress. Mother to Francois.

Martin - A guard in the Patras Palace

Michael - Myrgen's Nubian Slave. A very large man who is fiercely loyal to Myrgen.

Morgan Wolf - Viscount in St. Marguerite.

Myrgen "the Grey" de Sablonnieres (MUR-gun dee SAB-yon-air): Chancellor of Mervolingia, he is in charge of all funding and expenses for the entire kingdom.

Nicolai Moriarity - Husband of Catriona Moriarity. A guard in the Patras Palace.

Nigel - King Charles's Castellan before Myrgen.

Octavius - First mate of the *Enigma* under Captain Catriona Moriarity.

Pierre - A guard in the Patras Palace.

Pope Gregory - Head of the Augustinian Church.

Princess Isabelle - A Mandian Princess of marrying age

Princess Marie-Elizabeth - The three year old daughter of Elizabeth and Charles.

Queen Elizabeth of Krakte - Queen of Mervolingia, married to Charles Maximilian IX. Mother of Marie-Elizabeth. A school friend of Tanglwyst's along with Adriana Capaletti

Queen-Mother Catherine D'Medici - Mother of Charles and Alexander. Married to Henry II. Is currently away from Patras on business in the Papal City.

Simon - A young Valet of Tanglwyst's.

Tanglwyst de Holloway (TANG-gul-wist dee HALL-oh-way): Owner of the Tanglwyst Trading Company and Catriona's secret partner.

Tristram Wulfschlager - Captain of the *Righteous*, one of Catriona's ships.

Urien Atredes - Husband of Tanglwyst de Holloway, a Latian Merchant who owns The Atredes Trading Company, which along with the Tanglwyst Trading Company controls 73% of the Mervol - Mandian trade.

Appendix B: The Augustinian Calendar

The world of the Saintlands has four seasons, and those are the purview of the Fae Lords. Embertwist Apocraphix, the Vernal Monarch, rules over spring, Corrigan Starshadow, the Midsummer King, rules summer, Calpurnia Allegheri, the Autumnal Sovereign, reigns over fall and Gloriana Talnig, the Midwinter Queen, rules winter.

The combat these lords, the Church originally invoked the Archangels against them. These were sufficient but as Heaven gave the Church the Saints, these former humans were invoked in addition, adding to the strength of the protections against Fae trickery. The saints were originally celebrated upon the day of their ascension and delivery by Heaven into the Rolls.

However, 300 years ago, the Church, in the aftermath of a great war, decided to write down a formal calendar, honoring saints for their purviews instead of their date of ascension. This was to battle non-church beliefs, unify the masses and establish lines of Church control.

Pope Richard I told the cardinals to which he assigned this task to begin the year prior to the apex of Gloriana's control, so as to get ahead of the rise of her power. The Cardinals discussed it and Cardinal Cosimo of Pardua offered up Genevieve, invoked against disasters, to start the year. Richard approved and the calendar was begun.

Genevary became the first month and the months were divided into 31 day sets with 10 day week. In the center of the month, the 16th, is the Devotional Day, where all work stops for a day to pray and invoke the saints of the month. This strengthened the divinity in the realm, repelling anything not Heaven related. Although the new calendar reorganized the role of Saints during the year, many days are still known by the saint who ascended upon that day, though the Archangel's days were established during the Augustinian Calendar.

Months

1st: Named after Saint Genevieve, **Genevary** 16 honors Sebald, Martin of Tours, and Raphael the Archangel. Genevieve is invoked against disasters, which abound in the Saintlands during the winter. Sebald once burned icicles in a poor woman's home to produce heat. Martin of Tours cut his cloak in half to give to a naked beggar. Raphael brings the heat of the sun and dawn to battle freezing cold.

2nd: Named after Saint Vitus, **Vitusary** 16 honors Medard, Catald, and Barbara. Vitus is invoked against storms, but is also the Patron saint of dancers so balls abound in Vitusary. Medard is invoked against bad weather because he sheltered the beautiful queen Angelica, granddaughter of Saint Marie Angelica, when she fled the intrigues of the Mervol court during a storm. Medard gave his own tent so she would be safe and dry. An eagle sheltered him from the weather, creating an umbrella for him as he rested. Catald cured the ill and is invoked against plagues, which often abound from bad weather. Barbara was saved when lightning struck her attackers during a siege.

3rd: Named after Saint Florien, **Florias** 16 honors Vincent, Jude, & John of Nepomuk (bridges & flooding). Florien is invoked against floods, a common problem in the Saintlands the third month. Saint Vincent Ferrer is the patron saint of builders, often put to work during this time. Jude helps the hopeless. John of Nepomuk strengthens bridges during floods to save the towns.

4th: Named after Saint Elmo, **Elmos** 16 invokes Fiacre (gardeners), Phocas (market gardeners), and Uriel the Archangel. Elmos starts the sailing season, so Saint Elmo, patron saint of sailors marks this month. Fiacre and Phocas bring the first harvests from winter, began indoors or in warmer climes to feed the masses while Uriel protects the people from the lies and trickery of thieves.

5th: Named after Saint Walburga, **Walpurgisnacht** 16 invokes Valentine, Rose of Lima, & Theodore of Sykon (reconciling the unhappily married). Walpurgisnacht 1 allows the young and amorous to pursue each other unhindered and as such, this month marks the beginnings of many marriages. Valentine honors true love. Rose of Lima honors florists and flower growers. Theodore, known for his counseling skills, reconciles the unhappily married, reminding them of the way they felt their first month of marriage.

6th: Named after Saint Wilgefortis, **Vilgfort** 16 honors Felicity (women wanting sons), Monica (wives), & Marie Angelica (nun who married). Felicity is invoked by women wanting sons, usually royals, due to her miracle of delivering sons whenever she was a woman's midwife. Monica honors wives as she was Heaven's example of a perfect wife and Marie Angelica was a nun who married for the sake of the world. A vision held that Marie Angelica would have a daughter who would alter the church and though she was a nun, she was persuaded to leave her vows to fulfill this vision. Her daughter, Tanglwyst Angelica, inherited a powerful shipping company which was destined for the hands of a corrupt Church. Her sacrifice honors all women who must abandon their own dreams for the sake of a greater good.

7th: Named after Saint Maurice, **Maur** 16 honors Elizabeth (war), Clara (savior in the Soulless War) and Michael the Archangel. This is the season of war, and thus, the people invoke Saint Maurice to keep their soldiers safe while away from home while Elizabeth is invoked to find peaceful resolutions to wars. Clara was a woman whose role in the Soulless War enabled the plague to be destroyed through the spreading of soil she had walked upon, preventing the plague from crossing it. Michael fought the creatures of Hell to preserve the faithful during the great wars.

8th: Named after Saint Francis, **Franco** 16 honors Hubert (hunters), Andrew, and Sebastian. Saint Francis honors all animals and those who tend them. Hubert honors the hunters. Andrew the fishermen and Sebastian protects archers.

9th: Named after Saint Thomas Aquinas, **Aquin** 16 honors Ivo, Augustine, and Albert. The season of scholarly pursuits, Aquin honors those who devote themselves to study. Ivo honors lawyers. Augustine honors theologians and his ideals of Heaven are the basis for the Augustinian Church. Albert honors scientists and herbalists.

10th: Named after Saint Benedict, **Benedine** 16 honors Gabriel the Archangel, Giles, & Margaret. As this is a time of darkness descending upon the land and things turning cold, people were often creating tales of ghosts and fear. Those who had died in the wars of the summer or in the professions of the year were often "seen" wandering the desolate places during this month. To counter these tales of fancy, the church brought in their strongest saints against fear and superstition. Saint Benedict fought his greatest fear, being homeless, and opened his home as a shelter. As such, he is their patron saint. Giles protects against night terrors. Margaret defends against those being attacked by devils, enabling their escape. Gabriel the Archangel heralds Heaven's will, driving away doubt and fear.

11th: Named after Saint Ferdinand, **Ferdin** 16 honors All Saints (Fer 1), Eloi, and Anne. To celebrate the survival of the month of fear, All Saints Day was noted as the first Church holiday. It also honors those responsible for the greatest achievements of humanity: Ferdinand for Engineers, Eloi for jewelry and metal smithing and Anne for pregnancy.

12th: Named after Saint Brigit, **Brig** 16 honors Cosmas & Damian, Raymond, and Roch. A most notable saint, Brigit was one of the first saints ascended to Heaven after giving her life to heal others. Her blood created a fountain by which those who were ill or damaged could be restored. This fountain is in the center of the Papal Palace in the Papal City. Cosmos and Damian are conjoined twins who became doctors. Raymond honors midwives. Roch is invoked against epidemics.

Weekdays

Day 1: Honorasday: named from Honoratus, for bakers.

Day 2: Bernaday: Named after Saint Bernadette, shepherds.

Day 3: Rufinasday: Named after Saint Rufina, potters.

Day 4: Simproniday: Named after Four Crowned Martyrs, stonemasons.

Day 5: Julianusday: Named after Saint Julian, boatmen.

Day 6: Vincentsday: Named after Saint Vincent Ferrer, builders.

Day 7: Wencesday: Named after Saint Wenceslas, brewers.

Day 8: Genesday: Named after Saint Genesius, Actors & Comedians.

Day 9: Columbasday: Named after Saint Columba, poets.

Day 10: Dismasday: Named after Saint Dismas, undertakers.

Appendix C: Religions

Augustinian (AHG-us-TIN-ee-uhn)

The Augustinians believe God made the world and made Heaven. God set up the ability for Man to ascend to Heaven body and soul by doing good works. If a human is good enough and helps enough people, they can become a Saint. Each Saint in the Augustinian Rolls was once a human and their name appears in the Heavenly Roster when they ascend. The Heavenly Roster is a book kept in the Papal City on the Official Altar in the center of the Cathedral under constant guard.

In the 1300s, the Church stopped acknowledging new names in the Roster after The War of the Soulless which they blamed upon the heathen religions. The reason cited for this denial was the War made it difficult to believe all the reports of ascended Saints. At the time, it was unknown by the populace about the Heavenly Roster but after the declaration and an investigation by nobles outside the church, this information was revealed to the public. Regardless, once the Pope responsible passed away and the scandal was uncovered, the new Pope acknowledged the updated Rolls and the new Saints were canonized.

The main Tenant of Faith in the Augustinian religion is the Saints are the world's connection to Heaven. It is only by praying to the Saints that one can communicate with Heaven. It is against the Laws of the Church to pray directly to God, bypassing his appointed representatives, to make requests, though one can offer praise unto Heaven without invoking a particular Saint. However, if one prays to a particular saint for guidance or assistance and they receive it, it is against the laws of the Church to not acknowledge the Saint who answered the prayer.

Emilianite (uh-MEEL-ee-uhn-ITE)

After the War of the Soulless and the Scandal of the Unacknowledged Saints, a group of followers broke away from the Church. Citing corruption in the dictations of the papacy, it was determined that apparently the Church could communicate directly to Heaven without the help of the Saints since they refused to acknowledge the Saints received in the Rolls. They called these Saints "the Abandoned Children" and called themselves Emilianites, after Emilio, the patron Saint of abandoned children.

The Emilianites believe that man cannot be trusted with the will or intent of Heaven through a conduit, for that can be hidden or destroyed. Instead, they believe man can be more assured of correct information if he prays directly to Heaven. If Heaven wants the Emilianites to pray to a Saint, they will communicate that Saint's name to all the Faithful. Until that happens, the Emilianites will pray directly to Heaven. Since the Scandal of the Unacknowledged, no Emilianite has ever noted a Saint's name being given to them. As such, they continue to offer prayers only to Heaven.

Land Worship

The Maker split in two, creating the Heavens and the Land. Both are sentient and great entities unto themselves. Heaven holds the Well of Souls and deals with all things ethereal such as dreams and thoughts, ideas and concepts. The Land deals with all things physical, be it body, plant or liquid. If it can be held, it is the purview of the Land.

When the body dies, the Land takes it into itself and dissolves the flesh, leaving the soul. The soul is filtered and cleansed of the sins of its life and when all the sin is gone, the soul that is left is returned to the Well of Souls. The Land interacts with the people on a daily basis, feeding them, clothing them, healing them. They trust the Land and count on its gifts for life.

Calista's Call

Oceanus, Father of Waters, was alone and lonely. He wandered across the world without drive or direction. Sometimes, to relieve his boredom, he would slice through a mountain or sink an island he made but in the end, he was aimless and alone. Then, one night, he heard a stirring song. It beckoned him from across the Land and he fell upon a beach, kneeling before the singer. A beautiful maiden of silver hair and glowing pale skin sat naked on the beach, her voice filling the night. He crept up behind her and she saw him and screamed, then grabbed her clothes and fled to the sky.

Every night, he went to the beach to fall upon the shore, begging her to return. He brought her gifts from the sea and far away lands, creatures and stones, wood and plants. Eventually she peeked from behind the curtain of night and slowly emerged, a little more each night, until she fell in love with Oceanus and they made love upon the beach. They created a daughter of rich blue skin like her father and glowing white hair like her mother. They called her Calista and the salt from their tears of joy at the sight of her soaked her, making her touch turn water into salt water.

Calista watches the sea and keeps her secrets and those of her followers. She is a fickle goddess though, and prone to fits of fury that can seem unprovoked. When she is happy or dealing with honorable people, her hair is the white of sea foam. Mermaids gather the honored dead and if a sailor is a good follower, Calista recognizes them and grants them the ability to live underwater as merfolk in her cities. Her dolphins and sea mammals guide ships through treacherous areas and are always signs of her pleasure.

But she has her primal side as well and when dealing with the dishonorable, she sends her teeth to rend them. Her hair turns bloody red and her sharks and sirens call the evildoers to their destruction. If there is an argument in ship at sea and sharks arrive on the scene, it means someone in the fight is lying. If a criminal is sentenced to death at seas, the sharks will take him, but if the criminal is remorseful, they take him to the depths where he becomes a Marked One and serves Calista for as long as they breathed air. Sirens call the unjust to the sharks' maws so if one hears a siren's call, the heavier the sins on their soul, the harder it is to resist them.

If a body is rendered with fire at death, Calista will know them not and shall cast their spirit out of her mouth to walk the earth forever.

The Ancient Ones

Sovereignus was a good king. He loved Magic so much, that he mated with her, and fathered the Fae. The Fae were everywhere. They were the merfolk in the sea and the harpies in the air. They were the pixies and dryads in the trees and the white-furred talking animals in the snows. All the magical creatures, great and small, frolicked in the love of their mother and father. The Fae loved humans and played with them, guiding them to good places and punishing the lazy or wicked with their games and tricks.

But then a sickness came, one that threatened all the magical creatures. Dark men captured the Fae, torturing them to find the sources of Elemental magic. Sovereignus roared and rode to war against these dark men and felled them. In the battle, he was mortally wounded and returned home to die. He gave to his four eldest his power, divided as to their gifts.

To his youngest son Embertwist Apocraphix, he gave the powers of Spring. The Vernal Monarch is the quintessential thief and like a thief, it comes in the night, stealing the cold of winter and revealing the living things beneath her skirt. To his oldest son, Corrigan Starshadow, he gave the powers of Summer. As the Midsummer King, his paladin nature marches forthright towards the good and just.

To his oldest daughter, Calpurnia Allegheri, he gave the powers of Autumn. Calpurnia so resembled his beloved Magic, she channels the gifts of change and harvest during her reign as the Autumnal Sovereign. To his youngest daughter, Corrigan's twin, he gave the power of Winter. Gloriana Talnig, the Midwinter Queen, uses the cold to stop disease and preserve and heal, but also to punish the wicked and delay the unjust. The children split and went to different parts of the world to preserve their realms from the followers of the Dark Men, but each season, they return to Sovereignlumin, the great Tower That Watches All to transfer the power of the seasons.

Karma

Karma is all about balance. For each act, there is an equal and opposite reaction in a person's life. As they get closer to the end of their life thread, they can find themselves bound by the threads they have thrown. Negative acts cause sticky threads, positive acts throw stabilizing threads. If a soul has cast more sticky threads than stabilizing, they can be caught up in the negative and it will strangle them. Thus are many of the symbolic gods of Karma multi-limbed creatures.

The Primordial Egg

The Primordial Egg twitched and cracked and from the shell, four Dragons emerged. They opened their mouths and breathed forth the world. The Earth Dragon formed land and grass, ore and metal, wood and dale. The Water Dragon formed oceans and rivers, lakes and streams, snow and ice. The Fire Dragon breathed the sun and stars to warm the world. And the Air Dragon gave life and the moon. As all things came from magic, all creatures upon the world were magical, and all things communicated with one another in the combined tongue of the elements.

But then, a threat loomed on the face of all and it tried to conquer the magic in the world. It's flashing sword and violent means crushed all but its own belief, slaying the dragons in the world. The Elemental Dragons Rose against it, but to destroy the threat meant to destroy all they loved as well. Instead, they seized their followers and sealed them away in special places. The Earth Dragon hid the giants and Dwarves in the mountains. The Fire Dragon hid her faithful in the ash and lava. The Water Dragon took her children and gave them the ability to breathe water. And the Air Dragon took his children to the sky, to the place between life and death.

At first they spoke aloud to one another, but monsters found their hiding places, so the Dragons broke the world and spoke only in secret languages so none could find their whereabouts. The Earth Dragon spoke through entrails and omens, the Water Dragon through storms. Fire claimed its own hypnotic power and Air spoke through the dead. Together, they all keep the legends and the magic safe, making certain that only those who wish to keep magic in the world can find them.

Fang and Claw

The practice of having an animal choose to join with a person's soul to guide them is standard practice in the followers of Fang and Claw. They also believe in the consuming a part of the animal allows for that animal's superior quality to enter the consumer.

As a rite of passage, warriors of the tribes will hunt a dangerous animal with which to partner. Shaman may not be lead by a dangerous animal, but by a wise one such as Snake or Owl. And those who become the Seers find themselves in the company of spiders.

Appendix D: Countries

Caratia (CUH-ray-SHEE-uh)
Capital City: Zara
Native tongue: Caratian (CUH-ray-SHEE-uhn)
Dominant Religion: Land Worship

Glarren (GLARE-uhn)
Capital City: Kilmory (kill-MORE-ee)
Native tongue: Glarren
Dominant Religion: The Ancient Ones

Krakte (KRAHK-tuh)
Capital City: Austra
Native tongue: Krakten
Dominant Religion: Augustinian, Emilianite, the Ancient Ones

Latia (LAH-tee-uh)
Capital City: Cheryb (SHARE-eeb)
Native tongue: Latian (LAH-tee-uhn)
Dominant Religion: Calista's Call

Mande (MAHND)
Capital City: Vincenzia
Other Cities: Pardua, Floren, Roma
Native tongue: Mandian (MAHN-dee-uhn)
Dominant Religion: Augustinian

Mervolingia (MER-vole-LIN-jee-uh)
Capital City: Patras
Other Cities: Rouen (ROO-en), St. Giles, St. Andrew, St. Marguerite
Native tongue: Mervol (MER-vol)
Dominant Religion: Augustinian, Emilianite

Nubia (NOO-bee-uh)
Capital City: Leeus Brul (lee-OOS bruul)
Native Tongue: Fangspek
Dominant Religion: Fang and Claw

The Papal City (PAY-puhl)
Capital City: None
Native tongue: Mervol
Dominant Religion: Augustinian Church Seat

Toledo (toe-LEED-dough)
Capital City: Tuscan
Native tongue: Toledan
Dominant Religion: Land Worship

York (YORK)
Capital City: Landen
Other cities: Canterbury, Kent, Oxford, Cambridge
Native Tongue: Yorkish
Dominant Religion: Emilianite

Yndia (YIN-dee-uh)
Capital City: Yantap (YAN-tap)
Native tongue: Yndian
Dominant Religion: Karma

Yokotama (YO-ko-TAH-mah)
Capital City: Kūki doragon
Native Tongue: Yokotaman
Dominant Religion: Dance of the Air Dragons

About the Author

Tonya Adolfson has been a member of the Society for Creative Anachronism since 1988 and has met thousands of people with very interesting personas. Many of these people have made it into these books and she is grateful to them for enriching her life.

Tonya lives in Boise, Idaho with her husband, two children, two housemates, four cats and two dogs and yet, strangely, the house is actually pretty clean.

www.ingramcontent.com/pod-product-compliance
Lightning Source LLC
Chambersburg PA
CBHW070748280626
47162CB00018B/2552